“You make m

to myself.

“I promise myself ... you,” Daisy continued. “I tell myself that one night with you is enough, that it’s all I need. And then…and then you ruin it all. Worse than that, you make me indecisive. I’m not indecisive, Jacob, I don’t make an important decision and then change my mind because of a kiss.”

“Are you inviting me in?” Jacob rested his forehead against hers.

“I am.”

“If I come inside, I won’t leave until morning.”

“You better not,” she said. “And I do hope you’re more prepared than you were last time.”

“I’m ever the optimist, so yes.”

Daisy pulled Jacob inside by the tie. “You and your suits,” she said as she closed and locked the door behind him. “Take it off.”

Dear Reader,

Small-town living in the South is rife with possibilities when it comes to writing romance. There are characters everywhere you turn, families who have made their mark, men and women who have chosen to make themselves a part of a community where everyone knows everyone else and secrets are hard to keep. A beauty shop and small-engine-repair business is not at all a stretch, when it comes to small towns everywhere.

Family is important to me, as it is to Daisy Bell and Jacob Tasker in this story. They're both willing to make sacrifices for family members, to endure personal pain in order to make life easier for those they love. But after making those sacrifices for others, is it time to let the mistakes of the past go and take time for themselves? Can they find a second chance at love?

I hope you enjoy your journey into Bell Grove, Georgia, and the chance to watch Daisy and Jacob find one another all over again.

Happy reading!

Linda

A WEEK TILL THE WEDDING

BY

LINDA WINSTEAD JONES

MILLS & BOON

First published in Great Britain 2012
by Mills & Boon, an imprint of Harlequin (UK) Limited,
Eton House, 18-24 Paradise Road, Richmond, Surrey TW9 1SR

ISBN: 978 0 263 89479 0
ebook ISBN: 978 1 408 97154 3

23-1112

Harlequin (UK) policy is to use papers that are natural, renewable and recyclable products and made from wood grown in sustainable forests. The logging and manufacturing processes conform to the legal environmental regulations of the country of origin.

Printed and bound in Spain
by Blackprint CPI, Barcelona

Linda Winstead Jones is a bestselling author of more than fifty romance books in several subgenres—historical, fairy tale, paranormal and, of course, romance suspense. She's won a Colorado Romance Writers Award of Excellence twice. She is also a three-time RITA® Award finalist and (writing as Linda Fallon) winner of the 2004 RITA® Award for paranormal romance.

Linda lives in north Alabama with her husband of thirty-seven years. She can be reached via her website, www.lindawinsteadjones.com.

For my niece Christy, a hairstylist who keeps me from going gray and living in ponytails. She hasn't yet added small-engine repair, but…maybe someday. :-)
Love you!

Chapter One

"Those women on Crime Stoppers never have good haircuts. Have you noticed? Maybe if they didn't look so unkempt they'd make better choices. You know, get a job, marry a decent man. Just look at those bangs, bless her heart." Sandra Miller was a talker; Daisy never had to work to make conversation when Sandra was in the chair getting her hair done.

Daisy paused, scissors in hand, and glanced over the top of her client's head to catch a glimpse of a mug shot on the twenty-inch television that was mounted on the wall. Bell Grove, Georgia, was a small town off the beaten path, north of Atlanta. They didn't have their own television station, but they picked up the Atlanta stations. "Yeah, those bangs are pretty bad."

"A woman just can't feel good about herself if her hair looks that awful." Sandra gestured to the television. "I swear, I'd be tempted to use drugs myself if I had bangs like that. She has to have something to dull the pain."

Another mug shot was flashed on the screen. "Oh, dear," Sandra said softly. "Her problems go so far beyond bangs I don't know where to start. Don't they sell conditioner in Atlanta? And what color *is* that, exactly? I have never seen a box of Miss Clairol with *orange* or *pumpkin* stamped on it." In the mirror, Sandra caught and held Daisy's eye. "You know, you could do a lot of good, if you were of a mind to help those poor, unfortunate women. You can't overestimate how important hairstyle is to a woman's confidence."

Daisy laughed. "Sorry, Sandra. My hands are full enough without adding in the occasional trip to the Atlanta jail to give beauty advice."

Yes, her hands were more than full enough. Daisy was the sole proprietor of Bell's Beauty Shop and Small Engine Repair. She had no employees, though her sister Mari—the youngest of the three Bell girls—came home on the weekends to help with the repair aspect of the business. Mari was in junior college, and Lily had recently started a new job in an Atlanta art gallery. Lily didn't make it to Bell Grove as often as she had when she'd been a student. These days her weekends were taken up with the new job and new friends and settling into her new apartment.

While Daisy missed seeing her sisters on a regular basis, it wasn't like she didn't have enough to do. In addition to the business, which kept her busy enough since it was Bell Grove's only beauty salon and repair shop, she did volunteer work. On Mondays, when her shop was closed, she delivered meals to a number of housebound residents in the county. Some were elderly, others were in bad health; a couple had just fallen on hard times and needed a little help. While she wasn't keen on the idea of inspiring prisoners to change their ways by providing free haircuts, she had spent more hours than she could count spiffing up the hairstyles of those who didn't get out much. The service—the meals, not the hair trimming and restyling—was sponsored by the Bell Grove Methodist Church, as was a food bank which Daisy also volunteered for when she could.

She gave some of these same people rides to town, when she wasn't working and they needed to go to the doctor—there was a grand total of one in Bell Grove—or the grocery store. There was just the one grocery store, too. Bell Grove provided all the necessary services; there just wasn't much to choose from. Anyone who wasn't happy with their limited selection could—and did—drive into Atlanta or one of the communities between Bell Grove and the big city.

Daisy didn't get out of Bell Grove often. Everything she needed was close at hand. She liked it here, and everything she needed was within reach. Well, *almost* everything.

Sandra asked about Lily and Marigold, and Daisy filled her in on all the latest news. As she did, her heart sank a little. Just a little. She tried not to let her sad reaction show. When their parents had been killed Daisy had stepped up and done what needed to be done. She'd put her life on hold, sacrificing her own plans to take care of her younger sisters. Lily and Mari had still been in school at the time, Lily in the county high school, Mari in the middle school. There had been no close relatives to take over as guardian to the younger girls, so that duty had fallen to Daisy. Now they were grown, they had lives of their own.

That was as it should be, right? But sometimes Daisy felt as if she was suffering from Empty Nest Syndrome at the ripe old age of twenty-eight.

She never would've considered staying in Bell Grove and taking over her parents' businesses if they'd lived.

Her plans had been grander than that. A college degree—she'd waffled between physical therapy and elementary education and had finally decided on education—and a job in the big city. Marriage, babies, the PTA and Little League. Maybe her plans had not been grand, but they'd been *hers*. More than once in the past seven years she'd spent a sleepless night wondering where she'd be if that eighteen-wheeler hadn't crossed the center line. She would've finished college, gotten that job, made a life of her own. Would she have been as content with that life as she was with this one? Would things have turned out as she'd planned? She'd stopped asking those questions years ago. There was no way to know what that alternate life might've been like; there was no upside for her in "what-if?"

She liked her life just fine, and those old plans seemed so distant they might as well have been someone else's.

Daisy gave Sandra's new, shorter cut a good blow-dry with a round brush, touched it up with a spritz of hair spray and whipped off the purple cape that had protected her client's clothing. Sandra was happy with the new style, and had just begun to gush about how much slimmer her face looked with the new cut when the door to the shop opened. Daisy didn't have anyone scheduled for another hour. She'd planned to grab a sandwich as soon as Sandra left. But she did take walk-ins, and since business wasn't exactly booming she'd gladly skip lunch to squeeze in another haircut. Maybe someone was dropping off a small item for repair, though if that was the case…

That was as far as her thoughts wandered before the person who'd opened the door stepped inside.

Jacob Tasker, the biggest "what-if?" of them all, looked her in the eye the way he always had, with confidence in his steady gaze. Dark brown eyes, like strong black coffee, caught hers and held on. He was bigger than he'd been when she'd last seen him. Not in a bad way; he didn't have the beginnings of a gut, or jowls, or a double chin. All through college he'd bordered on skinny. He'd been wiry, at the very least. Since then he'd put on a few pounds of muscle, filling his expensive suit well.

Not only did that suit cost more than she made in a month, but no one wore a suit in Bell Grove unless A) They were Mayor or B) It was Sunday.

His haircut was expensive, too. There wasn't a single hair out of place, no misbehaving cowlick or split ends. He was recently well-shaven. Damned if he couldn't've just stepped out of an ad for expensive cologne or a ridiculously overpriced watch. And that smile…even though she could tell it was somewhat forced, the smile hadn't changed at all. That smile had captured her when she'd been fifteen and he'd been eighteen. She'd fallen hard. She'd doodled *Mrs. Daisy Tasker* on the inside cover, and numerous pages, of every notebook and journal she'd owned, with swirly hearts over the *i* in Daisy. At that time he'd been too old for her, and she'd never confessed her feelings to anyone, not even to her closest friends. He'd been her secret crush, her heart's deepest desire.

Four years later, when she'd been nineteen and he'd been twenty-two, they'd attended the same college and the three-year age difference was no longer an impediment. Since he'd taken a year off between high school and college, and he'd changed his major—twice—they'd even had some classes together. The smile had done her in again, along with other attributes she hadn't been able to even imagine at fifteen. That had been a blissfully happy time of her life; she'd lived in a fairy tale.

And a little less than two years later it had all fallen

apart, and she'd been reminded that the original fairy tales always had a wicked twist at the end.

Crap. Daisy couldn't say she hadn't ever imagined seeing Jacob again, but in her fantasy she'd had time to put on something pretty and freshen her makeup. She'd been ridiculously happy; she hadn't missed him *at all*. In her daydreams she could barely remember what he looked like. She had no regrets, there were no "what-ifs?" On the other hand he'd been miserable, so very sorry he'd let her slip away. In her imaginings he had not aged well. Maybe there was a gut, or a softening of his features. Just enough of an unflattering change to make her glad that their relationship had ended when it had. Ah, fantasy.

But in real life she was wearing a minimum of makeup and a black smock over well-worn jeans and a sadly old Brooks and Dunn T-shirt. And he looked better than she remembered, more a man, harder. Sharper. She thought about Jacob too damn often. And he didn't look at all sorry. No, he looked as confident as always, as if he never had a single moment of doubt about any decision he'd ever made.

Not even leaving her.

He closed the door on the bright sunshine, said hello to her and to Sandra, who—thankfully—prattled about how long it had been since she'd seen Jacob, how she'd heard about his success, and how was California, anyway? She asked about his brothers and his cousins. He had plenty of relatives in the area, so that took a while. While the Bells had dwindled—only the three sisters remained of the founders of this small town—the Taskers had multiplied and flourished. You couldn't take two steps in the county without tripping over one of Jacob's cousins.

While Jacob and Sandra exchanged pleasantries, Daisy took a deep breath and tried to decide what she should say, when the time for her to speak arrived. Her hands fell to her thighs, where she wiped them on her jeans. Her nails weren't painted. She had sweaty palms. Great. He couldn't have called first? He couldn't have given her a little warning so she could brush up on her speech? How rude!

As Jacob and Sandra talked, the television news droned on, the announcer's words making no sense at all. Blah, blah, blah. Yada yada yada. The air conditioner whirred. Daisy was aware of every sound that filled the room, most specifically Jacob's voice. She'd always loved his voice; the timbre, the way she felt it in her spine.

She really should pretend that seeing him again didn't affect her at all, but it was probably too late for that. Her jaw had dropped when he'd walked in and she'd stared at him wordlessly for too long to pull off that lie. He'd probably noticed her wiping her sweaty palms on her jeans; he never had been one to miss much. She could just light into him and say all the things she sometimes wished she'd said. For a long while all the things she wished she'd said to him had kept her up at night. None of them were pleasant.

But when Sandra put cash on the front counter, waved at Daisy and left, and Daisy and Jacob were left alone, what she said was,

"What the hell do you want?"

Well, what had he expected? A parade?

Daisy hadn't changed much at all. She still had long pale hair, cornflower-blue eyes, long legs and flawless, lightly tanned skin. On the drive over Jacob had wondered if Daisy would look older, if sacrificing for her family and giving up her own dreams, seven years ago, had drained her.

But she looked as good as ever. Better, in fact. The years had been good to her. The girl he'd loved was gone, replaced by a gorgeous woman.

"I need a favor," he said, suspecting that her response to that simple request wouldn't be pretty.

"A favor." She shook her head in wonder, and her posture changed as if she were getting ready to do battle. Maybe she was. "From me? Is this a joke?"

"Just hear me out."

Daisy threw up her hands. Her cheeks flushed pink. "Whatever this favor is, I don't have the time."

Bell's Beauty Shop and Small Engine Repair was located in the heart of downtown Bell Grove, on the square across from city hall, sandwiched between an antiques shop and a family-run sandwich shop. All the buildings in the downtown area were old as dirt. The owners did their best to keep them in good repair, but there was no way to disguise the effects of a hundred years plus of use.

Bell's was small but clean, the walls freshly painted a welcoming pale green, the magazines neatly stacked. The chairs in the shop were mismatched, probably yard sale finds, but somehow Daisy had made it all look planned. The lace curtains and live plants pulled it all together. There was a counter in the back, just past the door to the restroom, and a dark green wooden door that he knew opened onto the area where her dad had once fixed mowers and other lawn-care equipment, as well as the occasional toaster even though there were no small engines in kitchen appliances. Business didn't exactly seem to be brisk.

"The favor is not for me," he explained.

"Oh, really." Her voice was cool, as if she didn't care.

"It's Grandma Eunice."

Her face fell, a little. She'd always liked his dad's mother, and Grandma Eunice had liked Daisy. Which was probably a contributing factor in this latest problem.

Like it or not, he was going to have to explain. "I came home for the big family reunion, and since I haven't been back in a while I decided to stay for a month." He didn't tell her that the only reason he was here now was that his mother had told him it might be the last reunion his grandmother would see.

"Can that big company you work for survive without you for that long?" she snapped.

He'd been getting up early and staying up late to take care of business via cell phone and computer while he was here, but that detail wasn't relevant. Might as well just get to the heart of the matter. "Grandma Eunice isn't well."

Daisy's face paled a little. She couldn't have known. The Taskers and the Bells weren't exactly the Hatfields and the McCoys, but they didn't run in the same circles, either.

"I'm sorry to hear Miss Eunice is not well," Daisy said, her voice cool but not without genuine sympathy.

"Physically she doesn't seem to be in bad shape, though she's not getting around the way she used to. She's been in a wheelchair for a while. But her mind…" Might as well spit it out. "Daisy, she thinks we're engaged and she's been asking about you."

Daisy had never had much of a poker face. Her blue eyes widened, her mouth puckered slightly. Maybe she even paled, a bit. Her pretty mouth opened and closed a couple of times before she asked, "Is it Alzheimer's?"

"The doctor says no."

"Then what…"

"She doesn't forget everything, she's functions very well and remembers what she had for breakfast, but there are certain times when her memory just seems to malfunction. She has a terrible time remembering Ben's wife, but most specifically, her memory malfunctions where I'm concerned."

Daisy looked as confused as he'd been feeling for the

past few days. "You'll just have to tell her the truth," she said.

If only it were that simple. "I did. I told her we broke up a long time ago, that we were never engaged. She got upset, I went to the kitchen to make her some hot tea, and when I got back she was completely calm. Smiling, serene, looking out her bedroom window. I thought she was fine, that she'd accepted the truth, but..." The matter still concerned him. "She'd forgotten. In just a few minutes' time, she completely forgot what I'd told her about us." He bit the bullet and dropped the bombshell. "She's planning our wedding."

Daisy reached out to steady herself by grabbing the edge of the counter. Jacob considered stepping forward to take her arm, but he quickly thought better of it.

"What do you expect me to do?" she asked, her voice rising sharply. "I can't...we can't...this is not my problem!"

"I don't expect you to marry me to keep my grandmother happy," Jacob said sharply. "But if you would play along for a while, come to the family reunion if she keeps this up, maybe hang out at the house when you can. She might wake up one morning and have forgotten all about this fantasy of hers, but at the very least once I'm gone she'll let it go." Out of sight, out of mind. "She's promised to see a new doctor, but not until *after* the reunion."

"Play. Along." Ah, there was the difference in Daisy, *that's* how she'd changed. Her eyes were harder, more cynical. They'd never looked at him like this before.

"It would make an old woman very happy. She adores you."

"Give me a break. You aren't doing this for *her*. No, you want me to get *you* off the hook so you won't have to try again to tell her that we're not getting married. Heaven forbid that Jacob Tasker should have to do anything that he finds unpleasant. Heaven forbid that anything that's not in your precious plans..." She stopped, choking on her words.

Jacob took a deep breath, he exhaled slowly. He wished—not for the first time—that he was back in San Francisco, where his days and the decisions he had to make made sense. This situation was maddening. "I've been home four days, and I've told Grandma Eunice ten times that we're not engaged and never were. She's upset by the news, and then a few minutes later she forgets. I'm getting damn tired of upsetting her again and again."

Daisy was already shaking her head.

"I'll pay you."

There were those daggers in her eyes again. Her posture changed, as if she were literally getting ready to attack. "You think you can buy me off? That I'll do anything for money? Oh, poor Daisy Bell, she'll do anything for a few bucks."

He'd be glad to pay her more than a "few bucks." And it looked as if she could use the money. Jacob had put Daisy firmly in his rearview mirror years ago, but he hated the idea that she didn't have more. She'd sacrificed a lot for her sisters; she'd given up her own education, the career she'd planned. She'd raised Lily and Mari, put them through college, and from all he could see she'd done nothing for herself. Why in hell was she still here? She should've moved on years ago.

He snapped out a ridiculously high amount, a number large enough to make Daisy take a stutter-step back.

"Are you insane?" she asked.

No, he wasn't insane; he was ridiculously rich. He worked eighty to ninety hours a week, and until now he hadn't taken a real vacation since he'd gone to work for The Hudson-Dahlgren Corporation seven years ago. He'd become a workaholic who had no time for anything else. But all his hard work had paid off. Very well.

"I'm afraid Grandma Eunice doesn't have much time left. She's deteriorated so much since I last saw her. Physically, mentally…the doctor says it's manageable, but I don't buy it." He'd talked to her doctor—an old codger who wasn't much younger than she was—and according to the doc there was nothing to be done. Eunice Tasker was simply growing old. Jacob had initially offered to bring in specialists, to fly his grandmother to a decent hospital for tests and treatment, but she'd refused both offers. *After* the reunion, she'd said, she'd see a new doctor. Maybe her mind was slipping, but she was as stubborn as ever.

"You could help to make her final days happy ones." And he could leave here knowing Daisy was in good financial shape. She could finish school, close this crappy shop, get out of town the way he had.

She considered his offer for a long moment, and finally said, "All right, I'll help. A couple of visits to your grandmother, a few lies…I can do that." She walked toward him, came close, reached out and punched him in the chest with the tip of her index finger. She didn't look him in the eye as she poked him there, hard.

Jacob didn't move, but he took a long, deep breath. Damn, she smelled good. The sight of Daisy brought back strong, old memories, but it was the way she smelled that triggered memories he had no right to cling to. She was the stuff of dreams, the kind of woman a man could never entirely let go of, no matter how hard he tried.

"But I won't take a dime of your money," she said. "I'm doing this for Miss Eunice, not for you. She was kind to me after my parents died. She's a good woman and I'll do this for *her*." Daisy lifted her head slowly, until her eyes met his. "Not for you and not for your money." She said the word "money" as if it was a bad thing.

He'd change her mind about the money, eventually, but he wasn't going to argue with her now.

"Dinner tonight with the family?"

"Not wasting any time, are you?" she countered.

"Might as well not."

After seeing her, smelling her, remembering their time together—the good and the bad—he knew the sooner they got this over with, the better off they'd both be.

Their time, their chance, had come and gone years ago. He didn't pine for anything or anyone, but a small, reluctant part of his brain recognized that Daisy Bell disturbed him on some primitive level. He didn't need or want to be dragged into the past, not by old memories, not by a surprisingly tantalizing scent.

Daisy was the past, and Jacob cared only about the present and the future. Only a fool would be tempted by something long gone.

Chapter Two

The Taskers had been movers and shakers in the county for as long as there'd been a county. The family home, a few miles out of Bell Grove, was stately and majestic and yet still homey. It wasn't a showplace, it was a home. At least, it had been home years ago when Daisy had come here often with Jacob as his girlfriend. Holidays, summer vacations...for nearly two years she'd spent much of her time away from school and her part-time job with her parents right here. She'd never told anyone how much she loved this old house. And she never would.

Through the years residents had tried to give it an appropriate name, a name befitting a fine home with a rich history. Now and then a Tasker would try to call it Magnolia Whatsit or Oak Something. But what it was always called, what stuck, was Tasker House. Daisy had always thought that made the fabulous, sprawling two-story mansion sound like something out of an Edgar Allen Poe story.

Apparently she was not alone in that belief, and that was why Taskers kept trying to change it.

For the occasion, Daisy had chosen her outfit carefully. She wanted to look good, for the family and even for Jacob, though where he was concerned it was intended in a "this is what you threw away, look but don't touch" kind of way. She wore a pale green sundress that hit the top of her knees, white sandals, and her hair down. Maybe she hadn't done anything spectacular with her hair, but she'd brushed until it gleamed. Jacob had looked at her more often than was necessary on the ride from town, cutting his eyes from the road now and then to study her. It was what she'd wanted, right? She wanted him to regret giving her up, she wanted him to suffer.

So why was she determined to meet him here next time and avoid being trapped in a car with him again?

The way he stared at her made her squirm. Sitting so close to him for so long was making her seriously antsy. In trying to punish him, she had ended up punishing herself. It was absolute torture to have him so close. And he didn't seem to be tortured *at all*.

The house was just as she remembered it, majestic and welcoming, perfectly positioned on a vast expanse of land that was lushly green. A portion of the land was flat and had once been farmed, but to the west there were gentle hills and ancient trees. She and Jacob had taken many a long walk in those hills…

He offered his arm at the porch steps, and she took it. She would not allow him to see how she was affected by his closeness. He couldn't know, not ever, that he made her squirm.

"Do you sleep in a suit?" she asked coolly as they walked up the steps, neither of them in a hurry. He looked good in the dark suit and crisp white shirt, she'd admit, especially since everything he had on fit him as if it had been made for his body, but the outfit seemed wrong here at Tasker House, especially given the season. Even late in the day, the summer heat remained. And the humidity… you could not dismiss the humidity! Besides, the stupid suit reminded her that he'd dumped her for his precious career. She didn't want or need his success rubbed in her face.

"Not usually," he said.

She shouldn't have asked that question. As she recalled, he usually slept in nothing at all. At least, he had when she'd been around. So had she, come to think of it. They hadn't lived together, though that step had been coming, but she'd spent the night at his place and he'd spent the night at hers—when roommates were away. It was a vivid memory she could do without, given the circumstances. She tried to think of other things, to push the memory of a naked Jacob out of her mind, but nothing else would stick.

Before she could wipe the image of a naked Jacob from her brain, Susan Tasker met them at the door. The screen door squealed as she opened it, and she smiled. Or tried. It was the most pathetic attempt at a smile Daisy had ever seen. Focusing on Jacob's mother helped; it was difficult to fantasize about the man naked while the woman Daisy had once believed would one day be her mother-in-law looked on.

Susan Tasker had married into the prominent and wealthy Tasker family, but she'd soon become one of its leaders. Her husband, Jim, Miss Eunice's only living child, was a quiet man who seemed to be happy to share the handling of the family business matters and properties with his wife. She had given him four sons and taken on an active role in the multiple Tasker concerns—there were a number of businesses across the South that were at least partially owned by the family corporation—as if she'd been born to it.

And now she cared for his mother, as well.

"Daisy," she said softly as she backed up to allow her and Jacob to enter the house.

"Mrs. Tasker."

The older woman—she had to be approaching sixty—turned around, waving a hand dismissively. "Oh, call me Susan. You're not a child any longer."

Susan had put on a few pounds in the years since Daisy had seen her, and whoever was styling her hair had done a terrible job. The color was flat and lifeless, and the cut was too severe for the shape of her face. She needed layering, and some highlights to soften the color.

Which was, Daisy reminded herself as they followed Susan Tasker toward the parlor, *not* her problem.

From first glance, it was clear to her that the house hadn't changed. Not a stick of furniture from the entryway had been moved, and she would swear that even the fresh flowers on the round table near the foot of the staircase were exactly the same as they'd been last time she was here. The ceilings were high, the furnishings antique, the pictures unexciting landscapes and old family portraits framed in gold. This place was a constant, never changing.

She loved this old house, even though Taskers lived in it.

Jim Tasker was in the parlor, enjoying a predinner drink. Jacob's youngest brother Ben was there with his wife, Madison. And Eunice Tasker sat in the center of the room. She managed to look stately and dignified, even though she was seated in a wheelchair. Even though she did not look well.

It broke Daisy's heart a little to see the elderly woman so confined, and so obviously unwell. Her color was sallow, her hands unsteady. Her face was more deeply lined than it had been the last time Daisy had seen her. Like Susan, she could use a decent haircut.

Eunice's face lit up when she saw Daisy and Jacob. She smiled, the expression erasing years from her wrinkled face. A little color crept into her cheeks. "Oh, I'm so glad you're finally here," she said, her eyes on Daisy. "We have so much to discuss!"

Daisy walked to Eunice, bent and kissed her on the cheek. The old woman smelled like baby powder and flowery perfume, and her skin was papery soft. Standing there, the last of her doubts about this ridiculous scheme fled. She'd do this, no matter how painful it might be. And she was *not* doing it for Jacob. "Miss Eunice, it's been too long."

"Yes, it's been several weeks, hasn't it?" Eunice said, taking Daisy's hands in her own. "That is far too long."

Daisy just smiled. It had been years, not weeks, but she wouldn't distress the ill woman with inconvenient facts.

Miss Eunice squeezed Daisy's hand. "You look even more beautiful than I remember." Her gaze—those eyes dark, like Jacob's—flitted past Daisy to look upon her grandson. "Doesn't your lovely bride-to-be get more beautiful every day?"

"Yes, she does," Jacob agreed solemnly.

"She's going to be stunning in my wedding gown."

The entire room went silent. Of course, everyone there but Eunice knew Daisy's relationship with Jacob had been over for a very long time. How hard must this be for the family?

Daisy couldn't feel too bad for them. This ruse was harder on her than it could possibly be on anyone else. She had to pretend not to hate Jacob for moving on without her, for not giving up his dreams for her the way she had given up hers for her sisters. He'd chosen his precious career over her. His determination to succeed at anything he chose to do had been one of the things she'd always admired about him, but in the end that determination had taken him away from her.

And then she looked around the room, taking in the pale faces, the thinned lips, the clasped hands. The Taskers were losing a beloved member of their family, not quickly and without warning, the way she'd lost her parents, but slowly. Painfully. And she had the power to make Miss Eunice's final days happier. Not for them, she reminded herself, but for a woman who had been good to the Bell family for as long as Daisy could remember.

She smiled, looking at Miss Eunice and ignoring the others. "I can't wait to see the gown. I'm sure it's lovely."

"Tonight, after dinner," Miss Eunice said with barely contained glee. "You must try the gown on! We have to make sure it fits properly."

It was as if the old woman was trying to make this as difficult as possible. Everything was happening too fast as it was! "Oh, there's no rush," Daisy said, making a real effort to keep her voice calm. The idea of trying on a family wedding gown, when at one time she had been so sure that one day this would be *her* family, was enough to give her hives.

Eunice leaned forward, gripping the armrests of her wheelchair. "No rush? What if alterations are necessary? And don't forget, we must choose a new veil that will complement the gown and your face. So much to do, so very much to do. If the wedding is going to take place during the Tasker Reunion in less than three weeks, we haven't a single day to waste."

"What?" She and Jacob responded in stereo.

"Surprise!" Eunice said brightly.

* * *

Jacob held his spine straight and kept his face impassive. In a few hours Grandma Eunice would forget that Daisy had been here. She'd definitely forget about a wedding she'd planned to be held during the reunion. In two and a half weeks. The delusion had come to life when she'd seen him, and it would go away just as suddenly, when something else grabbed her attention.

Daisy looked like she'd seen a ghost, and in a way she had. For a couple of years she'd been a part of this family. For close to two years he and Daisy had been together. For almost a year of that time, they'd been damn near inseparable. Christmas and Thanksgiving, family reunions, weekends at home…she'd been here. They hadn't discussed marriage, they had both been too young. But she'd fit in so well here, she'd become like a member of the family. Everyone had loved her. Including him.

Maybe they hadn't discussed marriage, but he couldn't say it hadn't been a part of his plans. He was certain it had been a part of her plans, too.

And then her parents had been killed and everything had changed.

Jacob had tried to be there for Daisy. He'd held her while she'd cried; he'd stayed with her through the funeral arrangements and—later—the legal details of the estate and guardianship. But eventually his new job had called him away, and he'd gone. He'd truly believed that they would be able to make a long distance relationship work until the time came when Daisy—and her sisters—joined him. The job offer he'd received had been too good to turn down, it had been exciting and he'd made enough money right off the bat to support himself, Daisy and her sisters. All he had to do was get settled and send for her.

But it hadn't worked that way. There hadn't been any

spectacular blowup, no emotional scene. They'd simply drifted apart. It had been easy to do, with him working night and day in San Francisco and Daisy caught up in raising her sisters and taking over the family businesses here in Bell Grove, Georgia. Her dad had trained the girls from the time they could walk to tune an engine. Beauty school had taken care of the rest. If she'd come to San Francisco or if he'd stayed here, maybe they'd still be together. But she hadn't and he hadn't. And they weren't.

So here they were, seven years later. They'd both changed. Everything had changed. Well, perhaps not *everything*. Jacob was annoyed to admit that he wanted Daisy. She wasn't like any other woman. She could look at him, and he felt it to the bone.

A long time ago he'd convinced himself he was over her, but as soon as he'd laid eyes on her he'd realized how wrong he'd been. If he was over her, the curve of her cheek and the sway of her hips when she walked wouldn't drive him wild. If he was over her, he wouldn't continually find himself edging closer so he could inhale her scent. Dammit, he wasn't *over her* at all.

The past was coming back to bite him in the ass, even though logically he knew they were no longer the same people. If he spent a significant amount of time with Daisy he'd soon realize that they had grown apart. He wasn't the same; neither was she. Whatever he felt was annoyingly lingering chemistry. Nothing more.

It was announced that dinner was on the table, thank goodness, ending the conversation about wedding gowns and family reunions and surprise ceremonies. Jacob took Daisy's arm and escorted her to the dining room, hoping that the meal would serve as a distraction. He didn't miss the slight tremble of her body, even though outwardly she did her best to remain calm. Dammit, he shouldn't have asked her to do this. He should've found a way to take care of the situation without asking Daisy to torture herself.

And him.

His mom didn't cook, but that didn't mean the family didn't eat well. Lurlene Preston had been in charge of the kitchen for thirty years, and no one cooked a good old-fashioned Southern meal like Lurlene. The meal that was laid out was definitely a welcome distraction. Jacob didn't eat this way when he was in California. Not that he could've gotten fried chicken, turnip greens, fried okra and fried green tomatoes, served up with a mess of cornbread, in San Francisco. Even if he could've found those foods in a specialty restaurant, they wouldn't have been the same. The smells and tastes transported him back to his childhood, to family dinners followed by the front porch swing or an hour or so spent working on whatever car he was remodeling at the time.

He and Caleb—they were the middle boys of the four, and Caleb was almost two years older than Jacob—had both had an interest in rebuilding cars from the age of fourteen or so on. It was something they'd enjoyed doing together, even though they didn't have much else in common. Jacob hadn't touched an engine since he'd moved to San Francisco. He didn't even change the oil in his own car. No, he paid someone else to do it for him. Jacob hadn't missed tinkering with engines at all, hadn't even thought about that old hobby until he'd come home.

Funny how the scents of his youth were the ones plaguing him this week. Food. Engine oil. Daisy. Daisy, most of all.

For a while they enjoyed a reprieve from wedding talk. Everyone talked about the weather, the food, baseball and the upcoming football season and the relatives who were not in attendance. Daisy was quiet in the beginning, and she just picked at her food. But after a while she relaxed. She ate, participated in the conversation and completely and totally ignored him.

Which was good, in one way. He could stare at her all he wanted, and she wouldn't realize that he studied the gentle curve of her jaw and the tempting length of her neck. He didn't dare look any lower—not for more than a split second here and there—for fear that she'd turn in his direction and catch him with his eyes on the swell of her breasts. He knew better. He didn't ogle women. But this was Daisy, and he might never get another chance.

Their reprieve ended as peach cobbler was served. Grandma Eunice began again to discuss her plans for the wedding. The ceremony would be held Sunday afternoon of the three-day Tasker Reunion, she'd decided. It would be the culmination of the annual event, a formal wedding to be held in the house. Family only, since space would be an issue. Besides, Grandma Eunice added with her nose in the air, family was all that mattered.

She looked at him as she added this last dig. It wasn't a secret that she was annoyed at Jacob for throwing himself so wholeheartedly into his career, for not coming home and taking his place here. The Taskers owned interests in several successful restaurants, a department store—there were three locations, now—a steel mill and a sock factory. Jacob's grandfather and great-uncles—three of them—had gone into business together. They'd done well. These days this branch of the family was the most prosperous, but Jacob had many cousins—close and distant—who continued to hold a portion of old family businesses.

He could've taken a job at any one of them, or else begun working with his mother with the objective of eventually taking the reins from her. But he was determined to make it on his own, to be independently successful. Yes, his ambition had taken him away from his family for too long, he could admit to that. Was that why when his grandmother's mind had started to go she'd immediately honed in on this wedding business? Was she, somehow, determined to see him married to a local girl before she died so he'd be tied to Bell Grove in yet another way?

Jacob had hoped his grandmother would forget about having Daisy try on her wedding dress before the meal was done, but no such luck. No, she was anxious to see Daisy in the gown, prepared to get Lurlene to take care of any alterations that might be necessary. Daisy paled at the thought, he caught a hint of a return of that tremble that told him how hard this was for her, but she played along. The four women left the table and headed for Grandma Eunice's suite of rooms. Years ago, when she'd first started having trouble with the stairs, they'd converted the library and sitting room on the ground floor for her.

When the women had gone, Jacob stared at his dad and his brother—one and then the other. "Why didn't you tell me she was this bad?" he asked, keeping his voice low.

His father shrugged his shoulders. "It happened so fast. She's had trouble remembering some things for years, but we thought it was normal, related to her aging. Then all of a sudden she's losing whole blocks of time. Months, years. The doctor says the memory loss could be caused by any number of things, but...I don't know."

Ben nodded his head. "I know we don't get here often enough, but I swear, one time when we saw her she was fine. Sharp as a tack. A couple of months later she doesn't remember who Maddy is."

They hadn't been paying attention, if they thought this had come on suddenly. That wasn't the way dementia worked, unless it was a sudden side effect of a medication or an infection. Those possibilities had been checked and rejected. Jacob couldn't very well complain to his father and younger brother about their lack of attention to the family matriarch. He hadn't been home in years, so he could hardly jump all over them for not understanding the small changes that had turned into big ones. But dammit, they were *here*.

"She needs a more competent doctor."

"Good luck getting her to agree to that," Jim grumbled.

"You have to make it happen," Jacob snapped.

"She's agreed to see someone after the reunion. She wouldn't even agree to that much until you came home. That's a step in the right direction."

A step that should've been taken months ago. Jacob decided not to argue any longer with his father, who was maddeningly laid-back about the entire situation. Arguing was a waste of breath, apparently.

"Daisy looks great!" Ben said brightly, happy to change the subject.

"Yes, she does," Jacob agreed sourly. *Too* great.

"How on earth did you get her to agree to this? I figured she'd tell you to take a hike."

He'd love to be able to tell Ben that he'd bought Daisy's cooperation, but she'd taken that option away from him. "She's doing it for Grandma Eunice, not for me. They always did get along well."

Ben snorted. "I wish she and Maddy could find a way to get along. Grandma Eunice never approved of my wife, she never liked her the way she liked Daisy. Not once did she offer to let Maddy wear her wedding dress." He shook his head. "Not that Maddy would've worn the old thing."

Ben's wife was very pretty, but she was also very flashy. Madison had made the mistake of wearing a very short dress to the house the first time she'd had dinner here.

According to Susan, Grandma Eunice had never forgiven that infraction.

The men retired to the parlor for scotch and cigars, an old tradition that had survived many, many years in this household. Jacob passed on the offered cigar but took the scotch. Just one. He had a feeling he was going to need the fortification in order to get through the rest of the evening.

Eunice watched as Daisy followed her instructions and very carefully removed the wedding gown from the wardrobe. Eunice had had the dress—more than sixty years old and as beautiful as it had been the day she'd worn it—removed from storage as soon as she'd heard that Jacob was coming home.

Daisy was a beautiful girl. More than that she was a sweet girl, and a strong woman. She'd make Jacob a good wife.

Playing at being completely off her rocker was easier than she'd imagined. And more fun. Maybe it was a little bit mean, but desperate times called for desperate measures. Jacob hadn't been home in five years. Five years! And that time he'd flown into Atlanta one day and out the next, barely home long enough to say hello to his immediate family. Family was important. Family was everything!

Only one of her four grandsons—Ben, who had not chosen wisely—was married. Caleb and Luke were both older than Jacob, and neither of them had married. Well, Caleb had tried when he'd been a younger man, but she'd had cheese last longer than that marriage. She'd deal with the other two soon enough, but the situation with Jacob was critical.

No one knew it, except for Lurlene and Doc Porter, but Eunice had become quite good at browsing the internet with her laptop computer. The family thought she used the laptop for playing solitaire, and sometimes she did. But when no one was watching she browsed the internet with the best of them. A few weeks ago she'd run across an alarming photo that had sent warning bells off in her head. Jacob, at some highfalutin event, a skinny brunette in a tiny black dress clinging to his arm…

If she didn't do something he would marry a woman just like the one in the picture. Maybe not her, exactly, but someone like her. Shallow. Bony. Caring about nothing but money and possessions. They'd have one or two spoiled kids who'd grow up to be totally worthless, and she'd be lucky to see Jacob again before she passed even if she lived to be a hundred and twenty.

He'd lost his way. It was up to her to help him find his way back again. Daisy Bell was a big part of the plan. Eunice didn't believe for a minute that they weren't still in love.

All she had to do was remind them of that fact. She had two and a half weeks to get it done.

"Try it on," she instructed. Eunice looked at Susan and Madison. She narrowed her eyes, squinting at Madison. "Who are you? Are you the seamstress? I thought Lurlene could handle any alterations, but Susan, if you think it's best that we hire someone…"

Madison's lips narrowed. "Grandma Eunice, it's me, Maddy. I'm married to Ben, remember? We've been married almost two years."

Eunice had practiced her confused expression in the mirror countless times, and she called upon it now. Her eyes widened and she blinked fast several times. She puckered her mouth, very slightly before saying, "Ben isn't married! Why, he's much too young." Seven years ago, when Jacob and Daisy had been together, Ben hadn't been married. He hadn't even known this whiny girl. Oh, if only she really could turn back the clock.

Eunice didn't like Ben's wife much. The girl didn't dress properly, wore too much makeup, didn't go to church every Sunday and couldn't carry on an intelligent conversation to save her life. The last thing she'd read had probably been the side of a cereal box.

But Daisy...Daisy was sharp as a tack. She had her priorities straight. She went to church every Sunday, and that was a plus even if she was a Methodist. She'd sacrificed for her family, and that made her the kind of woman Jacob needed. And fast.

Eunice reminded herself, not for the first time, not to get too carried away. If she seemed to have really lost it, they might decide to lock her away somewhere, or the doctors they'd threatened to call in would show up long before the reunion—and the wedding. She needed to appear to be just a little bit crazy, not entirely cuckoo.

One way or another, she *would* get what she wanted.

Madison stormed out of the room, near tears. Daisy stared after her. Poor girl. She was so upset about Eunice's condition.

Daisy carefully placed the gown across Eunice's bed. It was so old she was afraid to touch it, much less try it on! The satin was a soft ivory, and the cut of the gown was surprisingly sleek and simple.

"I want to see it on you, dear," Eunice said in a voice that held not a hint of dementia. She was matriarch of this family, and was accustomed to being obeyed. Always.

If the old woman hadn't been sick, Daisy never would've agreed to try on the wedding gown. It was painful, to be reminded of what she'd never have. It hurt, to have the past brought back in such a sharp, detailed way. She and

Jacob were never going to get married. Those "Mrs. Daisy Tasker" doodles were ancient history. All the plans they'd made, the simple dreams she'd had...gone.

She should hate this house and everyone in it. For a long time she'd been so sure that these people would one day be her family, that the house would one day be her family home as well as Jacob's. It hurt...but she couldn't hate the house or the people. No, it couldn't be that easy.

Daisy caressed the fabric then pulled her hand back, afraid the simple touch might damage the satin. "I can't do it," she whispered, and then she looked up. Jacob's mother and grandmother were both staring at her. She tried to smile. "I'm sorry. I simply ate too much for supper. I'm not accustomed to Lurlene's cooking, and I just know I'm two sizes bigger than I was when I sat down to dinner. Tomorrow?" she offered. "I can come by after I close the shop and try on the gown."

She half expected an argument from Miss Eunice, but Jacob's grandmother smiled sweetly. "Of course. You must come for supper again tomorrow night. I've already asked Lurlene to make chicken and dumplings. Oh, and you know what I'm in the mood for? Your dear, sweet mother's lemon cake. Bless her soul. She used to bring it to the annual Fourth of July picnic and I always looked forward to eating a big piece. Sweet and tangy and rich... so amazingly *rich*. Do you have the recipe?"

"I do." Not that she'd ever attempted to make that cake. It had taken her mother half a day to prepare!

"Lovely. Tomorrow night, chicken and dumplings and lemon cake." It was a command that left no room for negotiation.

Daisy carefully returned the wedding gown to the wardrobe, kissed Eunice on the cheek and left the room. Once she was in the hallway, the door closed behind her, she shut her eyes and leaned against the wall. The hall was deserted, thank heavens, and she took a moment to gather her senses, as best she could. By tomorrow night Eunice would surely have forgotten about the wedding gown and the lemon cake, and Daisy could pass the evening blessedly alone, eating a frozen dinner and watching something mindless on television.

This was torture, pure and simple. Her legs were a little wobbly and her heart was beating much too hard. Daisy pushed away from the wall and headed not for the parlor where she assumed Jacob would be waiting but for the front porch. She needed a few minutes alone, a little bit of time to rein in her jumbled emotions.

She pushed the screen door open and headed for the porch swing that faced west. The days were long, in the midst of summer, and the sunsets across the expanse of Tasker land were breathtaking. This sunset was no exception. She'd seen more than a few, from this very porch swing. Normally she had not enjoyed them alone. This porch swing, Jacob, a couple glasses of iced tea, whispers, a stolen kiss or two or twenty…

Daisy sat there and vowed not to allow an old woman's fantasies to drag her into the past. She'd moved on, made a new and good life for herself. She didn't think about what might've been. Very often. Oh, hell, who was she kidding? She thought about it all the time!

And her life wasn't new at all. It was old and familiar. Bell Grove was home and she belonged here. She didn't need or *want* her life to be new and exciting.

She pushed off with a toe and swung lightly, hoping the gentle movement would soothe her jangled nerves. Having the past thrown in her face without warning forced her to look long and hard at the present. The truth of the matter was, she thought about Jacob entirely too much. That's why she hadn't had a serious relationship since they'd broken up. That's why she never had more than two dates with the same guy, why she found something wrong with every man who expressed an interest in her. She wasn't as pretty as Lily, but she wasn't exactly a troll, either. She could've had several serious relationships in the past few years, if she'd wanted to. She might even have found a man who'd make a good husband and father. And it took having Jacob right under her nose to allow her to see what she'd done.

Sitting in that porch swing alone, Daisy could see that she'd put her life on hold for a man who didn't deserve it. Where romance was concerned she was marking time, stagnant, stuck in a rut. A man was really all her life lacked. A man was the only thing Bell Grove had not been able to provide. How incredibly stupid! She couldn't give up the opportunity to build a family of her own just because her first love had disappointed her.

That's all Jacob was; her first love. Not her last, not her only. She didn't try to fool herself into thinking that she'd never loved him. She had. Deeply and completely. But that was then and this was now. Somehow her *now* had gone seriously askew. If this little charade—painful as it was—helped her to truly put Jacob in her past where he belonged, then it would be worthwhile.

He must've heard her leaving the house, because she hadn't been in the swing long before Jacob stepped onto the porch. Of course he knew just where she was. The gentle squeak of the porch swing, as she pushed herself back and forth with her toe, was a dead giveaway.

"Sorry," he said when he saw her there.

For so many things... She didn't go there. What was the point? "Not your fault." *This time.* "Bless her heart, one minute she seems just fine and the next she's completely befuddled."

"Yeah." Jacob walked toward her, and for a moment she wondered if he would sit beside her on the swing. It was more than big enough for two, but she wished, very hard, that he wouldn't make that move. She didn't want him that close; she didn't want that stark reminder of the old days.

The old days were gone, and there was no getting them back. Now all she had to do was convince herself that she didn't want them back.

He stopped a few feet away, almost as if he'd had the same thought. "I didn't know about the…the…"

"Wedding," she said briskly, providing the word he apparently could not.

"She'll forget about it." It sounded like an order, as if he thought he could sway an old woman's memory by will alone.

"And if she doesn't?"

He didn't have an answer for that question.

Daisy couldn't be too angry with Jacob, much as she wanted to. He was a career-focused, ambitious workaholic who'd let her go when keeping her had become inconvenient. He'd chosen his career over her. He hadn't loved her enough to sacrifice his grand plans for her. Family obligation had kept her here, while a job opportunity had taken him far, far away. They hadn't been able to make her need to provide a familiar home for her sisters and his desire for a new career to work together. He'd moved on, and he hadn't looked back, and she shouldn't hate him because he'd managed to do what she could not.

But he loved his grandmother and would apparently do anything to make her final days good ones. Maybe he did have a heart under that expensive suit, after all. That heart just wasn't meant for her.

"So," she said softly. "How's your life?"

He seemed surprised that she asked. "Good. Busy, but good. You?"

"Spectacular," she said, her voice low. "I like my life. I *love* my life." Maybe if she said it often enough she'd be able to gloss over the lack of romance in her almost-perfect life.

"Good."

Daisy wished she was the kind of woman who could purposely hurt someone who had hurt her. She wished she could tell Jacob how ecstatically happy she was, how active her sex life was, how she'd never wanted for a man's attention in the past seven years, how she hadn't missed him at all. But while she could lie to protect an old woman, she couldn't make herself lie to purposely cause pain.

As if he cared…

Jacob looked at Daisy as if he were seeing her for the first time. When she caught his eye he didn't turn away, didn't try to pretend that he wasn't studying her as if he could see beneath her skin. He looked at her with an intensity that was so much a part of the man she'd once loved.

"I'd forgotten," he said.

"Forgotten what?" she asked, her heart skipping a beat.

"I'd forgotten how you get to me." He looked her in the eye, shifted slightly as if suddenly uncomfortable in his own skin, though he still didn't turn away or drop his eyes. And Daisy could see what was coming so clearly it hurt. He'd get to *her;* they'd end up in bed; he'd break her heart all over again.

And she could *not* allow that to happen.

Chapter Three

Perhaps he'd made a mistake when he'd let Daisy go. He hadn't had a choice, he couldn't see how his life could've unfolded in any other way, but dammit, had he made a mistake?

This was the thought that plagued Jacob as he pulled his rental car to a stop in front of Daisy's home. He never second-guessed his decisions, never looked back and wondered.

The sooner he finished up here and got out of town, the better off he'd be.

Daisy still lived in the house she'd grown up in, a yellow cottage a mere five blocks from the shop where she worked. The house was square and wide and one-story, with a large wraparound porch complete with a pair of matching white rockers and healthy ferns. The yard was dotted with ancient trees; the branches intertwined overhead, and while he couldn't see it from here he imagined there was still a vegetable garden out back.

Her car was parked in the driveway, but instead of pulling in behind it he stopped at the curb. A concrete sidewalk ran in front of her house, and a leg of that sidewalk shot from the street to her front porch. This was a neighborhood where the residents walked, both for exercise and for more practical reasons, where they visited one another—on special occasions and sometimes for no reason at all. Both sidewalks saw a lot of wear. Or at least, they once had. He imagined that hadn't changed.

Daisy's entire life was right here, a general store, doctor's office, pharmacy—and her work—within easy walking distance, while he flew from one time zone to another on a regular basis. He was good at what he did, a whiz with numbers and an unshakable faith in his own instincts. The men he worked for trusted his instincts, too. They trusted him with billions of dollars in investments, and he hadn't let them down yet. In fact, he'd made them all lots and lots of money.

In the early days they'd called him a whiz kid. These days he was a highly valued member of a company that continued to grow, in large part thanks to him. And what had it gotten him? Insomnia. An almost nonexistent social life. And a fat bank account.

The second he stopped the car at the curb Daisy threw open the door and jumped out, as if she couldn't wait to escape. He should wave, let her go and hurry home. But instead he shut down the engine, jumped out of the car and followed her.

She glanced over her shoulder as his car door slammed. She was not happy. "What do you think you're doing?"

"Walking you to the door."

"If a man in a suit follows me around my neighbors are going to think someone is suing me for a bad haircut, or maybe the tax man is after me."

"The tax man? Really?"

"Shoo," she said, waving her fingers in his direction.

He ignored her dismissive order and took two long steps to catch up with her. "What's your problem with the suit?"

She didn't look at him. Her chin was in the air, her hair whipped as she glanced in the opposite direction. "I have no problem with what you wear. I don't care *at all* what you wear."

"Then why have you mentioned the damn suit so often?"

"It's summertime in the Deep South," she said. "Unless you're headed to church or a funeral, the suit is downright unnatural."

Daisy stopped in front of her porch steps, then spun around to face him. She was no longer trying to avoid him. No, instead she looked him in the eye, unflinching. She was stronger than he remembered. Tougher. "On second thought, wear a suit every day for all I care. It will serve as a constant reminder that you don't belong here."

"I don't need a constant reminder that I don't belong here." No, he'd felt it every second of every day.

"Neither do I." She took a step back and up, onto the bottom step.

Jacob matched her step, moving forward but not up. He wasn't ready to let her move away. They were nose to nose, now, eye to eye. "Then who am I supposed to be reminding?"

"I don't know and I don't care."

"You're not making any sense at all…."

"I don't have to make sense if I don't want to."

Jacob shook his head. "When did we start arguing?"

"Seven years ago," Daisy snapped.

Jacob reached out, took her face in his hands, stepped into her space and kissed her. He wasn't sure why, he just couldn't help himself. He had to kiss her; he had to press his mouth to hers. He'd thought her scent was maddening, but her taste…he had forgotten…how the hell had he forgotten this…

She tensed for a moment then she melted. Her lips molded to his, her eyes closed and they kissed. Long and soft and easy.

He never should've let her go.

She tasted so good, so warm and right. Her face in his hands was soft, and he loved holding her almost as much as he loved kissing her. She kissed him back, well and deeply. She leaned toward him, into him and when he swept his tongue just inside her mouth she gasped and moaned and deepened the kiss. The years melted away, the miles that had come between them no longer mattered.

Daisy pulled away from him sharply. Her lips were swollen and wet, her eyes wide and surprised. Was she surprised by the kiss, or by her response?

"Don't do that again," she ordered, backing up the front porch steps, toward the front door and escape.

"Why not?"

"Because it's a very bad idea."

He didn't follow her onto the porch; he'd pushed his luck enough for one day.

"Tomorrow night," he reminded her. "Lemon cake and chicken and dumplings."

"Surely Miss Eunice will forget all about those plans by tomorrow morning," Daisy said as she stopped by the front door and grabbed her house keys out of her small purse. "I hope," she added beneath her breath.

"If she doesn't…"

"She *will,*" Daisy said, almost as if she was commanding it to be so.

"Maybe. Probably." Jacob stood on the walk for several minutes after Daisy had closed the front door. When he'd heard about his grandmother's condition and decided to come home for a long visit, he hadn't expected this. He hadn't expected to have the past come to life again, to look at Daisy and suffer a deep regret for what he'd lost.

He shook his head, as if he could shake off unwanted thoughts, and turned around sharply to make his escape. Coming home had been a mistake. He'd had his reasons, and it was too late to turn back now. But the truth of the matter was, his life was no longer here in Bell Grove. It hadn't been for a very long time. Daisy and the reactions she elicited were a part of another life, and no matter how pleasant—and frustrating—it was to see her again, he had to remember to leave her in the past. Where she belonged.

Daisy didn't think she'd be able to sleep, after everything that had happened in the past twenty hours, but after Jacob dropped her at home she slept amazingly well. She dreamed about the kiss, which was very annoying because in her dream that kiss didn't end too soon. In her dream she got a lot more than a kiss from Jacob. She woke with a start, sweating and shaking and most of all angry with herself for allowing her badly neglected physical needs to wipe away every ounce of common sense. First the kiss, then the dream. Where was her self-control? Why couldn't she just be angry with him and leave it at that?

She should've bolted when he'd moved in for a kiss. She could have. Should have. But she'd wanted that kiss so much, and at that moment the want had been a lot stronger than her sense of what she *should* do.

Her dad had always been philosophical. Everything happened for a reason, he'd said on numerous occasions. There was a purpose in every heartbreak, in every decision, in every coincidence. She'd dismissed that way of thinking for a long time, because she hadn't been able to believe that her parents had died for some lofty reason that she didn't understand.

But as she walked to work she convinced herself that Jacob had returned to Bell Grove for a specific purpose, that Miss Eunice had lost her mind to put Daisy in this very position. Why? Easy. So she could get over Jacob once and for all and move on with her life.

They'd never had it out, had never really ended their relationship. They'd simply drifted apart, fallen into lives so different there was just no way to make them mesh. If she ever wanted to move on she had to get over Jacob, once and for all. Oh, she'd insisted to anyone who would listen that she'd gotten over him years ago, she'd even convinced herself, for a while. But now she knew that was a lie. If she'd really gotten over him, the unfortunate kiss wouldn't have affected her the way it had. Looking at Miss Eunice's wedding dress wouldn't have given her shivers. As well as a bout of unexpected nausea, if she were being completely honest.

She should have a few days to come up with a plan. As bad as her memory was these days, Miss Eunice had surely already forgotten about chicken and dumplings and lemon cake. What were the odds that she'd also forget that her grandson and Daisy were "engaged"? Daisy could hope, but the engagement seemed to be a thing Miss Eunice had grabbed on to, and she likely wasn't going to let it go easily. There was such joy on her face as she planned a wedding that would never take place.

Jacob seemed to think he was humoring his grandmother by playing along—and by dragging Daisy into the family mess—but what would happen if Miss Eunice's fantasy didn't fade? Did he really expect that she would go through with a fake wedding ceremony at his family reunion? No, something had to break before that happened. This charade couldn't go any further.

Much as she wanted to get Jacob out of her heart once and for all, Daisy knew very well that pretending to be his *wife* would shatter that heart beyond saving.

The morning was an easy one, until her eleven o'clock cut and color started talking about Jacob. She supposed it was inevitable that everyone would find out he was back, but you'd think people would have better manners! Not Amanda Williams, who had never met a silent moment she liked.

She started while Daisy was applying color to her hair. "I hear Jacob Tasker is in town."

Daisy made a noncommittal humming noise that sounded affirmative enough to her.

"I also heard that he was in your shop yesterday. Did he need a haircut or did he just stop by to chat? I'm sure none of the Taskers handles their own engine repair—they have people for that sort of thing. And really, why on earth would he want someone from Bell Grove to cut his hair?" She laughed, not realizing that she'd just insulted Daisy—Daisy, who had scissors and a variety of interesting hair dyes within reach. "Oh, you two were *such* a cute couple, back in the old days." She barely took a breath, much less leave spaces in the conversation for Daisy to actually respond. Which was just as well, in Daisy's opinion.

"Everyone always knew Jacob would light out of town as soon as he got the chance. He was always so smart, so driven to succeed. I didn't think he'd go without you, though."

Well, he did. Daisy wondered if it was too late to add some purple to the color she was putting on Amanda's honey-blond hair. Maybe a Mohawk…

"I hear he looks good. Is he married, do you know? Still

working for that same company that hired him right out of college? I haven't heard much about him for a couple of years, but that doesn't mean anything."

He looks damn good, I don't know for certain if he's married or not but I don't think so and last time I checked he was still working for that soulless money-hungry company that stole him out from under me. "I need you to sit under the dryer, now," Daisy said.

Sadly the noise of the dryer didn't shut Amanda up. She raised her voice and continued, thankfully moving on to the other Taskers. Sure, a beauty shop was a great place to gossip, but Amanda's rambling made Daisy wonder what the residents of Bell Grove had been saying about her lately. All gossip concerning Daisy Bell probably began with "That poor girl, bless her heart…"

She didn't want to be a poor girl, didn't want people to bless her heart behind her back. What the hell had she done to herself? Mari and Lily didn't need her anymore. Well, they needed her as a sister and she'd always be there for them, but her years as guardian were behind her. She loved Bell Grove, loved her job and her friends, but she no longer had her sisters as a barrier keeping her from pursuing romance. Maybe there wasn't exactly a glut of handsome, available, appealing men in town, but not every man in the county was an ogre or a jerk. Why was she alone after all this time?

Jacob's return was making her question everything! Just what she didn't need: a man to screw with her head.

But she did need a man in her life. That was becoming clear. She wanted to be kissed, wanted to have sex outside of a dream, wanted to marry and have kids and make a life for herself. Maybe that would happen here in Bell Grove, and maybe it would have to happen somewhere else. She should make more trips to Atlanta, broaden her horizons.

But it wouldn't happen at all until she ended things with Jacob once and for all and allowed herself to start over.

Jacob left his grandmother's room with a frown on his face. Great. Just great! Her memory issues were pretty damn selective. And inconvenient. She had told Lurlene to prepare chicken and dumplings for supper, and she'd already started talking about how much she was looking forward to Daisy's lemon cake.

Daisy couldn't cook. She was good at a lot of things, but cooking wasn't one of them. Maybe he could drive to Atlanta and buy a lemon cake. Not that a store-bought cake, even a spectacular one, would fool Grandma Eunice even on her worst day.

It had been seven years since he'd been with Daisy, and in that time she'd raised her sisters, taken over the family business, basically grown up. Maybe she'd learned how to cook. Maybe she *did* know how to make that lemon cake. He called the shop, and she answered with a sharp,

"Bell's."

"It's me," he said.

"Me? I'm afraid you'll have to be more specific, sir." Her voice was sweeter, now, a little lower and calmer, but with an edge he couldn't dismiss. "Would you like to make an appointment for a haircut? I do have an opening this afternoon."

"Dammit, Daisy, it's *Jacob*."

"Oh, so sorry." She didn't sound sorry at all. "I didn't recognize your voice. You sounded a little bit like Old Man Johnson, but I was afraid to assume…"

"We need a lemon cake," he snapped, without arguing that he sounded nothing like Old Man Johnson, who was ninety-seven years old and had the deepest Southern drawl of any man for miles.

The moment of silence told him Daisy was as bothered as he was. "She didn't forget?"

"No. You're expected for supper, and you're expected to bring a lemon cake. She's been talking about it all morning."

"I'll call you back in fifteen minutes," she said. "I have a customer." She disconnected without a goodbye, and for a few seconds Jacob stood there with the phone in his hand, staring at it as if somehow Daisy was still there, harassing him. Driving him crazy.

Making him pay.

He hadn't purposely left her behind, it had just happened. Like that made a difference. He'd planned to send for her, to send for them all, but the one time he'd mentioned moving, Daisy had been horrified. She wouldn't uproot her sisters, she'd said, wouldn't drag them away from their friends and the only home they'd ever known. He'd planned to come home for Christmas that year, to convince her face-to-face to return to California with him.

But he hadn't made Christmas that year. There had been a business emergency—in hindsight so unimportant that right now he could not remember what it had been—and he'd canceled his travel plans.

And that had been that, though there had been a few awkward phone conversations in the early months of the new year. Not many and nothing had been said that could break through the distance between them, distance both physical and emotional. He and Daisy had no longer wanted the same things. They'd drifted apart. His life was there, her life was here. Simple. She'd faded in his memory, as he was certain he'd faded in hers. Life went on.

Dammit, that hadn't been entirely his fault. She'd played a part, as well. Maybe he hadn't fought for her the way he should have, but she hadn't exactly fought for him, either.

When Daisy called back he was still holding the cordless phone in his hand, ready for her. Her words were sharp. "Grab a pen and paper. I'm going to tell you what I need, and you're going to put on that fancy suit of yours and head to the Piggly Wiggly."

A part of her wanted to kick Jacob out of her house and tackle this chore alone, but two things stopped her. One, she needed the help. Two, she'd never get over him if she didn't kick this annoying habit of being downright twitchy when he was around. Not twitchy in a bad way. No, he made her squirm in a way that was annoyingly pleasant. She felt like he had literally worked his way under her skin.

He looked good in khakis and a golf shirt. She'd kidded him about his suits, but he did look sharp in them. The more casual outfit he wore this afternoon showed off the muscle he'd built up since he'd left her. Not massive muscle, thank goodness, but he did have some interesting definition.

More reminder that they weren't the same people they'd been seven years ago. Of course they weren't! They'd been little more than babies, untouched by the real world, unshaped by loss and hardship and responsibility.

Daisy tried to keep her mind on lemon cake, but she really wanted to touch Jacob's forearm to see if it felt as hard as it looked. She wanted to look under that shirt—just a peek—to see what muscles he'd added there. He'd probably added some chest hair, as well. He hadn't had much at twenty-four. Oh, she really hoped he hadn't turned into one of those guys who worked out in a gym and waxed his chest....

Her mind could not wander there.

"Do you actually play golf?" she asked, pointing at

the dark blue shirt with the little embroidered doodad on the pocket.

"No."

"Doesn't that make your outfit false advertising?"

He'd didn't answer, but he did give her a frustrated look that made her smile as he unpacked everything he'd bought at the Piggly Wiggly down the road, a small grocery store that served the next town over as well as two communities that were too small to support their own. His purchases lined the counter in the Bell kitchen, a boxy room with a small table that was older than she was and appliances that weren't much newer. They worked. And it wasn't like she cooked all that often anyway.

He picked up a box. "I'm pretty sure your mom's famous homemade lemon cake didn't start with a cake mix."

Daisy shot him a cutting glance. "No, but I don't have time to make a homemade cake, and besides, it's the icing that makes it special."

"It's a good thing you were free this afternoon."

She glared at him. Again. Still. "I wasn't *free*. I had to reschedule a regular for tomorrow afternoon. Remember Miss Hattie?"

"How could I forget. Did you tell her why you had to cancel?"

"No, I lied and told her I didn't feel well. Do you know how much I hate lying to my clients?" She didn't point out that she hated the idea that the facts of this charade might get out much more than she hated fibbing to her customers.

"Sorry. I'll be happy to pay you for any income you lose because you're helping me."

"I still don't want your money, Tasker." She made sure she sounded sharp and certain. And annoyed.

He sounded pretty annoyed, himself. "I don't want you

to lose money because you're helping me out of a tough spot."

"I'm not helping you. I'm helping your grandmother." He could drown in his *tough spots* for all she cared.

"Sorry," he said sharply. "I forgot."

The tension in the air was almost unbearable. It hung between them, like every unspoken word that haunted her, still. He was angry. She was antsy.

"Are you married?" She'd planned to ask, needed to know, but the question could've come at a better time and been delivered more graciously. Instead she'd just blurted it out, standing in the kitchen with an apron worn over a pair of denim shorts and an old red tank—she always made such a mess when she did try to cook—feet bare, a box of butter in one hand and a sack of lemons in the other. The question did diffuse the tension, a bit. Maybe because it apparently took Jacob by surprise.

He shook his head. "No."

His answer was sadly insufficient, so Daisy pressed on. "Engaged? Dating seriously? Involved with any woman on any level?"

"No."

"Why the hell not? I'm sure you're quite the catch, even in California. I'll bet the women *looooove* your Southern accent."

"I lost my Southern accent years ago," he insisted.

Daisy laughed. "Yeah, keep telling yourself that."

Jacob's lips thinned. His jaw twitched. Finally he asked, "Would I have kissed you last night if I was married, engaged, or involved?"

"Maybe," she said sharply. "Some men don't seem to have a problem with that sort of thing…they don't find it a conflict of interest at all."

"I'm not one of those men. You should know that."

She should, but it had been so long. She didn't know him at all, not really. How much had he changed? Her task of kicking him out of her head and her heart would be so much easier if he'd turned into a jerk.

"So, there's no significant other waiting for you on the other side of the country, no woman sitting at home alone, waiting for your phone calls," she said calmly. "I can't help but wonder, why not?"

Daisy wanted, more than anything, for Jacob to convince her that he didn't deserve to visit her dreams and send her well-ordered life spinning out of control. The boy she'd once loved was gone. What kind of man had he become?

She studied him, up and down. *Be a complete ass, please. That will make this so much easier.*

Chapter Four

Why not? *No time, no inclination.* He'd dated, but never the same girl more than twice. Jacob hadn't questioned that MO until Daisy had come back into his life, however temporarily.

He was forced to consider that the reason he'd never met a woman who really did it for him wasn't because he worked so many hours, wasn't because he was so focused on his career that he didn't have the time for a serious relationship. Maybe the sad truth was that no one else had ever affected him this way because no one else was Daisy.

"Can we just make a cake?" he snapped.

Daisy switched on the oven, collected a large bowl and a small pot from a lower cabinet and then she turned to face him. "Sorry to pry. Amanda asked today if you were married, and I was horrified to realize that I didn't know."

Because he'd kissed her, and she'd kissed him back, and Daisy Bell would never have knowingly kissed a married man that way. "What about you?" He'd know if she was married. Someone would've told him, he supposed, and if she was married this charade never would've gotten off the ground, but… "Are you seeing anyone? Is there a boyfriend I should be on the lookout for?"

"Not at the moment," she said coolly.

Jacob found he was sharply relieved to know that there wasn't another man in Daisy's life. He also wondered about the qualifier. Not at the moment? Who had she dated in the past? Had any of those relationships been serious? A surge of jealousy almost knocked him on his ass.

No, not jealousy. Envy. He had no right to be jealous. He'd had his shot and he'd blown it. He wanted Daisy to be happy, to have everything she wanted and needed. At the same time, he couldn't say he'd be happy to see her with another man.

It annoyed him to realize that in spite of all the obstacles, he wanted Daisy again. While he was here, while they were forced to endure one another's company…he wanted her. The certainty of that wanting hit him low in the gut, as they worked together in her warm, cozy kitchen. His presence here, in her kitchen, wasn't really necessary, but he didn't back away, didn't come up with an excuse to bolt. He fetched things for her. He washed and dried bowls, and he moved out of her way when she started to dance from one counter to another, from the sink to the stove to the counter. His mind was *not* on cake.

He wanted to kiss Daisy again, but this time he wouldn't stop. He wanted to make love to her. He wanted to watch her laugh in bed, wanted to dance with her, naked, the way they once had. More than reliving old memories, he wanted to make new ones. With her.

He was old enough now to understand why she hadn't been able to come to him. She'd done what she had to do, what she'd believed to be best for her family. Maybe in hindsight she understood, too, why he hadn't been able to stay here. They couldn't go back and undo what had been done, but that didn't mean they couldn't forget that pain and get to know one another all over again.

He wanted her, Daisy the woman, Daisy who had said she wouldn't kiss him again, Daisy who occasionally looked at him as if she was willing him to disappear.

Jacob wasn't afraid of a challenge. Never had been. In fact, he loved a challenge more than just about anything.

Daisy licked a dollop of icing off the tip of her finger. The cake looked a little rubbery—maybe it had cooked too long—but the icing was awesome. How could it not be? Confectioners sugar, butter, lemon juice, whole milk. It was the icing that made the cake, anyway. Maybe Miss Eunice wouldn't remember exactly how the lemon cake used to taste. Maybe fabulous icing alone would be enough. She could hope!

"My turn." Jacob leaned in, looked down on the pot that had bits of icing clinging to the sides and waited.

"Go ahead," she said, starting to back away. He was too close for comfort. Just having him so near made her skin itch as if it was resizing itself to fit over her body. But before she could move away, he placed a hand at the small of her back. That hand was firm, warm and steady. It held her in place without undue pressure. It grounded her. Her entire body seemed to thump, as if the earth had just shifted in a major way. She had never before been so keenly aware of a *touch*. She could move away, she could simply step to the side and that hand would fall. She didn't move. If anything, she shifted slightly closer to Jacob.

He put his other hand over hers, guided both into the pot, scooped a bit of icing from the side of the pot onto *her* finger and lifted it to his mouth. He wasn't going to... he wouldn't dare...

He did. Jacob placed her finger in his mouth and sucked. No part of the act, not even the sucking, was hard or violent or forceful; his touch was actually very light. Easy. Just west of casual. Again, she could've stopped him, could've moved her hand away, but *again* she didn't. Instead she watched his mouth close over her finger, felt the warm, moist flick of his tongue.

If she'd felt that touch only on her finger she'd be all right, but no—she felt the way Jacob touched her in her entire body, from the top of her head to her curling toes. She felt it in her scalp, in her breasts, between her legs. She took the opportunity to place her free hand on his forearm. Yep, hard as rock and wonderfully warm to the touch. If she had even a tiny bit less self-control, she'd throw him on the floor and strip him naked and have her way with him here and now.

She was still curious about his current chest hair situation.

Thankfully she *did* have some self-control. And dignity. Both were fading fast, though. "I told you..."

Jacob slowly pulled her finger from his mouth. "You said no kissing. You didn't say a word about licking icing off your finger."

"Do I have to be *that* specific?" She dropped her hand, but didn't back away. She'd never admit it, at least not aloud, but she liked having him so close she could see the stubble on his jaw, see each and every hair on his forearm. She liked that she could smell him, and though he had changed and she had changed, his scent and her reaction to it remained the same. Like it or not she was drawn to Jacob the way iron was drawn to a magnet.

"I wish you would be specific," he said, his head dipped

down to bring it too close to hers. "What exactly do you not want me to do to you?"

He was teasing her, knowing damn well that she couldn't stand here and tell him not to touch her, not to make her feel itchy all over, not to invade her dreams. *Please, Jacob, don't look at me that way. Don't make me love you all over again.*

She backed away. Slowly. Reluctantly. "I have to change."

"Yes, Grandma Eunice will be shocked if you show up dressed like that. Not that I'd mind. You look amazing."

She should've worn old, baggy sweats instead of shorts and a tank, no matter how warm it was in the kitchen. Too much skin was exposed, and the way Jacob was staring at her…

She had to throw up a barrier between them, had to remind him—and herself—why they didn't work. "Too bad I don't have tennis whites or a matching golf shirt and a skort to wear. Wouldn't we make a fine preppy couple."

He didn't have a snappy comeback for that one. No, he just looked confused. "What's a skort?"

"Half skirt, half shorts. Skort."

It annoyed him when she criticized the way he dressed, she noticed. Funny. She didn't remember him caring much about such things in the old days. No, he'd cared about his grades, his plans for the future and her. He'd played guitar—as badly as she sang along—and he'd worked on old cars. He and Caleb had always had a project in the separate garage behind Tasker House, but these days she supposed he'd have a conniption if he wound up with grease under his fingernails. He'd been a whiz with the cars, but he'd never been able to master playing the guitar. He did everything else so well, he didn't fail at anything. Except playing the guitar. And keeping her.

These days he cared about clothes and work. That seemed like a huge step backward to her.

Daisy left Jacob in the kitchen while she all but ran to her bedroom to change clothes. She reached into her closet with a specific outfit in mind. Lavender slacks, matching blouse, strappy sandals. Too bad she didn't have a chastity belt in her closet, somewhere. She needed something to remind her why she couldn't have what she really wanted. Iron, lock and key…not a bad idea…

With her hand on the lavender outfit, another idea popped into her head. A *brilliant* idea, if she did say so herself.

She was in this uncomfortable situation for Miss Eunice's sake, not for Jacob's, not for any of the other Taskers. For some reason, Miss Eunice not only thought she and Jacob were engaged, she approved. Heartily. But she didn't approve of Ben's wife, Maddy. Not at all. She obviously didn't like the way Maddy dressed, spoke, or wore her makeup and hair. Maybe Maddy was a bit flashy and flamboyant, but everyone was entitled to their own style. Maddy's style was just kind of slutty, bless her heart.

Daisy let her hand fall. She stood at the open closet for a moment and asked herself…What would happen if Miss Eunice didn't approve of *her?* The wedding wouldn't seem so attractive and pressing, then. Daisy didn't want to shock Miss Eunice, didn't want to send the old woman into a conniption fit or anything, but if she started to disapprove of the match, even just a little bit…

Daisy closed her closet door, peeked into the hallway and jetted across to Lily's old room, a wide smile on her face. For the first time all day she felt as if she were in control. Not Miss Eunice, not Jacob, not her traitorous body. She was going to put an end to this debacle, once and for all.

* * *

She was trying to kill him. That was the only explanation.

At first, Daisy had insisted on driving herself to the house for dinner, but Jacob had talked her into riding with him again. He wanted her close; he wanted to steal glimpses of her as he drove down the deserted road between downtown Bell Grove and Tasker House. He wanted her in his presence for as long as possible; he wanted to be able to reach out and touch her, even if he didn't.

He wasn't sure why she'd eventually given in and agreed to make the short trip with him, in his rental car, he was just glad for it. She sat in the passenger seat, the lemon cake in her lap, her long, tanned, bare legs stretching out beyond the pale yellow, slightly lopsided dessert.

He'd like to think that maybe, just maybe, she'd agreed to come along for the same reasons he'd wanted her here. Did she like being near him, even just a little? Her words were sharp, and she'd given no sign—beyond her instinctive response to the kiss and his mouth on her finger—that she had any romantic feelings left for him. Still, he could hope. She'd never admit it, but chemistry like this couldn't be one-sided.

Jacob kept his attention entirely on the road for a few minutes. That final thought made him sound like a stalker. Like it or not, it was entirely possible that what he felt for her *was* one-sided.

But he didn't think that was the case.

When Daisy had stepped into the kitchen—after what seemed like an awfully long time to change clothes—she'd been transformed. She wore a floral print dress with a flirty skirt that was *very* short and a V-neck that was *very* deep. The four inch heels made her already long legs look incredibly long. Her hair was piled on top of her head in an artfully messy way, and she wore more makeup than he'd ever seen on her pretty face.

She was all boobs and legs and red lipstick. And what fine boobs and legs they were.

"You're a little overdressed for chicken and dumplings," he'd argued.

"Look who's talking about being overdressed," she'd countered.

Neither of them had said a word as he drove the final mile toward Tasker House. Daisy was up to something, he just didn't know what. Was she rubbing every gorgeous attribute she possessed in his face in order to torture him? If so, her plan was working. He was definitely tortured.

He pulled into a parking space close to the porch and shut off the engine of his rental car. Daisy—who was usually annoyingly independent—sat in the car and waited for him to round it and open her door. When he did so she offered him the cake. He laughed. She hadn't simply been waiting for him to open her door like a gentleman; she wasn't able to exit the car in those shoes with a layer cake in her hands. He took the cake from her, and watched as she grabbed her little purse and very carefully peeled herself out of the car. Slowly. Gracefully. *Damn.* His mouth went dry.

"What are you up to?" he asked as they approached the front door. He carried the cake, so his hands were full. Just as well.

"I have no idea what you're talking about," she said sweetly, and then she stumbled. As she recovered she tugged her skirt down as much as was possible. Which wasn't much. She wasn't accustomed to walking in those high heels, any more than she was used to a skirt that barely covered her butt. No, this was a show of some sort. She was in costume. For his benefit? He wasn't sure. What kind of woman told a man to keep his distance then turned up wearing a dress like that one?

As if he could understand how a woman thought.

Inside the house, he handed the cake over to Lurlene, whose eyes widened when she saw Daisy. Daisy dropped her purse on an entryway table and took a moment to once again adjust her teeny skirt. She twisted her body, as if she could realign her hips to make the skirt a bit longer. It didn't work. The cook who had been with the Taskers since before Jacob was born didn't say a word, not right away, but she walked toward the kitchen with the cake in her hands, shaking her head and mumbling something under her breath when she was too far away for them to make out the words.

Jacob and Daisy walked toward the parlor. Slowly, since she was unable to walk any other way in those heels. She pulled on the skirt again, and then adjusted the flimsy fabric that barely covered her breasts.

Again he asked. "What are you up to with that getup?"

"How do you know I don't dress like this all the time, these days?"

He didn't, so he kept his mouth shut.

"This is supposed to be a date, after all. I'm not a child anymore, Jacob, I'm all grown up. I'm certainly not the same naive girl I was when we dated. I've changed, I've matured." She lifted her chin and rotated her head slowly to look at him with ice-cold blue eyes.

They reached the parlor before he could respond, which was just as well since he had no idea what to say. The idea of Daisy dressing like this for another man was more than he could handle, even though he knew, logically, that he had no right to care how she dressed or for whom. Logic flew out the window where Daisy was concerned.

He found himself wondering who she'd dated, who she'd worn that dress for, who she'd kissed on the front porch....

As soon as he entered the room and saw Maddy pouting on the love seat by the bookcase, her own long legs displayed beyond a very short skirt, her own high heeled shoes dangling from her feet, he understood Daisy's motives in a flash that momentarily stopped him in his tracks. He should've realized immediately what she was up to. He turned to Daisy, narrowed his eyes and whispered, "Really?"

She just smiled back and walked into the room with confidence, those long legs and a nice swell of full breasts out there for everyone to see. The shock was evident on every face as they took in her new style. Even Grandma Eunice's face displayed disapproval and surprise. Ben's tongue was practically hanging out. His mom's eyes widened and she took a step back. His dad narrowed his gaze, squinting in Daisy's direction as if he couldn't believe what he was seeing. Jacob wouldn't have been surprised if his dad literally hit the floor.

Maddy didn't get it at all. She was completely oblivious to the reactions around her as she smiled widely, straightened her spine and said, "Oh, I love that dress."

Grandma Eunice muttered beneath her breath, "Of course you do."

Okay, so it wasn't the best idea she'd ever had. Her feet hurt, she could feel the blister on the big toe of her right foot taking shape and she was already tired of Ben checking out her cleavage every time he got the chance. He wasn't even bothering to be subtle about it! They weren't halfway through the meal, and Daisy already regretted her impulsive decision to take her cue from Maddy Tasker.

She needed to have a long, big sister talk with Lily. This

dress should never come out of the closet again! And the shoes, how did Lily walk in these things? Surely she didn't dress like this for her new job, or for dating in Atlanta, or for, well, anything.

Even worse, her plan hadn't worked. At all. Miss Eunice was still talking about the wedding. She hadn't mentioned the scandalous dress or the makeup or the shoes, not once. She repeated herself often, but she never veered from her purpose. At this rate there would be a wedding at the Tasker Reunion whether she and Jacob agreed to it or not. Miss Eunice would probably sit there in her wheelchair, front and center, shouting at the top of her lungs, "They do! They do!"

Would that be legal? Surely not, but if Miss Eunice could find a way to make it legal, she would.

The Tasker Reunion seemed very far away, at the moment. It was only one issue in a mountain of problems Daisy faced. For now, she needed to focus on surviving this night.

It wasn't going to be easy.

Jacob, having figured out her plan, was making her pay for her foolishness. He sat to her left, and one hand had found its way to her thigh not long after they'd taken their chairs. For a while that hand had just rested there, warm and heavy, and then, about the time she attempted to take a bite of the chicken and dumplings, that hand began to move. Not a lot, but it was movement, his fingers brushing against her bare leg. She'd jumped in response, once, then shooed at a nonexistent fly to explain away her twitch.

That hand was still on her thigh. It was warm, and heavy, and large. The fingers molded to the shape of her leg, brushing her inner thigh. She couldn't eat, not with Jacob's hand resting on her thigh as if it belonged there. A boulder had settled in her throat, so she didn't even try to take another bite. She reached down, put her hand over his, lifted it and placed that hand on his own thigh. Ten seconds later, the hand was back. Higher this time.

Like it or not, her body responded to Jacob's touch. Her body remembered, and long-neglected nerve endings danced just because his skin rested against hers. She wanted to throw that hand off her leg and move as far away from Jacob as possible. But she didn't want to make a scene at the table. Miss Eunice wouldn't understand why Daisy wouldn't allow her "fiancé" to touch her.

The dinner plates were cleared away, and the lemon cake was deposited on the table. Daisy hadn't been able to swallow more than three bites of chicken and dumplings, so she was still hungry. Unfortunately her throat was about to close up and she wasn't sure she could swallow. One finger on the hand at her thigh began to rock back and forth, every sway taking it higher and firmer and closer to her center. Like it or not, she throbbed. Like it or not, she *wanted* Jacob to touch her there.

Muscle memory, she told herself, that's all it was. When they'd been together, the sex had been great. No other man could make her feel that way, could make her lose control and scream and laugh and shudder.

Not that she'd ever given another man the chance…

Everyone seemed to enjoy the cake, but her. She looked at the piece on her plate, lifted a glob of icing onto her finger and licked it off. That was it. She couldn't swallow another bite.

Jacob seemed to be enjoying his cake well enough, taking big bites, complimenting her as everyone else did. If anyone had figured out she'd used a cake mix instead of her mother's old recipe, they were too polite to mention it. How dare he smile and act as if everything was right in his world? How dare he sit there, with his hand up her skirt, and act as if nothing was going on beneath the table?

Almost too late, the shock wore off and Daisy decided two could play his game. She'd decided to take control of the situation by dressing this way and attempting to scare his grandmother into changing her mind about the wedding, and with a touch Jacob had stolen that control from her. She couldn't let him get away with that.

Beneath the table, she placed her hand on Jacob's thigh. High, firm, familiar. Her fingertips moved, just a little. He almost choked on his last bite of cake when she stroked, allowing her hand to travel higher than was proper. But they were "engaged," after all. For all intents and purposes, they were a couple. She let her hand slide to his inner thigh. To his credit, he didn't jump out of his chair. But he tensed, and his neck turned red.

How much did her touch affect him? If she let her hand travel higher, would she find further evidence of his reaction? She wasn't brave enough to check, but the slight tremble she felt in his thigh gave her a good indication that he was not unaffected.

Good. She wasn't the only one vulnerable to this kind of torture.

Instead of being properly chastised and realizing—with regret—what he'd been doing to her throughout the meal, Jacob recovered and retaliated. His hand squeezed her thigh then it moved boldly higher. Slowly, firmly. Full of talent and promise and memory. Daisy couldn't breathe. The room got small and too warm, and someone was speaking but she couldn't make out the words. Her knees were all but knocking, her skin grew overly warm. His hand, big and warm and assured, slipped so far beneath her short skirt he was *right there*. Her thighs fell apart, just slightly.

Before Jacob could touch her where she ached for him, where she wanted him to touch her, Daisy pushed her chair back, broke all contact with him and excused herself from the table. She rushed from the dining room, headed for the guest bathroom down the hallway.

What had she been thinking? Why the hell was she even here? Had she really thought she could play chicken with Jacob and win?

In the small bathroom, she put down the toilet lid and plopped onto it. Pretending was exhausting. She wasn't an actress; she was a good hairdresser with enough mechanical skill to handle a simple engine repair. Acting was not her strong suit. She couldn't pretend to be someone she was not, to love someone who had hurt her. And somewhere along the way the pretending that nothing had changed had turned into full-out undeniable lust.

She wanted Jacob. She didn't love him anymore, she didn't want him to be a part of her life, she was still so mad at him that she could spit. But like it or not she wanted him in her bed. He had her aching and shaky and…dammit…needy. And really, why not? They were unattached, healthy, consenting adults. Obviously the spark that had come to life between them nine years ago was still there. And plenty strong. Why shouldn't she…why couldn't she… Oh, no, this was such a bad idea.

She had to get away from Jacob until her head cleared and her body became her own again. Maybe they could tell Miss Eunice that the bride had fallen deathly ill and the wedding was off. It was pretty clear that she wasn't going to forget about it, at least not as long as Jacob was here for her to see every day. For some reason Jacob's marriage had become a focal point for his grandmother, something she clung to while her health was deteriorating.

But Daisy knew she couldn't take this much longer. It

was torture, pure and simple. She could've lived the rest of her life without wanting Jacob Tasker this way! She'd planned to do just that, and now here she was, trembling to her marrow, throbbing, aching. And all it had taken was one stolen kiss and a hand on her thigh. Was she so easy? So desperate for affection?

"Daisy?" the tentative knock at the door was accompanied by his voice. Not Old Man Johnson's distinctive drawl, but Jacob's unforgettable voice, a voice she would remember with great clarity until the day she died. "Are you all right?"

"I'm fine. I just need a minute."

"I'm coming in."

"Good luck with that," she snapped. "I locked the..."

The cheap lock on the door popped, and Jacob walked inside. Suddenly the tiny guest bathroom was smaller than it had been before. He took up all the air in the room, all the space, and again, she couldn't breathe.

She didn't bother to stand. "Really, Jacob? What if I'd been using the facilities? Can't a girl get a little privacy around here?"

"This was a bad idea," he said, staying by the door and ignoring her questions.

"Tell me about it."

"I told everyone that you hadn't been feeling well and that I'm taking you home right away."

"No trying on my wedding dress tonight?" she asked, trying to come off cool and uncaring, instead sounding merely sad and frustrated.

"Not tonight."

Daisy stood quickly and brushed against Jacob. He caught her, held her firmly. She looked up, caught his eye, and heaven help her, she wanted to be with him here and now, in a teeny bathroom, while his family ate cake just a few yards away. She was inches away from begging him. *Please, Jacob, help me remember how good it was.* She actually scooted her body up slowly, moving her mouth closer to his, parting her lips. All rational thought was just about gone. Soon there would be nothing left but a primitive need she wouldn't be able to deny, an ache only he could satisfy.

Just about. She stopped before her lips touched his. "I need to go home."

He nodded, but didn't say a word.

"I want you to give me the keys to your car, and let me drive myself home, because I can't be with you right now."

She expected him to argue, but he surprised her. He reached into his pocket, withdrew the keys and handed them to her without a single word of argument. "Call me when you get home."

Daisy shook her head. She didn't want to talk to him, didn't want to hear his voice…didn't even want to think about him.

"If you don't, I'll show up at your house to make sure you made it home all right. Don't make me worry about you, Daisy," he added, and he sounded sincere.

She didn't want to believe he cared about her at all, didn't want to think he had a single attractive quality, beyond his obvious physical attributes. He was cold, hard, uncaring. As long as she believed that, he wouldn't be able to hurt her again.

"Fine, I'll call." If she didn't he probably would show up at her door. If he showed up at her door she'd ask him in. She'd ask him in, and she'd kiss him, and it wouldn't stop there. She wouldn't be able to help herself, and what did that say about her? How desperate was she for a man in her life when the one who'd broken her heart had her all but writhing in need?

They stepped into the hallway then moved apart. Daisy kicked off her shoes, grabbed her purse from the entryway table and headed out the door. She didn't look back.

Eunice watched from the window for several minutes after Jacob's rental car had disappeared from view. Without Jacob in it. She bit her lip. Frowned. Drummed her fingers on the armrest of her wheelchair. Everything was *not* going according to plan. She'd been so sure that as soon as Jacob and Daisy were in the same room their love would bloom to life again. They'd been so very much in love before life and career and far too many miles had driven them apart. But apparently it was not happening as she'd planned. Otherwise Daisy wouldn't be driving home alone, and Jacob wouldn't be sitting on the front porch. Also alone.

For years her grandson had made a very good living analyzing businesses, finding their strengths and weaknesses and advising his employer on whether or not the business under scrutiny could be salvaged or should be dismantled. He had an analytical mind that allowed him to see all sides of a situation, to detach himself from emotion and find the best approach. He'd gotten that ability from her, though he likely didn't realize it. In her generation a woman hid her strengths, especially if she was considerably smarter than her husband.

It had taken Jacob some time in college to find his calling. He'd changed his major twice, early on, and had ended up spending more than four years in school. But it had been worth it. He was smart, he had honed his innate skills and now he was amazingly successful.

And he was alone.

Jacob wanted Daisy; Eunice knew that to be true. Daisy wanted him, too, even if she wouldn't admit it to herself. But the truth was, Daisy Bell was too comfortable here in Bell Grove; her roots were too deep. How could she be convinced that she was better off with Jacob than she was staying here? She would always have ties to Bell Grove, and that meant Jacob would share those ties. But having ties to a place and being rooted there were two different things entirely.

Eunice pondered the possibilities. Daisy wasn't the kind of woman who could be influenced with gifts. She could not be bought; she would not swoon over diamonds and gold. No, she was made of stronger stuff than that.

The girl was very stubborn when it came to following her heart. If she'd followed her heart she would've wound up in Jacob's arms by now, and that hadn't happened. If they'd slept together, Jacob wouldn't be wound tighter than a two-dollar watch and Daisy wouldn't have sat at the dinner table looking as if she was on the verge of literally exploding.

Stubborn young people.

As far as Eunice could see there was only one way to go. Uproot Daisy. Remove all other options. And she had to make it happen fast. This had to happen *yesterday.* She was determined that the fake wedding they were planning to patronize her wouldn't be fake at all, and that when Jacob returned to San Francisco he wouldn't be going alone.

Chapter Five

Jacob had forgotten what it was like to live in his childhood home. In San Francisco his day was tightly scheduled from the moment he woke to the late hour he fell into bed. There was no time to reflect on the choices he'd made, no quiet time where his mind wandered to dangerous—and foolish—"what might've been" territory.

It had almost killed him not to see Daisy for the past two days, but she'd made it clear that she needed time. Time was something he didn't have enough of. The clock was ticking, his time here was rushing past. He'd been so tempted to go into town just to manage a quick and "accidental" moment with her, but he hadn't. He owed her the time she'd asked for.

Preparing the Tasker property for the annual reunion meant clearing fallen limbs and cutting those which were suitable for firewood into the proper lengths to dry for the coming winter. Winters were short in Georgia, but when the occasional ice or snowstorm came through there was nothing more comforting than a wood fire in one of the many fireplaces. Unfortunately, physical labor that didn't require much in the way of actual thinking gave Jacob's mind an opportunity to wander. His mind *never* wandered. There were so many aspects of his past that he'd given little—if any—thought to until he'd come home. Family, of course. His mother was under a lot of stress; his father didn't seem to be much help. His grandmother was aging before his eyes. Ben, the youngest of the Tasker boys, had grown up. Physically he was bigger, sturdier. Mentally he was sharper, less distracted than Jacob remembered, and he seemed to be doing a good job for the family company. He still needed some maturing, but Ben was a far cry from the kid Jacob remembered. Jacob had to admit, he didn't really know his little brother anymore. Time had changed them all.

He wondered if he'd notice the same kinds of changes in Caleb and Luke, when he saw them. Of course, they hadn't been kids when Jacob had left. They'd been grown men, so the changes shouldn't be as dramatic. Still, you never knew what the years would do to a person.

Jacob had borrowed suitable work clothes from Ben, who had joined in on this hot, summer weekend to take care of the chores that had been assigned to them by their mother. She enjoyed ordering them around like they were still teenagers.

After they took care of the limbs they needed to address the fire ant hills and a wasps' nest. When that was done, Susan would give her two younger boys another list of chores. In two weeks this land would be crawling with relatives. Young and old, from near and far…the property had to be made safe. Heaven forbid that anyone might find a flaw.

Jacob hadn't been assigned chores for a very long time. He couldn't say that a day in the sun, working and thinking as little as possible, was necessarily a bad thing. Physical labor outside his usual three days at the gym proved to be invigorating and more challenging than he wanted to admit. Even if his mind did wander to unfortunate what-might've-beens.

He wouldn't allow himself to admit that he'd missed Daisy. Her smile, her eyes, her walk. The simplest things grabbed him and wouldn't let go. Not that it mattered how much she appealed to him. Even though her sisters were grown and on their own, he didn't think for a minute that Daisy would ever consider moving to San Francisco. Even if she did forgive him for not sticking with her when she'd been forced to quit college and come back home, there was the simple fact that Daisy was a small-town girl. She loved it here; she was a part of the community. This was her *home,* in every sense of the word. He'd heard it in her voice when she'd called to let him know she'd arrived home safely and told him about the neighbor girl doing cartwheels on the lawn. And when he'd spoken to her that morning and she'd mentioned stopping by the farmer's market and running into an old mutual friend, someone who'd asked about Jacob.

While he could admit to perversely enjoying his simple chores, while talking to Daisy reminded him of what it was like to truly have a home town, giving up a very lucrative career to come home and work for his mother was not an option. Tasker Enterprises was diverse and there were a dozen positions he could take, if it suited him. But no matter what he chose to do, if he was employed by Tasker Enterprises he'd be working for his mother. No, thanks.

Which left the situation with Daisy entirely unworkable. A long distance relationship hadn't worked seven years ago, and it wouldn't work now.

Ben wiped the sweat from his face, grabbed a couple cold bottles of water from the ice chest and headed Jacob's way. "Slow down, bro. The faster we get this done, the sooner we'll get new marching orders. I swear, I don't know why Mom won't hire this out. It's not like we can't afford a crew of yard men and exterminators to get this done. Why don't you convince her that she'd be assisting the local economy by hiring a couple of unemployed guys to do the grunt work?"

Jacob set his chain saw aside and took the offered water. "Either she doesn't think workmen she'd hire would do a proper job, or she just likes ordering us around like we were still kids."

Ben smiled, and for a moment he almost looked like he was no more than thirteen again, gangly and awkward. The boy was still there, barely disguised by the years. "Probably both."

"Probably." Jacob drank the water too quickly, glad for the moment of rest and the much-needed hydration.

Ben's smile faded, and he glanced toward the house as if he was afraid someone might be headed their way. "So, how's it going with Daisy?"

"How the hell do you think it's going?" Jacob snapped. "This is the worst scheme I ever agreed to participate in, and if I could take it back I would do it in a heartbeat. Daisy's miserable, I'm miserable and Grandma Eunice seems to forget about everything else *but* the wedding plans, which remain clear as a bell. I wanted to give her a few good days, I wanted to see her not so upset, but what's going to happen when the reunion rolls around and she's still set on this wedding?" Had he just made matters worse by trying to do something nice for his grandmother? Maybe he should've left well enough alone. Too late, now.

Daisy still had his rental car. He hadn't bothered to try to collect it because it wasn't like the Tasker family was lacking in modes of transportation. There was a separate four-car garage out back and every bay housed a vehicle of some sort. Besides, Daisy had been so upset when she'd left the house a couple of days ago. She seemed better on the phone, but she was still cautious where he was concerned. And the days without her slipped by.

As soon as the reunion was over, he had to get back to San Francisco and back to work. He'd been trying to keep up by cell and computer, but it wasn't the same as being there in the thick of things.

"I talked to Daisy this morning," Jacob said. "Grandma Eunice has been asking for her, so she'll be here tomorrow for lunch." He didn't mention that he'd had to gently twist her arm.

"Good! I've gotten used to seeing her on the other side of the dining room table."

Jacob stared at his little brother. "I noticed that. Stare at her boobs the way you did the last time she was here, and I'll kick your ass."

Ben laughed. "You can try." His laughter faded. "Seriously, you can ditch the macho act anytime, bro. This isn't the real thing, remember? You aren't supposed to get possessive about a woman you're not actually involved with. It's all pretend, remember?"

"Yeah, I remember," Jacob said then he gave his brother a level glare. "But that doesn't change what I said. I *will* kick your ass."

Maybe Ben was right and he had no right to feel possessive about Daisy, but that didn't do a thing to squash what he was feeling. Regret and frustration…with a little bit of unexpected hope thrown into the mix.

Mari swiped her hand back, trying to move a stubborn strand of hair out of her eyes, and ended up smearing grease across her cheek. Daisy smiled as she looked on. This was Mari's normal weekend look. Coveralls, a crooked ponytail and grease. When it came to repairing engines she was as messy in the shop as Daisy was in the kitchen.

There were some repairs Daisy could handle, but for the more complicated jobs she needed Marigold. The youngest Bell sister had always had a magic touch with engines large and small. She could've made a career of it without going to college, but she'd decided to pursue a nursing degree, instead.

Always the fixer.

"So, what's up?" Mari's eyes were on her work, but repairing engines came so naturally to her she had no problem multitasking.

Oh, where to begin. *Jacob is home. He kissed me. His grandmother thinks we're getting married. I want him so badly I can barely keep my hands off of him.* "Same ol' same ol'. You?"

"You remember that guy I met at that thing? He asked me out."

"Did you say yes?"

Mari shrugged. "I said maybe. He's cute, but who has time for dating? Between school, my part-time job and coming home on weekends, my calendar is full. Besides, there's nothing wrong with making him work for me if we do end up dating." Mari smiled. Grease and all she was a princess, the baby girl of the family, the charmer who could do no wrong. She shifted her attention away from the engine on the workbench and settled it squarely on Daisy. "Are you dating? Please say yes. You need a man, big sister. If you can't find one in Bell Grove then we'll get you to Atlanta and do some shopping for a suitable penis."

"Mari!"

"Well, one with a man attached to it. Believe it or not, you really can get them unattached. That's *not* what I had in mind. Just so you know."

Her sisters weren't blind to the sacrifices Daisy had made for them. They'd tried numerous times to fix her up with a friend, or a friend of a friend. A time or two Daisy had agreed, but it never worked out. Thanks to the current charade she finally realized that it never worked out with anyone else because she'd subconsciously compared every man she met to Jacob. Dammit, any man who gave her the time of day should come out well in that comparison.

Daisy's mouth went dry. She scooted her chair back a foot or so, tapped her foot against the plain concrete floor and finally worked up the nerve to say, "Jacob is back."

Mari dropped her wrench. The clatter of metal on concrete made Daisy jump. "What do you mean, *back?*"

"I mean, he's at the Tasker place for a couple of weeks. He's in for the big family reunion."

Mari's eyes hardened; she squinted. "That snake."

Yeah. Snake. Why couldn't she just agree with that statement and move on? Mari didn't need to know everything. She really didn't need to know anything. At the same time, Daisy was dying to talk to someone. "We've...kind of dated a couple of times since he's been back."

Mari clapped her hands on her cheeks in an expression of extreme frustration. "What's the difference between dated and *kind of* dated? Oh, Daisy, any man but him. He really is a snake. Mom would call him a scalawag. Dad would call him a lot worse. Jacob Tasker left you when you needed him most!"

"We left each other," Daisy said defensively, recognizing the words as painful but true. "Besides, it's not serious." She gave a dismissive wave of her hand. "It's just, kind of, sorta..."

"Spit it out," Mari said sharply.

Daisy did, telling everything. Well, almost everything. She wasn't about to tell her little sister that she still had the hots for her first love, that she was seriously considering sleeping with him just because she could, that when he'd put his hand on her leg she'd almost come apart.

She couldn't possibly admit to her sister that no matter how she tried to fight the feelings, she enjoyed seeing Jacob. She liked touching him, looking at him, hearing the timbre of his voice wash over her. Painful as it was, she liked pretending that they were still together. Was she a glutton for punishment or what?

The changing expressions on Mari's face, as Daisy filled her in on most of the details, told it all. Sadness, horror, frustration, indignation. All the emotions Daisy herself had suffered since Jacob had walked through her door.

But eventually the pretty face of the youngest of the Bells settled into a smug expression. Daisy knew that look, and she couldn't remember a time that anything good had come of it. Mari leaned back in her chair, forgetting her work for the moment. Her blue eyes sparkled and her lips quirked in a half smile. "Sunday lunch tomorrow afternoon, yes?"

"Unless I beg off." Daisy was considering doing just that. The thought of seeing Jacob again was both terrifying and exciting. She dreaded and anticipated the next date. "Since you're in town I really should just call and cancel…."

"Don't you dare." Mari smiled. "I'm going with you."

Jacob showered, washing off the sweat and dirt of an oddly satisfying stint of yard work. After that he spent most of Saturday afternoon in his room, working via computer and cell phone. The desk where he'd once done his homework now served as a place for his laptop. The chair was uncomfortable, but it would do, for now. Both were antique, as most of the furnishings in the house were. So were the bed, the bedside table and the lamp on that table. Everything in the room was older than he was, and a stark contrast to his modern apartment in San Francisco.

His job was one emergency after another, and had been since he'd signed on. That had never bothered him before this moment. In fact, he'd fed off the intensity. He'd learned to love being indispensable.

But now he realized that the job had stolen years of his life. He was home for the first time in a very long time, and he should be visiting with his parents, his little brother and his ailing grandmother. In a few days his older brothers were coming in. He hadn't seen them for years, and he didn't intend to spend the short time they were here sitting in his old bedroom, working.

What among the mountain of emails couldn't wait? What couldn't be handed over to someone else if it was critical? This was supposed to be a vacation, and he'd spent hours working from a distance when he should've been *on vacation*.

When he thought about abandoning work for a while, more than his family crossed his mind. Daisy. She had crawled under his skin, and the only way to take care of that would be to spend some time with her. Alone. Without the charade, without his family watching every move. He could forget that she wanted time and space, find an excuse to go to town, drop by her shop, and maybe walk her home. They could stop by the ice cream shop for a cone or a sundae. She used to be fond of strawberry sundaes…

Like she was going to go for that.

They were different people than they'd been seven years ago. They'd grown, matured, moved on. But he was discovering that neither of them had moved on entirely. A spark was still there. They weren't finished, not yet.

He wanted to get to know the new Daisy, the woman. He wanted her to get to know him. For that, he was going to need time, and dammit he didn't have much time left. Two weeks, and a large part of those weeks would be devoted to family. No choice there. But he'd make time for Daisy, he'd find a way. The odds were, they'd spend some time together and find out there was nothing left but that unexpected spark which was nothing more than an echo of the past. They'd have nothing in common, most likely. Normally Jacob knew exactly what he wanted and how to get it, but since coming home life had become more complicated. *The odds, most likely…*qualifiers that were not a normal part of his thinking process.

There was only one way to proceed. He was going to court Daisy and see what happened. Did he even remember how to do that?

Would she allow him to court her? When was the last time he'd even considered "courting" a woman? These days there was the hookup, the blind date, the one-night stand. Courting indicated something else entirely. Something more.

Another email came in, another minor emergency. Jacob read the email and then, he answered.

I'm on vacation. See you in two weeks and two days.

He pulled his cell phone out of his pocket and turned it off then he stored both the laptop and the cell on the top shelf of his closet, right above the acoustic guitar he'd left behind years ago. Would he have taken that guitar with him if he'd been any good? He'd always loved music, and really wanted to play, but he'd never gotten the hang of it. Had he given up too soon?

He slammed the closet door on the guitar, the cell phone and the computer.

It felt good. It felt really good.

He couldn't truthfully say that he had no second thoughts. There was the perfectly reasonable concept that if the company could do without him for two weeks they could do without him forever. He might not have a job to go back to. He didn't think that would be the case, but in the corporate world anything was possible.

In the end he decided he didn't care. Maybe he'd change his mind in a few days, maybe he'd panic over the possibility that his company would find out he wasn't indispensable. Maybe once he and Daisy were alone for an extended period of time, the echoes of the past would fade away and they'd be left with nothing.

At the moment what he wanted more than anything was to concentrate on Daisy without distractions. Hudson-Dahlgren paid him an excellent salary and incredible bonuses. He enjoyed his work.

But for the next two weeks, his project of choice was Daisy Bell.

Chapter Six

Daisy glanced in the rearview mirror. It wasn't that she thought Mari might get lost, no. She just felt a little surge of much-needed comfort as she was reminded with a glance that she wasn't alone.

She drove Jacob's rental car, and Mari followed in her own small pickup truck. Not only did Daisy have a way to get home without Jacob, once Sunday dinner was done, she felt as if she were going into battle with a staunch ally at her side. Until now she'd been on her own, one Bell against six Taskers. Those weren't good odds for any Bell. There were only two of them today; they were still horribly outnumbered, but Daisy felt empowered. Mari might be slight and deceptively cute, but she was also blessed with determination and loyalty. She wouldn't let her big sister down.

Their weapons of choice for this particular battle were Mississippi Mud Cake and Cajun Shrimp Pasta Salad. Mari was a great baker; Daisy had made the pasta salad, which was tasty but simple to prepare. When it came to cooking, Daisy was a big fan of simple. She'd put the pasta salad together early that morning and then stuck it in the fridge to chill.

They parked in front of the house, Daisy purposely choosing the parking space to the right, where there was a place for Mari to park directly beside her. She recognized Ben's car, which had been pulled in slightly crooked as if he always took up two spaces with his flashy little car. The others were likely out back, parked in the separate garage. Today would be another small family gathering of familiar faces. Only this time, Daisy wasn't alone. She had backup.

For Sunday dinner Daisy had opted for long pants and a lightweight long-sleeve shirt, leaving as little skin as possible exposed. She wasn't worried about what the Taskers thought about the way she dressed, wasn't trying to make up for Lily's scandalous little dress by covering up every inch of skin. She was just making sure there was nothing exposed for Jacob to touch.

Even if she wanted that touch, she knew it was a bad idea. No matter how out of control they were, her hormones would not rule her. She was master of her own desires. Captain of a long-neglected body. She was in charge of her own hoohoo. It was not in charge of her.

A thought that lasted until Jacob stepped onto the porch. No suit today, she noted. Jeans. A pullover shirt that clung to those muscles she wasn't quite used to. His hair was a little mussed.

This was the Jacob she remembered. Her heart lurched and thumped against her chest; for a moment she couldn't breathe. How dare he? Where was the blasted suit that reminded Daisy that Jacob wasn't hers anymore?

Mari, huge Mississippi Mud Cake in hand, walked briskly up the steps and placed herself directly in front of

Jacob. "Long time no see," she said, smiling sweetly. And then she kicked him in the shin.

He flinched, not because it was a particular violent attack, but because Mari had taken him by surprise. "What the hell was that for?"

"As if you don't know," Mari said softly. She was smiling when she continued. "Hurt my sister again and I'll gut you."

Jacob looked past Mari's shoulder and caught Daisy's eye as she came up the steps, the large bowl of pasta salad in her hands. "I think she means it."

"I do," Mari said. Five foot two and not much more than a hundred pounds, she was surprisingly fierce. Lily might be the sister people thought could take a biker in a bar fight if necessary—she was tall and dark-haired (by choice, if not by birth) and sharp-tongued and had a low threshold for bull, and there had been a short period of time when she'd worn nothing but black—but it was Mari they should've been afraid of. She might *look* harmless, but beneath the Barbie-doll exterior she was tough as nails.

Susan came to the door, and Mari scooted around Jacob to greet her and hand over the cake. Susan wasn't surprised to see Mari. Naturally Daisy had called to ask if it was all right if her visiting sister tagged along. The two women exchanged hellos and smiles. The screen door squealed and then snapped shut behind them, as they stepped into the house.

And there was no longer anyone between Daisy and Jacob. All that remained between them was a large bowl of pasta salad and her determination to remain in control. Daisy clung to both for dear life.

"Y'all didn't have to bring food," Jacob said. "We have more than enough."

Daisy didn't respond that he should've known they

wouldn't show up to Sunday dinner without bringing something. She stepped toward the house, toward him, steeling herself for the day ahead. "So, in spite of your insistence that the accent is gone, San Francisco hasn't cured you of your 'y'all.'"

Jacob smiled. "I wasn't home long before it came back." When she reached him he took the bowl from her hands. Their fingers brushed, and lightning shot through Daisy's body. She dipped her head, looked down at the boards beneath her feet so he couldn't read the emotions on her face.

The truth wasn't easy to accept. In fact, it was damn hard. Standing there with her heart in her throat, Daisy accepted the ugly truth. In spite of all her affirmations and determination, when it came to Jacob she wasn't in control of anything.

To Jacob's relief, there was no talk of weddings or wedding gowns over the dining room table. Maybe Grandma Eunice was distracted because Mari was there, and goodness knows this could not possibly be the same very young girl she remembered. Maybe Grandma Eunice was still sharp enough to realize that there was a reason Daisy hadn't been to the house for a couple of days, and she'd wisely decided not to push—for once. She likely wouldn't guess that Jacob had scared Daisy off with a hand up her very short dress, but she might assume there was trouble in the fictional paradise she'd created.

Strangely enough, it was Mari and Maddy who dominated the conversation. They didn't talk about the reunion or Tasker family business or the wedding. Instead they talked about people they both knew. Maddy was a couple of years older than Mari, but they had several acquaintances in common. And then they started talking about football. Yes, even in June college football was an acceptable topic of conversation at the dinner table. The others soon joined in the discussion, and everyone had an opinion. They talked about coaches and players and the fall schedule. Ben and Susan both made predictions about win-loss records. They were both *very* optimistic. It was nice; nothing was forced or false and there was lots of laughter around the table. Jacob was able to relax. After a while, so did Daisy. It was good to see her genuine smile, to watch her unwind, to hear her laugh.

When dinner was over, Jacob pushed his chair back and offered Daisy a hand. He wasn't sure she'd take it, but she did. Tentatively, and after a pause the space of a heartbeat, but she wasn't afraid to touch him.

"Walk with me?" he said, imagining a stroll around the property. Alone. He wanted to have Daisy to himself, even if it was just for a few minutes. The courting process had to begin somewhere....

"I can't." She slipped her hand from his, slowly, and then hid it behind her back as if he wouldn't dare to reach for her if he couldn't see that hand. "Mari is heading back to school this afternoon, and she needs to get packed and on the road."

"She can't pack without you?"

"I told her I'd help. Besides, she's my ride home."

"I'll be your ride." It was an offer touched with command. Not a question, but a very polite order.

"No, thank you." Her response was delivered in a calm voice, so sweet and unmistakably insistent.

He should've remembered that Daisy had always hated being told what to do. She could dig in her heels with the best of them. How the hell was he supposed to court her if she wouldn't spend even a few minutes alone with him?

Mari glared at him and mouthed, *Remember what I said.* Then, for effect, she drove an imaginary knife into her own stomach and stuck her tongue out in a brief, expressive demonstration of his upcoming, violent demise. The entire warning, if you could call it that, took less than five seconds, and if anyone else saw her they didn't let it show.

Of course, Grandma Eunice was the only one who needed to be fooled, and she was being wheeled out of the dining room. She always took an afternoon nap, and today she appeared to be fading fast.

"We really should go," Mari said as she rounded the table to collect her sister. "Remember, we need to call the critter man this afternoon."

"The critter man?" Jacob asked.

"Sammy Jenkins?" Mari said, as if he was an idiot for not knowing who the critter man was.

"I have squirrels in my attic," Daisy explained. "Mari and I both heard them last night, scurrying above our heads." She shuddered, a little. "Sammy doesn't work on Sundays, but he will take calls in the afternoon and set up appointments for next week."

"I didn't realize critter men were in such demand," Jacob said.

"You wake up to the sound of little paws dancing a jig overhead and you'll understand why," Daisy said.

Maybe this could be his way in. "There's no need to wait. I'd be happy to take care of your squirrels."

Mari laughed. So did Maddy.

"What's so funny?" Jacob snapped.

"Jacob Tasker, critter man trainee?" Mari said. "Yeah, like you'd get your hands dirty crawling into the attic."

How hard could it be? "I'd be happy to help, and I *do* work on Sundays."

"No, thanks," Daisy said, without her sister's venom or humor.

"But I could..."

Daisy glanced around the room and then lowered her voice. "Eunice isn't here, Jacob. We don't have to pretend for anyone else."

Those who remained in the room—Ben, Maddy and Mari—went still and quiet. Maybe they'd forgotten that this was all pretend. Maybe they could hear the pain in Daisy's voice the way he did. It was enough to put a man on his ass.

How could he convince her he was no longer certain he was pretending?

Not here, not now.

"Oh, your dishes," Maddy said. "Let's wash them up real quick…"

"I'll get them later," Daisy said. She backed away, obviously anxious to leave. No, not to leave, to escape.

To escape him.

"Gotta go!" Mari took Daisy's arm and they left the dining room together, their steps quick as if they really were escaping. And he supposed they were. It was Mari who glanced back, once, to stick out her tongue and flash a particular finger in his direction.

Jacob couldn't help but wonder exactly what time Mari would be headed back to school.

Finally they were gone! Eunice had pretended to be asleep, but her daughter-in-law had hung around for a few minutes, sitting in the chair by the bed, sighing now and then.

Perhaps she should feel guilty for putting the family through all this drama. Maybe one day, after Jacob and Daisy were married and had a child or two, she'd confess and they'd all have a good laugh.

Eunice rolled up and reached for her bedside phone. She dialed the number she'd memorized. A man answered.

"Is everything in place?" she asked, her voice lowered in case anyone was in the hallway outside her door.

"Yes, but Ms. Tasker, are you sure…"

"If I wasn't sure would I be calling you?" She put a command she'd worked years to master into her voice. If you looked up Steel Magnolia in the dictionary, you might find her picture there.

"No, ma'am, but…" The man wisely stopped speaking, and then he sighed into the phone. That sigh really carried over the phone lines.

"Do it," Eunice said sharply, "or I'll find someone else who will. I want everything to be put into motion this week. This needs to happen immediately." Anyone who had ever worked with or for her knew that if she wanted something, it happened. Maybe she didn't have a controlling interest in the business any longer, but she did control a large portion of the family fortune, and her reputation made it difficult for many old business acquaintances to refuse her requests.

She hung up the phone without a proper goodbye, leaving the man on the other end of the call sputtering a bit.

Eunice lay back down and relaxed. She smiled as she drifted toward sleep. By God, this was going to happen. One way or another…

Mari was gone, and the house was oddly quiet again. Even the squirrels in her attic were silent as dusk settled and the light in the house dimmed. Daisy had taken off her good clothes hours earlier, and had put on a pair of cutoff shorts and a blue tank top—an outfit more suitable for the late-June weather. She should be thinking about putting together a light supper, but she wasn't hungry. She'd eaten too much at dinnertime.

Then again, maybe her lack of appetite was Jacob's

fault. He had her turned inside out and upside down. As far as she was concerned, she could even blame him for the squirrels that had taken up residence in her attic. After all, she hadn't had any trouble with critters before Jacob had come back to town.

The knock on the door made her jump. Without looking through the glass, without asking "Who's there?" she knew who it was. It was as if when Jacob was near her body shifted into another gear.

If she opened the door and it was someone else, would she be relieved or disappointed? Did she *want* Jacob to be on her front porch? She did, even though she knew that letting him into her house was the worst thing she could do. Or the best. No, it would definitely be a bad idea!

She could refuse to answer, simply pretend she wasn't at home. She could yell at him to go away, and take the chance that she was right about who had rung her doorbell. If she prepared herself, she might even be able to sound as if she meant it.

She did neither of those things.

Daisy opened the door on a Jacob who reminded her too vividly of the boy she'd once loved. Tonight there was no suit, no preppy golf shirt. Even his posture had changed a bit, as if he'd finally remembered that he was home, and relaxed. He was still wound pretty tight, just not as tightly as he'd been the day he'd walked into her shop and asked for the favor that would turn her life upside down. He held a large woven sack in one hand, and a small paper bag in the other.

"Your dishes," he said, lifting the well-worn woven sack. He raised up the paper bag. "Strawberry sundaes."

Daisy hesitated a moment before she backed farther into the house, opening the door wide, silently asking Jacob to come inside. For a moment she actually convinced herself that they could share a strawberry sundae and then she'd send him on his way, but that delusion didn't last long.

It didn't last long at all.

Chapter Seven

Jacob hadn't been sure what kind of reception he'd get when he showed up at Daisy's door unannounced. Since his return to Bell Grove, she'd never been exactly happy to see him. But if he was going to court her, if he was going to try to reignite an old flame for the next two weeks, that would have to change.

So many emotions passed across her face when she opened the door to him, he wasn't certain he could register them all. Annoyance, anger, resignation, lust. Maybe the lust that seemed to flicker in her eyes was wishful thinking on his part. Maybe he used her as a mirror for his own emotions.

She invited him inside—a good sign, he thought—took the sack of dishes from his hand and set them down. After a moment's hesitation she took the sack of sundaes, too, and carefully placed it on the coffee table.

And then Daisy surprised him. She stepped into him,

wrapped her arms around his neck and pressed her body to his as she lifted her mouth to his and kissed him. There was no hesitation in the kiss, or in the way she melded to him. There was no uncertainty or anger in the mouth that devoured, in the tongue that danced. She was soft and certain, warm and gentle.

For a split second he was taken back to a time when he and Daisy had been together, when kisses like this one had been an everyday pleasure. But the flashback didn't last. That was then, this was now. And now was fine. Very fine. They were both different. Older, if not necessarily wiser. The past seven years had changed them both, had shaped the people they'd become. This wasn't an echo, it was something new. New and powerful.

Jacob's rational thoughts drifted away as he was swept up in the kiss, in the sensation of Daisy's hands on his neck and in his hair, in the feel of her soft, warm body against his, in the way her mouth and his connected. One small, soft hand slipped just beneath his shirt. Her fingers swayed there, matching the rhythm of her mouth. The kiss deepened; her breathing changed. He was lost, caught up in that place where nothing mattered but touching her.

If she stopped, she was going to kill him.

As that thought flitted through what was left of his brain, she did stop. She pulled her mouth from his—slowly, and with a reluctance he tasted—dropped her arms, and took one step away. It was all Jacob could do not to grab her and pull her back. He didn't. Instead he fisted his hands and took a deep breath. If this was her idea of torture, it was successful. He was definitely tortured.

And then Daisy surprised him again. She grabbed the hem of her tank top and pulled it over her head. After dropping the tank to the floor, she reached out and unsnapped his jeans.

"Daisy..."

"Don't talk," she said. "If you talk I might change my mind, and I don't want to change my mind."

He remained silent.

"Just this once," she said softly, not looking him in the eye. "I don't love you anymore, so don't go thinking this is anything more than it is, but we didn't end things between us properly. We never did really end us at all." She unzipped him, reached her hand inside his jeans, moved in close again. For a long, wonderful moment, he held his breath and allowed himself to just *feel*. "So we're going to get this out of our systems tonight. We're going to make love and say goodbye, and then we're both going to move on."

He would've agreed to chop off his right hand at the moment, if she'd just keep going, so he didn't argue.

"We were good in bed, Jacob," she whispered, her breath warm on his skin. "Maybe we screwed up everything else, maybe life screwed it up for us, but...we did this right."

He whipped off his shirt, as she had, and reached into his back pocket for his wallet. One condom wouldn't be enough, but it would have to do.

She wasn't wrong; they *had* done this right.

"You can speak, now," she said.

"Have I told you that you're more beautiful than ever?" he asked as he backed her toward the hallway.

"No." She smiled.

"It's true."

"You only say that because I'm mostly naked."

"Maybe."

"You're not looking so bad yourself," she said, walking backward very slowly, reaching up to brush her fingers against his upper arm, then his chest. "I'm glad you don't wax your chest. A little chest hair is a good thing on a grown man. You only had the one, when I last saw you without a shirt."

"You've been worrying about my chest hair?"

"Maybe just a little." She smiled, but then her expression changed, shifted slightly and he could see a concern there. Where had her mind taken her?

"No more talking," he said as they arrived at her bedroom door. She opened the door on the small bedroom, the same one she'd slept in as a child.

She sighed in relief as she backed toward the double bed. "Fine by me. Talking was never our strong suit."

For a moment, an unpleasant split second, Daisy had imagined what Jacob's life in San Francisco was really like. It wasn't a thought she'd wanted, wasn't one she'd reached for. But like it or not, she'd found herself wondering if he seduced other women with ice cream, if those other women seduced him with a kiss, if they touched his biceps and his chest—where thankfully a decent but not overwhelming dusting of chest hair grew—as he walked them to a bed to make love. She'd wondered if he looked at them this way, visibly on the edge of losing control, his dark eyes narrowing and going darker, his focus on her and her alone. When he looked at her like this she felt like she was the only woman in the world. Did he make other women feel the same way?

Then she let the unpleasant thought drift away. She forced it to disappear, she let it go. None of that mattered; nothing mattered but right now. One night, one last hurrah, and then she could truly let *him* go.

And she'd only lied to him once, when she'd told him that she didn't love him anymore.

By the side of the bed, illuminated by what was left of

the day's light streaming through the blinds, he finished undressing her, unfastening her bra and dropping it to the floor, pushing her shorts and panties down and off. He was anxious, but didn't rush. Ready, but not out of control. Naked, Daisy slipped her hands into his jeans again, this time shucking them—along with a pair of dark green good-heavens-was-that-silk boxers—down and off.

And there they stood with nothing between them but whatever lingering doubts might remain. Daisy had none. Did Jacob?

She was so ready, one touch and she'd be done. It had been so long, too long, and she already throbbed in places that she'd forgotten could respond this way. Jacob tossed his condom to the bedside table and laid her down on the bed. They kissed, easy and deep. It reminded her that until Jacob had come back to town she hadn't been kissed in a very long time. No one had ever kissed her like this, no one but Jacob. Was a kiss more intimate and important than sex? Was it the true moment of soul connection? It seemed that way, as their mouths came together and incredible sensations danced through her body.

She loved the feel of his skin against hers, loved the heat of his body enveloping her. Her body swayed up and into his, slid down as she attempted to bring them closer together. She was ready; she wanted him *now*.

But he was stubborn, moving just out of reach, making this moment last.

He gently spread her legs with his knee, lifted up and looked at her—his eyes holding hers for a long, powerful moment—and then he slid down and dipped his head between her thighs. Her heart thudded, and she grasped the sheet as he lightly flicked his tongue against her where she throbbed for him. One flick and then another, and then he moved away. It was maddening, and then he intensified his efforts and she crested hard and fast, with a jerk of her body and a cry of release and relief.

That done, he crept up over her body. "If I just have this one night with you, do you really think I'll make it fast?"

No, no, not fast, please. Slow. Easy. Stay a while. But she was breathless, unable to speak coherently. So she said nothing. She didn't need to say anything as Jacob kissed his way up her body. Slowly and well. She melted into the mattress, satisfied—for the moment—and languid. Happy to have Jacob with her, thrilled to have this fantasy come true. Maybe it wouldn't last, maybe it wasn't the way it had once been, but this was fine on its own.

More than fine. She felt alive, cherished, a part of something greater than herself. She felt like a woman.

Jacob had developed some serious and impressive control in the past seven years. For a split second she allowed herself to think about how and why he'd developed that control, but she let that go, as she'd let so many other thoughts go. Sex had always been fast and furious in the old days. This was different. Jacob took his time arousing her all over again, kissing, touching. Maybe his control wasn't perfect, though, maybe it wasn't as infallible as he'd like for her to believe. He was hard and ready and hot. When she touched him, when she attempted to wrap her fingers around him, he always gently but insistently moved her hand away.

The faint light that had been streaming through the window when they'd entered the room soon faded entirely. She could no longer see Jacob well. She couldn't see his face, or the way his hands looked against her skin. And still he played with her. No, not *with* her. He played her like she was his guitar and he was a talented musician, and she gave herself over to him.

And then he was inside her. Finally. Perfectly. Daisy

closed her eyes and let her body take over. They found a rhythm that was slow and easy, at first. It was nice, it was perfection. She had the brief thought that she could do this all night, happily giving herself over to the amazing connection of body to body, to the gentle movements that were so right.

All night? No. Her need and his grew, their rhythm changed, became more frantic, and she found herself gasping as he drove deep one last time and they both shattered. She clung to him, crying out softly, holding on for dear life as her body shook. *I love you* flitted through her brain and almost escaped, but she stopped the words from flowing out in the heat of the moment.

"You're amazing," Jacob whispered. "And to think, I came over here to volunteer to be your critter man."

"You would make a lousy critter man," she responded in a whisper, surprised she had the strength to speak at all.

Jacob raised up, propped his head in one hand and looked down at her. She could barely see his face, and she wanted to see that face while she could.

"Why's that?" he asked.

She smiled. "How do I count the ways? First of all, your suit would get dirty when you climbed into the attic. I suspect you have no squirrel traps or bait in your fancy rental car, and what on earth would you do if you came face-to-face with a squirrel or a raccoon or a possum? They don't negotiate."

"Do you think that's all I can do? Negotiate?"

"Analyze and negotiate. You've been doing it since you were twelve." She ran her hands down his side, reveling in the shape of him, his heat and flesh. "Of course, you do seem to have developed some skills you couldn't have dreamed of at twelve."

He leaned over her, and she could not miss the hope in

his voice as he asked, "Are you reconsidering your one night only stipulation?"

Daisy turned her face away, dipped her chin even though she knew he could see her no more clearly than she could see him. "No."

Get it out of our systems my ass. It was the middle of the night when Jacob woke. Daisy slept on beside him, out like a light. Naked. Rumpled and flushed and gorgeous. If he stayed in her bed he'd end up making love to her again, and without a condom. That was a chance they couldn't take. What kind of a jerk would he be if he came home, knocked her up and then left again?

So he grabbed his clothes and made his way out of her bedroom, being very quiet, though he didn't think Daisy would wake even if he slammed the door.

There was a night-light in the hall, giving off just enough light to illuminate the space so he didn't run into anything. Feeling like a thief, as if he were intruding, he crept down the hall to open the door on the master suite. It was just as it had been the last time he'd seen it. Same king-size bed, same blue and white striped bedspread. It had been seven years, and Daisy had changed nothing. This was her home, now, she lived here alone, and yet she hadn't moved into the master bedroom and made it her own.

If she hadn't done it yet she never would, and he was washed in a wave of sadness. What if she wasn't happy here, the way he'd thought? What if she was simply stuck?

He used the hallway bathroom, dressed and made his way to the living room. There on the coffee table, melted ice cream and pink strawberry topping leaked out of a white paper bag. Since there was no way he could sleep, Jacob cleaned up the mess, tossing the melted sundaes in the kitchen trash and wiping down the coffee table with a damp cloth. That done he placed the dishes he'd returned to her—his excuse for coming to her door—on the kitchen table. He had no idea where they should be stored, so that would have to do. All the while he tried to be quiet even though he was pretty sure nothing would wake Daisy.

As he puttered around the house, he thought about his decision to court Daisy. Courting was an old-fashioned term, but it was appropriate. And here he was, still smelling her, still feeling her. They hadn't had the first real date, and he hadn't brought her flowers or candy. The sundaes… well, they'd never gotten to the sundaes, so that didn't count. Where did they go from here?

Since she'd declared this was a onetime deal, maybe nothing had changed. He could still attempt to court her. Would she be receptive or would she kick him to the curb? Would she think the only reason he pursued her was that they'd slept together once and he was trying to get her into bed again? Not that he'd mind sleeping with her again, but he wanted more. He wanted everything. How could he convince her that a one-night stand wasn't enough?

That thought stopped him in his tracks. If a one-night stand wasn't enough, then a two-week affair wouldn't be enough, either. Not for him, hopefully not for her. If he still intended to court Daisy, to woo her, to win back her heart…what would happen after his time in Bell Grove was done?

When it came to business, he could analyze and plot and graph a problem into submission, but when it came to planning his personal life he felt woefully inadequate. And really, *what* personal life? Since he'd moved away from Bell Grove his life had consisted almost entirely of work and work-related events. It had taken seeing Daisy again to make him realize what he'd lost.

He'd be doing her a favor if he walked away and didn't look back. He wasn't here to mess up her neat, tidy life, hadn't intended to start something he couldn't finish.

Jacob collected his wallet and his keys and headed for the door. With his hand on the doorknob, he stopped. If he left, what would Daisy think when she woke alone? If he stayed, how could he *not* make love to her again? He stood in the dark, undecided. For a moment he noted the complete stillness. San Francisco was never still. All night long he heard traffic, sirens and people in the hallway outside his condo. In Bell Grove life didn't stop after dark, but it did grow still. He'd missed that stillness and hadn't even realized it.

He needed to go, to get out of here while he could. And yet his hand remained on the unturned doorknob. He made important decisions every day, but since he'd come home the decisions he'd been forced to make were different. This wasn't business, it was life. A life he'd ignored, a life he'd put on hold.

His grandmother, his parents, Daisy... Was this a temporary aberration or had his life just taken a sharp turn?

Chapter Eight

Daisy woke with the sun that cut through the miniblinds shining in her eyes. She blinked hard, rolled over to escape the annoying light, pulled the covers over her head and took a minute to remember what day it was.

Monday, her day off. She sighed, closed her eyes tight and settled into the mattress, still half-asleep and hoping to drift off again. Hadn't she been having lovely dreams?

Jacob hadn't been a dream. He'd been here. He'd been hers again, for a while. Since she had the bed to herself, she could only assume that he'd left in the night, while she'd been sleeping. Just as well. Given the situation, the morning after might be awkward.

Reality intruded and she couldn't go back to sleep. She didn't have to get up and go to work, but the critter man was coming to check out the attic. As if on cue, one of the cursed critters ran across the attic floor above her head.

Who cared about squirrels? She was still naked, a little sore and supremely satisfied to the marrow of her bones.

Jacob. She shouldn't give him another thought, but how could she not? Last night had been even better than she'd imagined it could be. Daisy opened her eyes slowly, threw back the covers and reached one curious arm out to sweep the other side of the bed. It was cold and empty. There wasn't even much of an impression on the pillow next to hers. He'd left a long time ago.

Well, what had she expected? She'd told him sex was a onetime deal, one last hurrah. Why would he stick around?

She rolled out of bed, checked out the clock and groaned. Sammy would be here in less than an hour, so she needed to shower and grab a bite to eat. Clothes would be nice. Daisy grabbed a robe from the closet on her way to the bathroom across the hall. She took a quick shower, pulled on the robe again and headed for the kitchen.

At the end of the hallway, she stopped. A right turn would take her to the kitchen, and that was the plan. But she glanced to the left, and there he was; Jacob, asleep on the couch. Dressed, his too-long body twisted to fit the too-short couch, sound asleep.

Daisy smiled. Relief washed through her, as real and tangible as the water that had washed across her skin moments earlier. Jacob hadn't left. He should have…she told herself she would have if they'd been at his place…but he was here. He'd stayed.

Why had she ever thought having sex with Jacob would make it easier to let him go?

Since he was sleeping, she allowed herself to just watch him for a few minutes. It wasn't like this was a chance she'd ever have again. Asleep he looked more like the man…boy…she remembered. In sleep he lost the facade he'd built around himself. That's what the suits were, she decided, a part of the facade that he'd built to keep others at a distance, to remind everyone, including himself, that he didn't belong here anymore.

But lately he'd been dressing more casually, relaxing, and last night there had been no distance—and no clothing—between them. None at all.

For a moment, a few seconds maybe, Daisy allowed herself to wonder what it would be like to throw everything away and leave Bell Grove to be with Jacob. She loved her home, her business, her friends, but had she mistaken serenity and a feeling of home for being stuck in a rut? Could she walk away from everything she had, could she leave her life behind? Not that he was going to ask her to do that, but if he did…

She no longer had her sisters to raise, that was true, but nothing else had changed. Her home was here; she belonged here. In California she'd be too far away from Lily and Mari, and dammit, even if they were grown they still needed her. And she needed them. She couldn't even imagine herself there, a small-town girl in a big city. And she couldn't imagine Jacob moving back here, leaving his job behind to work with his mother and Ben in the family business. If he'd been interested in that he would've done it years ago. No, Jacob would go back to work and she'd do…what? She doubted Bell's Beauty Shop and Small Engine Repair would successfully relocate to San Francisco. She found herself both excited and terrified by the very thought.

Not that Jacob would ask her…

Not that she'd go…

As she walked into the kitchen to start the coffee, she knew she should be sorry about last night.

But she wasn't.

She should kick herself for being weak, for giving in,

for taking what she'd wanted from—no, *with*—a man she still loved.

But she didn't kick herself. With a smile on her face she started preparing breakfast, wondering if Jacob was as ravenously hungry as she was.

Jacob woke to the smell of bacon and coffee. He was twisted into an unnatural position and his back hurt—damn couch—but he wasn't sorry he'd spent the night here. It would've been wrong to sleep with Daisy and then creep out of her house like a thief.

He rolled up, stood, stretched and walked to the kitchen. Daisy stood before the stove, turning bacon in an ancient iron skillet. She wore a short robe. He was pretty sure there was nothing beneath it. Her body clung to the satiny fabric. Did she know how sexy she was in that robe?

"Morning," he said, his voice gruff.

She didn't look up from her task, but she smiled. "Good morning. Are you hungry?"

"Starving."

"Me, too." She opened the oven door and peeked inside. "The biscuits are almost done. It'll just take a minute to scramble the eggs."

Jacob walked to the kitchen table. "I thought you didn't cook."

"This isn't cooking," Daisy argued. "It's breakfast."

He didn't argue with her, he just watched.

As she broke eggs into a bowl, she glanced over her shoulder and smiled. "The biscuits are frozen. Well, they *were* frozen before I put them in the oven. Full disclosure. I don't make homemade biscuits, so don't go thinking I've turned into Suzy Homemaker overnight. Eggs are easy. Anyone can scramble an egg."

"I want to spend the day with you." Jacob didn't want

to talk about biscuits and eggs. He had this suffocating sensation that time was much too short where Daisy was concerned. He didn't want to waste a single minute.

She shrugged her shoulders. "I suppose we can spend the day together, but be warned. I have an agenda. The critter man is coming by this morning, and then I have to go to the church and pick up some meals to deliver. That'll take at least two hours, more if anyone along the way needs their hair trimmed or styled. This afternoon I'm helping my friend Terry—do you remember Terry Hall? She's Terry Sanson, now, and she's got three kids!—anyway, I'm helping her paint her bedroom. Lavender. I don't approve of the color, but it's what she wants and it *is* her bedroom. Her husband doesn't care, so lavender it is. Then tonight…"

"Are you trying to scare me away?"

"No." She glanced his way. "This is my life…it's a perfectly ordinary start to the week. Monday the shop is closed, so I volunteer and help my friends and take care of problems around the house."

"And later tonight? After all that is done?"

Daisy turned and looked at him, squarely and strong. "I wasn't kidding when I said sex was a onetime deal for us. It was great, but don't think you'll be spending the night here on a regular basis, or well, *at all,* while you're in town."

Jacob kept a straight face as he said, "So, you're going to use me and then throw me away."

"Pretty much," Daisy responded in a bright voice, and then she turned her back to him to see to the eggs.

That robe was maddening. Short, clingy and beneath there were long legs and bare feet. Had he ever seen her in anything that didn't make her look sexy as hell? Daisy Bell would be tempting wearing a potato sack.

"What if I just want a date?" he asked, his eyes on the curve of her hip beneath the robe she wore.

Moving efficiently, ignoring his question for a moment, Daisy put breakfast on the table. Old china plates, silverware, cloth napkins. Coffee cups that matched the plates. Jam. Three kinds. She finally answered as she worked. "Why on earth would you want to go on a date? Men take women on dates with the hope that they'll *maybe* have a night like last night. We skipped the dating part and went straight to the real fun. I'd think you'd be grateful."

"Grateful?" He couldn't keep the edge out of his voice.

She frowned a bit, looked away from him for a moment. "Look, just eat. The critter man will be here in less than fifteen minutes, and I'm still not dressed. Oh, shoot, I didn't make grits. Do you want grits? All I have is instant, and they won't take…"

Jacob reached up and snagged Daisy's wrist. She went still and silent, but she didn't snatch her arm away, as she could have. "I don't want grits. I want you to sit down and eat with me." She sat, almost reluctantly, and grabbed a biscuit. Then she reached for the strawberry jam and butter, and set about fixing her biscuit as if all was right with the world and she had no other concerns beyond the butter to jam ratio. He glared at her. "And dammit, Daisy, I want that date."

Daisy took a bite of her biscuit, licked a dollop of jam from her lip and then she looked at him. She could glare, too. "No."

The critter man, Sammy, arrived right on time. If you had a snake, raccoon, fox, chipmunk or squirrel problem in the county, you called Sammy. He was in great demand, and the only reason he'd worked Daisy into his schedule today, so soon after her call, was that she cut his wife's hair.

Sammy was an odd man. Short and stocky, he had a face that was less than symmetrical and a complete lack of fashion sense. Today he wore baggy khaki pants, black socks and shoes, a Georgia Tech T-shirt, and his usual horn-rimmed glasses.

That made it a relatively good day for Sammy, fashion-wise.

"Come on in," Daisy said brightly, trying to ignore the fact that Jacob was standing right behind her as if he'd spent the night and they were a couple. That was half-right, she supposed. He *had* spent the night.

Sammy wiped his feet before stepping inside, his curious eyes landed on Jacob. He nodded. "Mr. Tasker. Good to see you."

They'd never met, at least they'd never been properly introduced, but it wasn't like everyone in town couldn't recognize a Tasker on sight.

"Call me Jacob." He stepped forward and offered his hand. Sammy wiped his hand on the side of his khakis before taking the offered hand and shaking briefly.

"Love what you've done with the place," Sammy said, turning back to Daisy and pushing his glasses up with his index finger. He leaned forward and glanced into the dining room. "The new window treatments are fabulous. Really fabulous."

Window treatments? She'd hung new curtains a couple of years back, but they weren't anything special. "Uh, thanks."

"This rug is new, isn't it?" He looked down, between his feet. "Beautiful, beautiful work."

"No. This rug has been here for twenty years." Maybe she needed to shop for a new one, but who had the time?

"The place looks great, really. Of course, it always did. I haven't been here in years."

Not since before her parents had died. How long before, Daisy had no idea. She didn't remember, but maybe her parents had had trouble with squirrels while she'd been in college and had been ignorant of the kinds of problems that came with caring for an old house.

"Do you want to check the attic?" she asked.

Sammy straightened his spine, looked around one last time and said, "Sure."

Daisy led the critter man into the hallway, grabbed the plain rope-pull at the end of the hall and with a yank released the attic stairs. For a moment she held her breath, half expecting the offending squirrel to run down the stairs and into the house. Wouldn't *that* be a disaster! But that didn't happen. Sammy turned on his flashlight, adjusted his belt and climbed up the creaking wooden stairs. As he neared the top he sniffed hard and often, and with his head stuck in the attic he said ominously. "I smell urine. Yep, yep, that's urine all right."

Great. She had squirrel urine in her attic.

"The next step is to determine what species of squirrel you have nesting here." With his body half in and half out of the attic, he shone the light of his huge flashlight around. "I don't see anyone here at the moment, but…ah, yes, that's how they're getting in, the little rascals."

Jacob asked, loudly enough for Sammy to hear. "What difference does it make what species of squirrel is nesting up there?"

Sammy took a step down, turned and poked his head out of the attic. The serious expression on his face was almost comical, and Daisy had to bite her tongue to keep from laughing.

"It's extremely important. What if the invaders are an

endangered species? What if the newest residents of this house are flying squirrels, or fox squirrels?"

Daisy tipped her head back. "First of all, I think *invaders* is more accurate than *residents*." They weren't exactly roommates. "And I'm sorry, Sammy, but I don't care if they're endangered or not." Daisy kept her voice calm but firm. She didn't want to annoy the only critter man for fifty miles. "I want them out of my attic."

"Flying squirrels and fox squirrels are not really endangered, not in these parts, but they're not exactly common tree squirrels, either." Sammy looked offended, perhaps on the squirrels' behalf. Daisy wondered how offended he'd be if he knew everyone—including his wife—called him the critter man behind his back.

"There are lots of places for small animals to hide up here," Sammy continued. "I'll set some traps, plug the entrances and we'll see what happens." He took another two steps up the ladder, moving more fully into the attic. He continued to sniff and ooh and ah. "Nuts!" he cried.

"Is something wrong?" Jacob asked.

"No, no, but I found a stash of nuts. Walnuts and pecans. Your little friends have been hoarding."

"They are not my little friends," Daisy said softly. Jacob looked at her. He smiled. Then he laughed, and a moment later Daisy was laughing, too. It felt good, not just to laugh but to laugh with someone, to share a joke. Daisy's laughter died quickly. She forced it to stop. The last thing she needed was to get any closer to Jacob Tasker than she already was.

Today should cure him of any misconceptions where she was concerned. If she was really lucky he'd be a jerk and that would make it even easier to cut him loose. She really, really needed to cut him loose, once and for all.

Sammy was in and out of the house for a while, up and

down the attic access ladder. He set traps and sniffed some more, and once again admired her window treatments. As he left he said he'd be back later in the day to repair the cracks that had allowed the varmints to slip into the attic in the first place. Those repairs he could handle from outside, so Daisy didn't need to be home.

When they were alone again, Daisy turned to Jacob. "Welcome back to Bell Grove."

"Is the rest of your day going to be as interesting as the morning?"

"Probably."

"Then I'm definitely in."

Daisy raised her eyebrows, crossed her arms defensively. Maybe this wasn't such a good idea, after all. "You know how word spreads in a small town. If you spend the day with me, by sundown word will be out that we're back together. Even though we're *not*."

"I can handle that. You?"

No, not really. "Of course."

Jacob moved closer, he lifted his hand as if to cup her cheek, or pull her in for a kiss. For a split second Daisy considered letting him continue. After all, last night had been wonderful, and she could still feel him, smell him. And here he was, willing and able and wonderful. But she pulled away sharply and ducked beneath his arm, making a cowardly escape.

Jacob had forgotten where he'd come from, and he'd apparently forgotten why they didn't work together for more than one wonderful night. A day driving around the most rural parts of the county should cure him of that forgetfulness. Those she delivered meals to were needy, but they weren't always easy to get along with.

"Don't get any ideas, Tasker. Spend the day with me or not, it's not a date and we're not sleeping together again."

"Whatever you say."

She could hear in his voice that he hadn't given up. Too bad, because she meant what she'd said. Jacob Tasker could break her heart all over again, but only if she allowed him inside it.

Chapter Nine

Eunice Tasker sat at the table in her bedroom where she usually took her lunch, munching on chicken salad and green grapes and drinking sweet tea. For dessert she'd have chocolate cake, because she was by golly old enough to eat whatever she pleased without worrying about calories or fat count or sugar. According to Lurlene they were almost out of chocolate-covered cherries, and that would not do. That wouldn't do at all. Eunice had three chocolate-covered cherries every night before bed, served to her on one of her good china plates, with a linen napkin in case any of the juice dribbled. Since she was an expert at eating chocolate-covered cherries, it had been a long time since she'd had need of that napkin. Susan complained that it wasn't easy to find her mother-in-law's favorite treat after the Christmas season had passed, but she managed.

Eunice was not going to sacrifice her chocolate-covered cherries.

The truth of the matter was, at better than eighty she was healthy as a horse. Her legs weren't as strong as they had once been, and her hips and knees gave her trouble every day—and would until the day she died—which is why she relied on the wheelchair. If it hurt to walk, why should she walk?

Doc Porter had told her she'd live to be one hundred or more, and she planned to prove him right. Not that she could share that tidbit of information with her family. Not right away.

Eunice looked out the window and smiled. Jacob hadn't come home last night. He'd left here with Daisy's freshly washed dishes, and he hadn't come home. Finally! Maybe Daisy wasn't as stubborn as she'd first thought.

For a few minutes, just a few, she considered calling her friend in Atlanta and changing her plans, but in the end she decided against making that call. One night of love might not be enough to push Daisy into Jacob's arms. She might still need a little extra incentive. Everything was playing out very nicely. Why take a chance by changing her strategy now?

Not for the first time, Eunice felt a little guilty. Just a little. She could see that her family was suffering, thanks to her game. She knew they were on edge, waiting for her to go completely bonkers or fall over dead. But the guilt didn't last long. She already had a plan to cover her tracks. After Jacob and Daisy were married, but before the family brought in the new physician Eunice had promised to see after the reunion, Doc Porter would discover that his patient didn't have dementia after all, that her confusion was the side effect of a blood-pressure medication. He'd change her medication, for appearance's sake, and Eunice would miraculously improve. Voilà.

Though she had to admit, playing at being bonkers had been a lot of fun. And Caleb really could use a wife…

Jacob had forgotten how different everyday life was in Bell Grove. In San Francisco he didn't know his neighbors. His life consisted of work, a couple early mornings a week at the gym and the occasional work-related social event.

In Bell Grove everybody knew everybody. Work was necessary, but so was church, and the occasional town social, and helping your neighbors when they needed it.

Daisy thought nothing of spending her only weekday off driving all across the county delivering meals. And it wasn't like she dropped the prepackaged meals off and ran. She visited, laughed and expertly repaired more than one head of disheveled hair. She cleaned one man's kitchen in record time, and removed a splinter from a woman's trembling hand. At one house, she fed three dogs and a cat.

He didn't miss the joy on the faces of those Daisy visited as she walked in the door. They genuinely liked her, and why wouldn't they?

She was gorgeous, she had a killer body and she had a laugh that Jacob felt to his bones. But it was her heart that set her apart, her heart that made her unlike any other woman he'd ever met. Every chore she took on, she accomplished with a smile.

Jacob found himself a topic of conversation among those Daisy visited. He was a curiosity, at the very least. So far they'd dropped off meals to two elderly ladies, one ancient gentleman and a middle-aged woman with a broken leg. He was familiar with them all, the names if not the faces, though he couldn't say he knew even one of them well. They knew who he was, but other than a name and the memory of a child or a young man who'd once lived in Bell Grove he might as well have been a complete stranger.

They knew *his people,* and that was enough to serve as an instant introduction. You'd think he was a long lost relative, the way some of them acted.

None of the older folks were very subtle. They winked and waggled their eyebrows, and the old man looked at Daisy then glared at Jacob and announced that it was "about damn time." Daisy insisted on telling them all that she and Jacob were just old friends, but none of them bought it.

He didn't buy it himself.

Their last stop was the most isolated on her route. The small house had to be close to a hundred years old, but it had been well maintained. From the bumpy dirt road that approached the house from the south, he could see a window air conditioner at the front of the house. Given the size of the place that one unit was probably enough to cool the entire house. The wide front porch was so overgrown, all that was visible from their angle, as Jacob parked in what might've been a designated parking space, were a few weathered steps.

Daisy jumped out, opened the rear passenger side door and retrieved the last meal and a bag containing a bottle of water, a soda and a carton of milk. She didn't seem at all concerned about entering the house, even though it looked like the setting for a horror story.

And that was *before* an elderly, stick-thin woman with an Einstein-ish hairdo burst into view, brandishing a shotgun. She held the weapon as if she knew exactly how to use it.

Instinctively Jacob jumped in front of Daisy. He threw out an arm to push her back and she stumbled. He heard her bounce against the car, mutter "ow" and "what the hell?" The woman on the steps lowered her shotgun.

"Sorry," she said in a gravelly voice. "I didn't recognize the car."

"Not a problem," Daisy said. She stepped around Jacob, glared at him and then looked at the armed woman and—strangely—she smiled. "This is my friend, Jacob."

The woman adjusted her grip on the shotgun as if she were thinking of lifting it up again. "Jacob *Tasker?*"

"Yes," Daisy said crisply.

"I shoulda known. He has the look of his grandfather at that age." She finished that observation with a spit to the side, as if she were ejecting the bitter taste of his name out of her mouth.

This crazy woman he didn't remember at all. Maybe when he heard her name…

Daisy moved toward the house with her offerings. Jacob stayed close behind her. "Yes, I suppose he does look like his grandfather. But now, that's not his fault, is it? It's not his fault that he's a Tasker, either. There's not a thing he can do about the name he was born with." Standing on the bottom step, now, too damn close to the shotgun, Daisy turned to him. "Jacob, this is Vivian Reynolds." She looked up again. "Miss Vivian, be nice to Jacob and I'll braid your hair."

The old woman sighed as if being nice to a Tasker was going to be a great sacrifice, but she did finally nod and head across the porch and into the house. Jacob sighed himself when they stepped into the house and the Reynolds woman set her shotgun aside, leaning it into a corner near the front door. "Can't be too careful when you live out in the boonies on your own."

Jacob glanced around the living room, which was clean and nicely furnished, though none of the furnishings were new. There were knickknacks, but not too many. An older television with a single recliner in front of it. A small bookcase filled with paperback books.

A smallish dog came running from the back of the house. A bundle of hairy energy, the brown dog danced and sniffed around one visitor and then the other, then finally returned to the feet of his mistress. They were a matched, scruffy pair, both of them in serious need of more care than a little time with Daisy would provide.

"Why do you stay out here all alone?" Jacob asked. "Wouldn't you be better off living in town?"

The shotgun-toting woman turned an evil eye on him. "Well, ain't you the nosy one?"

"Sorry. But you did mention being careful because you live out in the boonies on your own."

She huffed, and when she moved her head her wild white hair danced. "If I could afford to move, sonny, I would've done it years ago. This house is paid for, the land is mine. It's all my sorry excuse for a husband left me when he passed, near twenty years ago."

"I'm sorry to hear that."

"Sorry that he's dead, or sorry that he didn't leave me a pot to piss in?"

Jacob wondered if it was too late to head outside and wait in the car. Ninety-plus degrees and sunny, it was still not a bad idea. Nothing he said was right. "Both, I suppose."

Daisy directed Mrs. Reynolds to the chair in front of the television, which was dark, and slipped out of the room. Jacob was tempted to follow her, or else excuse himself and wait outside in the heat.

Vivian pierced him with a glare. "So, Eunice is your grandmother."

"Yes, she is. Do you know her?" Jacob racked his brain,

but he had no memory of the Reynolds' family. He couldn't recall ever hearing the name Vivian Reynolds.

"I do. Is she still a conniving, backstabbing bitch?"

"Miss Vivian!" Daisy said, as she returned to the room with a brush in one hand and a handful of bobby pins in the other. "What a thing to say."

"I'm old enough to speak the truth when it suits me," she argued, settling back in her chair as she awaited the brush. She closed her eyes and looked almost content as Daisy began to brush out the tangles. It wasn't an easy job.

"Have you been using that conditioner I gave you?" Daisy asked.

"Now and then."

"Every time you wash your hair, use it," Daisy instructed firmly.

"All right, all right, if you insist." Vivian puckered her lips. "Like anyone cares what I look like. Hell, like anyone's going to see." She looked down at her dog. "Buster doesn't care if my hair is tangled or not."

Jacob glanced around the room. The only pictures displayed were two snapshots of a young Vivian and a handsome man who had a rough look about him. No pictures of children or grandchildren. No smiling photos of family and friends. Did she have no family or had she chased them all away?

"*I* see," Daisy said, "and so do the volunteers who come by on Wednesday and Friday. You know I would be happy to take you to the grocery store instead of bringing your groceries in, and when you need to see Doc Porter there are always people in the waiting room. If you'd start coming back to church you'd see all kinds of people."

"Last time I was at church that dirty old man George Hayes made a pass at me."

Daisy laughed. "He asked you out for ice cream and offered you a ride home."

"Like he didn't expect something in return," Vivian muttered under her breath.

Jacob wouldn't allow himself to smile. With his luck the old woman would pick *that* precise moment to open her eyes.

"I do hope you're not sleeping with this…this *Tasker.*" Vivian didn't wait for a response. "First of all, you deserve better than a Tasker. And secondly, no man is going to buy the cow when he can get the milk for free."

Daisy sounded calm as she replied, but he couldn't miss the new tension on her face. "Jacob is just here for a visit. He lives in San Francisco."

"Hell, if I was a Tasker I'd move as far away as I could, too," Vivian said. She opened her eyes and glared at Jacob. "You had the good sense to run away from that sorry family of yours. Why did you come back?"

"My grandmother is very ill."

Vivian made a huffing noise and closed her eyes. She squirmed a bit and finally she said, "Good." But there was something strangely *complicated* in her voice. She wanted to be glad that Eunice Tasker wasn't well, but she wasn't. Not entirely.

Daisy quickly transformed Vivian's hair, taking her from Einstein to simply disheveled. For a few minutes, while Daisy worked, everyone was silent. Even the dog. Then Vivian spoke, and her voice was different. Reluctantly softer. "What's wrong with her?"

Jacob explained, about the wheelchair. About the dementia. He didn't tell her about the ruse he and Daisy were participating in. He'd prefer to keep that in the family, if he could.

When he was finished, the old woman said, "Eunice

and I used to be best friends, a lifetime ago. We grew up together." Her words were clipped, precise. "I thought of her as if she were a sister, until she stole my boyfriend out from under me." Her eyes hardened. "That would be your grandfather, sonny."

Well, that explained a lot. "I'm sorry. I didn't know..."

"Of course you didn't know," Vivian snapped. "I did marry, a few years after Eunice and Charles, and I loved my husband deeply. But we didn't have much, and we never had children of our own. Do you know how much it hurt to see Eunice..." The woman took a deep breath and exhaled slowly. "But that was a long time ago. I don't suppose I should blame you." And yet her voice made it clear that she *did* blame him...

In Jacob's mind, Grandma Eunice had always been an old woman. He couldn't imagine her as a young girl with a best friend. Maybe laughing and dancing, whispering about boys...stealing her best friend's guy. That part wasn't all that hard to believe. For as long as he could remember, his grandmother had found a way to get what she wanted.

"Tell me about her. And you," Jacob added. "Tell me about those days."

It took a while to comb all the tangles out of Miss Vivian's fine, white hair. It always did. As she brushed, Daisy listened. She didn't know a person alive who didn't like to talk about themself and times gone by. Jacob had smoothed things over considerably by asking the old woman to talk about herself and her friend.

And apparently they had been very good friends, once upon a time. Miss Vivian talked about sleepovers and dances, skipping school and fishing. She talked about the time before they'd had a falling-out over a boy, and before she was finished the older woman was smiling in a way Daisy had never seen.

She finished with a story about two sixteen-year-old girls and a litter of puppies.

Daisy finished the braid and secured it. Next week she'd have to do it all again. Without Jacob. He'd disappointed her by not turning his nose up at those she visited, by pitching in when he got the opportunity. He'd taken an infirm woman's garbage cans to the street and had swept a kitchen or two. He hadn't uttered a word of complaint or judgment.

But best of all, he'd asked Miss Vivian to talk about herself. And then he'd listened. Miss Vivian always looked and obviously felt so much better after Daisy's visits, it made her wonder if she wouldn't be a completely different person if she wasn't so isolated.

Daisy settled her hands on Miss Vivian's bony shoulders. "I have an idea. Why don't you come to dinner with us one night at the Tasker House?"

The answer was immediate and held no room for negotiation. "I'd rather starve than eat in that woman's house. I'd rather have ground glass for supper than eat at Eunice's table. I'd rather eat cat food out of the can than give her the satisfaction."

Jacob didn't look as if he thought it was a very good idea, either, but he said nothing.

Daisy didn't give up. "Don't be that way. I'll give you a ride. I can do your hair, maybe even your makeup, before we go to the house. Don't think of it as having supper with 'that woman,'" she added. "Think of it as visiting with an old friend who might not be here six months from now."

Instead of another immediate refusal, Miss Vivian pursed her lips.

Jacob said, "Think of it as an opportunity to talk about

the old days one last time. Fishing and dances, puppies and cutting class. It's been a very long time, and…"

"Fine, fine," Miss Vivian said. "If you two are going to twist my arm I guess I have no choice but to agree."

Behind the older woman's back, Daisy smiled.

"How about Friday?" Miss Vivian said. "Friday is a lousy TV night. I won't miss anything if we make it Friday. There's a baseball game, but I should be home in plenty of time to see the last few innings." She scoffed. "It's not like I'm going to hang around after dinner is over."

"Friday it is," Daisy said, heading toward the bedroom with the brush and what was left of the bobby pins.

Behind her, she heard Jacob add, "Leave the shotgun behind."

Chapter Ten

Jacob pulled his car to the curb and shut off the engine. Daisy turned to him, smiled, then leaned over to give him a quick, easy, perfectly natural kiss. He was right there, and she just couldn't help herself. It had been a good day; he'd been a good sport. He'd not only stayed with her as she delivered the meals to those who needed them, he'd helped her help Terry paint her bedroom a hideous shade of lavender. With the three of them working it hadn't taken long. Of course, Terry had started before they'd arrived, so there hadn't been all that much to do.

Wanting Jacob was one thing. Realizing that she still loved him…she could live with that. *Liking* him was another matter entirely. It was a complication she could do without.

Daisy pulled away. Slowly.

"Are you going to ask me in?" Jacob leaned toward her, mirroring her movement away.

Daisy shook her head. “No.” She couldn’t ask him in. If she did they’d end up in bed again, and she was determined to remain in control of this situation.

He didn’t press her. Maybe because he understood her reason.

“When do I get my date?” he asked.

Daisy laughed. “You don’t! I think I’ve made it clear…”

“I threw myself in front of a weapon for you today. Don’t you think that should earn me a little consideration?”

“It was just birdshot,” Daisy argued.

“Just birdshot,” he repeated.

“Not that Miss Vivian would’ve shot you.” She shrugged. “Maybe,” she added in a lowered voice. “She’s not particularly fond of Taskers.”

“One date or I’ll camp on your front porch.”

“That would be so uncomfortable for you. Maybe I can spare a pillow to make your stay more comfortable.” She tried to sound nonchalant, when in fact the idea of Jacob right outside her door was torture.

He didn’t give up. Had he ever? “One date or I’ll hire a mariachi band to stand in your front yard and play until you change your mind.”

“You know I hate mariachi music!”

“One date or…”

“Fine,” she conceded. “Though I’ll have you know it’s only the threat of mariachi music that made me change my mind. One date. Nothing fancy. Maybe this weekend…”

“Tomorrow.”

There was a note of finality in his voice, and she was forced to remember that Jacob was a master of negotiation. He was determined to succeed in anything and everything, and always had been. He didn’t always succeed—his poor guitar-playing skills proved that—but he didn’t give up.

She wondered if he still played the guitar or if he'd abandoned the pastime entirely, the way he'd abandoned her.

Daisy knew when she was fighting a losing battle, and to be honest she wanted that date with Jacob. This time they would end it finally and completely before he left for California. This time she wouldn't be left hanging and hoping and waiting.

It was going to end, *they* were going to end, but there was no reason she couldn't enjoy the little bit of time he was here.

He took her face in his hands. "I'll walk you to the door."

Daisy sighed. "You'd better not."

"I'm not ready to let you go just yet."

And she wasn't ready to let him go, which was all the more reason to make him stay in the car. Daisy shook her head as she turned away from Jacob and opened her door.

"So," she said as she exited the car, "when are you going to tell Miss Eunice about the guest you're bringing to dinner on Friday?"

"I think it should be a surprise, don't you?"

"We'll have to tell Miss Vivian about the fake wedding business," Daisy said, leaning down to look into the car. "Otherwise she'll be very confused."

"We'll fill her in on the way. I have a feeling she won't feel at all bad about putting one over on my grandmother."

"Probably not."

She pulled away, reluctantly, and Jacob called out, "I have the connections to round up a mariachi band and have them here in less than an hour. Don't forget that!"

Daisy laughed. She felt amazingly lighthearted and happy as she all but danced to the front porch. Jacob watched her go; she could feel his eyes on her. He didn't even start the engine until she unlocked and opened the front door.

Once inside the house, she leaned back against the closed door and shut her eyes. Listening to him drive away, she sighed. This was supposed to be helping; it was supposed to be a way of finally and completely letting go.

It wasn't working. And tomorrow night she actually had a date with the man she was still in love with.

A man who would never choose her over his career. Who would never put her first in his life. After all these years of caring for others, she needed to feel like the most important thing to someone.

The house was so quiet…so lonely. Even the squirrels had gone silent, or else had departed completely, leaving Daisy entirely on her own. She could feel and hear her own heartbeat, could hear the ticking of the clock over the mantel. It had never seemed so loud before, as if it were counting off the seconds of her life.

Or counting down the seconds of the little bit of time Jacob would be close by.

It took every ounce of determination Daisy possessed not to run outside and chase Jacob down the street. She'd smiled as she'd left him sitting in the car, but as she stood alone in the only home she'd ever known, a few annoying tears slipped down her cheeks.

"I called the house and told Lurlene that I wouldn't be home."

"Yes, she passed the word on. But she didn't say where you were, and I was worried sick!"

Jacob felt like a fifteen-year-old who'd been caught sneaking out. He was thirty-one, an adult who shouldn't have to explain to his mother where he'd spent the night. All things considered, it shouldn't be much of a mystery.

Lurlene wheeled Grandma Eunice into the foyer. It was likely not a coincidence that she appeared when she did. She'd heard his car, and come out to say hello. Jacob looked at his grandmother and, for the first time, saw her as a young girl. He tried not to picture the kind of young woman who would steal a good friend's boyfriend, but instead attempted to see the girl who'd fished and skipped school and babied puppies.

"Where's Daisy?" Eunice asked, looking past Jacob to the front door.

"She won't be here tonight. It was a long day and she wanted to get to bed early."

Eunice smiled, briefly. "Well, perhaps tomorrow. She still hasn't tried on her wedding dress!"

Jacob shook his head. "Sorry, it won't be tomorrow."

"Why not?"

"Tomorrow night we have a date." He winked at Eunice, who seemed very pleased by his announcement.

"Well, then, you two have a good time. Another day this week, then."

Jacob thought about Friday, and wondered if he should tell Grandma Eunice that an old friend would be joining them for dinner. He hesitated. He was already rethinking his impulsive invitation. If Grandma Eunice reacted to Miss Vivian the way Miss Vivian had reacted to her, then the night could turn ugly.

But he didn't think that would be the case. They'd been good friends, once, and now they were both alone. Alone in different ways, but still, surely an old friend would be welcomed. He said, "Tonight after dinner, why don't you get out some old photos and tell me about Grandpa."

She smiled. Like Vivian, talking about the old days was not a chore. And though her memory of recent events was fuzzy, at times, she remembered those old days as if they'd been just yesterday.

"Of course. It's such a shame that your Grandpa Charles passed before you were old enough to remember him."

"Yes, it is."

"He was very handsome in his day, you know. You look very much like him."

So he had been told.

Grandma Eunice seemed to be in a very good mood, bright and with it…until Ben and Maddy arrived, and she mistook her youngest grandson's wife for the new maid.

They didn't have a new maid.

The Tuesday workday passed quickly, customers coming and going while Daisy's mind was on the coming evening. It was a minor miracle that she didn't butcher a single head of hair while she was thinking of the night ahead. What should she wear? Where would Jacob take her? How would the evening end?

She knew how the evening *should* end. She'd leave him sitting in his car while she ran for the safety of her house. Alone. Again. After making it very clear that they were through. But oh, he made it so difficult to do what she *should* do!

Eventually she would have to end it. Truly end it this time, not just drift apart. She needed to look Jacob in the eye and tell him that they were done, that it had been nice while it lasted, that a part of her would always love him but they didn't have a chance of making it work so why put themselves through the misery of trying?

Daisy didn't want to think about that reality tonight. She wanted to let go of her worries and enjoy the evening for what it was. Old friends who made great lovers enjoying one another's company. Jacob would leave, and it would end, but maybe she should enjoy his company while he was close by, and hers to enjoy.

On her way home—it was such a pretty day she was walking again, in spite of the heat—Daisy pulled her cell phone from her purse and dialed the Tasker House. Jim Tasker answered, and he fetched his son without asking a single question or trying to engage in polite conversation.

"What should I wear?" Daisy asked after Jacob said hello.

"Do you have a little black dress?" She loved the timbre of his voice. Even over the phone it was sexy and powerful, and oh, she was in much too deep when the sound of his voice made her squirm.

"I do, not that there's any place in Bell Grove to wear it."

"I made reservations at a Brazilian restaurant in Atlanta. Wear the little black dress. I'll pick you up in two hours."

She didn't get to Atlanta often. A couple times a year to shop, maybe, and she had been to a few concerts and ball games in the past few years. But for the most part she lived her life right here in Bell Grove. She'd never had a date take her all the way to Atlanta to eat.

Okay, black dress. But which shoes?

The critter man's truck was parked in front of her house. Shoot! She wanted to have the entire two hours to get ready. What was she going to do with her hair? Which bra? There were three possibilities when it came to shoes. Did she want to go for wowza or comfort or something in between?

There were also three bra possibilities. Also wowza, comfortable or something in between. Decisions, decisions.

A neighbor who had a key to the house had let Sammy in, and he'd collected the squirrel traps from her attic. They had served their purpose. He promised to release the squirrel-invaders on the other side of the county. It was unlikely, he said, that they would find their way back to this part of town and if they did, well, he'd already taken care of the access to her attic.

He was disappointed that the varmints were common tree squirrels.

Daisy started to suggest that squirrel stew might be an option, but then she saw the cute critters in their cages. Even if they were rats with bushy tails and good PR, and even if she would never have kind and fuzzy feelings for the critters the way Sammy did, they were, well, not stew worthy. Catch and release was fine by her.

Sammy didn't stay long, thank goodness. She wrote him a check, asked about his family, and when he asked she told him where she'd bought her curtains. Okay, so maybe he was a little odd, but he *had* gotten the critters out of her attic. He even seemed to genuinely like the rodents.

Not every man could be like Jacob. Handsome, sexy, driven…and not content to live in a small town where everyone knew everyone else and the pace of life was slow and easy.

That thought put a damper on her mood as she got ready, but by the time she was done she was feeling bright again. She wouldn't have Jacob for long, so she might as well enjoy him while she could.

The wowza shoes won.

As did the wowza bra. Just in case.

She was gorgeous. She took his breath away.

"Tonight I like the suit," Daisy said as she stepped onto the porch. "It's dashing, and appropriate."

"I don't look like the tax man showing up at your door to harass you?"

She shook her head, and her long, soft, pale hair swayed. "Not at all."

What he wanted to do was take her back inside and make love to her again. Surely she had something to eat in her kitchen, even if she didn't cook any more often than she had to. He'd be happy with a bowl of cereal.

She locked the door, and he took her arm. He walked her down the sidewalk to the driveway, where he'd parked behind her car instead of on the street, as he'd been doing since returning to Bell Grove.

Jacob placed himself between Daisy and the car door, which he had every intention of opening for her.

But not yet. He placed a hand at the base of her spine, pulled her close and kissed her. Not a searing kiss, not a prelude to sex, but a tattoo. A brand. *You're mine,* the kiss said. *Deny it all you want, but you're mine.*

With his hand still on the small of her back, he felt her tremble. Her lips opened to him, she leaned in closer. He released her, because if he didn't they'd never make it into the car.

Daisy blinked fast a couple of times, and when he opened the passenger door for her she slid into her seat carefully, as if her legs were unsteady. She didn't say a word until he took his seat and started the engine.

"Do you think anyone saw that kiss?" she asked.

"I don't know, and I don't care," Jacob said as he backed into the street and pointed the car toward Atlanta.

"That's because you don't live here. I do." She looked at him; he kept his eyes on the road but he could see her out of the corner of one eye. Damned if he didn't also feel her eyes on him. "I thought I heard a car go by, but I'm not sure."

If the kiss affected her the way it did him, what she'd heard might've been the roar of an engine…or the rush of her blood and her heartbeat, spinning out of control. "I don't recall," he said calmly. "And let's be honest. My car was parked in front of your house all night a couple of days ago. The nosy neighbors are probably already talking."

She sighed. "I know. But if anyone saw that kiss there will be no doubt about what's going on."

Going on. As in continuing? "Do you care?"

She sighed, fiddled with the small black purse in her lap. "No, not really. I'm a grown-up. I suppose it's perfectly natural for me to have a man stay over on occasion."

I suppose. Which meant it was unusual for her to have overnight guests. He couldn't express how relieved he was to hear that. Not that he could tell her as much. "Your decision that it was a onetime deal…"

"Still stands," she said quickly. And then she sighed. "I suppose. Though you will be gone soon, and it's not like either of us is involved, and…dammit, Jacob, why did you kiss me like that?"

Dinner had been great, well worth the drive into Atlanta. Jacob's company had been even better. He'd talked about his job and all the traveling he'd done; she told him about running the shop and what was going on with her sisters. Jacob had been her friend before he'd been her lover, and even though she didn't want to, she still liked him. You could love someone and not like them much, and you could certainly like someone without loving them. Jacob was the complete package, for her. A friend. A lover.

And in a couple of weeks he'd be back in California, and she'd still be here. Alone. She'd thought if she could finish things with him she'd be able to move on, meet another man…build a life.

But she was finding herself falling in deeper and deeper,

more in love than ever. She couldn't even imagine building a life with another man. And wasn't that a shame?

Having Jacob in her life, however temporarily, was like having a gallon of death-by-chocolate ice cream in the freezer, knowing it was the last gallon of death-by-chocolate ice cream she'd ever have. Maybe one day she'd settle for vanilla, when she really wanted ice cream and that was the only flavor available, but when? Not until she no longer craved death-by-chocolate. Not until she could no longer remember how it tasted, how it felt on her tongue. And what if she settled for vanilla and it turned out to be butter pecan inside a vanilla carton? She hated butter pecan.

Why should she limit herself to one bowl of death-by-chocolate ice cream? Why should she have one bowl and then dump the rest? What a waste. Shouldn't she finish up the entire gallon before it was gone for good?

It was late when Jacob walked her to the porch. A few lights were on in the neighborhood, but no cars—or people—were on the street. He parked in the driveway behind her car again. The streetlamp lit their way to the porch, where her front porch light cast a yellowish light over them. At the door she opened her purse, removed the house key…and then turned to Jacob and lifted her face for a kiss. He obliged, and this kiss was as deep and moving as the one that had started the evening. But it was also more. It was a beginning.

She pulled her mouth from his, grabbed his tie and hung on. "You make me break every promise to myself," she whispered. "I promise myself that I won't like you, I promise myself that I won't care, I tell myself that one night with you will be enough, that it's all I need. And then… and then you ruin it all. Worse than that, you make me indecisive. I'm not indecisive, Jacob, I don't make an important decision and then change my mind because of a kiss."

"Are you inviting me in?" Jacob rested his forehead against hers.

"I am."

"If I come inside I won't leave until morning."

"You better not," she said. "And I do hope you're more prepared than you were last time."

"I'm ever the optimist, so yes."

Daisy spun around, unlocked the door and pulled Jacob inside by the tie. "You and your suits," she said as she closed and locked the door behind him, leaning against it and looking him up and down. "Take it off."

Daisy had crawled out of bed to put a CD in her portable player. The music was something new, a soft sound with a slow, relaxing beat. When she tried to crawl back between the covers Jacob intercepted her, took her hand, and drew her away from the bed and more closely into his embrace. They danced away from the bed and across her bedroom floor. Naked.

He wasn't a great dancer, and neither was she. They didn't have a lot of space to maneuver in the small bedroom. But they could move together—man, could they move together—skin to skin, swaying to the music in the half light that cut in from the bathroom across the hall. That light fell across her shoulder as he spun her around, it lit her face, and he wondered how the hell he'd survived the past seven years without her.

Maybe it was the feel of her skin against his, the memory of her beneath him, the lingering sounds of her laugh and her sigh and that catch deep in her throat, but Jacob had the sudden and unwanted revelation that a part of him had been missing all this time. He'd lost himself in work, and along the way he'd allowed himself to forget what it was like to be more. To have someone to talk to at the end of the day. To have a person in his life that he couldn't live without.

He didn't want her for two weeks, wouldn't be satisfied with a fling. He didn't want to court her, enjoy her company for a too-short period of time and then go back to the way things were. No, he wanted all of her, heart, body and soul.

"Come back to San Francisco with me," he said, the words pouring from his mouth without thought.

"Really?" She backed away sharply; her eyes caught his and held them.

"Really."

Daisy moved in again, resting her head against his chest. She drifted closer, and her hands skimmed his back. "Maybe you should think it over and ask me when we're not naked."

"Why?"

"Because you're not thinking with the big head, at the moment." It was meant to be a tease, he could tell, but there was also a touch of uncertainty in the words. He'd hurt her. He didn't want to hurt her ever again.

"I won't change my mind."

Her hands settled on his hips. They continued to dance, skin to skin, barely moving, caught up in the movement and in each other. "Don't you travel a lot?"

"Yes, but what..."

"What am I going to do while you're gone?" He heard the anxiety in her voice. "If I were to go with you, if you still want me in the morning and you ask again and I say yes, if..." Her breath caught on one of her many ifs. "I don't know anyone there. I don't even know anyone on that side of the country."

"You know me," Jacob argued. "You could travel with me part of the time, and you'll meet other people there. You'll make friends right away. Who wouldn't love you?"

She hesitated, but not for long. "I have friends here, a business…a home that's paid for. My sisters are close by. I can't just put my life on hold and move because the sex is great."

Did she think that was all they had? Was she right? "We can work it out." He'd said that seven years ago, but nothing had worked out. Did she remember that, as he did? His invitation had been foolish, not well thought out at all. He was never impulsive, but that's what asking her to come home with him had been. Impulsive, his heart speaking instead of his head.

"You don't need me, Jacob," she whispered. "This is just…old memories, the past, one last hurrah…"

"What if it's not?" He pulled her closer, dipped his head to whisper against her ear. He didn't have all the answers. He only knew he wasn't ready to let her go. Not yet. "I need to think about it," she said. "And so do you."

Daisy let her hands drop to his butt cheeks and squeeze gently.

"Are you trying to change the subject?" he asked.

"Desperately."

Maybe she was right. He wasn't thinking things through; he hadn't allowed himself to work out the details. He worked long hours; he traveled around the world. As much as he liked the idea of coming home to Daisy every night…she'd be miserable. He didn't want to make her miserable; he wanted to make her happy. So simple. Not so easy. He should've thought this through before asking her to come home with him, should've anticipated all her questions and had answers ready. Instead he'd just blurted out the invitation without a single thought beyond keeping her.

He didn't want his brain to get caught up in all the problems, not right now.

"I didn't realize how much I'd missed you until I walked into Bell's Beauty Shop and Small Engine Repair and saw you standing there," he confessed.

"I've missed you, too," she said, but there was a sadness in her voice that told Jacob she wasn't even considering leaving Bell Grove behind to be with him. She'd missed him; she'd miss him again, when he was gone.

The dance, her flesh on his, the maddening knowledge that they didn't have forever…his brain was spinning, and he didn't like it. Life was black and white, good and bad, right and wrong. When he was with Daisy, everything was washed in shades of gray.

Jacob lifted Daisy off her feet and carried her back to bed. He tossed her onto the mattress; she bounced and laughed and then he was on her, his mouth against hers, his fingers on and in her body. There was no question about *this,* no shades of gray when they were in bed together. And then he was completely inside her and nothing else mattered.

Who wouldn't love you? Jacob had asked as they danced, skin to skin, in her bedroom.

What Daisy had wanted to say was *You. Or am I wrong about that? Do you love me? Say the words, make me change my mind. Tell me I'm more important than any career. Tell me that you love me.* Instead she'd offered a logical argument.

For as long as she could remember, logic had been a large part of every decision she made. What choice had she had? Thrust into the role of guardian too soon, taking on a demanding job at a young age and with no warning, she'd done what she had to do. Logic told her that she and

Jacob didn't have anything in common anymore. Logic reminded her that no matter how wonderful it was having him back in her life for a while, it couldn't last. There was much more than the countless miles between them. They lived in different worlds.

She loved having Jacob in her bed, waking up, reaching out, touching his body. How would she ever go back to sleeping alone? It felt so right to have him beside her, as if he should've been there all along, as if he'd never leave her again. Tonight—this morning—he didn't creep out of bed and move to the couch. No, he stayed with her all night. They made love, they talked, they laughed. They danced.

As the sun came up, Jacob slept on. Daisy couldn't. Thoughts of what might've been, what might still be, kept her awake. Maybe she should've just said yes when Jacob had asked her to go to California with him. Maybe she just should've trusted her heart and her body and dismissed all the logical reasons why she shouldn't go anywhere with him. It wasn't like Bell Grove was going anywhere. If she went to California and it didn't work out, she could always come home.

With her tail between her legs and defeat in her broken heart. That was what held her back, the very real possibility that her heart would be broken all over again. But was that very real possibility any worse than not taking a chance?

Jacob was still sound asleep when she cuddled up against him, put her mouth next to his ear, placed a hand against his hip and whispered, "Yes."

Jacob wasn't sure what had awakened him, but slowly and surely he came awake. It was still dark out, but the clock told him morning was coming. Daisy was nestled against him. Her breathing and the way she held her body told him she was not sleeping.

He rolled into her, wrapped his arms around her and held her close. "You should get some sleep."

"I can't," she said, her soft words warm against his skin. "Am I keeping you awake?"

"Yes."

Had he been snoring? Taking up too much space in the bed? "I can move to another room, sleep on the couch if I'm…"

Her hold on him tightened, and she threw one leg over his as if to hold him in place. "Don't you dare go anywhere. Not tonight," she added in a lowered voice.

It was so natural to tilt her face up and kiss her. She was right there, in his arms, so close she was almost a part of him already. The kiss deepened, her hands wandered and so did his.

She's mine. I'll never let her go again.

Yet as much as he wanted to believe that, he knew that nothing had changed. The clear light of day dispelled some of the emotion from the previous night. Her life was here and his was not. She *wasn't* his anymore and might never be again; and when he left Bell Grove it was very possible he'd have no choice but to let her go.

Chapter Eleven

"What? Is this some kind of a joke?" Daisy felt the floor beneath her spinning. Why now? Everything had been going so well. She'd hummed like a complete loon as she'd walked to work today, leaving Jacob asleep in her bed. Naked and rumpled. Beautiful. She'd smiled as she'd waved to neighbors who were walking their dogs or sitting on front porches drinking coffee. Her body ached, but it was a good ache. The song she kept humming was one they'd danced to last night.

She'd wondered more than once if Jacob would ask her to go to San Francisco with him when they weren't both naked. She wondered if she'd say yes while he was awake and could hear her.

Logic was highly overrated when it came to love.

It had been such a wonderful morning…for a while. Her short-lived happiness had come crashing down around her without warning, as if the universe was displeased that she was content. As if it wasn't in the cards for her to have everything she wanted.

Daisy—and her parents before her—had rented this space from the Chestnut family for more years than she could count. They hadn't had an actual lease since before her folks had died. The rental agreement went month to month, and they discussed expenses if they went up or down. Of course, expenses never went down. Still, she'd never felt the need for a lease. In this part of the world a handshake was as good as a contract, anyway.

Well, apparently that was no longer the case. Martin Chestnut was standing in front of her, his face a little pale as he explained what had happened. Someone had bought up this entire side of the square. Every space, every store. Including hers. The offer that had come his way had been too good to pass up.

She had a week to get out. A week! The other tenants along the strip would be allowed to stay; they'd simply be paying a new landlord. But the new owner wanted *this* space emptied.

There was a lifetime of memories here, she made her living here! The house was paid for, but she did have living expenses. Mari was still in college. Daisy needed food, she had to pay her property taxes and that old house was in constant need of some sort of repair. She had savings, but not enough. Maybe she had been considering leaving town with Jacob, if he asked again. But facing the reality of leaving everything behind was very different from fantasy.

"I'm sorry," Martin said, not for the first time. "But I'd be a fool to let a chance like this one pass me by."

"Yeah, yeah, you said that already." She waved off his offered excuses. "Who's the buyer? What do they plan to do with the space? Do you know of another space I could move to, at least temporarily?"

Even as she asked, she knew another space wouldn't do. It was in *this* space that her parents had lived and laughed, *here* that she still felt their presence, some days.

All idyllic thoughts of a new life elsewhere had been ejected from her head. Another chance with Jacob wasn't a done deal anyway, it was just a dream. A lovely fantasy fueled by sex and memories. Belle Grove was home; this shop was *hers*. Well, apparently not as much hers as she'd thought.

"I don't know, I don't know, and no. Sorry." Martin backed toward the door as if he expected her to shoot him in the back if he dared to show it to her. "I'm thinking of retiring soon, and this was just..."

"Too good to pass up," Daisy snapped. "Yeah, I got that."

When he was gone, Daisy collapsed into her client chair, breathless. She felt as if someone had pulled a rug out from under her. Her business! Everything she'd worked for! Her home, her way of life, all of it just *gone*. For a while she allowed herself to panic, to imagine the worst—which included homelessness and complete destitution—and then her heart slowed and a strange clarity washed over her.

It wasn't hers, not really. This shop, her home, they were all she had left of her parents. This was *their* life, *their* dream. Had she been trying to keep them alive by stepping into the life they'd left behind? Was that what held her here?

Even though it was legally hers, this shop had never been her dream. She'd taken over because it had seemed the best choice at the time. The only choice, to be honest. She'd had sisters to raise and the insurance money had only gone so far. It wasn't like her folks had expected to die too soon and made plans accordingly. Daisy loved her home, but she still slept in her old bedroom because she couldn't make herself move into the master suite that had been her parents'. That was their home, still, not hers.

She had stepped in and taken over their life, and somewhere along the way she'd given up on building one of her own. Why had she never seen that so clearly before this moment when the business was being yanked out from under her?

Recognizing what she'd been doing made it possible for her to truly think beyond today for the first time in years. She'd loved her parents dearly, loved them still, but she couldn't bring them back. She couldn't replace them, either. Tears filled her eyes, dribbled down her cheeks, and she mourned her mother and father all over again. It still seemed wrong to walk away from everything they'd built, to let it die as they had died, but maybe it was time.

If Jacob asked her again to move, if he made the offer when they both weren't naked and thinking with something other than their brains, she'd definitely say yes. No second thoughts this time. Even if he didn't ask, even if that opportunity had passed…it was time for her to move on, time to start something new.

New.

Her initial panic faded away entirely. Yes, she'd miss her friends if she left Bell Grove, and she'd certainly miss her childhood home. But that's all it was, her *childhood* home. Her life had just opened up in an unexpected and oddly exciting way, and once she pushed past her initial panic she realized that she'd just been set free.

She had a little savings, and if she could sell the house quickly she and her sisters would have a sizable bit of cash to split. That would help with Mari's college expenses. She could sell the furniture, too. Looking at it objectively, there was very little in her home that she'd want to take with her. A few keepsakes, but other than that it could all go.

She was *free*. Daisy found herself smiling and crying at the same time, planning ahead as she mourned the past. Soon enough the tears stopped. The smile remained.

Daisy spent the afternoon calling her clients. She squeezed as many as she could into the next few days, but left a couple of days clear for cleaning out the shop. She called Lily and Mari, and explained to them what had happened. They were initially horrified on her behalf, but she was no longer horrified for herself and once she explained that to them, they were reluctantly happy for her. She heard the hesitation in their voices and wondered if they, too, hadn't felt as if something of their parents remained as long as Daisy kept the shop and house as they'd always been.

She didn't tell them that Jacob might be a part of her new life. That was still up in the air, a variable. She was hopeful that variable would work out the way she wanted it to, but until then she'd keep it close. If he broke her heart again she'd keep it to herself. There would be no need to burden her sisters with her pain—which would also mean sharing her foolishness with them. No, for now she'd keep Jacob and those possibilities to herself.

She called the house, but Jacob didn't pick up. Why would he? It wasn't his house. He had a cell phone, but she didn't have the number. Come to think of it, in the past few days she hadn't seen that phone at all. She'd tell him the news later, and maybe he'd take the opportunity to ask her again to leave with him when he left town. She had to admit, the timing would be perfect.

Daisy was putting her house up for sale.

She was closing her business.

It was scary, but there was also a strange sense of excitement inside her. She didn't know where she'd go, she wasn't even sure what she wanted to do, but one way or another the last of the Bells was about to leave Bell Grove for good.

Jacob drove out to Tasker House not because he wanted to leave Daisy's place but because he needed a razor and a change of clothes. Daisy had shared her shower, soap and shampoo, and she'd found him an unused toothbrush with the name of her dentist stamped on the side, but he needed more. If nothing else, the razors in her bathroom were unacceptable.

Before he'd left the house yesterday he'd made sure his mother had known not to expect him home. He hadn't added "If I'm lucky," though to be honest he hadn't been positive Daisy would ask him to stay.

Not until he'd kissed her.

Tonight he'd ask her again to come to San Francisco with him. While they were both fully dressed and she couldn't accuse him of asking only because he was carried away, caught up in the moment. It might take time to convince her. She had the house, her sisters…business concerns. He would have to make changes himself. He couldn't work the kind of hours he and his company had come to expect, couldn't devote himself entirely to work if he had a woman in his life. But he was suddenly certain they could make it happen. He *wanted* to make it happen.

He found his mother sitting on the front porch swing, drinking tea, looking as sour as the lemon slice in her beverage.

"Good morning," he said.

"Good afternoon." Susan's response was sharper than was necessary.

Jacob, wearing the suit he'd worn last night but without the now-rumpled tie, headed in his mother's direction. "What's wrong?"

There were new lines on his mother's face, a strain no amount of makeup could hide. "What isn't wrong? Your grandmother is more of a trial every day. In the past couple of years she's run off every caretaker we've hired to help, and will only tolerate me or Lurlene and we both have our hands full without taking care of her. Thank goodness Ben has taken on so many of the business responsibilities, but to be honest I miss it. I want to get back to work." She smiled a little. "Your little brother is more than competent but I enjoy working, and I like being needed for my brain. You know very well that the Cyrus Tasker branch of the family doesn't have the good sense of a fence post, and the Clyde Tasker branch has sold almost everything away. Uncle Carlton is the only one with any sense, and when he dies, well, I don't even want to think about it. He's pushing ninety, you know. Your father would rather play golf and drink beer with his friends, but he does help out at work when I need him. He's no help with your grandmother, though, because she still sees him as a child." Her smile was gone, and her eyes shone bright. She didn't let a single tear fall, though. "And Daisy. Really, Jacob, how could you take up with her again, after everything she put you through?"

Jacob leaned against the house and looked down at his mother. "Everything she put *me* through?"

"Yes! She broke your heart...don't think I didn't see that. She should've...she could've..." Her lips pursed and the line between her eyebrows deepened. "Oh, who am I kidding? Daisy didn't do anything wrong, and neither did you. It's all my fault."

Jacob was accustomed to his mother's dramatics, but this one surprised him. "Your fault?"

The dam broke and tears ran down Susan's face. This was a woman who never cried, no matter how bad things got.

"I didn't want you to be saddled with a ready-made family, not at twenty-four. I pushed you to move on, to leave Daisy behind. I did my best to make sure her sisters were not a responsibility you'd have to bear." She balled her fists. "I even…I even made sure she knew how happy you were in San Francisco, how well you were doing there. It's easier to blame her, to twist my memories of that time around and forget my part in it all, but…I did everything but tell her outright that you didn't need her."

His heart constricted. "Whatever happened between me and Daisy is on us, not you."

"You say that, but I could've helped. I could've made things easier for both of you, and I didn't. I sat back and watched Daisy give up everything. She did a wonderful job of raising those girls." She wrung her hands—another unusual gesture. "So I quit going to town to get my hair done. I started shopping in places where I knew I wouldn't run into her. I avoided Daisy, because every time I looked at her I felt guilty."

"We can all look back and see what we should've done," Jacob said calmly.

"I was so wrapped up in the business, in seeing that you boys got a good start to your adult lives, I convinced myself that I didn't have time to take on another responsibility. I loved the idea of being more businesswoman than mom, of not having a houseful to take care of, and I didn't want to take on raising two young girls. I was selfish, Jacob. Horribly selfish. Now Daisy is here, day after day, playing this ridiculous game with you and the guilt is worse because I see how much you two care for one another. If

I'd offered to take the girls in, if I'd pushed the two of you together instead of doing my best to tear you apart..."

"I don't think Daisy would've agreed to leave her sisters here, not even with you," Jacob said.

"But...but I could've done something to help. I should've done something. Anything."

Jacob sat beside his mother and put an arm around her shoulder. For a moment they just sat there. She sniffled, but her tears didn't last.

"The blame is mine, not yours," Jacob said calmly. "If it makes you feel any better, I never believed what you said about taking on Daisy and her sisters being too hard, I never took that argument to heart. That's not the reason it didn't work. I got caught up in a new life, and I suppose the same thing happened to Daisy. We were young, and we let what we had fall apart all on our own."

"I can hardly look at her without regretting all I did. And even more, I feel horribly guilty about what I didn't do. I didn't help...all I did was make matters worse. She'll never forgive me."

"You're going to have to get past this, Mom," Jacob said. "Because if I have my way you'll be seeing a lot of Daisy."

She looked up at him.

"I'm going to pack a bag and stay at her place for a few days, if she'll have me," Jacob said calmly. "And if I'm very lucky, she'll agree to move to San Francisco with me." If he left here without her, no matter how good his intentions were, he feared they'd grow apart all over again.

"The mother of my grandchildren will hate me," his mother said softly.

Grandchildren? "She doesn't hate you."

"She doesn't like me much, either. Not that I've given her reason."

"Daisy hasn't agreed to anything yet," Jacob said with

a tight smile. "And you're getting ahead of yourself talking about grandchildren." Way ahead. He was thinking of living together and seeing how things went, getting to know one another again, having Daisy in his bed at the end of every day.

"I'm not ahead of myself, you're horribly behind. No one can watch the two of you together and not realize that you're in love."

First *grandchildren,* then *love.* The words shouldn't come as a surprise to him, shouldn't hit him with an almost physical force, but they did. He liked Daisy, he wanted her, she was like no other woman. Was that love?

His mother sniffled, lifted her head and looked him in the eye. "Don't ask her to move in with you."

Not again! "Mom, I..."

"Marry her, Jacob. She deserves nothing less."

Daisy was about to head for home when Martin Chestnut came back into the shop. He looked every bit as serious, and nervous, as he had that morning. She'd have to let him know that she was no longer upset, that it was okay...

"I got to thinking, after I left," he began.

"It's all right," Daisy said.

"No, no, it's not all right at all. At first I was just excited about the money, because the offer was so good. I was thinking about paying off the mortgage on the house, and retiring earlier than I'd thought I could. But after you asked who'd made that generous offer I got to pondering. I called my lawyer and asked him to do a little digging. He made a few calls, he asked all the right questions, I guess." Martin fidgeted, he was sweating, and though it was a hot day it wasn't that hot. And she had the air cranked up high.

"What did you find out?" Daisy asked, suddenly curious.

"The offer was routed through a couple of lawyers, like, you know, there was something to hide."

Daisy's spine went rigid. She tingled from head to toe, not in a good way but with an instinctive fear. She knew what was coming; she heard it in his voice. *No. Please, no.*

"It's a Tasker," Martin said. "Someone with the last name Tasker is trying to buy the downtown buildings."

Chapter Twelve

Daisy walked home slowly. She didn't hum, as she had that morning. She didn't wave at neighbors as she passed by. Her body and her brain were both numb. She hoped with everything she had that Jacob wasn't still at her house.

She wanted to kill him. Even before he'd asked her to go to California with him, he'd set a plan into motion to make sure she had no choice in the matter. The offer had seemed so spontaneous, as if he'd been as carried away by the moment as she'd been, but that wasn't the case. As usual, Jacob Tasker had come up with a plan to get what he wanted. Her.

A part of her wanted to believe that he hadn't had anything to do with what was happening, but nothing else made any sense. She'd tried to come up with another reason, an alternative, but there was no other logical explanation. He was playing her, had been playing her since the moment he'd walked into her shop. And it *hurt*. It hurt more than she'd imagined was possible.

Why was she surprised? It was Jacob's MO to do whatever was necessary to get what he wanted. He didn't lose. Ever.

He'd rip her livelihood out from under her to make sure she had no options other than him. Did he really think she was so weak? Did he think he could frighten her into packing up and following him to the other side of the country? Well, he was wrong. She *wasn't* weak and she had options. She had plenty of options that didn't include his sorry ass!

Again, Daisy suffered a moment's doubt. It was true that Martin hadn't specifically said *Jacob* Tasker was behind the sale, but who else could it be? What other Tasker would go to the trouble? It didn't make any sense to buy the property for one of their businesses. Downtown Bell Grove was much too small and insignificant to be of use to the company. The fact that hers was the only space that had to be vacated immediately was definitely suspicious. She tried to think of anyone else besides Jacob who might be behind the purchase. Ben probably didn't have the money. He and Maddy were big spenders, and she couldn't imagine that his savings were impressive. Not yet. Caleb and Luke had cut their ties to Bell Grove long ago. Jim? No. If it had been a golf course...maybe. Susan didn't even like the idea of Jacob and Daisy together. She wouldn't lift a finger to push Daisy out of town, and perhaps into her son's arms, and given the timing Daisy couldn't think of any other reason for the unexpected sale.

It couldn't possibly be coincidence that a Tasker was driving her out of business. Yeah, there were a lot of Taskers around, but she'd ruled out everyone else in Jacob's family—but him—she didn't think any of the cousins were even aware of her existence. Downtown Bell Grove functioned, but it wasn't great investment property by any stretch of the imagination.

That left Jacob. He wanted her, he'd set his sights on her the way he did a floundering company he thought his employer could take over and fix. Or destroy. Would he try to fix her and then, when he discovered that he couldn't, dismantle her? Maybe he'd get bored with her, once she was entirely his and there was no more challenge. Maybe once he had her, he wouldn't want her anymore. Like a fool she'd fallen in love all over again, and he'd just been playing a game. A game he fully intended to win.

Jacob Tasker always won.

She couldn't believe she'd let him get under her skin this way, that she'd fallen in love with him, that she'd actually allowed herself to *like* him. Well, at least one part of her original plan was still in place. There would be no growing apart, this time. No nagging feeling of romantic matters left unfinished.

They were finished, all right. This time she would tell Jacob to his face that they were through.

Jacob packed a bag this time, before driving to Daisy's place. There was just a little more than a week until the reunion. They'd be moving back and forth between her home and Tasker House for the next few days, but he wasn't going to pretend anymore that he wasn't with her. One hundred percent, he was with her.

Maybe tonight she'd agree to move to San Francisco with him. His mother's mention of marriage had nagged at him all afternoon. She said that was what Daisy deserved, and she was right. But he wanted to wait. It was too soon; this had happened too fast. They didn't know each other as well as they should before he took that big step. He'd get her to San Francisco, see how they worked there, make sure what he was feeling wasn't entirely physical. He didn't think that was the case, but still, he tried to be more cautious these days than he'd been at twenty-four. He liked to take his time and think important decisions through.

If he'd done that seven years ago, he would never have left Daisy behind. But that was then, this was now. Life was more complicated than it had once been.

Jacob pulled into the driveway and parked behind Daisy's car, blocking her in. The car had been there when he'd left, so she'd obviously walked to work. Was she home? He had to assume she was, by this time of day. If she wasn't home he'd wait on the front porch, sitting in the rocking chair there, waving at neighbors who passed by. He grabbed his bag from the backseat, locked the car and all but danced to the front steps. Maybe tonight she'd give him a key, so when he locked the door behind him as he left he'd be able to get back inside.

Daisy met him at the door, and when Jacob saw her face he stopped in the middle of the big porch, several steps from the doorway. He no longer felt like dancing.

Her cheeks were flushed red, her lips thin…she was furious.

"What's wrong?"

She pushed the screen door back and stepped onto the front porch, poised as if headed into battle. "As if you don't know."

He didn't know what was coming, but it couldn't possibly be good. "I really don't have any idea…"

"I'll make it easy for you." She stopped two steps away from him. "I'm not leaving Bell Grove. I *will* find another place for my business, and I *will* survive without you. I have never needed a knight on a white horse to come riding into town to rescue me, and if I did, well, we both know you'd be lousy at the job. I could've used a little rescuing seven years ago, but that girl is long gone. These days I take care of myself."

Jacob dropped his bag onto the porch. "Daisy, tell me what happened." He tried to remain calm, because one of them needed to be and she was anything but.

She waved an agitated hand in his direction. "Martin Chestnut came into the shop today and told me I have a week to get out. A *week!* Someone with the last name Tasker bought the building, and I'm being evicted. Like I need to tell you that. No more games, Jacob. No more games!"

"You don't have a lease?" He was horrified, and that horror came through in his voice.

Her face turned a deeper shade of red. "That's all you have to say? No, I don't have a lease," Daisy snapped. "I haven't needed a lease until now. How was I supposed to know you'd buy the building and kick me out to make sure I can't stay here?"

The situation was looking increasingly ugly, and to be honest the comment about him being a lousy white knight still stung. Even if it was true. Before he could do anything, he needed to know more about what had happened between the time she'd left the bed and this moment where she looked at him with panic and fury in her eyes and in the set of her jaw.

"I have no idea what you're talking about. What makes you think I'd do something like that?"

She was angry; he was insulted.

"Who else?" Her voice was too high-pitched, too sharp. "I've tried to come up with another explanation, I really have, but nothing else makes sense. You've always been one to get what you want, one way or another. You asked me to leave here with you, I didn't immediately fall on my knees in gratitude and say yes, and the next thing I know…"

Now *he* was angry, and he remembered some of the arguments they'd had when they'd been together. Daisy could dig in her heels. So could he. "Do you really think I have the connections to put together a sale between two in the morning when I asked you to move to San Francisco with me and whenever you got the news?"

"I figured you were planning ahead, covering all your bases." Finally he saw a flicker of doubt on her face. The mouth softened, and she looked down at the floorboards of her porch. Her eyes narrowed, and her body seemed to unwind. "It wasn't you?"

"No." The word was clipped, and held no room for debate.

"You swear?"

Jacob's hands clenched into fists; he felt a tightening in his chest, as his temper rose. "Daisy, if I was going to do something so underhanded, would I use my *name?*"

Daisy shuffled her feet. Her cheeks flushed. She'd been angry, and apparently she hadn't thought through the details. She'd lost her temper, and now she looked to be regretting it. A little bit, at least. "Well, apparently the buyer tried to cover their tracks, but they didn't do a very good job of it. All Martin could find out was that the buyer was a Tasker, and I can only think of one Tasker who would…"

"Me." So much for remaining calm. The last of his taut control washed away. "Someone is attempting to run you out of town, and you assume it has to be me."

"Who else, Jacob? Who else would *care?*"

He took one step closer to her. "I don't know. It's not like the county isn't lousy with Taskers. Maybe a cousin decided to make an investment and you were just caught in the cross fire."

"Investment? Have you been to downtown Bell Grove lately?" she asked, but her voice was low. Her face had returned to a somewhat normal color. "Besides, Martin was so excited that someone was paying more than the land was worth, he all but danced into my shop to share the news."

It was an odd situation, he'd give her that, but at the moment he could only concentrate on one thing: she'd been given the opportunity to think the worst of him, and that's exactly what she'd done.

"If I was going to buy that building in an attempt to run you out of town, to come in here like some lousy white knight and create my own opportunity to rescue you, you can be assured that I could manage to do so without the Tasker name being involved. I could rip that building out from under you and you would never have a clue that I was the buyer. I'd run it through so many lawyers and companies that it would take a *very* long time to sort out the details. You'd never know. Chestnut would never know. Not that I'm so desperate for you to come with me that I'd try to force you into that position. Do I look desperate, Daisy?"

"No." There was a hint of concession in her voice.

He took another step forward; she matched him with a step back.

"No," he repeated. "I was hoping you would decide to come home with me of your own free will, I was hoping it might be a choice you'd gladly make. Judging by the look on your face, I was wrong." Judging by the look on her face, she was furious not only that someone had bought the building she leased, but that she might have to leave Bell Grove. He'd been right about that all along. Daisy belonged in Bell Grove. She wasn't going anywhere.

"I don't know what I want anymore," Daisy said.

"I was hoping you might want me."

She shook her head. "I did. I do. Dammit, Jacob, I'm so

angry right now, I'm so hurt and confused. I don't know what comes next."

He stepped back, picked up his bag and turned around, glad that he couldn't see the pained expression on her face anymore. Glad that she couldn't see his.

"I'll find out who's behind this," he said as he walked down the steps. "I'll let you know." So much for taking Daisy home with him. So much for seeing how things worked out for them. If she was so quick to condemn him without even asking a single question, if she really thought so little of him, they didn't have a chance.

It was dark out when the doorbell rang. Daisy jumped. Surely Jacob hadn't come back! If it really wasn't him who'd bought the building out from under her, and he'd found out who had, he would've just called. She hadn't missed the fury in his eyes as she'd accused him. She couldn't possibly have misread the way he'd closed off, shut down.

She still didn't know who else might've done it, but she'd believed Jacob when he'd said it wasn't him. Too late. He'd never forgive her for doubting him, and if she was so quick to believe the worst maybe that was just as well. All they had was a bit of history and great sex. Neither was enough to build a lasting relationship upon.

When she peeked through the security viewer, she sighed in relief. Then she opened the door and asked, "What on earth are you doing here?"

Lily Bell had always been the difficult middle child. If there was a disagreement to be had, she was right in the middle of it. She'd argue any point just for the sake of arguing. There had been a while, a tough while, when her idea of a good time had included too much beer and staying out all night. For the past several years she'd dyed her dark blond hair black—or red or platinum, though it was normally black and it was black tonight—because she wanted to be different from her sisters.

She didn't have to dye her hair to be different. Lily had always been edgier than her sisters. Tougher, through and through. And at the moment, she was steaming.

"Those bastards," Lily said as she walked inside. Then she explained. "Mari called and told me what was going on. She can't miss class tomorrow or Friday, so I took the rest of the week off and drove up." Hands on hips, she asked. "Why didn't you call me? I mean, the first call was fine. Getting out of the business, selling the house, blah, blah, blah. But the second call, the one I didn't get? The Taskers?"

"I know you're busy with the new job," Daisy explained weakly. "I didn't want to bother you."

Lily responded by giving Daisy a big hug. "It's never a bother to hear from you. We're family. We stick together." She kept her hands on Daisy's shoulders as she pulled away. "Do you have a plan?"

Daisy shook her head. A plan? She still wasn't sure what she was going to do about dinner Friday night! Miss Vivian was expecting a dinner at the Tasker House with her old friend and rival, but if Daisy didn't fix her hair and take her she wouldn't go. And the old woman might never get another chance.

"Well, *I* have a plan." Lily plopped down on the couch. "At first I was just furious, but on the drive up I did some thinking. You sell the house like you planned, and come stay with me. Screw the Taskers. They can buy all of downtown Bell Grove for all I care, and they can choke on it. Go back to school, Daisy, or better yet take a job styling hair in Atlanta..."

"I can't work in Atlanta! The competition there is..."

"You're as good as any of them," Lily said. "Better than most. I know styling hair isn't what you planned to do when you went to school, but you're good at it and I think you like it. Why do you think I drive all the way to Bell Grove to get my hair cut?"

"Because I don't charge you?"

Lily laughed. "Okay, there is that. But if you weren't the best I'd pay someone else to do it and save the gas money."

"I don't know…" Daisy sat beside her sister. It was nice, not to be alone with her out-of-control thoughts and regrets.

"Maybe this is a blessing," Lily said, sounding oddly calm and reasonable.

"How can you say that?"

Lily looked Daisy in the eye. "You're stuck here, you're in a rut. Face it, Daisy, you don't belong in Bell Grove anymore. What are you going to do here, even if you stay and find another location for the shop? Keep on running Mom and Dad's business, make enough to get by and eventually marry some local guy. Though, honestly, I can't think of a single man in town who's good enough for you. If you move to Atlanta you'll have so many more options. You can start over. The world is so much bigger than Bell Grove, Daisy, and you need to be a part of it. It's time."

Time. Past time. "Will you miss it?" she asked, watching Lily's face for a clue to her feelings.

"Miss what?"

"The shop, the house…" She almost choked on the words. "What's left of Mom and Dad. Once it's all gone there won't be any getting that back."

"Oh, Daisy." Lily leaned in for a hug. "Of course I'll miss it. But nothing stays the same, and it's been such a long time. Is that why you stayed here? Please tell me you didn't stay for us, for me and Mari."

"No, I stayed for myself, because I couldn't let what

was left of them go. I didn't even realize it until a few hours ago."

Daisy had been furious. Before that she'd been shocked, and sad, and relieved and hopeful. All in the space of a few hours. Talking to Jacob had settled her down some, even though their conversation hadn't ended on a happy note. Now Lily opened her eyes to options she hadn't considered. A spark of excitement grew where her fear had been. Everything and everyone in Bell Grove was familiar to her. She was safe here, and she felt her parents' presence everywhere. It had been comfortable, but it hadn't been right. She knew that, now.

It was time to set safety aside in the name of moving on. Not with Jacob, not to the other side of the country, but moving on just the same.

Daisy rested her head on Lily's shoulder. "I'm glad you came."

"Me, too."

Lily's voice brightened. "Now that we have that settled, who do we kill first?"

Jacob didn't see anyone when he entered the house, but he was sure they could hear him. He didn't try to be quiet, didn't soften the slam of the door behind him. He walked up the stairs to his bedroom, opened the door, threw his bag onto the floor and headed for the closet and his cell phone.

With a flick of his thumb he turned it on, and within seconds the icons for voice mail messages and texts popped up. He didn't have time to listen to or read a single message, not now. Maybe later, when he couldn't sleep. Jacob was pretty sure he wouldn't be sleeping tonight. He was too wound up, too disappointed. It was three hours earlier in San Francisco, and he knew Ted would still be in the office.

Ted didn't have a personal life any more than Jacob did.

He dialed on a direct line, and Ted answered.

As soon as Jacob spoke, Ted interrupted and began his rant. "Where the hell have you been! Hudson's been calling you, and he's furious that you haven't called him back."

"Hudson's always furious," Jacob said. "And I'm on vacation. I need a favor."

"A favor. You leave me here all alone..."

"You're hardly alone."

"It feels like I'm alone when they expect me to do your job *and* mine. So, what's it like to be on vacation? It's been so long I don't really remember."

"You should try it sometime. Now, about that favor. I need you to track down the purchaser of a particular property here in Bell Grove."

"You can't do that from your end?"

"Eventually, but with your connections through the office you should be able to find out details quicker than I can. Besides, I have my hands full here." Between Daisy and Grandma Eunice and the upcoming reunion...Jacob had to wonder how any man managed to balance a demanding job with a family.

"Blonde, brunette or redhead?" Ted asked with a smile in his voice.

Definitely blonde. But instead of responding to the question aloud, Jacob told Ted what he knew about the sale that had ripped Daisy's business out from under her. Daisy hadn't even considered that the name Tasker had been dropped like a bomb, when in fact no one from the family was involved. Someone was trying to set him up.

Why?

Daisy had been so quick to believe that it was him, that he'd stoop so low to get what he wanted. Her. She didn't have a very high opinion of him if she truly believed he'd manipulate her that way. After the way things had ended last time, maybe she had good reason. He'd chosen his career over her and Bell Grove. And he did do whatever was necessary to get what he wanted. But before he left town he wanted to make sure she knew he wasn't the one who'd bought a chunk of downtown and run her out of business. For all the good that would do him.

Jacob realized with a sinking heart he'd be leaving town alone, when the reunion was over and he'd done his duty to the family. But when he left Daisy would know without a doubt that he hadn't been the one to force her out of the building where her family's business had been operating for twenty-plus years.

Would she feel at all guilty when he proved himself innocent, or would she just be glad to see him go?

Chapter Thirteen

Lily hadn't bothered to pack much for her trip. The overnight bag she'd brought with her had some toiletries and a pair of pajamas. When Daisy asked, Lily said she had more than enough clothes in her old closet. They were going to have to talk about that, Daisy decided, thinking about the dress that had shocked the Taskers and driven Jacob into overdrive. Lily had never been shy, she loved the shock factor, but some of her clothing choices were outrageous.

They were too busy on Wednesday night to talk much about plans, but as Daisy cut and styled hair Thursday, and Lily made a Going Out Of Business sign and called customers who'd left things behind to be repaired and had never picked them up, Daisy's mind spun wildly.

Bell Grove was her safety net; this shop was her parachute. She was comfortable here, so comfortable she'd stopped growing. Now that she realized what she'd been doing by trying to keep her parents' memories vibrant by living their lives, it seemed so obvious. And so wrong. Maybe that's the reason Jacob had seemed so attractive to her, for a while. He had been a way out. Nothing more.

In between customers and friends who saw the sign and stopped by, she and Lily made plans. Lily's Atlanta apartment was a two-bedroom, two-bath, so no problem there—though she did note that eventually Daisy would want her own place. Having a big sister around would seriously cramp Lily's style. Lily had already chosen a couple of men she thought were Daisy's type, and had been talking about blind dates. These were men she'd rejected, most likely, though she didn't say so. Daisy didn't even want to think about men, but Lily was already talking about double dates, making plans for nights out in Atlanta.

Which made Daisy think of her date with Jacob, and how foolish she'd been to believe for a minute that they had something more. At the moment she couldn't even imagine dating another man, much less getting involved in a serious relationship. Apparently she didn't do relationships well. Maybe she was destined to be the spinster sister, always alone, watching while her sisters moved on with their lives and she remained stagnant.

The opposite mindset from the one she'd been searching for when she'd allowed herself to get involved with Jacob Tasker again.

At the end of the day, she and Lily walked home together. Daisy was still sad about Jacob, sorry she'd accused him of being the one to buy the building and still not a hundred percent sure he hadn't been involved, even though she wanted to believe him. Obviously she didn't trust him enough to pick up where they'd left off seven years ago. The sex was great, but it was all they had. How could she love him and like him and need him and not trust him? What was *wrong* with her?

Atlanta was sounding better and better. She'd get away, start fresh and leave behind this little town where she felt safe. Here she was sheltered from the outside world. She didn't want to be sheltered anymore.

But apparently she was not averse to running away…

Lily was preparing dinner when Daisy decided to call Jacob. It wouldn't be easy, but she needed to talk to him. No matter what had happened, they needed a plan. Miss Eunice, Miss Vivian…all the plans they'd made that involved more than the two of them…she couldn't just walk away. Naturally he didn't answer the phone, and Susan—who'd answered with a formal "Tasker residence"—was less than cordial. No surprise, there.

It didn't take Jacob long to get to the phone, and when he spoke his voice was cool.

"I've been thinking about tomorrow," Daisy said, trying for a nonchalant voice. "I don't want to disappoint Miss Vivian, and we do have your grandmother to think of, so I suppose one more dinner is in order."

He agreed.

"And after dinner, we will tell Miss Eunice that we're not going to get married." *Not now, not ever.*

"It won't take," he said sharply. "Trust me, I've tried."

"Maybe if we tell her together she'll understand."

After a short pause, he said, "We can try."

She paused herself, for a long moment. "I know I said I'd help, and I do feel so bad about the situation with your grandmother, but we need to make the truth stick. Somehow." She took a deep breath. This should be easy, but it wasn't. "I'm not sure how much longer I'm going to be in town. I hope to be gone by the time the Tasker Reunion rolls around."

"Where are you going?" His voice was emotionless, distant.

"To Atlanta, with Lily. With the shop closing…"

"The shop doesn't have to close," he interrupted sharply. "I'm trying to find out who's behind the sale, and then… dammit, Daisy, I'll buy the place myself so you can stay. You don't have to run away."

"I'm not running away," she argued without heat, denying the accusation even though she'd had the same thought. "Not really. I'm moving forward. It's time. To be honest it's very much past time."

"Is that what you want?" His voice was crisp, distant. Was this the same man who'd whispered in her ear, held her, danced?

"Yes."

"All right, then."

"Dinner tomorrow," Daisy said as she prepared to hang up. "The regular time?"

Lily called out from the kitchen. "Tell them to set another plate. There's no way in hell I'd miss this shindig." She should've known her sister had been eavesdropping.

"Did you hear that?" Daisy asked.

"I'll make sure a place is set for your sister. It'll be a big night. Caleb is arriving tomorrow, too."

"The more the merrier, I suppose." Daisy wanted to tell Jacob that she was sorry, that she'd made a terrible mistake…and she would. But not over the phone. And not when he sounded like he was already more than two thousand miles away.

Caleb arrived shortly after lunchtime, parking his pickup truck next to Jacob's rental car. Dressed in jeans that had seen better days and in need of a shave, he made his way reluctantly to the front door. Those long legs could take much longer steps. He didn't have to look as if he were marching to the electric chair!

Eunice watched from her window. Caleb had so much potential. He'd had a good education, but he'd wasted his knowledge on starting a small construction company. A Tasker, working with his hands! Caleb was no dummy, she knew that, but he was as stubborn as the day was long.

He needed a wife himself, one more suitable than the first bimbo he'd been married to for a few weeks. When she was finished with Jacob she'd fix Caleb's life for him. First a decent job, then an appropriate wife.

Eunice felt as if she were the hub of a creaking wheel that was on the verge of falling apart. Three of her four grandsons were so far away; they had separated themselves from the family. And Ben…bless him, he tried hard, and he had remained near home and with the company, but he didn't have the strength to hold the family together when she was gone. Jim…well, she'd given up on her son long ago. He wasn't exactly a wastrel, but he didn't miss the mark by much. The future of this family rested squarely on the shoulders of her grandsons.

Maybe she was faking this latest illness, but Eunice was very well aware that she wouldn't live forever. She had a few good years left, God willing, and she wanted to see her family solidly knit together before she left this world.

First Jacob…then Caleb. She wondered if he'd be as cooperative as his younger brother.

Daisy tried to convince herself that this would be easier than it had been so far. Knowing that she wouldn't be here much longer, knowing there wasn't a drop of truth in the charade, should make playing the part of Jacob's bride-to-be a little less painful. Oh, she still wanted him, she still yearned for him in a place she tried very hard to deny, but now she knew that when he left—again—she wouldn't be staying behind. She'd be moving on, too. There would be no time for moping.

Away from Bell Grove she'd be able to completely leave the past behind. She wouldn't be reminded of Jacob Tasker everywhere she looked. She'd have a new life, in a new place, where she'd meet new people and make a new home. It was a little scary, she'd admit, but it was also exciting. With Lily there she wouldn't be entirely on her own, so she'd have the best of both worlds.

She'd been working toward a degree in elementary education, seven years ago, and she *could* go back to school. But after suffering through hundreds of children's haircuts, she wasn't sure teaching was the career for her. She could pick a new field of study, or do as Lily suggested and try her luck as a hairdresser in a more competitive market.

The world was wide-open; her life was unplanned.

Lily let Miss Vivian have the front seat; she happily climbed into the back. Vivian's hair was brushed and braided and twisted. Lily had insisted on applying a little bit of makeup, and the older woman had not protested. She wore a Sunday dress, squat black pumps and pearls. Daisy was surprised; she'd never seen Miss Vivian wear any jewelry other than her wedding ring. She looked downright respectable, every inch the proper Southern lady.

As they drove toward Tasker House, Daisy gently told Miss Vivian how she and Jacob were pretending to be engaged to placate Eunice. She should've done it sooner, but it wasn't an easy thing to explain! Vivian was shocked to hear that her old friend—and enemy—had degenerated to such a point. She was silent after that, thoughtful as she stared out the passenger window.

Lily wasn't at all silent. She never was. She talked about Atlanta, the apartment, selling the house. As they turned onto the long driveway with Tasker House at the end, Miss Vivian turned to look—no, to *glare*—at Daisy.

"You're moving to Atlanta?"

Lily answered. "She doesn't have much of a choice. Some Tasker bought the building out from under her."

"There are other buildings," Vivian argued.

It was Lily who responded. "Yeah, but it would be a hassle to move, and there would be expenses involved in getting a new place set up, and besides, Daisy needs to get out of Bell Grove."

Daisy added. "I'll come visit you, Miss Vivian. Atlanta isn't all that far away."

The old lady huffed, and looked out the window again. Her chin came up defiantly, and her voice was harsher than it had been. "You won't visit. Oh, maybe you'll make it to town once or twice, not long after you move away, but eventually you'll stop coming."

"I won't," Daisy insisted.

"You'll escape this little town and you won't look back. I don't blame you. I should've gotten out years ago." She turned and stared at Daisy. "Good for you, girlie. I'll miss you, but it's past time you got out of this place."

"See, Daisy?" Lily said brightly. "I told you so."

Daisy didn't respond. She knew leaving town was right, she knew a better life was waiting for her. But a boulder of doubt had settled in her gut and it wouldn't go away.

The dining room was crowded tonight. Jacob and Caleb, their parents, Ben and Maddy, Daisy and her sister Lily—who kept glaring in Jacob's direction and had even stuck her tongue out once, when she'd thought no one else was looking. Vivian Reynolds was there, too, looking very different from the wild-haired, plain woman who'd pointed a shotgun in his direction earlier in the week. She cleaned up well and looked downright respectable.

Lurlene wheeled Grandma Eunice into the room. The family matriarch made a grand entrance, which she very much enjoyed. As usual. Her eyes scanned the room, lingering for a moment on Lily. She frowned as introductions were made, but recovered quickly, perhaps realizing that she needed to be welcoming to Daisy's sister, even if Lily did have a reputation as a bit of a wild child.

Then she looked at Vivian, puzzled for a moment. After that moment, recognition showed on her face in shock and even horror. "Dear God, what are *you* doing here?"

"Miss Eunice," Daisy said sweetly, "I thought you might enjoy seeing an old friend again."

"An old friend? Is that what you think—" She stopped short, raised a hand to her forehead and blinked quickly several times. "Who are you?" she asked Vivian. "You do look vaguely familiar."

Vivian smiled oddly and took her seat. "We used to go fishing together, many years ago." She remained calm. Of course, she'd been forewarned about her old friend's mental condition.

"I don't fish," Eunice responded coldly. "Fishing is for men and small boys. Ladies do not fish."

"Well, you once did." Vivian smiled at the hostess. "Susan, this meal looks just wonderful. It's very gracious of you to have me." She hardly looked, or sounded, like the harridan who had threatened him with a shotgun and called his grandmother an "old bitch."

Tonight, after dinner, he and Daisy would break the bad news to Eunice. They weren't engaged. They never had been. It wasn't going to be easy. Throughout dinner Grandma Eunice ignored everyone but Daisy. She talked about wedding plans—the wedding was just a week away!—the dress Daisy still hadn't tried on, food for the reunion and the wedding reception. Everyone but Vivian, who was thoughtfully quiet throughout, tried to change the subject. The weather, the cousins who would be coming in the following weekend, sports, recipes. But there was no swaying the very determined woman.

Grandma Eunice wanted to talk about the bridesmaids—Daisy's sisters, she assumed, looking pointedly at Lily as she suggested matching yellow gowns. Reverend Ashton would perform the ceremony, of course. Grandma Eunice said she'd already ordered the cake, and mentioned who was going to take care of that task. Jacob made a mental note to call the cake maker first thing in the morning. Monday, if they were closed on Saturday. The last thing he needed was a tiered wedding cake showing up during the reunion.

When that was done and Grandma Eunice sighed in satisfaction, Vivian and Lily turned the conversation around. Finally. They drew Caleb into their discussion, asking about his business in Macon. Lily talked about her new job, about life in Atlanta…though she did know better than to mention that her sister would soon be joining her there. Maddy added in her two cents; she loved Atlanta, loved the shopping there and thought that Lily's job at an art gallery sounded very cool.

Daisy didn't say much at all. Neither did Jacob. He was having a hard time choking down much in the way of dinner, and judging by the way Daisy played with the food on her plate, maybe she had a lump in her throat like the one that had formed—and stayed—in his.

Jacob never suffered this way at home, in San Francisco. He never felt as if the world around him was spinning wildly and there wasn't a damn thing he could do.

There was still a week until the family reunion began.

A full week. Jacob was suddenly anxious to get back to work, back to a world he knew and could manage. Here everything was out of control; including him. He wanted Daisy; he missed having her in his life. But she'd proved that she didn't trust him, and they couldn't have a long lasting relationship without trust.

Maybe he'd lost the right to expect her trust years ago. Maybe he'd never deserved it.

Daisy didn't look forward to telling Miss Eunice the truth, but it had to be done. She'd agreed to this farce in order to placate the delusional woman, but she was having second thoughts over a difficult dinner. Had she just made matters worse by playing along thus far? Would finding out that there would be no wedding at the Tasker Reunion send the matriarch into a downward spiral? She didn't want to be responsible for causing problems, but the truth of the matter was, she might not be here for the Tasker Reunion. Not that she'd ever planned to let this ridiculous scheme go that far.

They would break the news gently, and then Daisy would leave and Jacob would be left behind to deal with the fallout. Daisy looked at Caleb, who sat directly across from her. Why hadn't Miss Eunice fixated on him? He was older than Jacob, lived closer—though from what she'd heard he didn't make it home often. Maybe he needed a little polishing, but there might be a gem in there. Somewhere.

As dessert was served—a choice of strawberry or chocolate cake—Miss Vivian launched into another tale of the old days. Miss Eunice just looked confused, as if she had no idea what the other woman was talking about. Fishing. Hikes in the woods. Skipping school.

Miss Eunice fanned herself with her napkin as if she

were suddenly warm, and even said, at one point, that their guest must have her confused with someone else.

And then Miss Vivian put her fork down, took a sip of her decaffeinated coffee and looked squarely at Miss Eunice. "Have you ever told your family about the time you pretended to sprain your ankle to get my fella to carry you home?"

Miss Eunice sputtered. "I have no idea what you're talking about."

Vivian laughed. "Come on, Eunice. It's been more than sixty years and you have the same tells when you lie. You drum your fingers and your right eyelid twitches. You cock your head to the left." Miss Vivian turned to Daisy and glared with strong, certain eyes. "You *do* know she's lying about the memory lapses, don't you?"

Chapter Fourteen

Everyone at the table went silent and still. For a long moment you could've heard a pin drop. Then Caleb coughed, and Lily put a hand over her mouth and muttered a soft, "Oh, my God."

Jacob stared at his grandmother and tried to recall how often he'd seen the "tells" Vivian spoke of, since he'd returned home. He would dismiss the bitter old woman's accusations as a mean-spirited joke, if not for the expression on Eunice Tasker's face.

She was horrified. Chastened. Guilty. *Caught.* Those fleeting expressions didn't last long. She tried to recover and insist that she had no idea what their guest was talking about, but it was too late for proclamations of innocence. It didn't help matters at all that as Grandma Eunice pretended to be ignorant, her eyelid twitched. She tried to catch the telling tilt of the head—a half second too late—and she clutched at the armrests of her wheelchair, apparently to keep her fingers from tapping.

"Miss Eunice?" Daisy said softly. Even she—who was so willing to look for the good in everyone but him—could see the truth, now. The color drained from her cheeks. "Did you really…all this time…oh, my God, it makes a sick kind of sense." Tears welled up in her eyes. "That's why you never spoke of my parents as if they were still alive, even though when Jacob and I were together they were still with us. You couldn't bring yourself to be *that* cruel." She pushed away from the table, stood and ran out of the room without looking back. Lily followed.

Jacob started to rise and follow, but he didn't. Not yet. Daisy hadn't been happy with him when the evening had started; she surely didn't want anything to do with him now.

Maddy looked from her husband to her mother-in-law to the matriarch. It took her a moment but soon she, too, stood. She did *not* cry as she directed her attention to her husband's grandmother. "So all this time you've been pretending you didn't remember me, when you've been mistaking me for a cook or a seamstress or a maid, it was a *joke?* You have got to be kidding me," she added under her breath as she threw her napkin to the table.

She left the room, storming out with her head held high and her husband on her heels. Ben shot one last glance at his grandmother. Jacob read the shock on his brother's face, the disbelief and condemnation.

"Really, Mother?" Jim Tasker said, sounding both resigned and sad. It was telling that he didn't sound particularly surprised.

Maybe if she'd been prepared for the bombshell, Grandma Eunice would've handled the situation better. But as it was she sat there, guilt written all over her face. She didn't say a word in her own defense, didn't attempt to pretend that she had no idea what everyone was talking about. She hadn't been losing her mind; she was sharp as a tack and as ruthless as ever.

Susan put her palms on the table and took a deep breath. In an instant she left behind her role as hostess and became the woman who'd taken on the family business affairs as if she'd been born to them. The fixer, a level head the family could rely on. "This revelation is distressing, that's true, but the reunion starts next weekend and we *will* move on and get past this. No one outside this room has to know..."

Jacob finally stood. "I won't be here for the reunion." He didn't feel the need to say anything more as he left the room.

At the moment he longed for an uncomplicated life filled with work and nothing else. He longed for a schedule he could follow; command and control over the events that ruled his days.

But most of all, he longed for Daisy, and after this... after this he figured there was no way she'd ever speak to a Tasker again.

He couldn't say he blamed her.

"You battle-ax," Eunice said sharply as Vivian rose and stepped in her direction. "How dare you come into my home and interfere in family concerns? Can you see what you've done? You've ruined everything."

Those few who remained in the dining room were talking among themselves, ignoring her as they discussed potential ways to fix the damage she'd done. At least, that was the way they phrased it. Eunice didn't see that she'd done any damage. All she'd done was put Jacob and Daisy together so they could find their way. That wasn't so bad. Was it?

Susan moved to Jim's side and put her hand on his shoulder. Jim patted Susan's hand then left his hand sitting there, on hers. Funny, but she didn't see them this way often. Together. United. Good heavens, different as they were—imperfect as they were—they were still in love. Maybe her son had done something right, after all.

Jim and Susan, even Caleb, talked about the reunion, Doc Porter and all those who had left the dining room table with hurt feelings.

Eunice only felt guilty about one of them. Daisy.

"What *I've* done?" Vivian repeated. "I told the truth. Not that you'd recognize the truth even if it bit you on that overly generous ass of yours."

Eunice gasped. How dare this woman come into her home, disrupt all her plans and then insult her? She tried to come up with a proper response, but words failed her. She hadn't had time to plan for this, to mull over her words, to script the evening.

"You're the one who's been lying to your family, Eunice. You're the one who has once again woven a tale in order to get your way." Vivian leaned over and gripped the handles of the wheelchair Eunice sat in. "Do you even need this contraption? I can just see you, using the wheelchair to get sympathy, then getting up at night and walking around the house when no one else can..."

"I do need this chair, dammit. I wish I didn't."

Vivian placed herself behind the wheelchair and pulled Eunice sharply away from the table. Eunice gripped the armrests and screamed weakly for help. Vivian—her oldest friend, her oldest rival—stopped and looked toward Susan, rightly sizing her up as the one in charge.

"I'll just take her to her room, if that suits you. Y'all have work to do and I don't think Eunice will be of much help here, given the circumstances."

Susan agreed, dismissing Eunice without giving much thought to the obvious peril she was putting her mother-in-law in. The hateful woman who had ruined everything might decide to push an old, helpless woman down the front porch steps, or dump her in the hallway and leave her there to flounder and call for help that wouldn't come. Panic welled up and she gripped the armrests of her wheelchair and held on. For the first time in a very long time, she was not in charge of the situation.

"Where to?" Vivian asked as she pushed the wheelchair into the wide hallway.

Eunice pointed, half expecting Vivian to turn in the opposite direction out of spite. That didn't happen.

Vivian pushed the chair slowly, even gently. She sighed. "If I was lucky enough to have a family, I wouldn't lie to them," she said. "You should be ashamed of yourself."

That truth hurt, even though Eunice was still convinced she'd done the right thing. Jacob needed Daisy. If not for the very necessary lies she'd told of late, he'd still be in San Francisco! Didn't the end justify the means? That wasn't a discussion she intended to have with this interloper. "Surely you have some family, somewhere."

"No." There was sadness in Vivian's voice. "Frank and I never had children. I had two miscarriages, and after that I just didn't get pregnant. There are a few nieces and nephews scattered about, but we were never close. I doubt they even know I'm still alive."

"I'm sorry," Eunice said. "I lost three myself…two stillborn before Jim and one who died at a few days old when Jim was three." She thought about how nice it would've been to have the support of a friend in those tough times. She wondered if Vivian had had a friend to help her when she'd lost her babies. There was no way to describe that pain to someone who had not been there.

Claiming the man she'd loved had cost her a good

friend. She'd thought the trade a fair one, at the time. Now she was not so sure.

The past was still between them, a living thing after all this time. "I loved him," Eunice whispered. "You had Charles, for a while, but you never truly loved him. Not like I did."

"I know." Vivian stopped pushing, positioned Eunice, set the brake and walked around the wheelchair to sit in the occasional chair in the hallway. Now they were face-to-face, and for the first time Eunice looked her old friend in the eye without lies between them. Vivian was a strong old bird, stringy and wrinkled and healthy, for her age. She wore a life of hardship on her face; it was clear in her eyes that she had struggled. And yet the face was still much the same. Eunice saw the girl she remembered in those eyes, in the set of the mouth. "But he was still mine, and you took him."

"If it makes you feel better, I don't think he ever entirely got over you."

Vivian smiled. "That does make me feel a little better."

"Not that he didn't love *me,*" Eunice felt compelled to point out.

Vivian waved that statement off with a dismissive gesture of her hand. "We can talk about the past later, if it suits us to do so. For now, we need to fix this mess you've made."

"May I point out that there would not be a mess to fix if you had kept your mouth shut?" Eunice couldn't help it that her voice was sharp. As far as she could see, Vivian had ruined a perfectly good scheme.

"You may, but that's not the case. Your ridiculous plan wasn't working."

"What do you mean it wasn't working?" It had been working perfectly!

"On the way here Daisy told me that she's moving to Atlanta to live with her sister. Is that what you had in mind?"

Eunice pursed her lips. "No."

"I didn't think so. Daisy is crazy about that grandson of yours, and he's definitely got a thing for her. We can't let this mess you've made pull them apart."

"We?"

Vivian sighed. "Maybe I should've kept my mouth shut, but you were so obvious I just couldn't do it."

"I wasn't obvious to anyone else."

"They don't know you the way I do." Vivian stood, kicked off the brake and righted the wheelchair. "Your room?"

Eunice pointed. Before they could enter the room, Lurlene came around the corner, moving as quickly as possible, for her old bones.

"Lurlene, thank goodness you're here," Eunice said dramatically.

Vivian sighed and stopped pushing.

Eunice caught Lurlene's eye. She could have Vivian kicked out of the house. It was her house after all. But even though there were things to be settled between them, she was very aware that life was moving quickly by, and she didn't have many friends left. She didn't have any as close as Vivian had once been, and none of them would dare to buck her.

"I'll need six chocolate covered cherries tonight, three for me and three for my friend. Vivian, would you like another cup of decaf? Perhaps some tea?"

There was a moment's hesitation before Vivian answered. "Sure. Decaf. Cream and sugar, please."

"So tell me," Eunice said as Vivian wheeled her into her suite. "How can we fix this?"

* * *

Daisy ran. Out of the dining room, out of the house, past the cars parked by the front porch. She kept running, realizing on some level that Lily was right behind her. Lily didn't try to catch up to her sister. She could have, but instead she kept a short distance between them. She was close, in case she was needed, but far enough away to allow Daisy to have some privacy.

Daisy knew she could turn and run into her sister's arms, she could pour out all her fears and anger and frustration. But she was unable to speak…unable to stop running. She ran up a gentle hill toward the cover of trees that were in stark contrast to the brilliant colors the setting sun had left behind.

At the base of an old oak tree, she stopped. She was out of breath and her legs shook from the effort. She put her hands on the trunk, leaned forward and took a deep breath. For a moment she thought she might throw up, but she didn't. Her stomach pitched and rolled, and her heart pounded—from the run and more.

She was such an idiot! A gullible fool. She hated the Taskers, each and every one of them. If she never saw a Tasker again it would be too soon.

Lily placed a comforting hand on her back, and with that touch tears came. Daisy didn't want to cry, but she did. The tears that ran down her cheeks weren't tears of sadness; they were tears of anger.

Getting out of town seemed even more attractive than it had before. Attractive? Hell, it was *necessary*.

Then Lily asked the question that had been plaguing Daisy. "Do you think Jacob knew all along?"

It was her greatest fear, that Jacob really had been playing with her from the moment he'd stepped into her shop, that it had all been a game. But she'd seen the look on his face when Miss Vivian dropped the bombshell. She didn't think a single person at that table had realized what was going on. If any one of them did, they were a great actor.

"No," she whispered, sniffling. "I don't think he knew. I think Miss Eunice lied to get him home, and then she lied to try to force us together." If she'd thought Jacob was involved, if she believed for one second that he'd been in on the ruse, she'd never recover. She'd never trust anyone again. "How the hell far was she willing to go?"

"All the way, I'm guessing," Lily said, her voice sharp.

Daisy turned, leaned her back against the tree trunk and slid down into a sitting position. She didn't have the strength to stand, at the moment. Her knees were knocking; her heart was beating too hard. She wiped away her tears, angry at herself for allowing them to fall in the first place.

She was going to have to find strength, and she'd need it for more than standing and walking away. She was going to have to find the strength to start a new life, say goodbye to Jacob, say goodbye to everything she knew. At the moment, escape sounded really good. More than good, she was coming to accept that escaping from Bell Grove, a home she truly loved, was necessary.

Lily sat down in front of Daisy, crossed her legs and leaned forward. "You can't let one old bat's sick game send you into a tailspin."

"What makes you think I'm…"

"You're pale, your hands are shaking, you're crying, and instead of heading for the car when the truth came out you kept running. In case you haven't noticed that we're sitting in the middle of nowhere."

Daisy stared at her sister in the dying light. "I'm not as strong as you are."

Lily's response was a single word that would've shocked

their parents. It even shocked Daisy, a little. "You're the strongest of us all. You're a rock for me and Mari, and you always have been. There was a time I almost hated you for being so damn perfect."

Daisy snorted. She was so *not* perfect.

"It's true," Lily snapped. "You gave up everything for us, and don't think we don't realize that. Mari and I never wanted for anything after Mom and Dad died, we had a stable home, food on the table, clothes. More than that, we still had a family. Thanks to you. That's strength, Daisy."

She leaned forward, and so did Lily. They hugged, tight.

"You really are the strongest person I know," Lily whispered.

And in the distance she heard a frustrated Jacob calling her name.

Chapter Fifteen

Her car was parked right where she'd left it, but where was Daisy? Jacob circled the house. As soon as complete darkness fell he'd have a hell of a time finding her and worse, she'd have a hell of a time finding her way back, if she'd wandered far. He checked out the garage and the gardens. Nothing.

The look on her face as the truth sank in and took hold had broken his heart. And he was to blame. He hadn't lied to her, he hadn't purposely hurt her, but he'd dragged her into this charade that had hurt her so badly. Where would she go, if she didn't jump in the car and make a quick escape?

After searching the immediate property as thoroughly as he could without a flashlight, Jacob rounded the house to the front, again. Daisy's car was still here. She wasn't in it, and neither was Lily. She couldn't have gone far. In frustration he shouted her name. Would that call her to him, or scare her away?

Jacob was embarrassed and angry; he felt as if he'd been betrayed. So how did Daisy feel right now? Wherever she might be, he imagined she was experiencing all of the same emotions. And more.

If she hadn't hated him before tonight, she did now. Not that he'd known what his grandmother had been up to, not that he would ever condone that kind of trickery, but still…he was a Tasker, and the head of the clan had screwed Daisy over in a big way.

After a few very long minutes, movement caught his eye. Finally! Two women—Daisy and her sister—approached from the west. They didn't seem to be in a hurry. Dusk made a colorful pastel backdrop for them as they headed slowly in his direction. Skirts fluttered in the breeze, and as they came closer and saw him standing there, Lily reached out and took Daisy's hand.

Comfort offered because he was close.

Jacob was glad Daisy had her sisters; he was grateful to know they would always be there for her. He wished he could be the one to comfort her, wished she would let him take her hand in tough times. And good times, too.

When they reached him, Lily shot daggers his way with her dark eyes. Daisy turned and dipped her head and whispered something to her sister, and Lily reluctantly released Daisy's hand and headed for the steps, a path that took her right past Jacob. As she brushed by him she muttered, "Addams family."

He ignored her. She had every right to be angry.

"I'm so sorry," he said when he and Daisy were alone. "I didn't have any idea what she'd done."

"I know," Daisy said, her voice so low he could barely hear her. "Everyone at the table looked so surprised. This mess appears to be all your grandmother's doings. Maybe she really is unwell, just not the way we thought."

"Maybe. Personally I think she's just a world-class control freak and she wanted what she wanted and would do anything to get it." His words were sharp, condemning. And, he was certain, right.

Daisy nodded. "That's probably so. I suppose I'd prefer to think that a woman I once admired was sick, rather than cruel and manipulative. All evidence to the contrary," she whispered. She lifted her head and looked him in the eye. "So, are you still sticking around for the reunion?"

"I don't think so." He walked toward her, but the way her body stiffened when he moved in her direction stopped him from closing the gap between them. He wouldn't do anything to make her more uncomfortable. He wouldn't stay for his family, but he'd stay for her, if she asked him to. What were the odds of that happening? Slim to none, he figured.

"I don't have any proof, but I suppose it was your grandmother who bought my downtown space."

He would have proof soon, if Ted did his job. "I'd guess so. No matter who it was, I can make it right for you. I can stop the deal before..."

"Don't," Daisy said sharply. "She can have it. Martin wants to retire, and it's a good deal for him. Besides, I'm not staying in this town, no matter what."

His heart sank, a little. Bell Grove without Daisy in it was just wrong. He didn't have the right to try to change her mind. "You're going to Atlanta with Lily?"

She nodded. "Not right away. I still have to finish cleaning out the shop, and there will be papers to sign to get the house on the market. Someone will have to replace me on my Monday meals run, and…well, there are a million small details to take care of before I go."

She looked so vulnerable, so sad. He didn't think she really wanted to leave Bell Grove: she was being forced out of town. He felt helpless, and he was angry for her. His mother had been right; he'd just been slow to accept the truth. He did still love her. Not the same way he'd loved her years ago, not in a way he could explain. But there it was. Too late.

Maybe not too late. If Daisy knew that he still loved her, if she knew he'd do anything to keep her…

"Daisy, I…" he began.

Lily came storming through the door. "You won't believe it! Miss Vivian and that psycho are chatting it up like lifelong buds, and she's not ready to go. The psycho said she'd have someone drive her guest home later."

"Miss Vivian was okay with that?" Daisy asked, more than a little confused.

"More than okay. She's fine here, trust me." The middle Bell sister stormed past Jacob without acknowledging his existence. "Let's get the hell out of here."

Daisy nodded, and Jacob watched as she got in the car. The passenger seat. Lily jumped behind the wheel and took the keys from her big sister. Just as well, Jacob supposed. Daisy was badly shaken and had no business driving. He could see the women through the windshield, watched as the engine revved and the car slowly backed away and made a sharp one-eighty. Daisy never so much as lifted her head to look his way.

Jacob stood there and watched the taillights fade away. His frustration grew, second by second. He wanted to do something; he needed to fix this mess…but it wasn't an easy fix. He couldn't buy a solution or hire a team to make things right.

They were back to square one, just like that. He was leaving town without Daisy. And this time, she was leaving without him.

Everyone who came into the shop on Saturday wanted to know about Daisy's move to Atlanta. Daisy smiled a lot. She never hinted that the relocation was anything other than something she desperately wanted to do. She didn't complain about the space being sold out from under her, or an old woman's lies to get her way, or Jacob breaking her heart all over again. Instead she talked about being closer to concerts and ball games and shopping. She told everyone she'd probably lease a chair at a salon in Atlanta. More than a few customers said they'd still come to her to get their hair done, even though they'd have to pass a lot of salons along the way to get to her.

She was flattered, and pleased, and more than a little teary-eyed. Maybe her subconscious motives for staying put had been wrong-minded, but she had a lot of friends here, friends who had become like family over the years.

It was Lily who called a local real estate agent and made an appointment for that afternoon, after the shop closed. Houses didn't exactly fly off the market in Bell Grove, but by signing the papers she'd set things into motion.

Daisy only thought about Jacob every ten minutes or so, which was an improvement over the mostly sleepless night before, when she'd almost felt as if he were still lying beside her.

Her anger had faded as she'd tossed and turned, and by morning she'd been left more sad than anything else. Still embarrassed to be such a fool, hurt that she'd been used as a patsy, but mostly she was just sad.

As she walked through the house the real estate agent—a middle-aged man who was fond of telling bad jokes—

suggested improvements that would make the house more attractive to potential buyers. New wall colors, decluttering, new appliances. He told her how much more she'd get for the house if she made those improvements.

He made a suggestion about paint color as they stood in the doorway of her bedroom. Daisy couldn't see a new color on the walls. Instead she saw Jacob in her bed. She saw the two of them dancing in the dark, her skin against his, the music washing over them. She saw herself, thinking—*knowing*—that she still loved Jacob and couldn't live without him. It would take weeks, maybe months, to make all the changes the agent suggested. She didn't want to drag this painful process out any longer than was absolutely necessary.

She'd kept the house almost exactly as it had been when her parents had died. Someone else would have to remake it into something new and different.

"Put the house on the market as is," she said as she and the real estate agent sat at the kitchen table with a stack of papers between them.

"But you could get..."

"I don't care," she interrupted sharply, not caring—too much—that she sounded almost rude. She just wanted out, as soon as possible. She didn't want to spend weekend after weekend here painting and remodeling. No, she wanted to escape every memory—the good and the bad. Now. "Get what you can for it, that's all I ask."

He shook his head and pushed some papers toward her. She signed, blinking twice to clear the annoying tears from her eyes.

Jacob was accustomed to sleeping in hotel rooms, but the one he woke in late Saturday morning was not exactly up to his usual standards. The bed was hard, there was the unmistakable hum of the interstate too close by and the walls were so thin he could hear the television—and some of the conversation—in the room next door. The hotel he had chosen was close, right off the interstate in between Bell Grove and Atlanta. He was tempted to get in his car and head a little farther south so he could get on a plane and return to San Francisco today.

Instead of hopping out of bed and doing just that he lay there for a while. Running away was too easy; it was the coward's way out. It would be so easy to fly away from this mess and tell himself that he and Daisy just weren't meant to be. Soon enough he'd be back in the swing of things, and he'd relegate her to the back of his mind, as best he could. He'd bury himself in work, and tell himself it was all for the best. But Daisy was worth fighting for. He knew that, now. He wasn't at all sure that she wanted to be won—not by him, at least—but if he didn't try he'd always wonder.

He wasn't going to San Francisco without her, not without a fight. The life he'd lived for the past seven years, the job, the money, the travel, the excitement…it didn't look very attractive to him anymore. In fact, from a distance it looked downright sad.

It would be very easy to hop on a plane and resume his life as it had been before. Daisy would be fine. She had her sisters, and a million friends who would be there for her if she needed them. No matter what had happened in the past couple of weeks—the good and the bad—they could both return to the lives they'd made in the past seven years. And they'd grow apart all over again. It would hurt more, this time, but life would go on.

Jacob showered, he dressed, he walked to the restaurant next to the hotel for a big breakfast. Back in the hotel room he sat at the faux-wood desk with a crappy cup of in-room coffee and answered a few of the emails that had piled up during his vacation. There were enough messages in his in-box to keep him busy for a week.

When Ted called that afternoon, Jacob wasn't at all surprised to hear that it had been his grandmother who'd set the sale of a strip of downtown Bell Grove into motion. And all this time he'd been feeling sorry for her…

"Thanks," Jacob said. He wheeled the creaky desk chair around and ran anxious fingers through his hair, trying to decide what to do. Usually he knew exactly what should come next. That was his job, after all. In business, though, not in life. His life held no surprises, no tough personal choices.

Before he hung up the phone he said, "There's something else…"

Eunice sat in her favorite spot, staring out the window. It was a beautiful summer day, bright and green. She half hoped to see Jacob's rental car heading down the long, winding driveway, but no such luck.

He hated her. She couldn't blame him. Well, she could blame him a little. Why couldn't he—and everyone else—see that her intentions had been good? She wondered if he'd ever give her the opportunity to explain herself. If he'd ever forgive her.

It was after lunch when she saw a bit of dust kicked up in the distance. With her eyes squinted so she could see farther, she waited to see who was coming this way. She hoped for Jacob. She even said a quick prayer that her grandson was coming home to make things right. Instead her tired old eyes eventually identified an ancient pickup truck she had never seen before. It was one Jacob wouldn't be caught dead in, she knew that much. The vehicle she watched left the driveway often, jerking off the asphalt and then back on again, sending dirt and dust flying each time the wheels left the path.

A drunkard, Eunice thought. A lost drunkard who could not keep control of his vehicle. It was a rusted pickup, she noted as it jerked to a stop at the front of the house. Perhaps it had once been red; it was difficult to tell.

The very loud engine was silenced with a sputter. The driver's door opened with a rusty squeal, and—surprise—Vivian stepped out of the truck.

Eunice was at once envious of her old friend for being so limber—and able to drive at all—and at the same time she was furious that someone who drove so badly would get on the road. She could've been killed!

A small brown dog followed Vivian out of the vehicle. Eunice was horrified. She would not allow that filthy creature into the house!

She heard the doorbell, moved her chair away from the window and pretended to be surprised when Lurlene knocked on her door and introduced the guest.

The dog followed Vivian into the room, ran toward Eunice and—horrors—jumped into her lap.

"Oh, oh, oh." Eunice attempted to move her face away from the mutt's slobbering attempts to lick her on the mouth. She failed miserably.

"Settle down," Vivian said with a smile. "Buster is an affectionate animal. And besides, you should be glad that *someone* still likes you."

"Take him! Take him! Get this creature off me!"

Vivian chuckled as she reached out and grabbed the dog, who gratefully turned his attentions to her. She smiled as Buster licked her face and then settled into her arms, a dirty bundle of long brown hair. The animal apparently didn't have a care in the world.

"What kind of dog is that?" Eunice asked with disdain.

"Buster is a mutt."

"I see."

"Don't turn up your nose that way. There's nothing wrong with being a mutt. You need to get that stick out of your ass, Eunice." Vivian sat on the edge of the bed and placed the dog beside her.

Eunice bit back a command to get the *mutt* off her bedspread. But the damage was already done, and since the animal settled down in one place and didn't seem inclined to romp further, she let the infraction go.

"Did you apologize to Jacob?" Vivian asked.

Eunice felt her lips tighten and thin. "No. He left last night without seeing me, and he's not answering his cell phone." Not to her, at least. He had caller ID—everyone did these days—and he might be purposely avoiding her. Might be? Of course he was purposely avoiding her.

"Did you call Daisy?"

It took everything Eunice had not to drop her head in shame. "No. I…what can I say to her? How can I explain over the phone what I did and why? I really did have her best interests at heart, but she won't believe that." Besides, Daisy was almost certain to screen her calls just as Jacob did. If she tried calling from another phone, well, Daisy would surely just hang up when she answered and heard Eunice's voice on the line.

"You can start with *I'm sorry.*"

Those words did not come easily to Eunice. They never had.

"You need to stick with the truth," Vivian instructed dryly. "Think of telling the truth as a new experience. Prove to your family that you're an old dog who can learn new tricks."

Eunice was tempted to kick Vivian and her mangy dog out of the house. No one spoke to her this way! But she couldn't deny that she perversely liked having the plain-spoken Vivian back in her life. Last night they'd talked for hours, catching up on the time that had passed. It made Eunice regret deeply the lost years, the years they could've been friends if she'd only made the first move and said she was sorry.

"That's not going to be easy."

Vivian snorted. Such unladylike behavior! "Try actually having dementia, if you want to imagine something that's not easy. Remember Jean from our class? She died five years ago, but not until she'd forgotten everyone in her family, not until she'd completely lost touch with the world she lived in. You *pretended* because it suited your purpose. She lived with it. For years. Her family truly suffered, the way you made your family suffer because you wanted to get your way."

A sharp retort was on Eunice's tongue, but she bit it back. Jean? She hadn't seen or heard about Jean for years, but she still remembered her as a pretty young woman with a husband who loved her and a handful of rowdy kids. The family had moved to Chattanooga years ago, but maybe she'd moved back. Maybe Vivian had kept in touch all these years. Eunice fought back tears. Had she lost touch so completely with the world around her?

"I didn't mean to make light of…I just didn't think… was it bad for her, really?" Pretending not to remember had been convenient and—yes, she'd admit it—occasionally fun. But even to imagine truly being in that state was painful.

"It was bad." Vivian stroked her mutt's fur and looked away for a few moments. The silence that followed was maddening.

"You'll stay for dinner," Eunice said as she regained complete control of her emotions.

Vivian's head snapped around and her eyebrows shot up sharply. "I will?"

Eunice took a deep breath. Good heavens, this was difficult. "Vivian, would you *please* stay for dinner?"

"I don't know. I don't like to drive after dark."

"From what I saw, you shouldn't drive by the light of day, either," Eunice snapped.

Vivian glanced toward the window that looked out over the front of the house. "You saw me coming and then pretended to be surprised. Why?"

"I don't know," Eunice admitted. Had lying become the norm for her? Was it her natural mode of operation? "I suppose I don't want everyone to know that I sit here at the window and watch life pass me by."

Vivian nodded as if she understood. "I don't drive often, and I will admit, that old thing doesn't steer the way it used to."

"I'll ask Caleb to look at it," Eunice said. "He's always been quite good with cars. He and Jacob both, though of course Jacob isn't here." She cleared her throat. "Caleb can drive you home later tonight." She added, in a lowered voice, "If that's all right with you, of course."

"Fine by me." Vivian looked pointedly at the wheelchair. "Since I'll be here for a while, I have some exercises I want you to try."

"Exercises?" Eunice repeated sharply. "I'll have you know, I do *not* exercise."

Vivian harrumphed, and there went those eyebrows again. "Maybe that's why you're in a wheelchair."

Dogs, exercise, apologizing. Eunice very much wanted her old friend back in her life, but she had a feeling that if she gave in nothing would ever be the same. Exercise! Horrors.

"The Braves are playing a day game today," Vivian said,

heading for the small television Eunice rarely bothered to turn on. "You do have cable, don't you?"

Baseball? Oh, the sacrifices...

"Of course," Eunice said.

"We'll exercise between innings, and after the game we'll try making those phone calls."

As much as Eunice hated the thought of talking to Jacob or Daisy, of facing what she'd done, she knew her old friend, who was perhaps going to become a new friend, was right.

Chapter Sixteen

Daisy wanted to be happy about leaving Bell Grove; she wanted to be excited about all the changes that were coming to her life. Goodness knows she needed a few changes!

But after Lily left—she didn't have any more time off from her new job—Daisy found herself sinking deeper and deeper into a funk. She waffled back and forth between trying to psych herself up, and being in the dumps about leaving home. Mari and Lily didn't complain about getting homesick. They didn't pine for Bell Grove. They hadn't put their lives on hold to keep what was left of their parents alive. She had. What was wrong with her?

Then again, they both knew this house and their big sister would be here, waiting for them, if they ever did get the urge to come home.

No more. As she packed knickknacks and doodads that hadn't been moved in many years, Daisy found herself getting maudlin. Every piece she touched had a memory attached to it. They'd gone in together and given their mother this figurine for Mother's Day one year. It was cheap and, yes, a little tacky, but Mom had loved it. At the very least, she'd pretended well to love it. It had been sitting on the same shelf for seventeen years.

This vase was chipped, thanks to a rambunctious four-year-old Lily. It was always placed with the chipped side to the wall, so no one would see the defect. This cat figurine had belonged to their grandmother—their father's mother. Mari had always loved it. Every dish, every plate, every cloth napkin had a memory attached to it.

Packing things away was torture. Daisy wasn't ready to sell or toss the worthless treasures, but where was she going to store it all?

She tried to make piles. Definitely keep, maybe throw away, Mari or Lily might want. But she kept moving things out of the *maybe throw away* pile and into one of the others. At one point she conceded that she was a hopeless pack rat and her sisters were going to have to help her make decisions about all this *stuff.*

She sat cross-legged on the living room floor, a trio of small framed pictures lined up before her. Mari, Lily and Daisy, each of them at one year old. These she'd take with her, she decided. No matter where she lived, she could look at these photos every day. They were a part of home she could take with her.

There wouldn't be room for everything, though, and she didn't want her new home to look exactly like the old one. It wouldn't look new at all, if that was the case. And oh, she really needed *new.* A fresh start, a new life. She'd decided that was such a good idea, and now it terrified her. Just a little.

Daisy lifted her head when she heard a car pull into her driveway. The engine was unfamiliar. Funny how it didn't take long to identify the particular sound of a car. It wasn't Lily's car, not Mari's truck, not Jacob's rental—thank goodness. Who else could it be? If the real estate agent wanted to show the house, he really should've called first. A pile of knickknacks on the living room floor wasn't exactly proper staging.

She stood and went to the window, brushing her dusty hands on her shorts as she went, and pulled back the curtain to peek outside. The car parked behind hers was a large black sedan, a few years old but in pristine condition. The black paint shone, the chrome grill sparkled, as if no bug would dare to die there.

Caleb Tasker stepped out of the driver's side of the tank of a car that was parked in the driveway, and Daisy's heart did a sick flip. Had Jacob sent him? No, that would be so unlike Jacob, to send someone else to do his dirty work for him. Well, unless this was a new MO for him. Maybe the business hotshot ordered people to do his dirty work all the time. She couldn't imagine Caleb stopping by to chat with her; they didn't know one another well at all. All they had in common was Jacob.

The rear passenger door opened, and Miss Vivian stepped out. She wore a Sunday dress and her hair was braided. Not as neatly as if Daisy had done the job, but she had made an effort.

Daisy was surprised. She never would've guessed either of the two of them would come to see her at the house, and together? No way. Had Miss Vivian called Caleb and asked him to give her a ride to town? Did she think Daisy would leave without saying goodbye?

The big surprise came when Caleb opened the front passenger door and assisted an unsteady Eunice Tasker from the vehicle.

Daisy let the curtain drop. Of all the people she didn't

want to see right now, Miss Eunice was second only to Jacob. Maybe if she'd taken one of the phone calls from the Tasker House earlier in the day, she wouldn't have Miss Eunice knocking on her door.

It took several minutes for the doorbell to ring. Daisy stood in the center of the room, away from the window and the door. She seriously considered not answering the door, the way she hadn't answered the phone. She didn't want to be a coward, even if she felt very cowardly at the moment.

She finally took a deep breath and walked to the door, just as the doorbell sounded again. Just because they were on her front porch, that didn't mean she had to invite them in. This was still her house. She'd find out what they wanted, then coolly and calmly send them all on their way.

"Thank goodness," Miss Eunice said breathlessly as the door swung open. "I desperately need to sit."

Caleb supported her on one side, Miss Vivian on the other. The unsteady woman really did look as if she were about to fall.

Daisy held the door open and allowed the three to walk inside. So much for her grand plan of sending them away! The two on either side of Miss Eunice led her to the nearest chair, where she sat carefully and with evident relief. She closed her eyes, took a deep breath and sank down into the chair. Finally she opened her eyes and looked directly at Daisy.

"Vivian has insisted that I *walk,*" Eunice said with disdain.

"She's got no strength in her legs at all," Vivian said.

"It's hard!" Eunice argued.

"Well, it'll only get harder if you don't move."

"She made me exercise and watch *baseball,*" Eunice grumbled, pursing her lips in evident displeasure.

Vivian responded. "The exercise is good for you, and trust me, baseball will grow on you."

The two women bickered like sisters. It was very odd. And why did they have to bicker *here?*

"May I help you?" Daisy asked formally. That seemed better than what she really wanted to say. *What the hell do you want*?

Eunice looked up at her grandson. "Caleb, go wait in the car."

Caleb couldn't get out of the house fast enough. He did cast Daisy an apologetic glance, but there was too much humor in his eyes for her to believe he was truly sympathetic. When he was gone, Miss Eunice looked at Daisy again. Her eyes were hard, inflexible, which made her words all the more surprising.

"I'm sorry." The simple words were clipped and emotionless.

Daisy didn't know what to say to that, so she said nothing.

"For…" Vivian nudged gently.

"For interfering, for lying, for basically sticking my nose in where it didn't belong." Eunice's words were sharp. Apologizing was obviously a new experience for her. She wasn't very good at it, and she had to follow up with a qualifier. "But that doesn't mean I wasn't right. You and Jacob do have feelings for one another, and if I hadn't done what I did you'd never know."

I don't want to know.

"Tell her the rest," Vivian urged.

"If you'll stay, I'll let you remain in your space downtown rent free."

"Eunice!" Vivian snapped.

The woman in the chair waved a dismissive hand. "Fine, I'll give it to you, free and clear. I'll put that entire side of downtown Bell Grove in your name and you can do with it what you please. If you stay, of course. I considered just calling off the deal to buy the property, but I understand that's not what you want."

Daisy shook her head. "I'm leaving town, and nothing you say or do will change my mind." And the truth was, she didn't want anything from the Taskers. She tried to sound tough and uncaring as she added, "I don't care what you do with that building." What she didn't say was *Choke on it.*

She looked at Vivian, who was obviously a part of this ridiculous scheme because she wanted Daisy to stay. "Don't worry, Miss Vivian. There are lots of other volunteers, and I'll make arrangements for someone else to get your groceries and take you to the doctor."

"I can drive myself."

Daisy shook her head. "Miss Vivian, I've seen you drive. Please let me make other arrangements."

"That won't be necessary," Eunice said sharply. "Vivian will soon be moving into Tasker House."

"I don't think so," Vivian grumbled.

Eunice didn't back down. "Lurlene is getting on in years and she needs some help. With Vivian as my live-in companion, Lurlene will have more free time. And I'll have someone around who makes me do things others won't."

"Like exercising," Vivian said.

"And apologizing," Eunice added. "There's always someone around to drive, so we can save the county from Vivian's dreadful attempts behind the wheel. Besides, we get the Braves games in that High Definition television. Vivian likes that. She likes looking at the players' butts in those tight pants."

"Eunice!" Vivian actually blushed a bit.

"Well, it's true enough. Besides, I don't like the idea of her living out there in the middle of nowhere all alone."

"I'm not alone. I have Buster."

Daisy didn't feel the need to walk on eggs, not with these two. "I thought y'all hated each other!"

"We got over it," Vivian said. "Life is too short to spend it wallowing in regret. Mistakes were made on both sides, but we've decided to move on. It's not like either one of us has so many friends left that we can throw one over in the name of spite."

Eunice gave Daisy her full attention once again. "So, will you consider staying?"

Daisy shook her head.

"Think it over," Miss Vivian said. "You'll be missed if you leave. Bell Grove won't be the same without you. You're the last of the Bells here and that means something."

Eunice looked squarely at Daisy, her old eyes still strong and smart. "Tell me you don't love Jacob. If you can do that, I'll walk away and never bother you again."

Daisy opened her mouth, fully intending to say the words, to tell Miss Eunice, and herself, that she didn't love Jacob. Didn't need him, didn't want him. But she choked on the unspoken words. They lodged in her throat, left her helpless and scared. She did love him, but what good had that done her?

The old woman nodded once, satisfied.

Vivian went to the front door, opened it and called to Caleb. Together they assisted Eunice from the chair and held on to her as they moved across the porch and down the stairs—carefully and slowly—and finally into the car. Daisy stood on the porch for a long time after the car had driven away.

She left her piles of stuff sitting on the living room floor, unsorted and unpacked, and sat in the front porch rocker. When she moved to Atlanta, there would be no quiet moments like this one. Atlanta was always hopping; there were so many *people* there. At the same time, she knew moving on was the right decision.

She also admitted, reluctantly, that she was still in love with Jacob and probably always would be. Tasker or not, lousy white knight, horrible guitar player who had the bad judgment to wear suits in Bell Grove in the summertime… she loved him. That was the reason she suffered doubts about moving away, that was why starting over in Atlanta practically gave her hives.

In her heart she had never imagined she'd leave Bell Grove and start over without him.

Jacob returned to Tasker House, moving back into his room and avoiding family members as he did what needed to be done. In between phone calls and long emails, he attempted to play the guitar that had been sitting in his closet for seven years. He'd lost his touch, and he had no calluses on his fingers, but there was something there, still. If he made the effort, if he practiced regularly, he'd soon be playing again. He'd never play in public, but that had never been his ambition anyway. He just wanted to make music, now and then.

He hadn't taken the guitar with him to San Francisco, but it wasn't like he couldn't have bought another guitar there. He hadn't done that. He'd given up the pastime, years ago, maybe because he had never been all that good at playing, maybe because he would never be more than adequate when it came to music.

How many nights had he played for Daisy while she'd sung along? After class, before bed, in the middle of the night…in their rare spare time, while they'd pursued an education. She sang as badly as he played, just slightly out of tune and with the occasional missed lyric or note. And yet, those had been good times. Maybe the best.

When his fingers gave out, Jacob returned the guitar to the case that had been sitting in his closet for the past seven years. He opened the small compartment built into the case for picks, and found something else he'd stored there. Something else he'd packed away and all but forgotten.

He had a lot to relearn, after spending seven years chasing a career that had been financially rewarding while it suffocated everything else in his life. More than playing the guitar and getting grease under his fingernails and learning to deal with his dysfunctional family more than once every five years. He'd gotten so sucked into the corporate lifestyle he'd forgotten that there was more to be had from life. Much more. He'd set the most important aspects of life to the side.

It was almost dark when he made the final arrangements and left the house, headed into Bell Grove to make the most important deal of his lifetime.

Daisy sat on the couch, numb and lost. She didn't turn on the television, didn't pack her suitcase...didn't fix herself supper, trying to use up the rest of the fresh food in the kitchen. There were still three piles of stuff on the floor. The pile of things to throw away was dismally small, but time was running out and she had to get busy.

Yeah, time was really running out. The house had sold. She'd hoped it would, of course, but houses didn't move that quickly in Bell Grove and she'd expected to have more time. Time to get ready, maybe even time to change her mind. She couldn't even turn the offer down, because it was for more than she'd asked. The buyer hadn't even bothered to look at the inside of the house! The real estate agent was thrilled. Two offers on his listings in one day had put him over the moon.

She wondered who else had sold their home, who else, besides her, was leaving Bell Grove.

She was so tempted to get in her car and drive out to Tasker House, see if Jacob was still there. If she found him there, would she be brave enough to tell him what she really felt? Was she brave enough to go after what she wanted?

Maybe *she* could be the white knight.

No, he'd said he wasn't going to stay. He was probably back in California, already putting the disastrous events of his trip home behind him.

Everything hadn't been disastrous…

When the car pulled into her driveway, her heart skipped a beat. Her ear for engines—thanks to her dad—told her that was Jacob's rental car. As she had earlier in the day when Miss Eunice had come calling, she sat there and considered not answering the doorbell when it rang. What could he possibly want? Had he left something behind? A razor, a toothbrush…*her?*

She waited, and waited, but the doorbell didn't ring.

After several minutes she heard the muted strum of a guitar, the sound faded since the windows and doors were closed, but unmistakable. One slightly out of tune guitar playing a tune that reminded her vaguely of mariachi music. And playing badly.

She sat there a moment, her emotions in a jumble, then jumped off the couch and ran for the front door and the porch just beyond.

Jacob sat on the steps, dressed in jeans and a T-shirt, his back to her as he gave his full attention to the less-than-perfect notes. He didn't turn to look at her, though he must've heard her. She hadn't tried to be quiet, didn't try to sneak up on him.

Looking at his back, and the slightly mussed dark hair and the cut of his shoulders, a certainty washed over her. Certainty and relief and a sense of being whole for the first time in a very long time. He'd broken her heart and made her love him all over again. His family was big and interfering and, simply put, a pain in the ass. He might break her heart all over again, if she gave him the chance.

But she couldn't imagine moving forward without Jacob in her life in some way. As a friend, as more than a friend. She needed him.

The mariachi attempt ended, thank goodness, and he started something new. She remembered this song, recognized it even though he pretty much butchered every note. It was the song they'd danced to just last week.

"You were never very good, but I have to say, you've gotten worse," she said as she approached him.

"I know. I need more practice." He glanced over his shoulder, and his dark gaze cut through her. "I need to practice quite a few things I've lost touch with."

Daisy sat beside Jacob, not too close, but close enough. She'd been running away, not just from Miss Eunice's lies, not just from a life that had gotten stale, but from Jacob and everything he represented. She'd never stopped loving him, and in spite of everything that had happened here he was literally on her doorstep.

Her gallon of death-by-chocolate ice cream. Her first love. Her past. Maybe her future?

She blamed him and his family for the fiasco, but she had to face the truth that she shared some of the blame. When she'd heard the name *Tasker,* she'd been so certain Jacob was the one behind the sale of that downtown property. She'd condemned him without asking for an explanation.

She'd torn them apart before he could break her heart again.

All day she'd been thinking about her life, her mistakes...the rut she was in of her own free will. After Miss Eunice's visit, she'd been forced to think about other things, as well. Most of all she'd thought about Jacob. She loved him and she always had. She was in a rut because he was no longer hers. Since Lily and Mari had left home, she hadn't just been keeping their old life alive, she'd been sitting here *waiting* for Jacob to come for her. She hadn't realized it, and if she had she would've been horrified, but it all made sense to her now.

"Ask me again to go to San Francisco with you," she whispered. This time she'd say yes, she'd throw away everything to be with Jacob.

"I can't," he said. He stopped playing and put the guitar aside.

Daisy's heart broke all over again. He hadn't forgiven her for not trusting him, for thinking the worst. Why should she expect anything different? Thank goodness he didn't allow her to suffer for very long.

"I'm not going back to San Francisco. Not for very long, anyway. There will be things to take care of, I suppose."

"What are you talking about?"

"I quit my job," he said. Jacob looked at her, really *looked* at her for the first time since she'd walked out of the house, and her heart flipped wildly in her chest. She loved him, she liked him; she could even forgive him for being a Tasker...

"You did *what?*"

"Well, I tried to quit. I've been on the phone all day, and as it stands now I'm going to work freelance for the company. I'm now a consultant. That means I can live wherever the hell I want to. My boss is very unhappy, but he'll learn to live with the change. We'll make it work."

He sounded so calm, so reasonable, and the truth became clear to her. "You're the one who bought my house!"

Jacob nodded. "I did. I also bought the old Hamilton place. We need a home of our own, Daisy, a home that's *ours,* but I thought you might want to hang on to this house, too. Your sisters might want to stay here, now and then."

The old Hamilton place was a grand two-story colonial on the edge of town. She'd always loved that house, and Jacob knew it. No one knew her the way he did.

"A home of our own?" she repeated.

"I also bought a condo in Buckhead. The Hamilton house needs a lot of work, and I wasn't sure where you'd prefer to live, here or in Atlanta. If you want to live somewhere else just tell me. We can live anywhere, and when I do have to travel you can come with me, if it suits you. Or you can stay here and we'll talk on the phone for hours while I'm gone, or you can visit your sisters, or stay at the condo. Whatever you want, whatever you need. You're my number-one priority, Daisy, you will always come first. I won't forget that again."

Her mind continued to spin. "You bought a house and a condo? For *us?*"

"If you'll have me." Jacob reached into the open guitar case, opened a small compartment that was built into one side and drew out a small velvet box. He got on one knee so they were face-to-face. Daisy's heart thumped. This was happening too fast! She wasn't ready! It was too soon!

She took a deep breath and her heart resumed a fairly normal rhythm. No, it wasn't too soon, not at all. In fact, this was overdue. They'd both waited more than long enough.

Jacob opened the box and offered it to her on his open palm. A simple diamond solitaire set in yellow gold winked at her. The stone was a good size, but was far from ostentatious. "Daisy Bell, I love you. I have always loved you. Will you marry me?"

Her heart caught in her throat; her mouth went dry. Finally she choked out a soft, "Yes."

Jacob smiled, as he crept up the steps to take her hand and place the ring on her finger. "I hope you like it."

"I do, very much. It's perfect." She kissed him, once. Again.

Jacob drew away slightly and looked into her eyes. "Good. It's been sitting in this guitar case for seven years." He leaned in and kissed her again, his lips soft and warm against hers.

She enjoyed the kiss for a moment then she pulled away. "Seven years? Jacob!"

He shrugged his shoulders, and with one finger moved a strand of hair off her shoulder. "Seven years. I saw the ring and knew it was right for you, so I bought it. I kept trying to plan the perfect proposal, but nothing ever seemed quite right. Besides, I wasn't in a rush. I thought we had all the time in the world. We were so young, and all I could see ahead of us was blue skies."

"And then my parents died," Daisy whispered.

Jacob nodded. "Everything fell apart after that. I couldn't give you an engagement ring right after your folks died, and I didn't want to propose and then move to the other side of the country. My plans to come home at Christmas didn't work out, but for a long time I still believed that we had all the time in the world, that nothing would change for us. I waited for the perfect moment, and it never came. You know the rest. I'm sorry it took me so long to put that ring on your finger, where it belongs. I love you, Daisy. I need you. I don't care where we live, as long as I get to live with you."

She draped her arms around his neck. "I love you, too."

Her last name was going to be Tasker. Maybe that wouldn't be so bad, after all.

She kissed Jacob again, wallowed in the kiss, and when she pulled away she placed her forehead against his and smiled.

They'd waited long enough, and this moment was as perfect as it could possibly get.

"I hope you don't have a long engagement in mind…"

Chapter Seventeen

"I told you so," Eunice whispered to Vivian, as they sat near the foot of the stairs, waiting. She was seated in a comfortable wing chair, as was her friend. The wheelchair was parked in her bedroom, and while she might need it by the end of the day, she didn't need it right now. Eunice had been surprised by how much she could do when her friend pushed her.

"Don't brag, Eunice," Vivian responded, her voice low. "It's not attractive."

Vivian had moved into Tasker House a few days earlier, at Eunice's insistence. She'd brought her little dog, Buster, with her. The mutt was not as annoying as Eunice had initially thought it would be. In fact, Buster was a very loving and loyal animal, and he was surprisingly smart. She allowed the dog to sit on the foot of the bed when they ate chocolate-covered cherries, or watched a baseball game. She and Vivian were already planning a trip to Atlanta to watch a game in person, as soon as Eunice was able to get around a bit better. With Vivian's help, she grew stronger every day. Caleb, who loved baseball, had promised to take them.

Eunice had to admit—silently and only to herself—that she wasn't always right. Maddy hadn't forgiven her the way Daisy had, but she was here for the reunion. Eunice had watched and listened a lot during the reunion. Others in the family seemed to genuinely like Maddy. Maybe she didn't dress properly, and maybe she did wear too much makeup, and goodness knows she'd never be a brain surgeon, but she was friendly and sunny. She and Ben had shared big news this weekend; they were going to have a baby. The Tasker family was growing once again. Eunice hadn't given up on earning the girl's forgiveness. One day.

Finally the music began. Not a recording, but a live string quartet. Eunice could get things done right *and* in a hurry, if need be.

Lily and Mari walked down the stairs slowly. Daisy's sisters both wore yellow sundresses, though they were not identical. Jacob elbowed his brother in the ribs when Caleb whistled and muttered an appreciative, drawled, "Damn." Those who were close enough to hear laughed lightly.

Eunice was not amused. Neither of the available Bell girls would be appropriate for Caleb! Mari was too young, and Lily was too harsh and outspoken. No, she'd need to look elsewhere for a bride for Caleb. And soon.

When Lily and Mari reached the foot of the stairs, Daisy appeared at the top. Eunice smiled. Her wedding gown fit Daisy perfectly. No adjustments had been required. That was a good thing, given the short time they'd had to pull this wedding ceremony together. The bride's hair was down, simple and unadorned, and she carried white and yellow roses.

Daisy walked down the stairs slowly. Even though the foyer and the hallways beyond were filled with people, her smile and eyes were for Jacob alone. When she reached her waiting groom she whispered, before the preacher said a single word, "I do, I do, I do."

And Eunice turned once more to her friend, a smug smile on her face. "I told you so."

* * * * *

Daisy walked down the stairs slowly. Even though the [illegible] and the hallways beyond were filled with people, her aunts and [illegible] [illegible] [illegible] alone. When she reached the [illegible] [illegible] [illegible] [illegible] [illegible] [illegible] and a simple word. "I do. I do, I do."

And [illegible] [illegible] once more [illegible] friend, a sunny smile on her face. "I'll do you."

repeated. “Just you an

“And if I say no?”

“I’m not above kidnapping you.”

“I don’t know, Ry. Could I at least think about it?”

“Of course.”

And that should have been his cue to haul his sorry ass through the door and out to his car. If he’d been inclined, that is, to listen to his head and not whatever made him instead lift one hand to brush his thumb across her rapidly cooling cheek, a move that sent his stomach into a freefall.

Mel sucked in a breath, her eyes going even bigger. “What the hell are you doing?”

“Seriously thinking about things I’ve got no right to think about.”

inspiration can grow into a whole story. Or, as with SUMMER SISTERS, an entire series. In this case I'm talking memories of childhood vacations spent in North Carolina with my two close-in-age cousins, when my father would take me to visit my grandmother nearly every summer.

I still remember long, jostling rides in the back of somebody's Country Squire station wagon, cannonballing into assorted swimming pools and jamming out to the Beach Boys (guess that decade!).

Of course, this is fiction, and my cousins and I aren't anything like Mel, April and Blythe. High Point, North Carolina, turned into make-believe St Mary's Cove on Maryland's eastern shore, and heaven knows none of us went on to lead lives anywhere near as tangled in secrets as those three. But the love and camaraderie, the shared silliness and laughter—those, the six of us had in common. Like all three of my heroines, I, too, was an only child, who cherished those weeks every summer when I had "sisters." And writing these stories has allowed me to pay tribute to those gals…and those wonderful memories.

Enjoy!

Karen Templeton

THE DOCTOR'S DO-OVER

BY
KAREN TEMPLETON

MILLS & BOON

First published in Great Britain 2012
by Mills & Boon, an imprint of Harlequin (UK) Limited,
Eton House, 18-24 Paradise Road, Richmond, Surrey TW9 1SR

ISBN: 978 0 263 89479 0
ebook ISBN: 978 1 408 97155 0

23-1112

Harlequin (UK) policy is to use papers that are natural, renewable and recyclable products and made from wood grown in sustainable forests. The logging and manufacturing processes conform to the legal environmental regulations of the country of origin.

Printed and bound in Spain
by Blackprint CPI, Barcelona

Since 1998, two-time RITA® Award winner and Waldenbooks bestselling author **Karen Templeton** has written more than thirty novels for Mills & Boon. A transplanted Easterner, she now lives in New Mexico with two hideously spoiled cats and whichever of her five sons happens to be in residence.

To Amy and Lainey
Here's to memories of hot summers,
frigid swimming pools,
sighing over boys
and more good times than I can count.
Miss you guys.

Chapter One

Her nostrils twitching at the putrid mix of mildew, ancient grease and whatever it was that had died in her grandmother's Nixon-era refrigerator, Melanie Duncan could only gawk in horrified amazement. Holy cannoli—Amelia Rinehart had apparently kept every glass jar and plastic container she'd ever touched.

Along with—shuddering, Mel thunked shut the grimy, mustard-yellow cabinet door—decades' worth of magazines, newspapers and junk mail stacked in teetering piles throughout the eight-freaking-bedroom house. And just think, she thought sourly, shoving up the nasty water faucet with her wrist and waiting for-*ev*-er for the hot water to meander up from the basement, it was all hers. Hers and April's and Blythe's, that is.

With that, her gaze also meandered, out the dirt-fogged window and beyond the weed-infested backyard sloping down to the inlet beyond, to the slate blue water glittering in the late September sunshine…and she could almost see those three girls sunbathing on the pier, stretched out on Walmart-issue beach towels as Green Day blared from somebody's old boom box. Blythe's, most likely.

The water suddenly went blistering hot, making Mel yelp. Cursing, she adjusted the handle, thinking maybe she was still in shock. Not so much about her grandmother's passing—she had been nearly ninety, after all, even if Death probably had to hog-tie her and drag her away kicking and screaming. But, yeah, inheriting the Eastern Shore property, especially since her grandmother and she hadn't spoken in more than ten years? That was strange. Far more strange than that, however, was finding herself in the last place she'd ever expected to set foot again.

Or wanted to.

Anxiety prickling her chilled skin—the thermostat didn't appear to be working—Mel scrubbed her hands with the dish soap still sitting on the back of the pock-marked sink and turned, only to grimace at the M. C. Escher-like towers of long-since-expired bottles of herbal supplements smothering the chipped Formica counters…the jungle of dead plants at the base of the patio doors leading to the disintegrating back porch…what appeared to be hundreds of paper bags, undoubtedly loaded with mouse droppings, wadded between the fridge and the cabinets. Dis*gust*ing, as her daughter would say. Thank God the washing machine was working—go, Maytag—because no way in hell was she letting her child sleep on any of the musty sheets she'd found all jumbled up in the linen closet.

Had her grandmother always been that much of a packrat? Or had the three of them turned blind eyes to the clutter during those long, lazy summers when the world as they all knew it simply didn't exist?

Shaking her head, Mel tromped to the dining room and

yelled for her daughter, who, being made of sterner stuff than Mel, had gasped in utter delight the moment they'd set foot inside, then immediately taken off to explore.

"Quinn! Where are you?" she bellowed again, fighting images of the child fending off a posse of rats, breathing a sigh of relief at Quinn's faint, but strong, "Coming!" in reply.

She glowered at the behemoth of a buffet across the room, the blotchy mirror behind it nearly obliterated by more…stuff. Doodads and knickknacks and tchotchkes galore. And in every corner, packages of all shapes and sizes—some unopened, even—from every purveyor of useless crap on the planet.

So much for a quick in-and-out. What had clearly taken years to accumulate wasn't going to simply go *poof* in a couple of days. And then what? What the hell were the three of them supposed to do with the place? Yes, St. Mary's Cove was picturesque and all, but even divested of all the *stuff,* potential buyers would take one look and laugh their tushies off. And she sincerely doubted that either of her cousins had the funds, let alone the wherewithal, to fix it up. She sure as hell didn't, a thought that only shoved Mel back down into the Pit of Despair she'd been trying—with scant success—to climb out of for what felt like forever.

With a mighty sigh, she hiked through the House of Horrors and outside to her trusty little Honda to unload the backseat, the tangy, slightly fruity bay breeze catching her off guard. Oh, no. Not doing nostalgia, nope.

And just like that, there he was. In her head, of course, not in person, since there was no reason for him to know she was even here—and God willing, that's how this little episode would play out—but…damn.

She hadn't allowed herself to think of him in years.

Had almost convinced herself it didn't matter anymore. *He* didn't matter anymore, that what they'd shared was as firmly and irrevocably in the past as those long ago summers—

"Mom? Whatcha doing?"

Mel glanced up, smiling for the slightly frowning ten-year-old—her life, her love, her reason for living—standing on the porch, all turn-of-the-century charm fallen on hard times, and her heart turned over in her chest. Heaven knows she'd made a boatload of mistakes in her life—oh, let her count the ways—but the skinny fifth-grader with the wild red hair currently standing with her hands planted on her skinny, not-at-all-like-Mama's, hips wasn't one of them.

Although the circumstances of her conception? In a class by itself.

"Unpacking. And good news! You can come play pack mule." Because there was no way she was leaving that half-finished cheesecake to rot back in Baltimore while they were here. Or the pumpkin soufflé. Or the...

Okay, she liked her own cooking. So sue her.

They carted the various Tupperwared goodies into the kitchen, at which point Quinn gasped, bug-eyed, then shook her head."Looks like you and me have got some *serious* cleaning to do."

"You might say," Mel said as she cautiously opened the doors under the sink to find—booyah!—six half-empty containers of Comet and as many boxes of garbage bags, a bucketload of desiccated sponges and enough Lysol to disinfect a cruise ship. And, praise be, two unopened packages of rubber gloves. *The good Lord will provide,* she heard her mother say, and tears threatened. *Not going there, either,* Mel thought, standing and handing her daughter a pair of gloves, a sponge and one of the Comets.

"Start with the sink." Gloves donned, Mel yanked out a garbage bag and faced the fridge. "This puppy is *mine*."

"Got it." Quinn dragged over a step stool to better reach inside the sink, wriggled into her own gloves and got to it, determination oozing from every pore in her little body… as she started to sing, loudly and very badly, a song from *Wicked*.

What a little weirdo, Mel thought, chuckling. A little weirdo, she thought on a sharp intake of breath, she'd protect with everything she had in her.

Especially from people who wanted to pretend she didn't exist.

Looking up from Jenny O'Hearn's chart, Ryder Caldwell stared at his father's white-coated back, the words barely registering.

"What did you say?"

David Caldwell slid his pen back into his top pocket, then directed a steady, but concerned, gaze at Ryder before removing the coat and snagging it onto a hook on the back of his office door. "That Amelia left the house to the girls."

Not that this was any surprise, Ryder thought over the pinching inside his chest as he watched his dad shrug into the same tan corduroy sport coat he wore to work every day, rain or shine—much to Ryder's mother's annoyance—then yank down the cuffs of his blue Oxford shirt. Made perfect sense, in fact, Amelia Rinehart's bequeathing the house to the three cousins who'd spent, what? Nine or ten summers there? At least?

What was a surprise, was his reaction to the news. That after all this time the prospect of seeing Mel again should provoke any kind of reaction at all. After all, stuff happened. People grew up, moved on—

"You okay?"

Ryder glanced up at his father. Although David's lanky form stooped more than it used to, and silver riddled his thick, dark hair, it often startled Ryder that it was like seeing an age progression image of what Ryder himself would look like in thirty years. Unlike his younger brother Jeremy, who'd inherited their mother's fair skin and red hair. *Among other things.*

"Of course, why wouldn't I be?" he said, flipping closed Jenny's file, then striding down the short hall to the empty waiting room to leave it on Evelyn's desk to tend to the next morning. Outside, a light rain had begun to speckle the oversize windows of the small family practice clinic on Main Street his father had started nearly thirty years ago, where Ryder had joined him—again, much to his mother's annoyance—after completing his residency five years ago. The clinic, his practice, had been the only constants in a life clearly determined to knock him flat on his butt with irritating regularity. Good thing that butt was made of rubber, was all he had to say. "But how did you—"

"Golf. Phil," his father said behind him, rattling his keys. "Far as he knows they'll be here today or tomorrow. To decide what to do with the place." He paused. "Just thought you should know."

"Because of Mel?"

A slight smile curved his father's lips. "That little girl worshipped the ground you walked on. Never saw a pair of kids as close as you two were."

Slipping into a tan windbreaker nearly as old as his father's jacket, Ryder turned to the older man, now standing by the front door. "That was years ago, Dad," he said over the twist of guilt, an almost welcome change from the pain he still lugged around after nearly a year. "We haven't even spoken since that summer." Another twist. "After her father died—"

"There's a child, Ry."

Again, the words weren't making sense. How—why—did his father know this? And what on earth did it have to do with Ryder? "So she has a kid—"

"She's ten."

And that would be the sound of pieces slamming into place. "And you think she's *mine?* Excuse me, Dad, but that's not possible—"

"I know she's not yours, Ry," his father said wearily. Bleakly. "She's your brother's."

His head still spinning, Ryder sat across the street from the massive quasi-Victorian, set well back on its equally massive, and woefully neglected, lot. He'd been there a while, parked in the dark, dead space between the street lamps and not giving a rat's ass that the damp from the now full-out rain had seeped into his bones. He had no idea, of course, if the little white Honda with the Maryland plates was Mel's or not, if the lights glowing from the kitchen window meant she was in there.

With her daughter.

You know, you tell yourself what's past is past. That time inevitably fades reality. If not warps it into something else altogether. Then something, anything—a word, a thought, a scent—and it all comes rushing back.

His father hadn't said much, muttering something about how his tail was going to be in a sling as it was. Meaning, Ryder surmised, that his mother had been behind whatever had gone down. No shocker there, given her obsessive protectiveness of his younger brother. Who, according to Ryder's father, had known about the baby—

Holy hell. After an hour, the shock hadn't even begun to wear off. He pushed out a short, soundless laugh—he'd finally gotten to the point, if barely, where he no longer felt as though he had a rusty pitchfork lodged in his chest, and now...this.

Even if he had no idea yet what "this" was. If anything.

Frankly, if the child *had* been his—if that had even been a possibility, of course—he doubted he could have been more stunned. Or furious. Hell, Ryder couldn't decide which was eating him alive more—that Jeremy had knocked Mel up or that everybody had kept it a secret all these years. That Mel hadn't told him—

You feel betrayed? Really?

The front door opened. Ryder slouched behind the wheel like some creepy stalker, even as he silently lowered his window to get a better look, rain be damned. So, yeah, the car was Mel's—even over the deluge he could hear her still-infectious laughter before he saw her, and the memories flooded his thoughts like soldiers charging into battle. Somehow, he steeled himself against them as the kid emerged first, her tall, thin frame swallowed up in a lime-green down vest, the feeble porch light glancing off a headful of blazing curls before she yanked her sweatshirt hood up over them. She tramped to the edge of the wide porch to glare over the railing. At the weather, he guessed.

Crap. She looked exactly like Jeremy.

Ryder's heart thumped when Mel backed through the door, her translucent, bright pink plastic rain poncho making her look as though she'd been swallowed alive by a jellyfish. He couldn't tell much, other than she'd traded in those godawful Birkenstocks for even more godawful Crocs. In a bilious pink to coordinate with the poncho, no less.

Ryder felt his mouth twitch: fashion never had been her strong suit.

The door locked, Mel joined her daughter to give her a one-armed hug, laying her cheek atop her curls, and his lungs seized. Of course, between the downpour and the sketchy light from the streetlamp, he couldn't really see her face, although there was no reason why she wouldn't be as pretty as ever, her thick dark hair—still long, he saw—a breath-stealing contrast to her light, gray green eyes. Something he hadn't dared tell her then, despite how badly he knew she'd needed to hear it. Her posture, however, as she held her little girl close, her obvious sigh as her gaze drifted over what must have seemed like a bad dream, positively screamed *Just kill me now.*

It occurred to him he didn't know if she was in a relationship. Or even married. If she'd gone to college, or what she'd majored in if she had.

If she was happy, or heartbroken, or bored with her life—

No. Mel would never be bored.

He had no intention of ambushing her. Not yet, anyway. As it was, he was pressing an unfair advantage simply by being here, especially since he doubted she had any idea he knew she'd returned, let alone about Quinn. And he certainly wasn't about to confront her—not the right word, but the only one he could think of at the moment—before the million and one thoughts staggering around inside his brain shook off their drunken stupor and started talking sense. Or before he shook loose the full story from his mother—the next item on his to-do list, in fact. But for reasons as yet undefined he'd simply wanted to…see her.

The poncho glimmered in the sketchy light as Mel said something to the girl. He couldn't hear their exchange, but damned if Quinn's dramatic gestures didn't remind him exactly of her mother at that age, and it suddenly seemed incomprehensible, that he'd known absolutely nothing about the last ten years of her life when he'd been privy to pretty much all of it up to that point.

Those huge, curious eyes had hooked Ryder from the moment he saw her when she was two days old, as though—or so it seemed to his five-year-old self—she was asking him to watch out for her. Never mind that her parents lived in the groundskeeper's cottage and he in the main house, the oldest son of her parents' employers. He was hers, and she was his, and that was that, he now thought with a slight smile.

Images floated through, of her belly laugh when he'd play peekaboo with her, of helping her learn to walk, ride a tricycle, learn her alphabet. Then, later, how to throw a baseball, and cannonball into the swimming pool, and lob water balloons with deadly, and enviable, accuracy—activities his four-years-younger brother Jeremy, coddled and cosseted long after a full recovery from a severe bout of pneumonia as a toddler, found stupid and/or boring.

Of course, as Ryder grew older Mel's constantly trailing him like a duckling sometimes annoyed him no end, when he wanted to hang with his fifth-grade homies or build his model airplanes without some five-year-old *girl* yakking in his ear. A five-year-old girl with no compunction whatsoever about slugging him, hard, when he'd tell her to beat it, before stomping off, her long, twin ponytails flopping against her back.

Until he'd come to his senses—or his friends would go home—and he'd seek her out again, finding her in the kitchen "helping" her mother, Maureen, cook, or building castles out of his cast-off Legos.

And she always greeted him with a bright grin, his rejection forgiven, forgotten, Ryder thought with a pang as, shrieking the whole way, Mel and the kid finally dashed down the steps to her car.

His window raised, he watched the Honda cautiously take off through the downpour, thinking how he'd always been able to count on that grin, even after he was in high school and Mel barely up to her ankles in the first waves of adolescence, when their mothers began to cast leery glances in their direction. Although it was absurd, that they'd even think what they were thinking. Mel was his little *sister,* for God's sake, a take-no-crap punk kid who knew everything she needed to know about how boys thought…from Ryder. The boundaries couldn't have been brighter if they'd been marked in Kryptonite.

Until the summer after she turned sixteen.

He'd just finished pre-med. And oh, how grateful he'd been, after that semester from hell, for Mel's easy, no-demands company, even if the sight of her in that floral two-piece swimsuit seriously threatened those boundaries. She'd always been more mature than most girls his own age. That summer, when her body caught up to her brain…yowsa. And, yes, not being totally clueless, it was evident she no longer looked at him the same way, either.

However. He would have lopped off an appendage—in particular the one giving him five fits those days—before violating her trust. Except it had been that very trust that sent her into his arms, the day after her father's sudden death, for the comfort she couldn't get from anyone else. Especially not her wrecked mother.

Even after all this time, a wave of hot shame washed over Ryder as he remembered how desperately he'd wanted to accept what she was offering. How horrified he'd been. And he'd panicked, pure and simple. Pushed her away, walked away…*run* away, back to school weeks before he needed to be there.

She'd meant more to him than anyone else in the world, and he'd bungled things, big-time. Stomped on her already broken heart like a mad elephant. Worse, he'd never apologized, never explained, never tried to fix what he'd broken, partly because, at twenty-one, he had no clue how to do that.

But mainly because…he'd wanted her. And what kind of perv did that make him?

Groaning, Ryder let his head fall back, his own still-bruised heart throbbing inside his chest. This was the last thing he needed, to have that particularly egregious period of his life return to chomp his behind when his heart was still so sore. But chomp, it had.

He'd never expected to see Mel again, never imagined he'd have the opportunity to tell his side of the story. Not that there was any guarantee she'd even want to hear it after all this time. Nor would he blame her.

However—he finally started the car, eased down the road that led to his parents' house, on the other side of the cove—he did want to hear *Mel's* side. Which would be the side, he thought as bile rose in his throat, that explained how she'd come to have his brother's baby.

"You *told* him?" Knowing, and not caring, that she probably looked as though she'd been goosed, Lorraine Caldwell gaped at her husband as a brutal cocktail of emotions threatened to knock her right on her fanny. "Are you out of your *mind?*"

Settled into his favorite wing-chair in the wood-paneled den, the dogs dozing at his feet, David swirled his two fingers of Scotch in his glass and shrugged. Even after nearly thirty-five years of marriage, Lorraine still hadn't decided if his unflappability soothed her or unnerved her. Until she remembered they probably wouldn't still *be* married otherwise, considering…things. Things not given a voice for more than three decades, but which still occasionally shimmered between them like a ghost that refused to move on. Now, underneath blue eyes that had knocked her off her feet as a girl, a slight smirk told her that he had the upper hand. And wasn't about to let it go.

"And if you remember I was the one who said you were out of *your* mind, thinking you could keep this a secret."

David hadn't exactly been on board with the arrangement, Lorraine thought with a mix of aggravation and—dare she admit it?—admiration. Now. Then, however…

"She wasn't supposed to come back! Especially with…" She lowered her voice, despite their being alone. Even though they hadn't had full time help in years, old habits die hard. "The child. That was the agreement."

"Clearly you didn't consider all eventualities. Believe it or not, Lorraine, you can't control the entire world."

Lorraine's eyes burned. The entire world? There was a laugh. How about even her own tiny corner of it? "For heaven's sake, David—maybe they wouldn't even have run into each other. Why on earth did you jump the gun?"

"Because," he said, standing, "it didn't feel right to leave it to chance. Catching Ryder off guard if they did cross paths. Besides, aren't you even curious about her?"

Talking about being caught off guard. Lorraine sucked in a breath: she'd never, not once, indulged herself in pointless "what ifs?" After all, she'd made the best decision, the only decision, she could have made at the time. A decision circumstances had forced her to make. To change the rules now—

"What about Jeremy?" she said, grasping at rapidly disintegrating straws. "And Caroline. They've only been married six months—" At her husband's quelling look, Lorraine blew out a sigh. "What if Ryder confronts him? Did you think of that?"

"I imagine he will," David said with a shrug. "Hell, I was all for making the boy own up to his idiocy at the time—"

"Then why didn't you?" Ryder said quietly from the doorway, making Lorraine jump.

David waved his nearly empty glass in her direction. "Ask your mother."

Wordlessly, Ryder turned his gaze on her, his hands shoved into the pockets of that awful old windbreaker he'd had since college. Whereas her younger son had always been given to flying off the handle—her fault, she supposed—Ryder had always been the even-tempered one, even as a toddler. Just like his father. That had unnerved her, too, his seeming imperviousness to anything that would try to unseat him. Now, however, Lorraine could tell by the glint in his dark brown eyes, the hard set to his beard-hazed jaw—another "style" also picked up in college—that his customary calm masked an anger so intense she almost couldn't look at him.

Especially since that angry gaze relentlessly poked at the guilt she'd done her best to ignore for the past ten years.

Secrets, she thought on an inward wince. You would think she'd have learned her lesson the first time, wouldn't you?

Apparently not.

Ryder watched his mother, still attractive in an old-money, take-me-as-you-find-me way, sink into the sofa's down-filled cushions, sighing when one of the dogs heaved herself to her feet and plodded over to lay her head in his mother's lap. A pair of silver clips held her fading red curls back from her sharply boned face; in her rust-colored cardigan, jeans and flats, she gave off a certain Kate Hepburn vibe most people found intimidating. And, to a certain extent, fascinating.

Most people. Not Ryder.

"Well?" he prompted.

She distractedly traced the design of the Waterford lamp beside her before folding her hands on her lap. "The thing between Jeremy and Mel…we had no idea. None. Until Maureen marched Mel in here—into this very room, in fact—that fall and announced that Mel was pregnant." His mother shot a brief glance in his direction. "Frankly, we assumed the baby was yours." Her mouth twisted. "Until we did the math."

Too angry to speak, Ryder crossed his arms high on his chest. "And when you realized it wasn't?"

"Jeremy was barely eighteen," his mother said, her gaze fixed on the golden retriever's smooth head as she stroked it. "He'd just started at Columbia…" She pushed out a truncated sigh. "It was perfectly obvious it was all a mistake. That it meant nothing. To him, especially, but even Mel admitted…"

When Lorraine looked away, Ryder prodded, "Mel admitted what?"

"That she didn't love Jeremy. Oh, for heaven's sake, Ryder—don't look at me like that. It was a silly summer fling, nothing more. A silly summer fling with dire consequences," his mother finished on a grimace. "But then, Jeremy could hardly be blamed, could he? Not with the way M-Mel kept flaunting herself in those short shorts and tight tops—"

As in, cut-offs and T-shirts. Same as every other high school girl wore.

"And that *bathing* suit—"

"So, what? She's automatically the guilty party because she grew breasts?"

Twin dots of pink bloomed on his mother's cheeks. "Of course not. But she didn't have to be so, so *blatant* about them. She could have dressed less…enticingly. I mean, you know your brother—"

Behind them, his father huffed out a breath. "Lorraine, for pity's sake."

"Well, it's true. She played right into his hand."

"Literally," Ryder muttered, his own fisting inside his pockets. "You know, being neither blind nor gay, I was pretty aware of Mel's…assets, too. Assets she didn't flaunt any more than any other girl her age. Less, in fact, than most. That bathing suit—sure, it showed off her curves, but we're not talking a string bikini, for heaven's sake." Ryder glowered at his mother. "Yeah, I know Jeremy. But I would've thought…"

His mother stood. "You can't lay this whole thing at his feet, Ryder. Even though I know you'd love to do that. I never did understand why the two of you never got along, which is one reason we decided it was better to keep this from you. Because I knew how much it would hurt you, that Mel…" At Ryder's glare, Lorraine pressed her lips together, shaking her head.

"However, I refused to let one mistake derail Jeremy's plans. Not after he'd had to work so hard to get into Columbia. So we struck a deal—one Maureen agreed to, by the way—that in exchange for our financial support they'd leave St. Mary's for good and we'd never speak of any of this again."

As livid as he was, Ryder felt his eyes narrow. Something was off. Not so much what his mother was saying but how she was saying it. But right now he just wanted the facts.

"So it never occurred to you to make Jeremy own up to his part in this?"

"At eighteen? What on earth was he supposed to do?"

"And Mel was *six*teen. Something tells me she definitely got the short end of the stick—"

"I tried to make her see reason!" his mother said, and

he caught the flash of desperation in her eyes. "To explore her…options, but she was having none of it. She insisted on having, and keeping, the baby, although for the life of me I never understood why. That was her choice, Ryder. *Our* choice—"

"Was to let my brother off the hook by sweeping the whole thing under the rug?"

"There's a trust fund for the child. And we sent enough money through the years so they were never in any danger of starving. We honored our obligations, believe me. In the way we best saw fit. Your sister-in-law has no idea, by the way. And we'd appreciate it if you didn't tell her. It could ruin their marriage. And I'm sure you wouldn't want that on your conscience."

Ryder smirked: although the news had gobsmacked him, nothing coming out of his mother's mouth now surprised him in the least. To say Lorraine Caldwell was a control freak didn't even begin to cover it. As far back as Ryder could remember his mother had ruled the household—in her childhood home, the estate having belonged to her surgeon father, her D.C.-socialite mother, long before she'd married the gentle GP who'd stolen her heart, as lore would have it, that summer when she was nineteen. As far as Ryder could tell she'd been Daddy's spoiled little princess who'd seen no reason to change her modus operandi—as in, always getting her way—when she grew up. That she still seemed to have his father, as she'd had her own, so tightly wound around her little finger was a mystery he doubted he'd ever solve.

Except Ryder now looked to his father, seeing for the first time in David's chagrined, embarrassed expression the older man's constant acquiescence to his mother's whims for what it was—weakness, pure and simple. *For God's sake, grow a pair!* he wanted to shout, even as his heart cracked a little more, that the man he'd so wanted to believe in, look up to, apparently didn't really exist. For his dedication to his work, his patients, Ryder would always admire him. But respect him as a man? As someone he could count on to do the right thing?

Not so much.

Disheartened, he thought back to that silent promise he'd made to that chubby, bald, two-day-old baby, to look out for her. Protect her. Only he'd no idea at the time it would be his own family he'd have to protect her from. Or at the very least, try to undo ten years' worth of damage.

"No," he said to his mother. "I swear I won't breathe a word to Caroline. That's not my place, it's Jeremy's. Whose conscience, frankly, could use a good swift kick in the ass. But whatever. However, now that I know I have a niece, you better believe she's going to know at least one member of this family gives a damn about her."

"And what if Mel isn't on board with that idea?"

He looked from one to the other. "That's between Mel and me. Because you two officially have nothing more to say about it."

Chapter Two

All that food in the house, and Mel and Quinn both decided they'd rather have stir-fry. Go figure. But at least by the time they finished shopping at the only decent supermarket in town, she'd stopped looking over her shoulder, convinced Ryder—or worse, one of his parents—was going to appear at the end of every aisle. She'd driven by the clinic, seen his name beside his father's; a quick Google search on her phone revealed that Jeremy was a junior partner at some hot-shot law firm in New York.

"Hey, Virginia plates," Quinn said as Mel's headlights stabbed at the weather-and-time ravaged house, as well as the late model Lexus parked in the driveway. The rain had finally let up, although it had turned bone-chillingly cold. Welcome to early fall on the Eastern Shore. "Whose car is that?"

"I'm gonna guess April's," Mel said, all bittersweet ache at the prospect of seeing her cousin again after more than a decade. She and April had chatted briefly the day before, but only long enough to coordinate their schedules. And unleash a boatload of memories.

And laughter.

We were happy here, Mel thought on a smile, even as the backs of her sinuses twinged. *She'd* been happy here, during those summers when Amelia called enough of a truce with Mel's mother to allow Mel to hang out in the rambling old house with her close-in-age cousins. Summer sisters, they'd called themselves—

"Ohmigosh! There you are!"

In a flippy little plaid skirt and coordinating cardigan, April—still tiny and bubbly and strawberry blonde—burst out of the front door and down the steps before they'd even climbed out of the Honda, where she grabbed Mel in a hug hard enough to do damage, then let go to fan her now tear-streaked face.

"Honest to Pete," Mel said, laughing, digging in her gargantuan purse for a pack of tissues which she handed to her cousin. "Still?"

"I know, I know, I'm terrible!" Gal always had cried at the drop of a hat. "But I can't help it, it's just so good to *see* you…wait," she said, her soggy gaze turning to Quinn, standing off to one side. "Oh, my word—is that *your* little girl?"

"Little girl?" Mel said, pretending to look shocked. "What little girl? For heaven's sake, she must've crawled in the backseat while I was at the store—"

"Mo-om, geez," Quinn said. Rolling her eyes. Then she extended her hand to April. "I'm Quinn. The sane one—"

"Don't you go giving me your hand—come here, sugar," April said, hauling Quinn into her arms, and Mel's own eyes watered. Yes, April had cried more than ten girls put together, but this was what Mel remembered most about her cousin, that she *loved* more than any human being she'd ever known. That her tenderheartedness was only surpassed by an unfeigned generosity that put most people to shame.

Then she noticed how the feeble porch light glinted off the tasteful, but impressive, array of diamonds on April's ring finger. Between those and the car, Mel got the feeling her cousin was a lot better off than when they'd been kids. Not that they'd ever discussed such things, even when they were all old enough to figure out that while their grandmother obviously had money—then, at least—her three daughters had all somehow bounced well out of range of that particular tree.

"Aren't you the prettiest thing?" April now said, holding Quinn at arm's length before turning to Mel. "I take it she looks like her daddy, since I'm not seeing a whole lot of you in that face—"

"Quinn, let's get this food out of the car," Mel said, smartly going around to the trunk. "Stir-fry for dinner okay with you?"

April shot her a look, but took the hint and simply said, "Sure thing. I'm starved!"

Despite their earlier attack on the kitchen, the cloying dampness assaulted Mel's nose as they carted the groceries through the conglomeration of dusty wicker and sisal and faded pastels hunched together on scabrous floors in the large gathering room, every surface obliterated by their grandmother's "collections." Dusty paintings hung askew on walls gone cobweb-gray; mismatched shelves bowed under the weight of hundreds, if not thousands, of books and DVDs and videotapes. At least there weren't any cats.

That they'd found, at any rate.

"I had no idea the place had gone to seed like this," April whispered to Mel as they loaded the bags onto the now disinfected pine table in the middle of the oversize kitchen. Quinn dumped her bags, as well, then took off to continue exploring. Mel was half tempted suit up the kid in hazmat attire. And maybe a cross.

"Seed, hell," Mel muttered as she hauled two gallons of milk onto the top shelf of the fridge, which at least was no longer toxic. "The ancient Greeks had nothing on the civilizations growing in there."

"So you're saying it was worse?"

"Heh." April stared at one of the kitchen chairs; Mel chuckled. "Your butt might smell like Pine-sol when you get up, but you're good."

"The lawyer said Nana died virtually broke," her cousin said, sitting. "That the house…this was all that was left."

"Because she clearly spent everything she had on crap she didn't need," Mel said. "Have you been upstairs yet?"

"After seeing the gathering room? I didn't have the nerve. Not alone, anyway. And you let Quinn go up there?"

"She's an intrepid soul, she'll be fine."

April sighed. "I cannot imagine how long it's gonna take to sort through all this junk. Although I don't suppose it was junk to Nana. And who knows? There might be some valuable stuff in amongst all that…" She waved her hand, searching for the right word.

"Trash? I seriously doubt it. Frankly, my vote is for lighting a match." Mel lifted her hands. *"Oops."*

"Bite your tongue," her cousin said, coloring. "And you know she used to have good things. I remember the crystal. And the china. And some of the furniture dated back to when the house was built—"

"And sometimes, old is just old. April—the place is about to collapse, from what I can tell—"

"I'm sure most of it's cosmetic!" At Mel's snort, she added, "You mark my words, once we get it all cleared out..." Her eyes filled. "We can bring it back to life, Mel. I'm sure of it."

Too tired to argue, Mel changed the subject. "So... you're married, huh?" April frowned slightly. Readying the veggies for slaughter on a cutting board in the middle of the kitchen table, Mel pointed to her cousin's left hand with one of the knives she'd hauled from Baltimore. Because some things, a real cook doesn't leave home without.

"Oh," April said, touching the rings. "I am. Or rather, was. Clayton—my husband—died a few months ago."

"Oh, God, honey—"

"It's okay, he'd been ill for a long time." Then she squinted up at the forlorn schoolhouse-style fixture dangling in the center of the room. "That has got to go."

"And it will, when the flames reach the kitchen." Mel clanged her iron skillet onto the gas range, turned the heat on high, then returned to the table. "I take it you don't want to talk about your husband?"

"Not any more than you do the house, apparently."

"I did talk about the house, I suggested we level it and collect the insurance. That, or turn it into an annual Halloween attraction." At her cousin's silence, she frowned. "What?"

"Nothing."

"Nothing, my hiney." Mel waved the knife in April's direction. "I remember that look. All too well. That look spells trouble."

On a soft laugh, April reached across the table to briefly squeeze Mel's wrist, before grabbing a red pepper slice and nibbling on it. "It's nice, being here with you again."

"Ditto. Although...I'm not the same person I was then."

"Who is?" April said on a sigh. "Even so, despite the clutter and the filth and wildlife I don't even want to think about, being back here...it's like time stood still. Not that I feel like when we were kids—and heaven knows I wouldn't want to—but it's like the me I am now can feel the me I was then looking over my shoulder. Didn't expect that." She paused, then said, "So did you keep up with Ryder or what?" When Mel shot her a what-the-hell look, April grinned. "It's hardly an illogical question, Mel. Well?"

"No."

"Really? I mean, I know how close you two were—"

"We were childhood buddies, that's all," Mel said, wondering if it was too late to bake something. As if that was a serious question. "Besides, he went off to med school, and Mama and I moved to Baltimore after Dad died, and… we lost touch—"

Quinn bounded into the kitchen—Mel had often wondered if the child had springs on the soles of her feet—and straight to the table to snatch a carrot slice. "When's dinner? I'm about to *expire* from hunger."

"Ten minutes," Mel said, carting the chopped veggies to the stove to dump them into the sizzling oil. "You can set the table. Dishes are up there." She nodded toward the cupboard next to the sink. "Used to be, anyway."

After filching a pepper slice, Quinn swung open the cupboard door, nearly gagging when she pulled down an avocado-green Fiestaware plate that looked like it hadn't been washed in twenty years. "Gross!"

"Hey," April said with a laugh. "When we were kids we'd've rinsed it off and called it good."

"And you, child of mine," Mel said as she stirred, "used to lick the kitchen floor."

Shock and horror bloomed in Quinn's blue eyes. "Did not!"

"Got the video to prove it. You apparently have the immune system of an android. Palmolive's right on the sink, baby. Go for it."

After dinner, during which they talked, and laughed, and reminisced more than Mel had any idea they could, Quinn disappeared again to poke through those ten thousand books—heaven!—while April and Mel cleaned up. Her hands deep in Palmolive suds, April looked over at Mel, drying the dishes and stacking them on the counter rather than putting them back with their disgusting little friends.

"Dinner was fantastic. You always cook like that?"

"Thanks. And yes. Cooking's my thing."

"Really? Huh." Behind her, Mel heard sudsy swishing. "So…is Quinn's father in the picture?"

"Nope," Mel said lightly. "Never has been."

More swishing. Then: "Is she Ryder's kid?"

Yeah, she'd expected that. Still, the assumption needled. Especially since there were other people in town who'd be all too eager to leap to the same conclusion. "No. As I said, Ryder and I were friends. Good friends." She felt a tight smile tug at her mouth. "There was no way anything untoward would have happened between us. He would have never let it." At her cousin's silence, Mel turned. "What? You don't believe me?"

"Oh, I believe you. But I also remember that last summer we were all together, when Ryder took the three of us out on his dad's boat." Hauling the clean skillet onto the drainboard, April slid Mel a devilish grin. "I *also* remember the way he looked at you when he thought nobody would notice." A wet hand pressed to her chest, she released an exaggerated sigh. "And *I* thought if a boy looked at me like that? I'd absolutely die of happiness. *Die,* I tell you."

"And *how* many romance novels did you read that summer?"

April belted out a laugh, the sound unexpected from her

delicate frame. "Best. Summer. Ever," she said, and even Mel had to smile, at how they'd discovered their grandmother's stash of old, yellowing Harlequins in a trunk on the porch, clandestinely stashing them in their beach towels to read aloud to each other as they sunbathed. Damn books were probably still in the house somewhere. If they hadn't completely disintegrated by now—

"However," her cousin went on, "I also caught the way you looked at *him.* And don't you dare try to deny it. These eyes know what they saw, yes, they do."

Overhead, Mel heard the floorboards creak. "Fine," she said with a quick glance toward the ceiling. Either Quinn had changed rooms upstairs or there was a raccoon the size of Cincinnati up there. "So I might have had a little crush on him. I mean, I suppose it was inevitable, considering how kind he'd always been to me."

April laughed again. And flicked water at her.

"He was my *friend,* April," Mel said, zapping her cousin with the damp towel. "And that was the only thing that mattered."

Wringing out the sponge and laying it on the edge of the sink, April turned to her with a frown. "Then why'd you two stop talking to each other?"

"Because we just did!" Mel slammed the last plate a little too hard on the pile, then shut her eyes, thinking, *Yeah, hand her the gun to shoot you with, why not?*

She heard April dump the sudsy water into the sink, yank another dishtowel off the old "finger" rack under the counter.

"That's probably not dry yet," Mel muttered. "I just washed it this afternoon."

"It's fine." April wiped her hands and hung the towel back up, then leaned closer to the sink to look out the window at the plum-colored sky. "I didn't mean to upset you, honey. But being back here…guess it's made me a little melancholy. Like I want to recapture a little of that magic, you know?"

"I do, actually. But it's not possible."

"I know. Still, it's sad. You and Ryder losing touch." She turned to Mel. "Don't you think?"

"I don't. Think about it, I mean." Or at least she hadn't until a five-minute phone call once more snatched the rug right out from under her.

"You think you'll see him while you're here?"

"Not planning on it. And can we *please* change the subject—?"

The doorbell rang. After a fashion. "Oh! I bet that's Blythe," April said, heading out of the kitchen. "Last time we talked she said she didn't know if she'd get in tonight or tomorrow…"

Not at all sure if she was ready to deal with her older, bossier cousin, Mel turned on the old radio that had been in that same spot on the counter forever, fiddling with the dial until she picked up some oldies rock station from Dover…the same music her mother had listened to while cooking in the Caldwells' kitchen when she'd been growing up. Over Simon and Garfunkel's "The Sound of Silence"—heh—she heard April's cheery, non-stop prattle coming closer. Steeling herself, Mel turned, a forced smile stretching her cheeks.

And nearly passed out.

"That last thing you were saying? You might want to revise that," April said, clearly enjoying the heck out of the moment before she vanished, leaving Mel to face Ryder all by her little self.

Ridiculously handsome, all-grown-up, obviously angry-as-hell Ryder.

Yippee-skippy.

* * *

"How'd you know I was here?"

Mel had left Quinn with her cousin—since no way was she going to have this little reunion in her daughter's presence—but it'd taken her a good ten minutes to work up to the question. This being the awkward moment from hell and all. Now she sensed Ryder—who hadn't exactly been chatty, either—glance over as they strolled, bundled up against the frigid night air, along the marina at the edge of town. A trek they'd made innumerable times as kids, at all times of the day and night, in every imaginable kind of weather. Mostly just for something to do away from the adults, sometimes on their bikes or inline skates when there weren't too many people around....

And cocooning herself in the used-to-bes wasn't going to do a blessed thing to stop the vague nausea brought on by having to face the right-nows.

"Phil Paxton told my dad," Ryder said, that comfortingly familiar voice conjuring up so much of what she'd made herself forget, and there it was, the past colliding with her present, boom. Even his obvious irritation provoked memories, of when he'd get ticked off over some dumb prank or other she'd pulled as a kid. Man, this was doing even stranger things to her head than walking back into her grandmother's house. "Said Amelia'd left you three her place, that you were coming down to get everything in order."

"Big mouth," she muttered.

"Was it supposed to be a secret?"

At the word "secret," Mel flinched, then dug a tissue out of the down vest she'd thrown over her hoodie to wipe her drippy nose. "I don't suppose."

"Anything else you'd like to share?"

No need to ask what he meant, since the disbelief icing

his words said it all. Even so, she had no idea what she was and wasn't allowed to say, to admit to, even now. "Depends. What've you heard?"

"That you and Jeremy had a kid together."

She stuffed the tissue back in her pocket. "Jeremy may be Quinn's biological father, but to say we had her *together* is a stretch."

Silence crackled between them, far more biting than the damp air, until Ryder finally broke it with, "God, Mel—*why?*"

"Because I was a mess and he was there." *And you weren't,* she thought, startled at the residual anger after all this time. "Sad, but true." More silence, punctuated by the soft clattering of the docked boats, Ryder's steady footsteps against the wood. "When did you find out?"

"Late this afternoon."

"I don't mean that I was coming down—"

"Not talking about that."

"You really had no idea?"

"Nope."

"Wow," she said on a strangled half laugh, her breath misting around her face. "I can't believe they actually took it that far. I assumed you knew."

Ryder raised his arms to flip the collar of his jacket up around his neck. "Because I never contacted you again?"

"Yeah."

He shook his head, then thrust his hands into his pockets. "That wasn't the reason."

When no further explanation seemed to be forthcoming, Mel wandered out underneath the gazebo-like structure at the end of the marina to fold her arms across the top railing, deeply inhaling the tangy, bone-chilling breeze. Moonlight flicked at the black, rippling water below. Pretty. When Ryder mimicked her pose, the wind ruffling his short, dark hair, she said, "I can't even imagine how ticked you must be right now."

"No. You can't." He glanced at her. "My folks said Jeremy knows."

"He always has."

"And he's never—?"

"Nope. Far as he's concerned Quinn never happened."

He leaned harder on the railing to press his head into his palms, then dropped them again. "Does she ask? About her father?"

"Until recently? Not as much as you might think. Although..." Mel forced air into her lungs, annoyed that she still felt like she was breathing through broken glass. "I was seriously involved with someone for two years. Thought...this was it. *He* was it. Quinn became very attached. Enough that she didn't ask about her daddy because she'd assumed she'd found one."

"This isn't going to end well, is it?"

And there it was, despite everything, that same kindness and understanding that had seen her through her entire childhood, that made her eyes sting even now. "His ex popped back into his life. And right into the bastard's bed, apparently. Turns out he'd never really gotten over her. Our virtually living in each other's pockets notwithstanding. Although..." She twisted to lean one elbow on the railing, looking at Ryder. "He did offer to make me a partner. In his restaurant," she added at Ryder's quick frown.

"After...?"

"Oh, as in, right on the heels of. Consolation prize, yay," she said, then hmmphed. "Guess he figured that was the least he could do. Considering it was my mad cooking skills that'd made the place as successful as it was."

A hint of a smile played across Ryder's mouth. "And you walked."

"As fast as these cute little feet could carry me."

"Good for you."

"In theory, sure. In practical terms, not so much. Oh, I've managed, working for caterers off and on, but nothing's come along that even begins to compare. I really, really loved that job. Made me stretch as a chef, try new things. And the partnership would've been an incredible opportunity. If I'd had a heart made of stone."

"How long ago was this?"

"A few months," she said, even though the date was indelibly, and regrettably, forever etched in her brain. "Dammit, Ry—I never saw it coming. Neither did Quinn. And it was especially hard on her since my mother died last year. She and Quinn were extremely close, as you can imagine."

"Damn, honey. I'm sorry."

Mel nodded, then said, "Quinn's just now getting over it, I think. Hope. The breakup, I mean. She doesn't mention it, in any case."

"And you?" he said gently.

"I alternate between numb and mad-as-hell. Although I'm at least through the eating anything that isn't nailed down stage." She sighed. "But now that we're once again in daddyless mode, yeah, Quinn's started asking about her father. Not a subject I'm wild about discussing when I'm *not* wishing bad things on half the human population. Best I could come up with was telling her he vanished before she was born, he didn't know she was coming, that I have no idea where he is. How to find him."

"You lied?"

She snorted a humorless laugh. "How do you tell a child her father really didn't want her? That his parents paid me off to never contact him, or show my face in St. Mary's, ever again? And how in *God's* name..." She swallowed. "How do I explain that her mother was every bit as complicit in this little scheme as the people who've been paying her hush money since before she was born?"

"Mel, for God's sake—you were sixteen."

"Seventeen, by the time she arrived. But yeah. Even so, I can't pretend I didn't know what I was doing. That I'd more or less sold my soul—or at least, my integrity—in order to provide for my child. And it's eating me up, living this lie."

Expelling a harsh sigh, Ryder grasped the railing, not looking at her. "Not any more than it's eating *me* up, that when you get right down to it, this is all my fault."

"And how on earth do you figure that?"

"So you didn't hook up with Jeremy to get back at me?"

It was funny, really, if you thought about it: years of experience had taught Mel that few human males seemed ready, or able, to accept responsibility for anything. At least, the human males *in* her experience. To the point where she'd forgotten that Ryder had probably been the most responsible human being she'd ever met. Except, because Ryder *had* been stalwart and noble and honorable as all hell, in a convoluted way he had a point.

"Didn't say that," she said at last. "But it's ridiculous to blame you for my actions. No matter what I might have told myself at the time." She paused, then breathed out, "Please don't hate me, Ryder. Since I still hate myself plenty enough for both of us."

Ryder's chest constricted at the self-deprecation trying so damn hard to undermine Mel's tough bunny persona. He looked away, giving her the space she clearly wanted. And he needed. Because he had no idea how to bind up her wounds when his own were still so fresh.

Even as the old compulsion reared its head, refusing to be ignored.

"How could I possibly hate you when I'm the one who botched things so badly—"

"What you did was save me from making an idiot of myself." Her mouth twisted. "At least, that night."

Acid flared in his gut. "Still. I could've handled the situation with a bit more…grace. And afterwards…I should have called. Emailed, something. To check on you, make sure you were okay. I mean, I owed you that much."

"Owed me?" Mel gave him a puzzled look. "You didn't—don't—owe me anything—"

"You were *grieving,* Mel. Whatever else might have been going on, you came to me for comfort, and instead of figuring out how to give you what you really needed I pushed you away. Harshly, if memory serves. So you can't possibly be beating yourself up more than I am. On that score, I figure we're probably about even—"

Her sharp laugh caught him up short. "Did you really think my actions that night were solely motivated by grief? Yeah, that might've short-circuited my inhibitors, but I wanted you because I wanted you." She looked away. "Because I was sick to death of being treated like a little sister. Stupid, huh?"

Ryder looked up into the navy sky before saying, very quietly, "Then you have no idea how much of a struggle it was to turn you down."

He felt her eyes on the side of his face for several beats before a soft, startled laugh fell out of her mouth. "Holy crap. Are you *serious?*"

"Yep. And you can stop laughing," he said, even as chagrin pushed at the corners of his own mouth. Then he sighed. "All our lives, I thought of myself as your protector. A role I took very seriously—"

"Tell me about it."

"—and you were a kid. Legally, anyway. And what I'd

begun to feel for you…inappropriate doesn't even begin to cover it. No way on God's earth was I going to act on what I was feeling, but damn, it scared me. That everything our relationship was predicated on…" He scrubbed the heel of his hand across his jaw, then banged it against the railing. "What you wanted that night—hell, what *I* wanted—redefined *wrong*. You'd always trusted me. And I refused to violate that trust. Even though it nearly killed me."

She took a deep breath. "So you freaked."

"To put it mildly. No matter what I did, I was going to hurt you. Worse than you already were. And afterward, when I went back to school…" His gaze touched hers. "I had no idea how to fix it."

Yanking her sweatshirt hood up over her head, Mel faced the moonlight-stippled currents for some time before finally saying, "It took a while, but eventually I got over the rejection. Once the hormone fog cleared. Because, like you said, what else could you have done? Your silence, though… That devastated me, Ry. Not gonna lie."

His gut twisted. "So you got even."

"Not on purpose," she said after a moment. "I mean, I didn't set my sights on your brother. Small consolation though that might be."

Ryder frowned. "He came on to you?"

"Not blatantly, no. Not at first, anyway. He just suddenly seemed, I don't know. Interested. Like he cared. And I was hurt, Ryder. Hurt, and confused, and adrift…" One side of her mouth ticked up. "And, okay, mad. At you, for basically walking out of my life. At myself, for being an idiot. For ruining the one good thing in it."

She paused. "I made a terrible mistake, Ryder. Not that I don't love Quinn with every fiber of my being, but the rest of it?" Her head wagged. "I disappointed everyone, especially my mother. Who adored Quinn, don't get me wrong, but I know she never quite got over how badly everything ended. Then there was Nana, who never spoke to me again—"

"This being the same woman who cut herself off from her own daughter, right? For reasons known only to herself? You're not responsible for other people's grudges, Mel. And as far as that *agreement* goes—legally it's worth bupkiss."

"Yeah, well, it's amazing, how strong a motivator fear is. You want to talk freaked?" She pointed to herself. "Poster child. And if I'm being completely honest, at least it got me out of St. Mary's. Me, and my mother, even if she never quite saw it that way. Got both of us away from…everything."

"Meaning my family."

Several beats passed before she said, "In all fairness it's not as if they treated my parents badly—and I always did have a soft spot for your father. At heart he's a good man. In fact, I gathered he was behind the generous financial considerations. And as far as Jeremy and I went—we used each other," she said flatly. "And we both knew it. So there was never any *ohmigod, you can't separate us we're in loooove* thing going on. If the dude couldn't be bothered to acknowledge his own kid, I could live with that. I hated him for it, but I could live with it. For your parents, though, to turn their backs on their first grandchild…" She gave her head a sharp shake. "For your mother to go so far as to demand that I *take care* of the 'problem'—that was a lot harder to handle."

Of course it was. Because while he may have detected a glimmer of regret in his mother's eyes, he doubted it was any match for the stubborn pride that motivated every action and decision Lorraine Caldwell had ever made. And hearing Mel echo his mother's earlier admission…

Ryder shut his eyes, wrestling to control his breathing before saying, "I want to make things up to you."

"Forget it, Ry. What's done is done."

"Even if I say I'd like to get to know Quinn? Why not?" he said when her gaze slammed into his. "Just because my brother had his head up his ass—"

Mel pushed herself away from the railing and started back down the boardwalk. "Not gonna happen."

"She's still my niece."

"Which I can't tell her, brainiac."

"They can't legally—"

"*Legal* has nothing to do with it!" she said, stopping short, the wind whipping strands of hair that had escaped the hood across her face. "I know what my rights are, okay? I know what I could do. I also know what I can't do. And *won't* do. And that's anything that could potentially hurt my kid—"

"So you're tarring me with the same brush? When I knew nothing about it?"

"You weren't there, Ryder!" she said, tears shining in her eyes. "Weren't there when your mother called me a little tramp in front of my humilated mother, who'd been loyal as hell to yours for more than twenty years! Weren't there when she accused me of trying to worm my way into the family, saying that since clearly my plan to snag you hadn't worked, I'd gone after Jeremy, or when she made me do a DNA test before Quinn was born to verify that Jeremy was really the father!"

Ryder's stomach plummeted. "Dammit—I had no idea—"

"No, you didn't. Don't. So believe me, I want less to do with your parents than they want to do with me. And if you get involved with Quinn…" She jerked away. "It won't work, Ryder. Because the past…it doesn't go *poof* simply because you want it to. But here's the weird thing…"

Suddenly calmer, as though the storm had blown over, she started walking again. "Now that I'm a mother, too? In a way I get where your mother was coming from. About how you do anything to protect your kid. I didn't—don't—agree with her methods, but I understand her motivation."

Mel's mouth pulled flat, exactly the way she used to as a child, when she'd made up her mind, by golly, and nothing and no one was going to change it. "Quinn's already hurting, from her grandmother's death, from my breakup. At least one of those things I had some control over, and I blew it. Forgot, when I went and hitched my wagon to a rainbow, there was someone else involved. So you better believe I learned my lesson. Meaning I'd hack off a limb before I'd let Quinn anywhere near the people who wrote *her* off."

Even in the dark, the pain in her eyes, her voice…

"And you thought I'd written you off, too." When she shrugged, he said, over the guilt dammed up at the back of his throat, "I swear, things would've been different if I'd known."

"Right. What on earth would you have done?"

"I don't know. Something. Married you, if nothing else—"

"Oh, yeah," Mel said on a high-pitched laugh, "your parents would've been totally on board with that idea. Do you really think they would have let you jeopardize *your* education, *your* career, when they wouldn't let Jeremy jeopardize his? And Quinn wasn't even yours! Not to mention, what makes you think I would have let you do that?"

"You can honestly say you wouldn't have even considered it? Especially given—"

"That I had the mother of all crushes on you?"

"A crush I had a damn hard time not reciprocating!"

She blinked, then released another laugh, this one softer. Sadder. "And marriage would've made it all okay? Au contraire, my friend. It would've ruined everything."

"Except I did that anyway, didn't I?"

On a cross between a groan and a growl, Mel clamped her hands to her head, tromping down off the boardwalk to the parking lot. "God, why are we even talking about this? Like we can somehow change what happened? It's done, it's over, and the second this business with Nana's house is straightened out, I'm outta here. So you tell your mother she has absolutely nothing to worry about, the last thing I want to do is make waves."

Nearly to the car, Ryder grabbed Mel's hand. If she was shocked, she didn't let on. Instead she calmly met his gaze, her brows slightly raised.

"I know I can't even begin to fix what my family broke. Or even what I broke. But to at least honor what we had—"

"What we had doesn't exist anymore," Mel said softly, reclaiming her hand. "And it hasn't for a long, long time. We're not those two kids anymore, Ry." She smirked. "Can't go back, no way to go forward. So. Think this is what they call a non-starter—"

At the sound of some ridiculous ringtone, she dug her phone out of her pocket. "Huh. It's April..." She put the phone to her ear. "Yeah?" Ryder saw her brows crash, then she yanked open the car door. "We'll be right there."

"Everything okay?" he asked after getting in beside her, barely getting his seat belt fastened before she zoomed out of the sandy, unpaved lot and back onto the street.

"I didn't quite get it all, April wasn't making total sense, but apparently Quinn sliced her hand open on a nail or something." At Ryder's silence, she let out a sigh. "I suppose logically I should let you take a look, huh?"

"Up to you. But the nearest E.R.'s a good half hour away. And I have my bag in my car."

"Of course you do," she muttered as they flew into the weed-cracked driveway and she cut the engine. But before he could get out, she snagged his wrist. "Not one word—"

"Can I at least tell her we were friends? She's going to wonder why we were together," he said when she opened her mouth to protest. "She knows you lived here before, right? So we happened to run into each other—"

"Fine, fine, whatever." She shooed him toward the door. "Just get in there before my kid bleeds to death."

Ryder slammed shut the car door and trudged up the porch steps behind Mel, thinking he'd never been so angry, at so many people, for so many reasons, in his life.

With his own sorry hide easily taking first place.

Chapter Three

Mel was grateful to see that her cousin—who as a teenager would scream like a banshee if she nicked herself shaving—had either overcome her heebie-jeebies at the sight of blood or was doing a damn good job of hiding it from Quinn, seated on the counter and looking a little woozy herself. April had hidden the boo-boo, as well, wrapping it tightly in a paper towel and holding Quinn's arm up over her head.

"Oh, sweetie..." Mel rushed to her blood-smeared daughter—yeah, that top was history—forking her fingers through Quinn's curls as April, bless her heart, beat a hasty retreat. "What happened?"

"There's a dumb nail sticking out of the back door, I didn't see it," Quinn mumbled, then squinted at Ryder, who'd plunked his coat and bag on the kitchen table and was now rooting around inside it. "Who're you?"

"An old friend of your mother's," Ryder said with a

kind—and yet, still killer, go figure—smile for the kid as he carted a bottle of antiseptic and assorted packets over to lay beside Quinn on the counter. One hand propped on the edge of the worn laminate, he hooked the other on his hip. "I'm also a doctor. Convenient, huh?"

Quinn shrugged. "I guess."

On a soft chuckle, Ryder washed his hands and dried them on a paper towel, then ripped open a package of latex gloves, snapped them on. "Mind if I take a peek?"

"April said to keep my hand up 'cause of the bleeding."

"Lots of blood, huh?"

"Like you would *not* believe."

"Then April did good. But I think it's okay to lower it now." When she did, he carefully removed the blood-soaked towel. Aiyiyi. Mel told herself it would be very uncool to throw up, even if the sink was right there. "It seems to have pretty much stopped now, so that's good. You'll be back to playing the violin in no time."

Quinn giggled. "I don't play the violin, I play the piano."

"You don't say?" Another smile. "You any good?"

Not nearly as good as you are, Mel thought ruefully as her daughter's shoulders bumped. "Not really. But I've only been taking lessons for a year."

"Yeah. I took 'em for ten. Loved every minute of it."

"Really?"

"No," he said, and Quinn laughed again, and Ryder's smile melted Mel's heart, dammit to hell. Especially when he turned it on her and all—well, most—of her man-hating crazies scurried away, whimpering. "I assume her tetanus is up to date?"

"Not sure. She might be due for a booster?"

"We can take care of that, too. Okay, honey, I want you to hold your hand over the sink, I'm going to pour a bunch of this antiseptic over the wound to clean it. It's probably going to sting, but it won't last long. You ready?"

Quinn sucked in a deep breath, then nodded and gingerly stuck out her hand, wincing as Ryder cleaned it. "Almost done, you're doing great…there. Now I can see what's going on."

As he carefully inspected the gash, Quinn actually leaned closer to get a better look. As opposed to Mel, who was perfectly happy to let someone else tend to this side of things, thank you. Especially if that person was the same one who'd always been the one to patch up her various scrapes and cuts and owies when they were kids. That inline skating thing? Hadn't exactly been a natural talent—

"I'm gonna need stitches, huh?" Quinn asked, sounding more curious than worried.

"Oh, I'd say at least a hundred," Ryder said, deadpan, and Quinn giggled, and Ryder lifted his eyes—all sweetly crinkled at the corners, of course—to the little girl, and Mel saw in those eyes…too much. That while she didn't doubt that Ryder was every bit as kind and funny with all his younger patients, it was patently obvious Quinn had already grabbed his heart.

And, judging from the grin on her daughter's face, the feeling was mutual.

Ah, doom. You again, is it?

Then Ryder turned his gaze to Mel, all business, except not, and now that the urge to barf had passed she noticed a dullness in those dark eyes she hadn't noticed before, and it occurred to her how one-sided their catch-me-up conversation had been. That she had no idea what was, or had been, going on in his life. Was he married? Divorced? No ring, but that didn't mean anything—

"Actually," he said, "if the cut hadn't been where she's likely to pull it apart in normal use, I'd say we'd be good with a butterfly bandage. But to be on the safe side I think a couple of stitches are in order. Piece of cake," he said with a wink for Quinn, and Mel thought, *If only, buddy boy. If only.*

If only, Ryder thought, removing his gloves a few minutes later after stitching up his niece's wound, one could stitch back together the ragged edges of one's life, and heart, so easily. If all it took to repair the damage was training and skill and patience. A strong stomach wouldn't hurt, either.

The booster shot administered and the wound dressed, Quinn skipped off to watch the monster, old-school TV in the gathering room—after giving Ryder a hug that scraped his still-tender heart. His eyes fixed on the kitchen doorway, he asked, "Is she always that affectionate?"

"It depends." She paused. "On whether she feels she can trust someone or not. Guess you passed."

He lowered his gaze to hers, just long enough to make her blush, then walked over to the offending nail. "Then I'm honored. She's a fun kid." He opened the door, the chilly damp barely registering in the drafty old house. Now why the heck would somebody hammer through the panel from the outside? "You got something I can pound this sucker out with?"

"Probably." Watching Mel as she began yanking open, then ramming shut, assorted swollen drawers, guilt shuddered through Ryder that he was even noticing how the soft jersey of her hoodie, the even softer fabric of her worn jeans, hugged curves that had very nicely matured—

"Sorry about the house," she said, still rummaging.

"Why? Since I assume—" he scanned the mountains of detritus "—you didn't make the mess."

"True. Still. Oh, looky..." Amidst much clattering, she

hauled a decrepit-looking hammer from one of the drawers, her brows drawn as she inspected it. "Although Noah probably used this to build the ark."

Ryder extended his hand. "If it worked for Noah, I'm good." Two whacks and the nasty thing was history, safely disposed of in the trash where it no longer posed a danger. "Next question—why isn't the heat on?"

"The thermostat's not working—"

"Where is it?"

"In the dining room, but—"

"Be right back."

A few minutes later he returned triumphant, loving Mel's dumbfounded expression when the radiators started to clank. "How'd you do that?"

"Thermostat's fine," he said, opening cupboard doors until he found a half dozen flowery, albeit dusty, tin containers which still held an assortment of teas. "Boiler pilot light had gone out. All fixed now." He hadn't been in the house much when they were kids, and then only after Amelia had deemed her granddaughters old enough to be left on their own, but he remembered these. And, in the first one he opened, he hit pay dirt—a stash of Earl Grey. He dug out two bags and held them up. "Kettle?"

Mel frowned. "And I'm guessing those would be Mrs. Noah's tea bags."

"Eh, the boiling water will kill whatever needs killing." He waggled them, and Mel sighed. But she dragged the kettle off the stove, rinsed it out five times, then filled it and set it on the burner. "You actually went down into the basement?"

"I did. It's even scarier than it was when we were kids."

Mel sighed, then angled her head at him. "Why are you still here?"

Because the thought of going back to that empty house makes me crazy. Crazier.

"Because I'm cold as hell. And you'd hardly begrudge the man who just saved your daughter's life a cup of tea, would you?"

"Hey," April said from the doorway, wrapping a scarf around her neck. "Since the heat's on—" Mel pointed to Ryder, who waved "—the kid and I are gonna make an ice cream run. Any requests?"

"Chocolate chip," Ryder said smoothly, earning him a "Got it," from April and a glare from Mel.

"Thought you were freezing?" she said after they heard the front door close.

"I won't be by the time they get back. Especially since—" he leaned back in the chair, his arms folded high on his chest "—the heat's back on. You might want to close off the radiators in the unused rooms, though. To save fuel."

"Gah. Were you always this much of a pain in the butt?"

"No more than you were."

"Touché." ”

Okay, so it felt good, sitting here, giving her grief, letting her give him grief right back. Simply enjoying the company, he mused as he surveyed the woebegone—to the point of creepy—room. "Place needs a lot of work, doesn't it?"

"That would be our take on it, yep," Mel muttered, apparently fascinated with the flames licking at the kettle's bottom.

"Might be hard to find many buyers interested in it in this condition."

"Only need one," she said. Still watching that kettle. "And what's it to you?"

"Nothing. Nothing at all. Just making conversation."

Which sputtered and gasped for several seconds until she said, "Thank you." Her eyes touched his before veering back to the kettle. "For saving Quinn's life and all."

"Oh, that. Anytime. Although I do want to see her in a day or so, make sure everything's healing up okay."

"We can do that." The kettle whistled; seconds later she handed him a mug of steaming water. "Not sure there's any sugar—"

"This is fine," he said, dunking his tea bag. "For God's sake, Mel…sit. Talk."

She stood, her arms crossed, her mouth set. "About what?"

"The Orioles' chances at taking the Series this year, I don't know. No, wait, I've got an idea—how about you tell me all about Quinn?"

He saw her eyes fill. "Ryder—"

"Why *did* you decide to keep her?" he asked as gently as he knew how. "We get our share of teen moms at the clinic, I know how hard it is—"

"Do you?"

"Enough," he said, refusing to cow. "So, why?" He paused. "Especially considering the circumstances."

That got a tight little smile. "Hardest decision I ever had to make. Or probably ever will. But in the end I guess I just wanted her to know at least *one* of us thought she was worth keeping. Which I suppose sounds silly and romantic and totally impractical, and to be honest I don't know how I would have managed without my mother to help out, but there it is. She's mine and I'm hers and that's that."

Ryder smiled. "She's nothing like Jeremy, is she?"

After a long moment, she shook her head. "She's an awful lot like her mother, though."

"As in, silly and romantic and totally impractical?"

"Or we could go with headstrong, ruthlessly honest

and never knows when to shut up." At Ryder's laugh, Mel seemed to weigh her options for a moment before slowly lowering herself into the chair across from him, her eyes alight. "She is *so* smart, Ryder. Taught herself to read at four, she goes through library books like candy. I home-school her, so she can go at her own pace. She's reading at high school level, just finished eighth grade math. And she adores science—far more than I ever did, that's for sure."

"Wow."

"You said it. Except I don't know how much longer I can keep up with her. And now that she's so far ahead of other kids her age, putting her in public school seems pointless."

"What about a private school with a program that would challenge her?" When she got up to face the sink and the blackness outside, he took a scalding swallow of the tea, then carefully set down the mug. "There are scholarships—"

"I know. And I actually checked out a couple of schools in Baltimore, but…"

"But, what?"

She blew a short laugh through her nose, then turned back to him. "Despite our friendship, Ry, I was always extremely aware growing up that you were breaking 'the rules.' That I was the hired help's kid. And I pretty quickly figured out that people…well, we pigeonhole each other, don't we?"

"I don't," Ryder said evenly, his fingers strangling the mug's handle.

"Of course you do," she said on a sigh. "It's what human beings do. Even when we were kids, you knew you were breaking the rules, too, and don't tell me you didn't." When he glowered at the mug, she let out another little laugh. "It wasn't possible to be in the position I was in at that house and not feel 'less than.' A point more than driven home to me at the end. And I don't want Quinn to ever feel like that, as though someone was doing her a favor by 'letting' her go to a school with the rich kids."

His forehead pinched, Ryder lifted his eyes to hers. "It's not the same thing. True, my mother can be a snob, but—"

"You don't think I didn't hear your private school buddies give you grief about me? That I didn't know the real reason behind why you pushed me away when they came over? As long as our friendship stayed in the closet we were fine—"

"For heaven's sake—you were five years younger than I was! No bunch of twelve-year-old boys on earth is going to be okay with a seven-year-old hanging around with them!"

"And that's all it was?"

"Yes! Mel…where is this coming from?"

She bunched her mouth for a moment, then said, "One of your friends, I don't remember his name, brought his little sister with him a couple of times. I caught a glimpse of her from the hall when they arrived, she looked to be about my age—"

"That would've been Robbie Banes's sister. Sylvia or Sarah or something."

Mel nodded. "She saw me, too, even asked her mother if she could play with 'the little girl.' Your mother glanced in my direction, then mumbled something that sounded like 'That wouldn't be a good idea,' before steering them away."

"Oh, God…" Ryder scrubbed a hand through his hair. "Again, no idea. Although, if I'm remembering correctly we all would have been thrilled if the kid had been able to play with you. Man, what a little pill." He lifted the mug toward her. "Count yourself lucky you were spared."

"That's not the issue," she said, and he sighed.

"I know it's not. And maybe, if I'm being totally honest, there's more truth to what you were picking up on than I want to admit. Not that I didn't think my mother was full of it, but I guess I did try as much as possible to avoid rubbing her face in our friendship."

Her lips twitched in an approximation of a smile. "Thank you. For not giving me some BS."

"I would never do that. Not consciously, in any case. But believe me, our friendship was as real as it gets. Real enough to piss my mother off," he said, feeling one side of his mouth hitch.

"Which would prove my point, yes?"

"That my mother's a throwback to another era? Not going to deny it. That she speaks for her entire socio-economic class? I sure as hell hope not. And you are not going to like this, but it's not right to put your issues on Quinn."

"I'm her mother, I'll pile on whatever issues I damn well like. At least until she tells me to butt out, she can make her own decisions. Which I realize could be next week, at the rate she's going. Not a bridge I'm anxious to cross, but whatever. And she has friends, before you ask. I'm not raising her in a vacuum. We're part of a homeschooling support group, in fact. Just regular folks, happily owning our little middle-class lives—"

"And what if Quinn goes on to an Ivy League school? She's not going to live in that middle-class bubble forever."

"True. But by then she'll be old enough to handle it."

"To not be contaminated, you mean."

"Yes, I suppose." She shrugged. "It's a lot easier to pretend class differences don't exist when you're at the top of the food chain."

"Mel, this isn't making any sense. If for no other reason than your grandparents…this house…"

"Belonged to my grandfather's family. I didn't know this until a few years ago, but it seems Nana had been a store clerk or something when they married, well after his parents' deaths. But unfortunately, at least in her generation—and in this town—marriage wasn't some alchemic process by which a person's roots could be magically altered. An Irish peasant will always be an Irish peasant. So when my mother married your parents' groundskeeper..."

"Your grandmother had a cow."

"Try a whole herd. As though she saw my mother's decision as setting *her* back several generations, that her attempts to shake off her background had been for naught. That Mom and Dad's marriage was a happy one meant nothing." She blew out a sigh. "I just wonder," she said, more to herself than to him, "why people take everything so personally? Why we can't simply be happy for our kids without worrying about how their actions reflect on us?"

And Ryder found himself wishing he could somehow relieve her of at least some of the baggage crushing what had once been the brightest spirit he'd ever known, even if anger, crouched in the shadows of his mind, flashed razor-edged teeth at her stubbornness, her insistence about things he knew weren't entirely true. That they'd been so close in many ways, and yet seen things through entirely different lenses...not a damn thing he could do about that.

Or was there?

He got up, repacked his bag, slipped his coat back on.

"You're leaving?"

"For now."

"No ice cream?"

"Think I'll take a rain check."

She followed him through the cluttered gathering room, like a thrift store run amok, to the front door. Once there, Ryder suggested they exchange cell phone numbers, after which Mel asked, "How much do I owe you? For the house call?"

"I'll pretend I didn't hear that."

"I don't want—"

"Fine. Then…dinner. How's that?"

"And I'll pretend I didn't hear *that.*"

"This isn't about Quinn."

Her chin came up. "Damn straight it isn't," she said, and he thought, *There's my girl.*

"Mel…I'm not about to out Quinn. Granted, I hate this whole secrecy thing, and I know it's going to come back and bite everyone in the butt, but I also realize how delicate the situation is. For Quinn especially. So I promise you, she will not hear the truth from me. But you might want to hold on to that sigh of relief for a second, because I'm not done."

At her wide eyes, Ryder leaned one wrist against the door jamb, leaning close enough to see Mel's pupils dilate. "But you and I were friends, and you are back, and it's high time we opened *those* closet doors, don't you think? So. Dinner," Ryder repeated. "Just you and me. In the most public venue I can think of."

"And if I say no?"

"I'm not above kidnapping you."

Her mouth twitched. "Your mother would have kittens."

"Here's hoping," he said, and she actually laughed before slowly shaking her head.

"I don't know, Ry. Could I at least think about it?"

"Of course."

And that should have been his cue to haul his sorry ass through the door and out to his car. If he'd been inclined, that is, to listen to his head and not whatever made him instead lift one hand to brush his thumb across her rapidly cooling cheek, a move that sent his stomach into a free fall, that he hadn't touched anyone like that since Deanna. Hadn't wanted to. And his wanting to now confused the hell out of him.

Mel sucked in a breath, her eyes going even bigger. "What the *hell* are you doing?"

"Seriously thinking about things I've got no right to think about," he said, realizing how hard he was frowning. That Mel's pulse had kicked up at the base of her throat. He let his hand drop, and Mel released a shaky breath.

"Ryder—"

"I'm no more interested in trying to recapture the past than you are," he said with a short, point-to-you nod. "But just to set the record straight? I didn't hurt you back then because I was rich. I hurt you because I was stupid. We clear on that?"

"Sure," she said after a moment, the single word squeezed out as though she didn't dare say anything more, and Ryder finally made his feet carry him down the porch steps.

And away from madness.

Chapter Four

Quinn had thought it was kinda weird that Ryder was already gone when she and April got back from the store, since he'd *asked* for the chocolate chip ice cream. But then, considering how weird things already were? She didn't suppose she should be surprised.

Especially with her mom. At first Quinn had been focusing too hard on her cut hand to really notice, but once Ryder got her fixed up Quinn saw that Mom was sort of rattled. And not because of Quinn's hand, which wasn't nearly as bad as when she'd been a little kid and the window in their apartment had slammed shut on her fingers, breaking two of them. *That* sucked. This was messy and all—she hadn't been kidding about the blood—but nothing to get scared about, really. But Mom had looked like she was gonna throw up. So what could it be except Ryder? Except if they'd been friends and stuff…?

It made no sense. But then, the older Quinn got, the

less anything about grown-ups made sense. They were just weird.

And she really needed to come up with a new word before she wore that one out.

So last night Mom let her eat a boatload of ice cream, and then she and April and Mom watched some dumb old movie—only it was a tape or something you had to rewind when it was finished? Weird—and then the grown-ups made her go to bed way before she was ready while they stayed downstairs and talked. Only Quinn couldn't sleep, because she kept thinking about how Mom looked like Quinn had felt when they'd gone to that fake haunted house last Halloween—even though she *knew* it was fake, she was still all nervous from thinking something was going to jump out and scare her any second.

Except it wasn't Halloween and as far as Quinn knew her great-grandmother's house wasn't haunted, pretend or otherwise. Gross and dirty and disgusting, but not haunted.

At least today was sunny and warmer and Mom had said, yeah, they could go walking along the waterfront soon, but not until after her other cousin—Blythe—got there from D.C. So, since her hand didn't really hurt all that much, Quinn—who'd been up since the butt-crack of dawn, as Mom would say—dragged out some of her homeschooling textbooks and did a couple of assignments, which made Mom happy, she could tell. She'd also tried playing the old piano in the gathering room, but she gave up after a couple of minutes because it was so badly out of tune she couldn't tell if she was hitting the right notes or not. So now she was poking around in one of the upstairs bedrooms, even though she kept sneezing from all the dust. It smelled funny, too. Like Mrs. Davis's—her babysitter's—apartment upstairs when she kept her windows closed for too long.

She could hear April and Mom talking downstairs again, and even though she knew it was stupid her stomach started to hurt a little. Like it used to when she'd hear Mom and Lance whispering out in the living room, right before they broke up, the words sounding all sharp and pointy, like knives—

Quinn closed her eyes, imagining she could hear her grandmother, feel her heartbeat in her ear when she'd give Quinn a hug. Grams used to say thinking too much about your past, especially the parts that make you feel bad, keeps you from seeing the good things right in front of you.

Then she heard April laugh, and she smiled. April was cool. When they'd gone to the store, April had actually listened to her. Like she cared what Quinn thought about stuff. Mom told her April's husband died, a thought that tried to make Quinn sad about Grams dying. For a while she'd been bummed about Lance, too, but she got over it. Because now that she thought about it, his smile had been all fake. Like he was trying too hard. And why Mom couldn't see that Quinn did not know.

Ryder, though—now *his* smile had made her feel like everything was really going to be okay—

Holy cannoli, her great-grandmother had so much *stuff. Everywhere.* Mom had said to be careful, there might be spiders, but Quinn liked spiders. Actually she liked bugs, period, but especially spiders, although she wasn't a total dummy, and knew to stay away from black widows. Other than that, the house was way cool, especially being so close to the water. And all that sky…

She walked over to the bedroom's dirty window, thinking she felt like…like she wasn't stuck in her body when she looked at it. Not like she was in the sky, but like the sky was in her.

As she watched, she saw a boy—around her age, maybe,

it was hard to tell from way up here—walking along the edge of the water, a large black dog galloping ahead of him, barking its head off—

"That must be Blythe!" she heard her mom call out, and Quinn tiptoed to the head of the stairs—the floors creaked really badly—then crept down a couple of steps to sit where she could see the entryway through the banister, wishing *she* had a cat or dog or something to keep her company until life got back to normal.

Whatever the heck that meant, she thought with a sigh.

"Oh, dear God—" Blythe Broussard's perfectly smudged, smoky eyes darted around the gathering room, clearly not knowing where to focus first. "I had no idea it was this bad."

"And it's all ours, aren't we lucky ducks?" Mel grumbled as her cousin's gaze lifted to the gathering room's leprous ceiling, her multi-bangled wrists crossed over the charcoal-gray, dolman-sleeved sweater gracefully draping her angular, nearly six-foot-tall frame.

"Lucky's not exactly the word that first comes to mind," Blythe said, the sunlight fighting through the room's three large, filthy windows glancing off her spiky blond hair, the pewter-colored works of art dangling from earlobe to shoulder. Damn things had nearly lacerated Mel's cheeks when they'd hugged. "Right now I can't decide whether she hated us more or less than our mothers."

"Now, now," April said as she carted in a bamboo tray laden with teacups—real ones, not mugs—and a plate of baked goodies. "Hate is such a strong word." Honestly, between Blythe's designer glam and April's Barbie-doll vibe, Mel felt downright frumpalicious in her jeans, hoodie and Crocs. Pink and sparkly though they were. Not that Ryder had seemed to mind the night before, she thought on a what-the-heck? as she recalled the confused look in his eyes, the intensity in his voice. The way his hand shook when he touched her. And how her body had *mwa-ha-ha'd* in response…

"Yes, it is," Blythe said, flopping down in one of the chairs and jerking Mel back to the subject at hand. Although she'd never been particularly close to her aunts, apparently their grandmother had cut off April's and Blythe's mothers, as well, for various and sundry reasons….

Okay, clearly the dude wasn't married. Because he… um, no. No way. But for damn sure Mel needed to find out a salient fact or six before this phantom dinner. A thought which provoked more *mwa-ha-ha*-ing—

"At least it's a beach house," April said. "So the weathering is good, right?"

For the love of Mike, girl—focus!

"Honey, this goes way beyond weathered," Mel said, slamming shut the gate on her renegade thoughts as her gaze latched on to the dry-rotted sheers shivering like ghosts in the drafty windows. Now that she'd seen the place in the harsh light of day…oh, dear.

Then she looked at April, all twin-setty and such, a velvet headband keeping her long hair from tangling with the goodies as she set the tray on a small table nestled between a group of tatty looking chairs. As sweet and put-together as always—even as a child, she wouldn't dream of her undies not coordinating with her outties, never mind how cheap any of it was—her smile now did little to mask the sadness camped out in eyes not quite as bright as Mel remembered.

Because despite hours of catch-up conversation the night before, during which April had coaxed Mel into spilling her guts about her failed relationship with Lance, April had not been nearly as forthcoming about her own marriage, other than to admit how much she missed her husband. But if April wanted to hide whatever she was hiding behind a heaping plate of baked goods, who was Mel—insert ironic eyeroll here—to say?

"Where'd you get those?"

"I popped out to that new bakery on Main Street while you were still asleep. Y'all want coffee or tea? I've got both in the kitchen. And hot chocolate for Quinn, if she wants it."

Blythe and Mel exchanged a glance before Mel said, "What's with the perfect hostess routine?"

Artfully arranging her wares on the dinged table, April shrugged. "I like taking care of people. Makes me feel useful. So what'll it be?"

"Coffee," Mel and Blythe chorused before Mel bellowed, "Quinn! Breakfast!" which naturally got a "Who's Quinn?" from Blythe.

"Mel's little girl," April said before scurrying back to the kitchen. "Sweetest child ever…"

"Don't believe a word of it," Mel said to Blythe, selecting a muffin from the pile and settling into one of the chairs to feast. "The part about her being sweet, I mean," she amended as the child herself appeared, scrubbed her dusty palm across her butt to shake hands with Blythe and mumble hello, grab a muffin—but only after first ascertaining it wasn't contaminated with raisins—and bolt back toward the stairs.

"What are you doing up there?" Mel called after her.

"Nothin'. Exploring."

"You want hot chocolate with that?"

"No, I'm good."

Mel looked back at Blythe. "As I was saying."

Blythe chuckled, then said, "And why didn't I know you even had a kid?"

Their oldest cousin, even if only by a year, had always mother-henned her and April. To death. A more than decent trade-off, they'd finally decided, for Blythe's gleeful, detailed sharing of every adolescent rite of passage she'd scored ahead of her younger cousins. "S'okay," Mel said, biting into some kind of muffin. Oooh, oatmeal chocolate chip. Score. "April didn't know, either."

"And why is that, pray?"

Mel felt her face warm. "We hadn't spoken for, what? Two years by that point. I was hardly going to suddenly surface with that piece of news…this is pretty good," she said, pointing to the muffin. "But I can do better."

Which would have been Blythe's cue to follow Mel down a different conversational path. Had Blythe been anyone other than Blythe.

"Was there a husband?" she asked, buttering a corner of her scone, and Mel stuffed more muffin in her mouth.

"No," Mel said as April returned, bearing coffee. "What about you?"

"Do I have any kids?" Blythe shook her head. "Just as well, since the marriage experiment failed. Miserably."

"Oh, honey," April said with a touch to Blythe's shoulder before she sat, "That's too bad."

"Not really," Blythe said with a short laugh. "So," she said, clearly as eager to steer the conversation away from those pesky personal issues as Mel had been, "what are we doing about the house?"

"Since April's not on board with my initial plan," Mel said, "which involved a match and several gallons of strategically dribbled gasoline, I vote for selling. As quickly as possible. Although I suppose we have to…" She glanced around, then back at Blythe. "Do a little cleaning first."

"Can we even fit a bulldozer in here?"

"Maybe if we brought it through the French doors…?"

"Girls!" April barked. Well, yipped. "We are not going to toss this stuff without goin' through it! What if we throw out something important? Or valuable?"

"Then we'd never know, would we?" Blythe said. Then sighed at April's hurt expression. "Fine, fine. We'll..." She shuddered, setting her earring-sculptures to mad jiggling. "Sort. But I can't be here full-time, I've got clients lined up far as my iPad can see. I can maybe do some late afternoons and evenings, how's that?"

"Works for me," April said, even as Mel saw any possibility of her escaping this hell-hole in a timely manner disintegrate before her eyes. "But—"

"And I know we won't get top dollar for the place in the condition it's in," Blythe continued, "but some fresh paint might mitigate the ick factor enough to get *something* for it. I know a Realtor not too far away, I'll have her come do a market analysis early next week—"

"I don't suppose you could stage this for, like, cheap?" Mel asked.

Blythe laughed. An oh-you-poor-deluded-soul kind of titter. "Sweetie, I'm a decorator. Not God. Although some of my clients seem to think I am," she said with a grin, sipping her coffee.

"Actually..." April's baby blues bounced from one to the other. Like an adorable, fluffy kitten with serious mischief on its mind. "I thought maybe we could discuss, um, alternatives. To selling, I mean."

Another exchanged glance preceded Blythe's careful, "Such as?"

"Well...how about turning it back into an inn? Or at least a bed-and-breakfast?"

While Mel nearly choked on her bite of muffin, Blythe hooted. "Sorry, count me out. Not about to give up my life—let alone a career I busted my posterior to achieve—

to run a B&B. Anywhere. With anyone. Even you. An innkeeper I am not. End of discussion."

Then April turned her undeterred gaze on Mel, who shook her head as vehemently as she dared while her eyes were still watering. She lifted one finger before taking a swallow of coffee, then cleared her throat. "Don't look at me, I'd rather shove sharp sticks under my fingernails than move back here."

"Why, for heaven's sake?" April said, her voice all kitteny-soft but her eyes…not. "Okay, so I get that Blythe might not be able to change *her* life, but you already said you lost your job—"

"You lost your job? Oh, sweetie…"

See, this is why she never told people stuff. Because they used it against you.

"—and an inn has to have somebody to cook. And that can't be me, because I can't even make toast. And ohmigod," April said to Blythe, "you should have tasted this stir-fry she made last night, swear to God angels sang in my mouth—"

"Stop!" Throat cleared, hands lifted, Mel leveled her gaze on her cousin. "First off, it was a simple stir-fry, for heaven's sake, I didn't even make the sauce from scratch. And second…I'm sorry, hon. I really am—" Okay, she wasn't, but she didn't have to be mean about it "—but me staying here? Not gonna happen. There are too many…" She pressed her lips together before she tripped over her big mouth right into dangerous territory. Then—hallelujah!—she realized she had the perfect out. "Besides, if Blythe isn't interested—"

"Sharp sticks? Right there with ya, babycakes."

"—then we'd have to buy out her share of the property. And I don't have a cent to spare right now." Or ever—

"Um, not a problem," April said quietly. "Because if

you're absolutely sure you don't want to go into this with me—" she looked from one to the other, getting two vigorous head shakes in response "—I could buy both of you out. And have more than enough left over for renovations." At their gape-mouthed expressions, she blushed almost as pink as Mel's Crocs. "Since my attorney tells me I'm apparently stinking rich."

It was all still a bit much to take in, Mel thought as she tossed together this and that into her version of a salade Nicoise, that the cousin who'd barely had a pot to pee in, as Nana would say, had been able to assure Blythe that, yes, a six-figure budget to renovate the old house would not be a problem.

She'd known her husband Clayton was wealthy, of course—something about a family business which he and his mother had sold some years before—but she'd had no idea how wealthy until after his death.

And she still seemed a little gobsmacked about it all, unable—or unwilling—to say much more. Probably because the poor thing was still grieving too hard, Mel mused as she sliced boiled potatoes and dumped them into the wooden salad bowl. Although April did confess that as a child, her biggest wish had been to live in the house forever. Now, to get a shot at *owning* it, to have something that was completely hers, was a dream come true—

"Whatcha making?" Quinn said as she sashayed into the kitchen and plopped into one of the chairs, all big, blue trusting eyes and ingenuous grin, and Mel's heart fisted inside her chest, the truth relentlessly lapping at her consciousness like the waves against the beach. Being around her cousins again, slipping back into the easy, open relationship that had made those childhood summers so special, so free, only made her realize how much that damn secret was holding both of them prisoner.

"Salade Nicoise," Mel said over a spurt of anger. "You hungry?"

"Starving." Puckering her forehead, Quinn snitched a piece of cold asparagus from the cutting board and popped it into her mouth. Kid always had preferred "good" food, in fact, for which Mel had always been grateful. Sweet, no. Omnivorous, yes, the raisin phobia notwithstanding. "Mom…you okay?"

"What? Oh, fine. Just tired." *Smile,* she commanded her mouth. Grudgingly, it complied. "Didn't sleep particularly well last night." As in, not at all. *Thank you, Ryder...*

"Me, neither," Quinn said. "It was so quiet I could hear my heart beating." She shuddered, then filched another piece of asparagus. "So…what's going on? Like, is Blythe gonna decorate the house or something?"

Although both Blythe and Mel remained adamant that they still wanted no part of their cousin's scheme-slash-dream, it was obvious Blythe could not wait to get her mitts on the place, even as she insisted on waiving her fee. Said having it in her portfolio was more than worth the hassle of shifting around appointments to oversee the project—which they hoped to have done before Christmas, when the annual St. Mary's Cove Festival brought in tourists by the boatload. Literally.

"April's going to keep the house and pay Blythe and me for our part of it. So, yeah, Blythe's going to make it all pretty."

Quinn's brows flew up. "Does that mean we can come visit?"

More anger spurted. Accompanied by a healthy side order of fear. "I don't know, baby."

Brows dropped. "Why? Won't April let us?"

"Of course April would let us. That's not the issue—"

"It's Ryder, isn't it?"

And didn't that testify to the sorryness of the whole situation that Quinn's assumption that *Ryder* was the issue was actually a relief? Which didn't keep Mel's eyes from snapping to her daughter's. "What?"

"You already said you two were friends. When you were kids. So how come you act so strange around him?"

"I do not—"

"Mom." Huffed sigh. "Not blind, okay? Even if I don't exactly know what I'm seeing."

"Remind me to trade you in for a dumb model, 'kay?"

"So…does that mean I'm right? It's not that we couldn't come back, it's that you don't want to. Because of Ryder."

Sighing, Mel resumed her chopping. "It's complicated."

"He's not…ohmigod—is he my *father?*"

Mel laughed. Sort of. Then turned to get something, anything, out of the fridge. "No, baby. He's not your father."

"Swear?"

"On my life."

"Was he at least your boyfriend?"

Annoyance trumping embarrassment, Mel sucked it up and carted a couple of tomatoes to the table, along with a clean cutting board. "Not my boyfriend, either. Hon, Ryder's five years older than I am. I mean, when he was sixteen I was eleven."

"Oh. Ew."

"Exactly." *And can we please move on—?*

"So how'd you two know each other?"

Apparently not. The hacked, er, wedged tomatoes dumped on top of the salad, Mel inwardly sighed. And, okay, asked a God she wasn't exactly on speed dial status with for the right words. Not for her sake, for her kid's.

And you know what? Those truth-waves lapped a little harder, eroding her resolve a little more and making her curse her grandmother for leaving her the house—or a third of it, anyway—followed by another surge of annoyance, that they hadn't simply decided to dump the place. So future visits wouldn't be even be an issue. Then there was Ryder, showing up on her doorstep…and Quinn's timing for impaling herself on that nail…and her grandmother's lawyer spilling the beans…

Yep, this here was what you might call a perfect cluster…fluff.

The salad assembled, Mel set it aside—she'd do the dressing after the others showed their faces—and sat across from the little girl she'd sworn to protect with her last dying breath.

"Grams and your grandfather worked for Ryder's parents. Grams was the housekeeper and cook, my father was the groundskeeper."

Quinn's jaw dropped. "Really?"

"Really. We lived in a cute little cottage—" after a fashion "—on their property. After I was born, Ryder sort of appointed himself my honorary big brother."

"Why?"

Because that's Ryder. "You'd have to ask him that." Oh, hell. "I don't mean literally ask him, I just mean…"

"I know what you mean. Geez." Quinn stood to reach across the table and grab a tomato, cramming it into her mouth before she said around it, "So why'd you stop being friends?"

"Our lives changed," Mel said over her thumping heart. "We got older, he went on to college and—after my dad died—Grams and I moved to Baltimore."

"When was this?"

"Before you were born."

"And that's it?"

"Pretty much."

Quinn gave her a funny look, then shrugged. "For what it's worth? He seems really nice."

There was no mistaking the wistfulness in her voice. That cross between don't-want-to-be-hurt-again caution and sweet, sanguine hope…

Mel plucked out the unfinished thought before it could take root. "He's a doctor, he's supposed to be nice."

"Yeah, right. You remember the doc in the E.R. when I broke my wrist? Worst. Attitude. Ever—"

Her cousins' arrival at that moment blessedly ejected Dr. Ryder Caldwell from the conversation, if not the look in her daughter's eyes that said this discussion wasn't over yet. Not by a long shot.

Oh, yeah. She was fluffed, all right.

Chapter Five

Ryder rang Amelia's doorbell, telling himself it was only professional courtesy motivating him to stop by to make sure Quinn's stitches were healing up okay. But he knew that was a lie. As would Mel. Smart cookie, that Mel. Not to mention enough of a worrywart about her daughter that she would have called him if there was a problem.

This was dumb, he should just leave now—

"Oh!" said the tall, graceful blonde who answered the door, flashing him a full body scan before planting one long-fingered hand on a hip that was nothing but bone and dusty denim. A grin sliced her angular face as Betty Crocker aromas slithered from behind her. "Ryder?"

"Holy cow…Blythe?"

She laughed, then waved him in, her voluminous, blue-gray sweater sliding off one shoulder. After calling for Mel, she turned eyes nearly the same color on him, swiping at a smudge of dirt on her cheek. "My, my, my," she said on a low chuckle as she tucked a pointy wisp of nearly white hair behind one multi-studded ear. "After spending all day surrounded by rampant decay—" she swept one arm to indicate, he assumed, the decrepit state of the house "—you are a sight for sore eyes. Nice to see that at least *something* in this two-bit town actually improved over the last decade!"

Ryder smiled, even as he bristled at the dig. Of all the places he'd lived or visited, St. Mary's was still home, the place he'd deliberately chosen to establish his career. A point he might've been tempted to make had Mel not appeared, about a hundred expressions zipping across her face and pinking her cheeks. Which in turn made her eyes look brighter and Ryder realize that the big brother thing was definitely not working for him anymore.

She'd pulled her hair back into a ponytail—blast from the past—so she was all dark, messy, sexy bangs and big, pale, wary eyes. And those pink cheeks. But mostly the wary eyes.

"Hey," he said, "Thought I'd check on Quinn." From underneath a deep pink cardigan a lowish-cut white top hinted at cleavage, clung to what caused the cleavage. He looked up. Just in time to catch the arched eyebrow. "See how she's doing."

Aaaand time went into stop-action mode.

Blythe cleared her throat, backing away while jabbing a thumb over her shoulder. "And if you'll excuse me, I've got a hot date with an upstairs closet…."

They both watched Blythe's retreat, dust motes boogying around them for several seconds until Mel raked a hand through her bangs, provoking memories. "Quinn's fine."

"And that would be your professional medical opinion."

"After ten years of on-the-job training? As good as." Ryder lowered his chin; Mel sighed, said, "Fine, see for yourself." Then, with a nod toward the kitchen, she turned. "We've been making cookies."

Speaking of clinging…no mom jeans for this gal. And could we hear a hallelujah for that?

No, what he needed was someone or something to clobber some sense into him, stat. So Mel was back and they were all grown up now and he no longer had to feel like scum because he was physically attracted to her. Except he still did because this was *Mel* and the timing was no better now than it had been then, legal issues aside, and because, hello? Not…ready? Willing? Able?

Okay, *able,* maybe. Probably. But he still wouldn't feel right about it. Hell, even without the clobbering he knew this whole thing had *disaster in the making* written all over it.

And yet.

In the eclectically furnished dining room they passed a dusty-glassed, dark wood breakfront crammed with crystal and china, the matching buffet laden with tarnished silver. Good, if neglected, pieces at odds with the general tattiness of the rest of the furnishings.

"What happened to the other stuff? On the buffet?"

"Boxed. Pitched. Whatever."

"So…you guys going to hold an estate sale?"

"Haven't decided yet. Right now we're just trying to figure out what stays and what goes."

"Stays?"

Mel slowed enough for Ryder to see her mouth pull flat. "We're not selling. Or I should say, April's not selling. She wants to keep the place, turn it into a B&B. So she's buying Blythe and me out and turning it into something people might actually want to spend the night in."

"Oh. And how do you feel about that?"

"Resigned," she said after a moment. "And relieved, I

suppose. That I can walk away and never think about this place again—"

"Ryder!" From the kitchen table where she'd apparently been decorating cookies, Quinn grinned up at him, and from out of nowhere Ryder felt knifed, that she didn't know who he really was. Who *she* really was, for that matter. "Did you come to make sure my hand's okay?"

"I did." Shaking off the unsettled feeling—for the moment—he glanced around, taking in the supplement-divested counters, now smothered with plates of cookies in all shapes and varieties. "Although something tells me I needn't have bothered. That thing still works?" he asked, frowning at the stove.

"After a fashion," Mel said, then sighed, taking in the cookie explosion. "We might've gone a little overboard."

"You think?"

"That's because we couldn't decide what kind to make," Quinn said, then wagged her bandaged hand. "It doesn't even hurt, I swear."

"Glad to hear it," Ryder said, sitting at right angles to her. "But why don't you let me take a peek, anyway?"

"Knock yourself out," she said, extending her hand in a very royal gesture, and Ryder smiled, even as the knife twisted again, although for another reason.

He glanced up at Mel, who was concentrating on her daughter's hand, and way too many emotions collided in his brain to suss out. But one thing was absolutely clear—for both Mel's and her daughter's sake, this subterfuge needed to end, now. Or at least very soon. Because not only could he tell the whole situation was eating Mel alive, but the longer Quinn was kept in the dark, the worse it would be when she found out the truth.

And she would find out. Because these things always worked their way to the surface. Always.

A minute later, satisfied, he replaced the gauze with an antiseptic plastic bandage and gave Quinn a thumb's up, then Mel a grin which he didn't feel nearly as much as he would have liked.

"I do good work, if I say so myself," he said, and she sputtered a short laugh.

"Me, too," Quinn said, planting her hands on the edge of the table and pushing herself to her feet, giving Mel what sure as heck to Ryder looked like a pointed look. "C'n I take some cookies up to my room?"

Mel handed her an enormous plastic mixing bowl. "Go for it."

With a squeal, the child gathered enough cookies to feed Delaware and flounced out of the room, munching as she marched. Figuring whatever was left was fair game, Ryder plucked a still-warm oatmeal cookie from a plate in the center of the table. "Now you've gone and done it," he said to Mel's back as, with much clattering and banging, she washed several discolored, misshapen cookie trays at the chipped sink. "I may never leave. At least not until the cookies are gone."

The cookie sheets haphazardly stacked in a dingy plastic drying rack on the counter, Mel turned, drying her hands on an equally dingy towel, and Ryder suddenly flashed back to another kitchen, another woman drying her hands on a towel, smiling at the two kids sitting at the kitchen table, stuffing their faces with her oatmeal cookies. Odd, how easy things seemed back then.

At least, for him.

Ryder held up another cookie. "Your mom's recipe?"

He saw the flash of pain in her eyes before she nodded. "Although she didn't bake much after, um, we left. Or cook, either. Said she just didn't feel like it, with Dad not there. So I learned in self-defense." Her mouth pulled into a sly grin. "As you may have noticed, I'm not exactly a three-carrot-slices-on-a-lettuce-leaf kind of girl."

"I noticed." She rolled her eyes, provoking another memory flash, even though now, with a pang, Ryder saw it for the illusion it was. Chewing, he regarded the cookie with a gaze that probably bordered on worshipful. "I'm guessing you use real butter?"

Her eyes actually dilated. "Every chance I get. Well, um..." The towel slung over a door knob, she crossed her arms. "I've already played hooky with the cookie baking, I really need to get back to sorting and cataloguing. We only have Blythe through tomorrow, she has to get back to D.C.—"

"Need help?"

"Don't be—"

"Unless you *want* to spend the rest of your life going through your grandmother's things? Come on," he said, getting to his feet and yanking open the nearest cupboard door. "It'll be fun."

"In what universe?"

"Mine."

"You honestly have nothing better to do?"

He hefted a stack of chipped stoneware onto the counter, his heart pounding at the prospect of bringing up a subject he'd lay odds she was not even remotely ready to discuss. "It's Saturday. So not really, no."

"You do realize how lame that sounds?"

"And *you* realize," he said, clunking a second stack onto the counter, "the longer you stand here arguing with me the longer it'll take to get away again?"

He felt her eyes on the side of his face for a long moment before, huffing a sigh, she opened the cupboard door on the other side of the sink and started pulling out glasses, no two of which appeared to match. At her extended silence, he said, "You going to tell me what's bugging you or let me guess?"

"For God's sake, Ry..." She faced him again, a deep furrow between her brows. "What do you want?"

"From you?"

"Sure. Let's start there."

He grinned. "Dinner?"

She rolled her eyes. "Still thinking."

The smile dimmed. "Then...to regain your trust?"

The question mark at the end of his answer startled him more than it apparently did Mel, even though another flush washed over her cheeks as she turned back to pull out more glasses. "That might be tricky since I'm not really sure I completely trust anyone anymore," she said, and he felt like he'd been sucker-punched.

"Don't you sometimes wish," he said carefully, "that you could get a do-over?"

"No. Never. Especially if it meant I'd have to live through the same crap."

"But if it didn't?"

"Then there'd undoubtedly be different crap to live through. Right?" With a grimace, she tossed several of the glasses into a plastic-lined bin where they sadly shattered, their lives finally over. "Life is just...crappy."

"You didn't used to be so bitter."

"People change." Another glass met its demise.

"You're just in a bad place right now—"

"Now?" Her gaze lanced his. "You can't even begin to imagine what the last ten years has been like for me, Ryder. What my life has been like. Okay, I'm not saying it's all been horrible, that would be a gross exaggeration and totally unfair to people who've faced far worse challenges. Not to mention...I can't imagine not having Quinn. How could I possibly regret *her?* But still. Most days I feel

like I'm shoveling sand—I no sooner plug up one problem than another one appears, and the thing of it is, it's my own damn fault—" She abruptly turned away. "None of which is any of your concern. Sorry."

"For dumping on me?"

She shrugged, then dragged over a chair, climbing up on it to reach the upper shelves.

"Hey. If you can't dump on me, then who?"

"And you do not want to get me started on the folly that is letting myself lean on other people."

"Especially people who let you down when you needed them most, you mean."

"Or who might have hidden agendas. Good God, there's a dead bug the size of my head in here."

Ryder frowned. "Where on earth did that come from?"

"I'm thinking Jersey. Oh. You mean the agenda comment?" With a shudder, she swept the carcass off the shelf onto the counter. She hadn't been kidding—*biiiig* sucker. "The deep, dark recesses of my embittered brain." Her gaze met his. "Forgive me for being skeptical, but…" She lowered her voice. "Is your wanting to reconnect really about me, or about my daughter?"

"Are you deliberately trying to piss me off?"

"Is it working?"

"Heck, yeah, it's working. Wanting to patch things up with you and wanting to get to know Quinn are two separate issues, even if they're intertwined—"

"And what if I don't *want* to 'patch things up'? Because that's all it would be, some…some jury-rigged approximation of something that died a natural death more than ten years ago. And would have in any case," she said before he could protest.

"You don't know that," he said, and her brows flew up.

"Oh, really? What? You would have waited for me to

grow up? I mean, come on, Ryder—do you honestly expect me to believe you were saving yourself for me after you went off to school?" When he flushed, she let out a harsh laugh. "No, I didn't think so. And even after that night, even considering you *didn't* know what happened…you could have found me if you'd wanted to, it wouldn't have been that hard. But you didn't because, hello? That chapter in our lives…it was over. You'd moved on. And don't even think about apologizing for doing what you were supposed to do. Or for simply being a guy. Although that does beg the question—so why *are* you still single?"

"What?"

"You heard me. You're over thirty and straight and a *doctor,* for the love of Pete. No way have you made it this far unscathed. So, c'mon. Spill."

No, he sure hadn't. And everything she'd said…she was right, of course. As much as he'd valued their friendship, they had been kids, Ryder hadn't planned at the time on returning to St. Mary's and Mel sure as hell hadn't planned on sticking around. Part of the reason, he supposed, he'd let go—because, as she'd said, there would have been no point.

And there were no words for how little he wanted to talk about this. Because, God, it hurt. Like a sonuvabitch.

But without being totally open, what hope did he have of regaining her trust?

The dishes temporarily forgotten, he clamped his hands on the counter edge and blew out a long breath. "You're absolutely right, there were…others."

"Thank God, you had me worried there for a minute—"

"In fact, I was engaged," he said, taking an almost perverse pleasure in her flinch of surprise, even as the admission ripped open the barely healed wound all over again.

* * *

Well, you asked, dumbbutt, Mel thought, only to swallow hard when she saw the pain briefly flash across his face. A pain she suspected he didn't let a lot of people see.

"Was?"

"She died," he said softly, not looking at her, and Mel lost her breath.

"Holy hell, Ry—when?"

"Last year. A month before our wedding. Car accident," he said with a slight roll of his shoulders, a guy-trying-to-be-brave shrug she'd witnessed before, when some chickie or other in high school had done him wrong and he'd tried so hard to pretend it didn't matter.

This, though…crap. Because for all she'd meant every word about how tough things had been, that she was bitter and cynical and knew that rainbows were an illusion, that didn't mean she didn't care. Or couldn't feel anybody else's misery.

Especially Ryder's.

As a kid she'd watched him limp in from a soccer game, filthy and bleeding and grinning, heard him stand up to his mother without so much as a quaver in his voice, but when it came to romance damned if he didn't have the most tender, vulnerable heart of any male she'd ever known. That he'd suffered deeply—was still suffering—was more than evident in his wracked expression, and it made her feel like she'd swallowed lye.

Except then he gave her one of those pierce-her-soul looks and said, "No pity. Got it?"

Never mind that all she wanted was to take him in her arms and hug him for, oh, the next ten years. Instead she climbed off the chair, dragging over a box to pack the "better" stuff in until they decided what to do with it. "So riddle me this, Batman," she said, her gaze carefully averted, "since it's obvious you're still hurting, why are you looking at me like I'm, um, a girl?"

Loooong pause. Then, behind her: "Not a girl, honey. Not by a long shot. A woman."

Her eyes cut to his, saw something she couldn't/wouldn't/so did not want to handle and skittered away again. "Not answering the quest—"

"Because you're gorgeous and I'm *not* dead. Although I sure as hell felt like it until I saw you again."

Mel dumped two glasses into the box a little hard, breaking one of them. Not that this was a loss. "I see."

"I doubt it—"

"I know how hurting men act," she said, wheeling on him. "How they seek…solace—"

"And not to be crude, but if that's what I was looking for I certainly wouldn't seek it from you." When she barked out a laugh, he let his head drop back, then sighed. "That didn't come out right. I meant, if that's *all* I was looking for, I could find it easily enough from other sources. As it is I've had absolutely no interest in even casual dating since…then."

Mel raised her brows, waiting. Ryder sighed.

"Do I find you appealing?" His eyes darkened. "Oh, yeah. Am I going to act on that?" He shook his head. "Because it would be—"

"Wrong," Mel finished, then marched the broken glass pieces across the kitchen to dump them in the garbage.

"I'm not making any sense, am I?"

"Not a whole lot, no."

He picked up the top to a cow-shaped butter dish and skimmed his fingers along its back. "When I heard you were back, I didn't know what to expect. How I'd react, seeing you again. And to be honest I still haven't sorted it all out. But when I talk about wanting a do-over…"

He set down the top, his forehead crunched. "I don't mean literally. Obviously. God, I wouldn't want to be that kid again for anything. Let alone that frustrated, horny kid who didn't dare follow through on what he was thinking. But being around you again…it makes me remember a time when things were good. For me, anyway. I know—now—they probably weren't so good for you."

She could lie. Heaven knew she'd had enough practice at it. Except she was tired of lying. Damned tired. "When we hung out together, things were good for me, too. Good enough, anyway."

His smile was sad. "I thought I'd stopped missing you. Apparently I was wrong."

Oh, hell. She was going to cry. And that would never do. "Well," she said, after way too long a pause and in a voice she knew wasn't kidding anybody, "isn't that corny as hell?" and Ryder held out his arm and whispered, "C'mere, you."

And instead of running shrieking from the room like, you know, a sane person, she went, and he slung an arm around her shoulders and pulled her close, and it didn't feel nearly as bizarre as she might have assumed it would. In fact, it felt *pret*-ty good. Which of course wasn't good at all.

Especially when Ryder said, "Still friends?" and Mel sighed, knowing that despite all her protests, all her determination to pretend what they'd had as kids was dead and buried…it wasn't. Worse, though—much, much worse—was the what-could-be threatening to eclipse the what-had-been.

Because nothing ranked higher on the old follymeter than *two* people with broken hearts.

So she pulled away, or would have if Ryder hadn't caught her hand, forcing her gaze to his, and oh, dear merciful heavens, was the dude conflicted, or what? Maybe even more than she was, and that was going some.

"Ryder—"

"Because I've got a lot of making up to do."

Her brows slammed together. "I didn't ask—"

"You didn't have to."

She removed her hand and crossed her arms, his touch still making her palm tingle. Among other things. Because, fine, she'd missed him, too, whether she'd let herself think about that or not, and now that she was a grownup and knew how everything worked—and how much fun it was when they did—simply looking at the man made her entire body hum quite the merry little tune.

"I already told you," she said over the humming, "I'm totally over what happened between us. So no making up to do—"

"But you're definitely not over what my family did to you."

She almost laughed. "*You* can't make up for that."

"I sure as hell can try," he said, then stooped to snag her gaze in his. "You need a friend, Mel," he said, adding, when her mouth opened, "for Quinn's sake, if nothing else. Because it's not good, keeping all of this jammed up inside you. And I know the last thing you'd want to do is take out your frustration on your child."

"I would never do that!"

"You really want to take that chance?"

No, she didn't. Because—damn his hide—he was right. Already there'd been times when she'd been short with Quinn for no reason other than not having an outlet for all the junk bubbling inside her head. Even before her mother's death, she'd been loath to vent to the woman whose life had been turned upside down because of Mel's sketchy judgment. And if nothing else, Ryder had always understood her. Or at least, did a good job of pretending he did.

Which, perhaps, was what she'd missed most.

What scared her the most, too.

"And you know what?" Ryder said. "I could use a friend, too."

She hazarded a glance in his direction. "Even a temporary one?"

His grin shattered her heart. "I'm very good at working with what I'm given. Now. You got a box for these plates, or should we toss them?"

Quinn had just come down the back staircase and into the pantry when she saw Ryder take Mom's hand. She'd been so startled she'd frozen, not sure what to do. Although tiptoeing away had been pretty high on the list.

But then she'd caught bits and pieces of their conversation and she *couldn't* leave. Because nobody ever told kids anything. Or at least, not as much as there was to tell. Especially Mom, who considering the eleventy billion times she'd told Quinn she could tell *her* anything, sure as heck didn't seem interested in returning the favor.

So she'd ducked behind the wall outside the doorway, straining to hear what they were saying, her heart thumping like crazy that she'd get caught. Only the longer she listened, the more confused she got. What did Ryder mean, what his family had done to Mom? Keeping all of *what* jammed up inside her? And what did any of it have to do with Quinn?

Unfortunately, one problem with hearing a conversation you weren't supposed to was that you couldn't exactly ask for an explanation afterwards. Poop. But eventually Ryder and Mom went back to talking about dumb stuff, so Quinn scooted back upstairs, where she ran into April at the end of the hallway, her arms full of sheets.

"Hey there, baby girl." April dumped the sheets into a big box by the linen closet, waving her hand at the cloud of dust before giving Quinn a big smile. "Whatcha doing?"

"Nothing, I..." She glanced back toward the stairs, her face getting all hot.

"Hey...everything okay?"

No, it sure as heck wasn't, and that was a fact. Quinn frowned at her cousin. "If I ask you something, you promise not to say anything to my mom?"

After like half a second, April took Quinn by the elbow and marched her into the nearest bedroom, nodding toward a stuffed chair in the corner with ugly blue flowers all over it. She partially shut the door with her hip, then sat on the edge of the bed, although you couldn't pay Quinn to get anywhere near that yucky old bedspread. "I can't promise that whatever you tell me I won't discuss with your mama, that would depend on what it is. So you might want to think about that before we go any further. But if you need to run whatever it is by me first—like a rehearsal—I'm here for you. Okay?"

Quinn nodded, then decided if she didn't let it all out she'd pop. Looping a curl around her index finger, she shrank into the chair, not sure if she felt worse for what she'd done, what she'd heard, or that she was dragging April—whom she hardly knew—into it. But finally she whispered, "I kinda overhead my mom and Ryder in the kitchen, talking. I didn't mean to, I swear, I just went to get a glass of milk and..."

Shaking her head, she let go of the curl to fold her hands in her lap and look down at them. "Ryder's family...I know my grandparents worked for them and stuff, but Ryder said something about…wanting to make up for what they did to Mom. Do you know what he's talking about?"

April's eyebrows about lifted right off her head. "No, baby, I sure don't. I swear. He say anything else?"

"Not really, no. Not about that, anyway. But…I also saw them holding hands."

"Who? Your mama and Ryder?"

"Yeah."

"Oh." April touched the little gold necklace she always wore. "Um…you know they were real good friends when they were kids, right?"

"Yeah. Mama told me. But if you ask me he was not looking at her like a friend. I mean, they were *talking* about being friends, but…" Quinn pushed out a breath. "Something's going on, April, I know it. Something nobody wants me to know. Things just don't feel right." She smushed her lips together. "And they haven't for a long time."

"Don't feel right, how?"

"I don't know. But ever since I was little it's been like…" She let her eyes fall to her lap again, almost ashamed to say what she was thinking. "Like Mom's not telling me the truth."

After a couple of seconds, April said, real quietly, "Honey, look at me." When Quinn finally did, a tear dribbling down her cheek, April leaned over to take Quinn's hand. "Your mama and I haven't been close in a long time, so I'm as clueless as you are, what any of that meant. I'll tell you one thing, though—she loves you with all her heart, and she would die before hurting you. Or letting you get hurt. So my advice to you, sweet thing, is to come right out and tell her what you told me. You don't have to mention what you heard, or how you heard it, only that things are feeling a little strange and you'd like to know what's going on."

"So you think something *is* going on?"

"I didn't say that. But I do know..." She paused. "People—and everybody does this at some time or another, so don't feel bad—we hear part of a conversation and get to wondering about it, and before you know it we're making ourselves nuts, filling in the blanks with all sorts of things that only exist in our heads. And I know your mama would feel awful if she knew how confused you were right now. I bet she has no idea."

"So you think I should be honest with her?"

"Don't see any other way of getting answers, do you?"

Quinn nodded, feeling both better and more jumbled up at the same time. *Figure that one out,* she thought with a sigh.

By Sunday evening Mel had to admit that although they weren't done yet—not by a long shot, they'd barely sorted out the dining and gathering rooms—they'd made a lot more progress than she would've thought possible in only two days with three women whose takes varied greatly on what was worth keeping and what wasn't.

However, they not only muddled through without bloodshed, but there was a big old Dumpster in the driveway chock-full of crap not even worth donating. So go, them. Whatever April wanted to keep—the good china and crystal, a few pieces of furniture Blythe said would look terrific once reupholstered or refinished—would eventually get shoved into one of the downstairs bedrooms, the rest carted off to various charity thrift stores.

Which meant April would be more or less starting from scratch, a prospect that clearly excited her no end. In fact, after Blythe declared herself too exhausted to haul her butt back to D.C. that night, and that she'd get an early start in the morning, April had spent the better part of the evening blissfully poring over—and over—their cousin's first sketchy draft of the proposed kitchen remodel, currently laid out on the to-be-refinished dining table. Which is where Mel found her after tucking in Quinn for the night.

"She go down okay?" April asked, taking a sip of her tea from the mug hugged close to her chest and looking about ten years old with her hair pulled into twin ponytails, her size 5 Mary Janes peeking out from her flared leg jeans. She, too, was headed back to Richmond in the morning, but only long enough to pack up her clothes and put Clayton's house on the market. While Mel didn't relish the idea of it just being her and Quinn in the great big house, she'd promised to stay and continue chipping away at the upstairs bedrooms. And then there was the attic, which they'd glanced at, groaned, and quietly closed the door to again. Mel wouldn't be surprised to find the remains of Union soldiers up there.

Now she released a tired laugh. Every muscle in her body ached, although she was grateful she'd been too busy to mull over that "let's be friends" convo with Ryder, too tired at night to do anything but zonk out within seconds of hitting her bed. "She's ten. Not ten months. She likes to read herself to sleep."

"Not that this will come as a shock, I'm sure," her cousin said with a grin, "but I'm crazy about that kid."

"Yeah. Me, too."

Smiling, Mel dragged herself into the kitchen for a cookie—or three—to find Blythe standing at the counter, slumming it in a ratty T-shirt and ripped jeans as she polished off the leftover casserole, warmed up to go with the slow-cooker pork roast Mel decided to make after Blythe unearthed a still-in-its-box Crock-Pot at the bottom of the hall closet, of all places. Blythe's gaze swung from Mel to April, who'd trailed in behind Mel, shutting the swinging door behind her. When she crossed the room to push closed the door to the back stairs as well, Mel felt the back of her neck prickle.

"What's going on?"

With a sigh, April sat at the table, focused on her tea. Mel offered her a plate of cookies, but she shook her head. "I'm still stuffed from dinner. And I'll have you know I've never eaten three servings of cauliflower in my life."

"There's cauliflower in here?" Blythe said. "My brain shorted out at the bacon."

"And cheese," April said on another sigh. "You *sure* I can't talk you into—?"

"Positive," Mel said. "Not that I don't think if anybody can make this work, it'd be you. But count me out." Although she had to admit she wasn't relishing the idea of job-hunting when she got back to Baltimore. And/or making five gazillion bacon-wrapped shrimp appetizers for weddings every weekend. Not to mention Blythe's plans for the kitchen were…intriguing. But enough of that. "And I'm guessing you didn't close the doors so nobody would hear you extolling the virtues of my cauliflower casserole."

The cousins exchanged another glance before April took a cookie, anyway, nibbling at the edge for a moment before asking, "Has Quinn…talked to you?"

"Talked to me? Are you kidding, the kid never shuts up." Again with the glances. And the prickles. "Okay, guys—what's this about?"

Blythe burped the circa 1972 Tupperware container and turned, her hands braced on the edge of the counter behind her. "She came to April yesterday. While Ryder was here."

"And I thought I'd convinced her that she needed to bring up the subject herself," April said. "With you, I mean. But…"

She looked to Blythe, who pushed herself away from

the counter and pulled out a kitchen chair. "But since she hasn't…well. You should probably sit."

Mel looked from one to the other, trying to make sense of what they were saying. "For God's sake, you're scaring me—what the *hell* is going on?"

"That's what your daughter wants to know," April said, and Mel's gaze zinged to hers. "Believe me, I didn't ask to get in the middle of this, but she seems to think there's something you're not telling her?"

Ouch.

For all the catching-up chitchat they'd shared over the past forty-eight hours, Mel had handily diverted the conversation away from the subject of her daughter's paternity, partly because what her cousins didn't know they couldn't inadvertently let slip to certain small parties, and partly because Mel simply hadn't wanted to get into it with them.

Just like when she'd been a kid, she realized, when self-protection had made her keep things to herself—a knee-jerk reaction, she supposed, to always feeling relegated to the sidelines—even though neither of her cousins had ever given her cause to not trust them. Or think they'd judge her.

Any more than there was reason to believe they'd judge her now.

Finally she lowered herself into the chair, her fingers closing around April's when her cousin reached for her hand.

Then she pushed the plate of cookies toward her cousins. "It's a long story. You might need fortification."

An obscene amount of consumed cookies later, Blythe was all for an impromptu road trip to New York to drag Jeremy back by his 'nads to atone for his scumbaggery—a plan even sweet April appeared to consider for a moment before shaking her head. Even as she regarded Mel with genuine concern.

"My Lord, honey…what a fiasco."

"Tell me about it." Her stomach rebelling against all the sugar and butter—there was a first—Mel got up for a glass of milk. "Why on earth I even agreed to such a stupid scheme, I have no idea. And why the Caldwells thought it would work…" She shoved the milk carton back onto the shelf; the fridge wobbled when she slammed shut the door.

"You were scared, sugar," April said. "You didn't think you had any choice. And nobody's gonna fault you for doing what you did."

"Oh, yeah? What do you think my daughter's going to think when she finds out?"

Blythe stood and stretched, her hands propped on her lower back. "That you're the mom from hell, what else?" When Mel shot her a daggered look, Blythe shrugged. "She will get over it, sweetie."

"Providing I ever figure out how to give her something to get over."

"So you do want to tell her the truth?"

"What I want, is for this stupid secret to magically disappear. And, yes, I know that's not going to happen, but the *truth* is, her father's family wanted nothing to do with her. And since it's been more than ten years and they apparently still don't…" Mel forked her hands through her loose hair, then let them slap back onto the table. "At this point I honestly don't give a damn about what they'd think, or how they'd react. What are they going to do, sue me for breach of contract? And I know the longer I put this off the worse it's going to be. But…"

Blythe slipped a hand onto Mel's back to gently rub between her shoulder blades. "But you can't bear the thought of Quinn getting caught in the crossfire."

"Exactly."

"Does Ryder know?"

"He does now. But only because our grandmother died, bringing me inconveniently back to St. Mary's."

Blythe's hand stilled. "You're kidding—his parents didn't even tell him?"

"Nope. And God knows Jeremy didn't. You need somebody to ride shotgun with you on that road trip, Ry's your guy."

"Then there's your answer," April said.

"Letting Ry kill his brother?"

"Aside from that. Did he know when he came here that first night? After Quinn hurt herself?"

"Yes. Nana's lawyer had apparently told Ryder's dad we'd inherited the house. And he apparently thought it best to forewarn Ryder about Quinn."

"So the secret's beginning to unravel at the edges, anyway."

Mel's mouth pulled tight. "At one edge, anyway. But that makes things even trickier. That Quinn and Ryder have already met. She already adores him—"

"And he, her," April said. "Meaning I bet he'll do anything to help you straighten this out." Mel covered her eyes, groaning. "No, really. Let Ryder be the go-between. Especially since I assume he's not exactly pleased with his parents right now." April grinned. "And since from what little I observed I'm guessing Quinn's not the only one Ryder's keen to bond with."

At Blythe's snort, April turned on her cousin. "Don't you snort at me, Blythe Broussard. It's perfectly obvious Ryder's still got a thing for Mel."

Mel raised her hand. "Um, actually—"

"And now that you're all grown up," April said to Mel,

"he could actually do something about it. And so could you."

"No, you don't understand—"

"And we've already established how sweet you were on him that last summer we were all together. So this is a no-brainer, right?"

Momentarily giving up on wedging reality into the conversation, Mel looked at Blythe. "It was really that obvious?"

Her cousin laughed, and Mel sighed. Then Blythe said, "Although forgive me for being the voice of reason, but unlike Miss Stars-in-the-Eyes here, I'm not seeing this end well. Yeah, fine, maybe it would work to have him be the mediator between you and his parents, but anything else?" She shook her head. "Take my advice, don't even go there. Because no way this isn't all going to blow up in everybody's faces—"

"For heaven's sake," April said, soundlessly slapping her delicate little hand on the table. "Stop being so darn cynical—"

"*Guys!* Sheesh!" Mel clunked her empty glass on the counter. "April, sorry, but I'm with Blythe on this one. This really is a non-starter. About me and Ryder, I mean. Even if his fiancée hadn't died last year—"

April sucked in a little breath. "Ohmigod, you're kidding?"

"Nope. And he's still grieving. Then there's the little issue of my not being exactly gung ho about jumping into another relationship after my own disaster—"

"But maybe you're exactly what Ryder needs to heal," April said, and Blythe groaned out, "Oh, for pity's sake…"

"April! Not. Happening. Because no matter how this thing gets resolved—assuming that it does, which is not a given—do you really think I'd ever want a connection with that family again after what they did to me? To Quinn?"

"Not even with Ryder? But that's so unfair!"

"Dammit, April—nothing about *any* of this is fair! And you know something else?" she said, getting to her feet. "Nobody can figure out how to handle this but me, because I'm the one who bungled everything to begin with. So if you'll excuse me, it's late, and I'm about to fall over, so I'll see you two in the morning."

But before she got to the door, Blythe called to her. When Mel turned back, her cousins were standing side by side, both with their arms crossed, both clearly loaded for bear.

"First off," Blythe said, "so help me if I *ever* hear you take the entire blame for this on yourself, ever again, I will bitchslap you clear into next week."

"Yeah. What she said," April said, and Mel got all teary. Honestly, she was getting as bad as April.

"Thanks, guys—"

Blythe's hand flew up. "Not done yet. Quinn's your daughter, so of course it's ultimately your call. But, sweetie, this is your chance to resolve something that's obviously worrying you to death. And my guess is you're going to beat yourself up even more if you leave St. Mary's *without* resolving it. One way or the other."

Mel's mouth popped open, only to clamp shut again. Because her cousin was right. Eleven years ago she'd left because she'd felt she'd had no choice. This time the choice was hers—to continue running from the lie, or face it head on.

To—okay, might as well be honest—dodge her feelings about Ryder, or to face them head on, as well.

"Call Ryder, sweetie," Blythe said, as April bobble-headed beside her.

Agita, Mel thought on a long sigh. *I has it.*

Chapter Six

Monday decided to be one of those blue-skied, Indian-summer days that lured people outdoors. Or, in this case, prompted Ryder's father to invite Ryder to join him for lunch at a little café not far from the clinic, housed in what had originally been an eighteenth-century tavern. St. Mary's was nothing if not riddled with historic vibes. And, this time of year, sleepy to the point of comatose. Even the gulls that normally pestered the hell out of everyone during the height of the summer season couldn't be bothered to venture the few blocks inland.

But the sun was warm and the breeze balmy, so Ryder and David took advantage of the gulls' disinterest to dine al fresco in the deserted courtyard adjacent to the restaurant, even though Ryder knew not even the peaceful setting would soothe his jangled nerves.

"Beautiful day," his father said, tucking into his chicken

salad sandwich and not looking at Ryder. "Hard to believe winter's right around the corner."

"Happens every year," Ryder said, and his father smiled. Still gazing across the street at one of the many antiques shops lining Main Street, he said, "So. Have you met the child yet?"

Well, well.

Despite his father's being the one to alert him to Mel's return, since the subject had pointedly not surfaced during family dinner the day before, Ryder had assumed it would be up to him to broach it. But only with Mel's permission, which he'd yet to figure out how to get. Just like she'd yet to agree to have dinner with him.

"Yes, actually," he said, wiping his mouth with his napkin and studying his father's profile. "She hurt herself that first night, needed some stitches. I happened to be around."

His father's eyes cut to his. "So you went over there after you talked to us."

"Did you think I wouldn't?"

David looked away again. "What's she like?" he asked, and Ryder saw it, the chink in the armor. A chink he imagined had always been there, now wrenched wide open by the knowledge that his granddaughter was barely a mile away.

"She looks like Jeremy," Ryder said, and his father pressed his lips together. "But she's smart like Mel. Curious about everything. Funny. Bit of a smartass." He paused, then said, "You'd love her."

"I bet I would." He pushed his plate away. "And Mel? How is she?"

"Angry," Ryder said simply, his gut twisting that his family had done this to her, turned the always smiling girl he'd known into someone he almost didn't recognize. Except he knew—or had to believe, at least—that she was still there, underneath all that disillusionment. "She's also coming off a relationship that ended badly, which isn't exactly adding to her good mood at the moment."

"I swear to you, it wasn't my idea—"

"I know. But that doesn't change anything. The damage is done. And this isn't something that can be fixed with a dose of antibiotics or a few stitches. Good God, Dad—what were you and Mom *thinking?*"

Judging from the wounded look in his father's eyes, Ryder's blow hit its mark dead on. David ripped open two packets of sugar, dumping them in his iced tea as sparrows twittered in the Virginia-creeper-choked trellises nearby. "And I suppose you want to tell Jeremy. That you've seen her."

"Crap's gonna hit the fan eventually, Dad. And whether *I* tell him or not," he said, watching his father stir his tea, "Jeremy is an adult. Now, at least. And he will deal." Ryder paused. "And so will Mom. Man," he said with a dry laugh and a short shake of his head, "she's pulled some doozies over the years, but this one takes the cake—"

"It's not as if we completely turned our backs!" David said, clattering the teaspoon onto the edge of his plate. "We have been supporting the child all these years—"

"You bought Mel off! And making sure the kid didn't starve and had a roof over her head was the least you could have done—"

"I want to meet her," his father said on a rush of air, tears welling in his eyes.

Despite his father's obvious contrition, Ryder refused to let his plea derail him, or undermine the resurrected, all-consuming protectiveness that now included Quinn as well as Mel. They came first. As Mel should have then, had Ryder listened to his gut instead of his hormones. Even so, he was curious how far his father's change of heart went.

"Behind Mom's back?"

"If necessary."

Wow. And frankly the idea was at least momentarily tempting, not only for the satisfaction of getting one over on his mother, but because Ryder knew Quinn and his father would get on like gangbusters. However…

"Sorry, Dad, but it's not up to me. Nothing I can do."

"Can't you talk to Mel, feel her out…?"

"She's already made her feelings on the subject more than plain. Hell, if it hadn't been for Quinn's getting hurt she wouldn't even have let *me* meet her."

"But if your mother and I were the ones who set the conditions to begin with—?"

"Conditions you can't simply undo with a wave of your hand because you've changed your mind."

Shoving his trembling hand underneath his glasses, David rubbed his eyelids, then pushed the glasses back into place. "This is torture, Ry, knowing she's so close…" He glanced away, clearly trying to compose himself. "We made a terrible mistake, Ry."

"You think?"

David's gaze met his. "You'll never forgive us for this, will you?"

Anger fisted in Ryder's chest. "Forgive you for what, Dad? For writing off someone you *knew* meant a great deal to me? For rewarding Maureen's loyalty by treating her daughter like trash? For rewarding Jeremy's behavior by absolving him of any responsibility whatsoever—?"

"And if I could undo it, I would! I told you, we—"

"Screwed up. Got it." Ryder got to his feet to dump his unfinished lunch in a nearby garbage can. "But you know what? What I think, whether or not I can forgive you, is immaterial. Because this isn't about either you or me. It's about Quinn. And Mel. Who has no earthly idea what to tell her daughter when she asks about her father—"

"Then let Mel know it's okay to tell Quinn the truth!"

"Here's a better idea—how about *you* let her know that? No, wait—you and Mom. Together. In fact..." Suddenly, he saw the glimmer of a solution, one that kept eluding him as long as he'd kept thinking it was entirely up to him to bring it about. "I'll make a deal with you—you get Mom to admit this was a mistake, and I'll broach the subject with Mel."

Hope bloomed in his father's eyes. "So you'll arrange a meeting?"

"Not so fast. This wound's been festering for way too long to be cleared up by a single 'sorry, we blew it,' so I have no idea what Mel's reaction will be. She might still tell you both to go to hell. And she'd be completely justified."

"Good God, Ry—whose side are you on?"

He pushed out a dry laugh. "The side that would have never let this travesty get as far as it did." At his father's stung expression, Ryder said, more gently, "Dad...I didn't have to come back to St. Mary's, I chose to. Chose to risk Mom's wrath that I didn't become a specialist because I wanted to practice alongside you. Because I feel the work you're doing, right here, is important. And because in many, many ways, I admire the hell out of you. You're the whole reason I became a doctor, okay? So in that respect I will always be on your side."

He laid a hand on his father's shoulder. "But what you and Mom did to Mel was about as far from admirable as it gets. Which you've already admitted. Still, for reasons I've never understood—and don't want to get into now, believe me—you and Mom have each other. Mel..." He shrugged.

His father lifted understanding eyes to his. "You're it."

"Apparently so," Ryder said on a breath as his phone buzzed.

The one-word text was from Mel:

Dinner?

Despite her resolution from the night before, it had taken Mel until after lunch the following day to work up the cojones to text Ryder and take him up on his offer. But she needed to talk to him alone, where Quinn couldn't hear them. And when he texted back, suggesting Emerson's, the town's best seafood restaurant, her mouth watered.

Not that they'd ever been there together, she mused as she parked beside Ryder's sturdy little Toyota RAV in the lot and trudged up the wide plank to the dock bordering the weathered, flat-roofed building—although calling it a building was a stretch—set on pylons in the water. Nobody ever dressed up to go to Emerson's, either, except for the occasional, clueless tourist. Because when you're expected to eat until you pop, you may as well be comfortable. Hence Mel's jeans and faux Uggs now, although she had raised the bar with a dark rose cotton turtleneck and some dangly earrings she'd picked up on a whim at one of the shops in town. Oh, and she'd tossed on some mascara and lipgloss, too. Just for kicks.

Long before she reached the double doors, the scent of steamed crabs and fried fish, spicy crab cakes and hush puppies beckoned, stoking more memories. Inside, the aroma almost made her too dizzy to spot Ryder, seated at one of the oilcloth-covered tables—all the better to crack crabs on—beside a window overlooking the marina and the water beyond.

Shoulder-hugging, dark blue sweater: check. Furrowed brow as he apparently studied the menu he had to have known by heart: check. Huge, delighted smile when he glanced over and noticed her: check.

Hammering heart in reaction to the huge, delighted smile?

Uh-boy.

No sooner had she taken her first nervous steps in his direction, however, than Estelle Emerson, who with her husband Clarence had kept St. Mary's residents', not to mention thousands of tourists', bellies filled for more than thirty years, swooped down on Mel with outstretched arms.

"I don't *believe* it!" she sang out, her dark skin glowing from the steaming pots for the hapless crustaceans that filled those bellies. "Oh, my gracious, girl—aren't you a sight for sore eyes! I remember your daddy and mama coming in here with you when you were a bit of a thing. I heard about your grandma, honey…I'm so sorry. Although I suppose she lived a good long life. You here by yourself?"

"Um, no, actually I'm…" She nodded toward Ryder. One of maybe a half dozen patrons in the place, what with it being off-season. In fact, many of the local joints closed down between September and May altogether. But as Estelle had so often said, what else was she gonna do? Go to Florida for the winter? So she may as well feed whoever was left.

Now Estelle's gaze slid toward Ryder's, then back to Mel. If Estelle knew about their old friendship, Mel had no idea. No reason for her to, she supposed. But her eyes sure lit up now, even as she leaned close to whisper, "You be careful, baby—boy's still nursing a broken heart."

Mel whispered back, "It's okay. So am I."

Now, whatever made her say that, she had no idea. But Estelle's little moan of sympathy, as well as another hug, did feel pretty good, she had to admit. Then the older woman said, her voice even lower, "Just remember—blessings often come out of adversity. You hear?"

"Yes, ma'am," Mel said, polite as she could be, before finally making her way over to the table, blushing when Ryder—all five o'clock shadow and dark, soulful eyes, damn the man—stood to pull out her chair for her. Except Emerson's was not a pulling-out-a-chair kind of place. At least, not before this.

"You look great," he said, sitting back down, and a nervous chuckle burped from Mel's mouth, provoking an understandably curious look from Ryder.

She unwrapped the gigundo paper napkin from around the chintzy flatware. "You don't have to do that."

"Do what?"

"The obligatory 'you look nice' thing. This isn't a date, for heaven's sake."

His brows crashed. Over eyes determined, apparently, to hold hers hostage. Uh-boy, again. "I can't give you a compliment?"

Mel grabbed the Ten Commandments-tablet-sized menu, feeling her cheeks go about the same color as her sweater. Let's hear it for coordination, yay. "It feels… weird, coming from you. I didn't expect it."

"You needed a warning?"

She blubbered out a laugh. "No, I…" Her eyes lowered to the menu. To get away from his, if nothing else. "Just not used to them, that's all."

"From me?"

"From anybody."

His fingers hooked over the top of the menu and yanked it down.

"Hey, I was reading that—"

"You are crazy beautiful," Ryder said. Frowning. "You always have been. I just couldn't say it before."

"But you can say it now."

"Yes. So. What do you want to order?"

You?

Blushing again—this was getting to be a really bad habit, yeesh—Mel cleared her throat as Estelle appeared to take their order. "This," she said, pointing to a combination platter of friend oysters, fried shrimp, fried perch, hush puppies, and Estelle's famous potato salad.

"You want a salad with that?"

As in, iceberg lettuce with some shredded carrots and a tomato wedge.

"Sure. With ranch dressing."

"To keep the arteriosclerosis theme going," Ryder said with a bemused smile after Estelle left.

"Hey. I'd rather shave a few years off my life and die happy than live to a hundred eating cardboard and grass clippings. Although," she said as he chuckled, "if it makes you feel any better I actually love veggies."

"Drenched in butter, I presume."

"Is there any other way?" When he rolled his eyes, she reached over and patted his hand. "I also run and ride a bike. Not to mention cleaning out my grandmother's house is the best cardio workout *ever.* I'm thinking we should charge. But if God hadn't meant for us to eat butter he would've made cows give skim milk. And are we both tap-dancing around why we're really here, or what?"

Ryder leaned back in his chair, one wrist on the edge of the table. "By that, I assume you mean Quinn? Who I assume is with April?"

"No, April's in Richmond. But the Harrises still live next door, and their granddaughter's a year or so older than Quinn, so I pawned her off on them. They were thrilled, she was thrilled, so it was a win-win."

When Ryder chuckled, Mel let her gaze drift outside,

where the sky was turning a deep periwinkle-blue. "But anyway…yes. Quinn."

Who had yet to initiate the "things don't feel right" conversation, even though—as much as the prospect of said conversation freaked her out, because she still had no idea what the heck she was going to tell her—Mel had given the kid several openings throughout the day. So, yeah. Time bomb.

She huffed a sigh, then let her eyes meet Ryder's again, seeing the same compassion that had always been there, but coming from a much deeper place than before. A place of grief and loss that made her ache for him. "My cousins finally knocked some sense into me, that somehow or other I need to lay this issue to rest."

"Really."

"Yep. Like it or not, I can't protect my daughter forever. And she's apparently indicated to April that she can sense that something's off, although she doesn't seem anxious to talk to me about it."

"You think maybe she's afraid of what she'll find out?"

"I have no idea. But she deserves to know who her family is. And it might be better to do this before she hits puberty," she said with a slight smile. "And…I need your help."

After a moment, Ryder leaned forward to slip his hand around hers and her throat went dry. "You got it." Then he released a breath, although not her hand. "Dad wants to meet her. Asked me to arrange a meeting, in fact."

Mel started. "You're kidding?"

"Nope." He gave her hand a brief squeeze before letting go to take a sip of his water. "Not really a surprise, since apparently he was never particularly on board with this, anyway."

"And what did you say?"

Estelle brought them their food; Ryder waited until the steaming, fragrant plates were set in front of them and Estelle was gone, before continuing. "That it was up to you. And that I wouldn't even say anything unless he got Mom to admit *she* screwed up. But since you brought it up first..." He lifted his hands.

Mel dunked a shrimp into a plastic cup of cocktail sauce. "You really think your mother would ever do that?"

"I haven't talked to her since that first night, so I have no idea what she's thinking. But stranger things have happened, I suppose."

"Stranger than your mother actually conceding she was wrong? I doubt it." Fork in hand, Mel tackled the tender, flaky perch, remembering how she'd been the only one of her cousins who actually preferred her fish to taste like fish. Although the things she could do with sole and tilapia had been known to make people weep.

Ryder forked in a bite of his broiled salmon. Weenie. "So how do you feel about letting Quinn and my dad meet?"

"With or without your mother knowing?"

"Either." When Mel hesitated, Ryder leaned forward again. "Honey, there's no way out of this but through it. And maybe if Quinn got to know us—Dad and me, at least—it might diffuse the shock. At least a little?"

For several seconds, Mel stared at her food, twirling her fork in her fingers and wondering why, if she'd already made the decision to move forward, the idea of actually making that move was twisting her up in knots. Finally she lifted her eyes to Ryder's again. "It's just been the two of us for so long. Well, yes, my mother had been part of that, but she's gone, and..." She swallowed. "This is hard—"

"I know it is, sweetheart—"

"No, I mean what I'm about to say." She took a breath, letting it out on a tiny laugh. "Damn, Ry, I am so conflicted about all of this. Sure, finally coming clean about what happened...I know that will be a relief. At least, once the dust settles from the ka-boom. But to be honest, the idea of sharing her isn't sitting all that well."

Ryder's brows pulled together. "You're not going to lose her, Mel."

"No, I know that. Especially since I'm going back to Baltimore as soon as possible. So that's not even an issue, really. But it's more than that. Watching her with Lance—my ex—and then, worse, seeing how torn up she was when it was over...I'm sorry, but your mother is still the unknown quantity in all this. And your father..."

"Is likely to do whatever she wants."

"There is historical precedent."

One side of Ryder's mouth pushed up. "True. So you're concerned Quinn will become attached to my dad and then my mother will find out and put the kibosh on the relationship?"

Mel dunked the next shrimp. Like it'd been accused of witchcraft. "Not only your father."

He frowned, then pushed out a sharp laugh. "Mel, whatever happens, whatever kind of relationship I end up having with Quinn, is up to you. Not my mother. If her opinion didn't sway me then, it sure as hell won't now. If I do become part of Quinn's life," he said carefully, his gaze riveted to hers, "it's for the long haul. Whatever she needs, whatever *you* need, it's yours." Smiling, he raised his hand, three fingers extended. "Scout's honor. *I'm* not going anywhere. Not anymore."

The sincerity in his eyes, his expression... Mel ripped her gaze away from Ryder's to the other diners enjoying their meals, their lives, secure in those lives, while her traitorous heart whispered things that could break that heart, if she let it.

"You don't trust me," he said quietly, and her head snapped back to find something like hurt etched into his features.

"You, I trust. It's all the rest of it..." She shrugged, then let out another little laugh. "I may regret admitting this, but I am *so* tired of doing all the thinking."

"Then lucky for you I'm really, really good at thinking," he said, and she laughed again, and he reached for her hand, again, and that no-account heart started up with the whispering—again—that she'd wasted ten years looking for a clone of what was right in front of her. Especially when he said, "You don't have to do this alone, Mel. I'm right there. Right here, for both you and Quinn. We'll get through this, I promise."

"How?" she squeezed out past the lump in her throat.

"Well...tell you what—Dad and I usually play hooky on Wednesday afternoons, anyway. If the weather cooperates, how about Dad and I take you and Quinn out on the boat for an hour or so? No pressure, just an opportunity for friends to hang out. That way Dad gets to meet her, and, if my hunch is correct, you get an antsy kid out of the house for a little while."

"Oh, Lord," Mel said on a short laugh. "You got that right. Child's about to drive me nuts."

"Then...is it a plan?"

"O...kay. Deal. But I'm gonna need some of that coconut cream pie for fortification."

Grinning, Ryder signaled to Estelle. "Anything for my girl," he said, and Mel seriously considered asking for two pieces.

For the second time in a week, Lorraine's husband had flabbergasted her.

"You're going to do what?"

"Meet our granddaughter," David said mildly as he slipped on his favorite old tennis sweater over a plaid shirt. "Ry thought it might be a good idea for us all to go sailing. And Mel agreed. Reluctantly, though. Can't say I blame her for that."

"Are you saying they've told the child—"

"Quinn."

"They've told…Quinn the truth?"

"Not yet. But that's the plan. At some point."

"And this was Ryder's idea."

"Meeting Quinn?" Tugging down the sweater's sleeves, David shook his head. "Nope. Mine. Now what on earth," he said, vanishing into the walk-in closet, "happened to my deck shoes…?"

"You decided this without even consulting me?"

The found shoes dangling from one hand, David dropped onto the edge of their four-poster bed. "Here's the funny thing, Raney—when I first mentioned to Ry that I wanted to meet Quinn, he said no. Flat out. To protect Mel as well as Quinn, I imagine," he then said, his gaze drifting across the room, as though talking to himself more than Lorraine.

Then his eyes touched hers again, until he dropped them to this shoes, lying on their sides on the thick ivory carpeting, and something about the slump to his shoulders, the more pronounced gray in his hair, made Lorraine suck in a tiny breath. Almost without knowing she was doing it, she braced one hand on the mattress to lower herself to the floor, slip his shoes on his feet. David chuckled.

"What on earth are you doing, Raney?"

"I'm not sure," she said, rapidly tying the first shoelace. "Best not to question it too hard." Then she looked up into the face she loved more than life itself, into the face of the man she knew loved her the same way, even if she often felt she didn't deserve it. "What made him change his mind?" she said, finishing up the second shoelace and awkwardly pushing herself back up to sit beside him, their shoulders touching.

"He didn't. In fact, he first said he wouldn't even consider asking Mel if I could meet Quinn unless I talked to you first. Got you to admit what you—we—did was wrong."

Her face flamed. "I can't do that."

"Of course you could. If you'd just set aside that stubbornness for more than a half second."

She stretched out her hands, blinking at the three-stone diamond ring David had given her for their twenty-fifth anniversary. If only it were that easy. "So why didn't you say something earlier?"

"Because I knew what *you'd* say. And anyway, as it turns out he and Mel had dinner together that very night, and she said she was ready for this all to be over."

Lorraine's stomach clenched. "That's not her decision."

"Yes, Raney," David said, laying a hand on her knee. "It is. Can't protect the kids forever, you know—"

"So, what? You're simply going to rip this whole thing wide open? What about Jeremy? What about *me?*" she said, pressing a hand to her pounding heart.

"What about you?" David said calmly, gently stroking her leg.

"I'll…I'll look like…"

"A fool?"

"David!"

With a final pat to her knee, her husband got to his feet, standing straighter than she'd ever seen him. "It's okay, honey, we can look like fools together. Because for what it's worth—which isn't much at this point, I'll grant you—when the truth does come out, I promise I won't tell

Quinn whose idea it was. That, she doesn't need to know." He pocketed his keys and cell phone, then cut his eyes to hers. "I suppose I'd need to clear it with Ryder, first, but… you could come with us, if you like—"

"What?" She practically jumped to her feet. "No! Are you *mad?*"

"Clearly. Although you'd only be there as Ryder's mother, of course. Not Quinn's grandm—"

"I said no! I can't…I couldn't…" Her eyes stinging, Lorraine walked over to the window overlooking the expanse of lawn interspersed with soaring loblolly pines, the wharf jutting into the inlet beyond. Her own reflection stared back at her, pale and distorted. Accusatory. "I can't," she whispered.

"I understand," David said, dropping a kiss on the top of her head. Except how could he, when she didn't fully understand herself?

She whipped around, clutching the front of her sweater. "So tell me something," she said, her heart hammering against her knuckles, "if you think what we did was so wrong, why did you agree to begin with?"

When he turned back, regret flooded his eyes. "Because there would have been hell to pay if I hadn't. Only, what I didn't realize, was that the debt would still have to paid, someday. With the kind of interest my stockbroker can only dream about." He ducked his head slightly to peer at the sun streaming through the pines. "Shaping up to be a pretty day—the dogs might appreciate a nice, long walk, hmm?"

His gaze glanced off hers before he walked away.

Chapter Seven

"She'll be fine, Mama," Ryder said as the twenty-foot-long boat, with his father at the helm, smoothly sliced through the cove and out toward the slate-blue, sun-flecked waters of the open bay. "All the times we went out as kids, nobody ever fell overboard."

"You're not just saying that to make me feel better."

Ryder's laugh cut through the motor's whine. "Of course I am. But it's true."

Mel wrenched her gaze from the curly-headed, life-jacketed pumpkin squealing with delight in the seat beside David only to have that gaze slam into the windblown glory that was Ryder. One foot up on the side bench, an arm slung lazily across the back—putting it within scant inches of Mel's shoulder—he was clearly in his element.

And she had to say it made her feel good to see him looking even a little relaxed. Content. She had to resist reaching over, taking his hand. Because that would be entirely inappropriate. Not to mention *stoo*pid.

There'd always been a boat, Mel recalled as she looked away, although David had clearly traded up since the night Ryder had clandestinely taken her out for a short spin when she was thirteen or fourteen—an event that would have frosted *all* their parents had they known. And Mel couldn't deny that the thrum of the motor through her veins, the gentle sting of breeze-blown spray in her face as the sweet little cuddy skimmed the water's surface…fed something inside her as much now as it had on that moonlit night when everything felt possible and it had been enough to simply enjoy that whole big brother-little sister thing they'd had going.

Overhead, an eagle soared, the sun glancing off its white head, its low *kak-kak-kak* competing with the rush of wind in her ears. Spotting it, Quinn pointed.

"Is that an eagle?"

"It is," David shouted. "There's a pair with a nest at the very top of one of the pine trees over there. Watch…"

The magnificent bird dove toward the water, snatching a fish in its talons before flying off again.

"Cool!" Quinn said, and Ryder's father laughed. Quinn hooked a hand over her eyes to watch the bird flap back to its nest. "Mom said the bay's home to lots of birds."

"Yep. More in the warmer months, but still plenty that hang around all year. Or even winter here. You like birds?"

"You kidding?" Quinn said, shoving her more tangled than usual hair behind her ear, where the wind whipped it away again. "I *love* birds…"

"Uh-oh," Ryder said, sliding close enough for Mel to hear him. For his breath to make her skin prickle. "She's got him in the palm of her hand now. Dad took up birding a few years ago, spends nearly every Sunday morning traipsing through marshes and the forests farther inland with binoculars and a guidebook…."

Sure enough, David was grinning to beat the band. "Me, too."

"It's going well, don't you think?" Ryder said, his voice low.

Tensing, Mel glanced away. "That they've bonded like Krazy Glue, you mean?"

"I thought that was the point?"

"I know, I just…sorry," she said, giving her head a sharp shake. "Ambivalence blows. I also keep thinking…" She sucked the inside of her cheek. "How much I wish *my* father was here. That he could have met her." Tears bit at her eyes. "He would've been nuts about her, too."

"I'm sure," he said, then chuckled when Quinn laughed again. "But then, who wouldn't?" He paused. "She's definitely your kid."

Mel smiled. "Does she remind you of me at that age?"

He tilted his head, as though thinking it over. "Some. Not nearly the little pest that you were, though."

"Hah. Wait until you get to know her better."

Too late, she realized what she'd said. Implied. Thankfully Ryder either didn't pick up on her oopsie or decided to take the honorable route and not mention it. "I've got great memories of your father. Seeing him and your mother together, the way they'd kid around…and *fool* around," he said with a grin, and Mel sighed, remembering they'd had no problem with expressing their affection for each other, despite Mom's oft-giggled, "Tony! Not around the children!" "They always seemed so comfortable together."

Mel nodded over the sting at the back of her throat. "I always thought they had the perfect marriage."

"Yeah," Ryder said, his gaze fixed on his father's back six feet away. "Me, too." The rest of that unspoken thought—and Mel had no doubt he'd left things unsaid—trailed out behind them as his father began to circle a grouping of small islands, chatting away to her rapt daughter. "It must've been so hard on your mom, after Tony died."

"It was. He was her rock. Mine, too," she said, then huffed out a breath. "Then I go and get myself knocked up…" Suddenly chilled, she tugged her hood up over her mist-damp, flyaway hair.

"What did she do?" Ryder asked. "After you guys, um, moved?"

Mel allowed a tight smile for Ryder's word choice. "She surprised me, actually. She started her own business, vetting and referring household help for families that still wanted their own domestics rather than using a maid service. It took a while to get it really up and running, of course, but between our survivors' benefits from Social Security and…funds from your parents, we managed. And it gave her something to focus on, keep her mind off things. And once Quinn was born…" She smiled. "She was the best grandmother ever."

"What about yours?"

"Amelia? What about her?"

"She really never spoke to you again?"

"Nope."

"Not even at your mother's funeral?"

"There wasn't one. Mom didn't want anyone to 'make a fuss.' Said, since the family had drifted apart, anyway, what was the point?" She snorted. "Just like Nana, who apparently didn't want a service, either."

"I know."

"Oh, right. Of course," Mel said, thinking that she had no earthly idea what to do with the ashes she'd picked up from the funeral home the day before.

"So I take it she and your mother never patched things up between them, either?"

Mel shook her head. "Not that Mom gave her the chance, since she refused to even tell Nana she was sick. And threatened me within an inch of my life if I did."

Ryder hooked his elbow over the back of the stern, watching the rooster-tail of spray for a moment before saying, "What is it with humans and their damn pride?"

With a short laugh Mel said, "I know, right?" Then she linked her hands over her knees as she watched her daughter, who was clearly having the time of her life. "Why Nana deliberately severed ties with all of us, why we all isolated ourselves from each other, I have no idea. But I'll tell you this—I can't imagine there's anything—*anything*—that Quinn could possibly do that would make me cut her off. Any more than my mother did me, even though I will never, ever forget the look on her face when I told her I was pregnant." Her gaze drifted to Ryder, watching her with a calm intensity that sent a shiver scuttling up her spine. "I'd sliced her heart wide open, and we both knew it."

"Hearts heal," Ryder said. But looking away, as though trying to convince himself of that fact.

"So I hear," Mel said gently, shivering again when he gave her a small smile. "In any case, I don't suppose I'll ever know why Nana never accepted my parents' relationship. Other than the obvious, that she simply didn't think my father was good enough for her daughter. That Mom could have done better." She tucked a stray hank of hair behind her ear. "As if. Hey, cutie-patootie," she said as a grinning Quinn wedged herself between Ryder and Mel with what Mel guessed was a profoundly happy sigh. "Having a good time?"

"Uh-huh," she said with an enthusiastic nod, then twisted to Ryder. "This was the best idea, ever, Ryder!

Thank you! And your dad is so cool! He knows, like, everything about birds and the bay and stuff. He said, if I want, I can go with him the next time he goes birding." She wiggled back around to give Mel the Pleading Hound Dog look. "Can I, Mom?"

Mel's eyes shot to Ryder's, then back to Quinn. "Um, I don't know…we're not going to be here much longer—"

"He said Sunday. That's only a few days from now. So please?"

"We'll see, hon," Mel said, cringing even as the words left her lips. Fortunately, Quinn was too spellbound to call her on the prevarication, instead turning her attention to Ryder, with whom she chattered non-stop the rest of the ride, giggling right on cue in response to his benign teasing.

Just as Mel had done with her father, she realized with a bittersweet pang. And as she listened to their easy, natural interplay, Quinn's sparkling giggles juxtaposed to Ryder's rich laughter, as she caught his delighted glances over her daughter's head—glances that made her heart knock in her chest—she realized she was liking all of this far too much for her own good. For anybody's good.

And yet, as they neared the marina again, she felt like a kid herself, not ready for the outing to end. So when Ryder suggested she and Quinn tag along when he drove out to check on a housebound patient, Mel was hard pressed to find a reason why they couldn't. Shouldn't.

'Course, his smiling right into her eyes and tripping a breaker in her brain might've had something to do with that.

"I've got a better idea," David said to Quinn after they'd disembarked. "You like hot fudge sundaes?"

Quinn's brows dropped. "Dude! Is that a trick question?"

"Not at all," David said, chuckling, as Mel gasped out a mildly horrified, "Quinn! You don't call grown-ups 'dude!'"

Still laughing, David turned to Mel. "Finnegan's decided to stay open year 'round. Thought I'd treat my g—… my new friend while you two go on out to the Washingtons'."

Her stomach jerking at David's slip, Mel reached for her daughter's hand. "Maybe another time, it's kind of cold for ice cream, anyway—"

"No, it's not!" Quinn said, pulling away from Mel to clasp her hands under her chin. Above which her teeth were chattering. "P-please, M-mom?"

"We still have all those cookies at the house. And the cheesecake—"

"And they're all stale and gross!"

"It's only for an hour," David said, his eyes every bit as imploring as her daughter's. Although for completely different reasons, she knew. Reasons that could easily trip him into saying something to Quinn Mel wasn't ready for her daughter to hear. But how was she supposed to do her Mama Bear act with Quinn standing right there? Then Ryder touched her shoulder, making her look up to see that *It's okay, I've got this* look in his eyes before he called to Quinn.

"Hey," he said, holding out his hand to her, "wanna go take a look at that big yacht at the end of the pier?"

Amazingly, she went, although not before lecturing him on how she hadn't held hands with a grown-up since she was six, geez.

After they were a safe distance away, Mel faced Ryder's father again, his yearning expression as he watched Ryder and Quinn mosey on down the dock almost making her wish they didn't have to have this conversation. But before she could speak, he said, "I know. What I almost said." Finally his eyes met hers. "And you have every right to be ticked. And concerned. But I swear it won't happen again."

Mel glanced at her daughter, who was happily yakking poor Ryder's ears off, then back at David. "'Concerned' doesn't even begin to cover it, Dr. Caldwell. 'Worried sick' is more like it, that this whole thing's going to blow up in our faces, that I have no idea how Quinn's going to take this news as it is. At least I'd like to control the when and how." She smiled weakly. "A deluded concept though that might be. Even so," she said on an exhaled breath, "why should I trust you?"

Behind his glasses, self-reproach burned in David's eyes. "Because I already love that little girl with all my heart. I promise you I'd never do anything to hurt her. And the last thing I want to do is get on your bad side."

"A little late for that, isn't it?"

"I know, what we did to you, and her...if you never forgive us for that, I doubt anyone would fault you. Including me. But now that I've met Quinn, I can't imagine not having a relationship of some kind with her. And I daresay neither can Ryder," he said, nodding toward his son and granddaughter walking back toward them, and Mel's breath caught in her throat at Ryder's besotted expression as he watched Quinn zigzag from one side of the dock to the other, still talking a mile a minute. Even a moron could tell how good she'd already been for him.

Or, in her case—big sigh, here—how good *he'd* been for a baggage-ridden chick who'd made "don't trust the bastards" her mantra.

"We only want what's best for Quinn, too," David said quietly. "But how can we prove that if you don't give us a chance?"

She met the older man's gaze. "And Mrs. Caldwell? Is she included in that 'us'?"

"Right now she's all wound up in that damn pride of hers," he said, and Mel thought of Ryder's earlier comment. "It's hard for her…" Clearing his throat, he glanced down, then lifted sheened eyes to Mel. "To admit she made a mistake. Or to ask for forgiveness. Doesn't mean she's not thinking about it, though. Thinking about it hard, too, if you ask me. Mel," he said when she turned away. "There are certain…things you don't know."

Her head snapped back around. "What things?"

"Things I'm not at liberty to discuss at present. All I can say is, there might have been more behind Lorraine's actions than appeared on the surface. Not that she said anything directly, but I know my wife. And right now, I know she's struggling."

As Mel gaped at David, a red-cheeked Quinn bounded up to them. Followed by an ambling Ryder, hands in pockets, his relaxed smile at odds with the obvious longing in his eyes. Eyes which connected with hers, rife with undefined questions.

"So did you decide?" Quinn said, grabbing Mel's hand. "If I can go get ice cream with Dr. David?"

No mean feat, making a decision when your brain cells were in roller derby mode, slamming against the inside of your skull, taking each other out, *splat!* But a decision she made, based on two things: one, that she truly believed David wouldn't spill the beans, if for no other reason than she doubted he'd want to deal with the fallout by himself; and two, that letting Quinn hang out with Ryder's father gave Mel the perfect opportunity to grill Ryder about his mother.

"How long do you think we'll be?" she asked Ryder.

"Hour, hour and a half—"

"Take your time," David said, smiling down at Quinn. "We're in no hurry. Are we, Quinn?"

Then two sets of eyes canted to Mel's. Sheesh.

"Oh, all right," she said, and Quinn gave Mel a hard hug before falling in step beside David, chattering away and matching him stride for stride as they marched down the dock and into what Mel suddenly realized was her future.

Like it or not.

Ten minutes later, after she'd taken advantage of the marina's facilities to "freshen up," as Nana used to say, they were whizzing past vast, flat fields of just-harvested farmland and Ryder had once again fallen into pensive mode. Not somber, she didn't think, but definitely contemplative. Not unheard of even when he'd been a teenager. Although then, according to her mother when Mel had complained about his crazy mood swings, he'd been at the mercy of some vicious hormones. Now he had cause—

"I know that wasn't easy," he said, making her flinch. "Leaving Quinn with Dad."

"There's an understatement," she grumbled.

"I'd say it's going to be okay, but I don't want to get smacked."

"Good call."

He chuckled. Good to know she hadn't lost her touch. Except he sank into silence again, making Mel think maybe this wasn't the best time to get chit-chatty about his mother. So instead she said, "Where are we going again?"

"You remember old Moses Washington? Used to have a fruit-and-vegetable stand out on the highway—"

"Where Mom used to take us?" *All* of them, Mel thought with a half smile—Blythe and April as well as Ryder, piled like puppies in her parents' Dodge Caravan, wearing flip-flops and terrycloth coverups and smelling of sunscreen and cherry Popsicles. "You bet." Then she frowned. "Is he sick?"

"Just old, mostly. Turned eighty last month."

"Get *out*. Really? Wow."

"Yeah. His heart's not what it used to be. Or his mind, unfortunately. Which is why I go out there, since bringing him into the clinic confuses him. He still lives in his house, but his oldest daughter Nina and her husband live with him now, since his wife died five, six years ago." He flashed her a grin. "Fair warning—there will undoubtedly be pie of some kind. Which Nina will expect you to eat."

"I can do that," Mel said, then laughed. "Gosh, it seems like a million years ago. Those summers." She blew another, shorter laugh through her nose. "How on earth—*why* on earth—did you put up with three teenyboppers like that? The giggling alone must've driven you insane."

"Speaking of understatements."

"Then—"

"I don't know, really. I never really thought about it. I guess because those outings…they were fun. You guys were fun. *And* you let me boss you around."

Mel sucked in a shocked breath and gently swatted his shoulder. "We did not! Take it back!"

"Hey," Ryder said, laughing, "cut it out, I'm driving! And I did, too, boss you guys. And you *loved* it."

"You are *so* dead," she said without thinking, only to mentally swat herself when his smile faded. "Sorry, sorry, sorry…God, what an idiot—"

"You are many things, Mel," Ryder said in a very low voice, "but you are not, and never have been, an idiot." His eyes bounced to hers, then away. "Is that clear?"

Unable to speak, she could only nod.

Then they rounded a bend in the road, startling a small flock of Canada geese into flight against the hazy blue sky. Ryder's gaze followed for a moment, his expression tense when he returned his attention to the road. And Mel thought, *Ah*.

"It takes a long, long time," she said at last, "before you stop feeling like there's a blunt instrument lodged inside your chest. Before everything stops reminding you of them."

A faint smile stretched his lips. "Dang. You're good."

"Familiar territory. I'd recognize it blindfolded."

Another two, three fields zipped past before he said, "For what it's worth, the constant pain faded months ago. But it still has a nasty way of blindsiding me when I least expect it. The geese…Deanna loved them. Noisy, obnoxious birds with no sense of personal space whatsoever, barely one step above pigeons as far as I'm concerned, but…" Smiling, he shook his head, then blinked, too quickly. "We wanted three kids. One of each, she used to joke."

"Sounds like my kind of gal."

"I think you would have liked her very much. She was very down-to-earth, despite—"

When he stopped, Mel's eyebrows lifted. "Despite what? Oh. Being pedigreed, you mean?" She scratched the side of her neck. "Bet your mother adored her."

"Although I had no idea when we met," he said, and Mel didn't miss that he'd sidestepped her last comment. "She did a lot of volunteer work with wildlife conservation in the area. One of the other volunteers got hurt one day, and she brought him to the clinic, the pair of them wet and filthy and smelling like the marsh."

"And you fell like a ton of bricks."

"Something like that."

Mel laughed, picturing Ryder getting emotionally side-swiped by this mud-drenched goddess reeking of rotten eggs. "I take it she cleaned up okay?"

"Yes," he said after a moment. "She did."

Mel's eyes filled. "I'm so sorry, Ry."

"Thanks."

Several more seconds passed before she said, "And you really haven't dated since?"

"No. Oh, once or twice my mother foisted someone on me and I took her out to dinner, but I'm sure I would have won a Worst Date award. Even though intellectually I know I need to move on."

"Meaning your parents are pressuring you to."

"No. Well, maybe a little."

"Hey." She poked one finger into his arm. "You'll know when the time's right. And nobody can know that *except* you. So don't you let anybody bully you into something you're not ready for, you hear me?"

"Yes, ma'am," he said, his grin coming out from hiding.

"And in the meantime…you can be as much of an uncle to Quinn as you want."

His eyes cut to hers. "You sure?"

"Yes."

"I'd like that. But…" He paused. "I can only accept if you're part of the package."

Mel started. "I…? What?"

"I'd forgotten how easy it is to talk to you. I know, I know—we can't go back to what we had. And I don't want to." He glanced at her, then away. "But what we've got now…well. I like it. And I'd like to keep it. If that's okay with you."

"Even long distance?" she said softly.

"Whatever works for you. And Quinn."

Sighing, Mel faced front. "I suppose that depends on all the other stuff. And according to your father," she said, figuring she might as well go for it, "there's apparently more 'stuff' than I'd at first realized."

"Like…what?"

"Not sure. Since all he said was, that there were 'things'—" she made air quotes "—he wasn't at liberty to discuss. About your mother."

His voice lowered. "Really?"

"Yeah. Got any idea what he's talking about?"

"None." Ryder flexed his hands on the wheel. "Although I suppose you want me to find out."

"Oh, right. And how exactly do you propose to do that?"

"Ask her?"

Mel laughed. "This is your mother we're talking about—"

"Mel. As insane as this all is, it's also the first thing in nearly a year that's made me focus on something besides myself. And I'll do anything in my power to make this right. You have my word."

It'd been so long since she'd felt as though someone was truly and completely on her side. Not since she'd been a kid, in fact, and she'd known she could trust Ryder with her life. As far as that went, he was right—nothing had changed, even if both of them had. But as she said, "Thanks," and he nodded, determination sharpening a jaw that didn't need any more definition, she felt a wave of something trickle through her that she sure as hell hoped was gratitude.

Because anything else would be disastrous.

"So I take it you had a good time?"

Bouncing a little in the slippery red booth after the waitress took their order, Quinn nodded for Dr. David, even though her head felt like it was about to explode from all the questions inside it. 'Cause you better believe, after what she'd overhead? She'd been watching her mom and Ryder's dad *real* closely. Especially when Ryder had taken her away so Mom and Dr. David could talk—like *that* wasn't obvious, geez—Quinn had kept sneaking peeks at them. Not that she could tell anything, although Mom had seemed kind of nervous, maybe. But then Mom had let Quinn go with Ryder's dad, right? So how bad could it—whatever "it" was—be?

"On the boat, you mean? Yeah, it was cool."

"Good," Ryder's dad said with a smile as he dug his phone out of a pocket over his chest, texting something before putting it away again. "Thought you might like it."

"Mom'll probably make me write a report, though," she said, making a face, and he laughed, sounding a lot like Ryder.

"Ry tells me your mother homeschools you."

And why she couldn't just do what April said, and tell Mom what she was feeling, she didn't know. But it was like the words would get stuck in her throat or something. Like she wanted to know what was going on, yeah, but she was also scared of what she might find out. And besides, it wasn't like there was any guarantee Mom would tell her the truth, anyway, right?

"Yeah. Since I was four."

"Have you ever been to regular school?"

"Once. When I was in the second grade. Because Mom thought maybe I was missing out by not being around other kids."

"Were you?"

She shrugged. "Not really. For one thing, I like being by myself—at least sometimes—and for another I was already so far ahead of everybody else that I kept saying stuff that made them mad. Not on purpose, I don't mean that. But like I'd be all surprised when they didn't know how to do something I'd known for a year already. Not the best way to make friends," she said on a sigh. "And anyway, I was bored to *tears,* and the teacher didn't really know what to do with me, so Mom asked me what I wanted to do and I said I wanted to go back to being homeschooled."

Dr. David's phone buzzed; he pulled it out, checked the message, then set it on the table in front of him just as the waitress brought them their ice cream. Wow. That was a lot of whipped cream. Not that this was a problem.

"What's your favorite part about being homeschooled?"

Quinn picked up her spoon and dug in. "Not having to get up early," she said, and Dr. David laughed again. "And staying in my pj's, if I want. Sometimes Mom does, too. Because that's how we roll. This," she said, jabbing the spoon toward the ice cream, "is seriously excellent."

"It is that—"

"Can I ask you something?"

Dr. David gave her one of those oh-heck-now-what looks like she'd seen on Mom's face a gazillion times. "Sure."

And to be honest, for a second Quinn thought about asking him straight out about what she'd overheard. Only, for one thing, she wasn't really sure what to ask. Or how. And for another, whatever it was, she was pretty sure she needed to hear it from Mom. But there was this one question about to burn a hole in her brain, and she figured if anybody could answer it, it would be Ryder's dad.

"Mom says she and Ryder were friends when they were kids."

"They were. Very good friends."

"Like, best friends?"

The doctor rubbed a knuckle over his chin. "I think Ryder thought of your mother like a little sister. It made him feel good, having her to look out for. Take care of."

"Oh. He didn't have any brothers or sisters of his own?"

Dr. David went real still, except for twisting his spoon around and around over his sundae. Hot fudge, like hers. "Actually, he does. A younger brother. Jeremy."

"So how come he didn't play with him? Instead of my mother?"

The doctor's eyes bounced to hers, then back to his ice cream. And there it was again. That weird feeling. Like she was playing the hot-cold game with the truth, and she was getting really warm.

"They had—have—very different personalities. They never did get along particularly well. That happens sometimes. In families."

Quinn spooned a gooey spoonful of ice cream into her mouth, barely catching the runny fudge before it dripped all over her chin. "So what you're saying is," she said around the coldness, "Ryder liked my mother better than his own brother?"

The doctor's mouth moved, like he couldn't decide whether to smile or not. "In many ways, yes. I suppose he did." Now he frowned. "Is that what you wanted to ask me?"

"What? Oh, no. Sorry. I guess I got off track. Mom is always on my case about that, she said if I'd ever actually finish the conversation I started she'd fall over in a dead faint. But anyway, that couldn't've been my question, anyway, right? Since I didn't even know Ryder had a brother. Does he live here?"

"No. In New York. We don't see him much."

"How come?"

"Just living different lives, I suppose."

"That is so sad. I mean, maybe because it's only Mom and me, since my grandmother died, but I think it would be so cool to have more family. *Anyway,* sorry, I did it again—my question *is*...do you think Ryder and my mom maybe like each other more than just friends?"

The doctor half coughed, half laughed. "And there's a question I don't dare answer, because no matter what I say I'm bound to get in trouble." He looked up as the door jangled open behind her, then back at Quinn. "But how would you feel if they were?"

"Me? I think that'd be the coolest thing ever," she said on a sigh, mushing her ice cream so the fudge sauce got all mixed in. "And since they're friends already, it sorta feels like a no-brainer, if you ask me. That they'd get together." She grinned. "And then I could stay here and you and I could go do all that cool birding stuff, huh?"

For the first time, Dr. David's face relaxed. "That would be nice. Very nice." Smiling, he lifted his glass of water, like Mom would do with the sparkling cider on holidays. So Quinn picked hers up and toasted him back as he said, "Here's to everybody's dreams coming true."

Giggling, Quinn clinked glasses with him, then concentrated on what was left of her sundae, on feeling *good*, for once, good enough that the spooky feeling was almost gone.

Although the questions? They weren't going anywhere.

Lorraine doubted Quinn had seen David's glance over her head when the child refocused on her sundae, her gingery curls bobbing in time with her swinging feet. Just as she clearly hadn't seen the brief flicker of surprise in David's eyes when she came in, lifting a finger to her lips before sliding into a booth far enough away to not be seen, but close enough to observe. To listen.

He probably didn't know what to make of it, since low key had never been her style. After all, what was the point in arriving someplace if people didn't *know?* Not this time, however. Goodness, she'd even dressed in all beige, as though to become as invisible as possible.

All the better to get her heart shredded, she supposed. Even more than it already was.

Truth be told, when David had first texted her, telling her where they were, giving her the opportunity to change her mind, she'd texted back, *No way.* Except curiosity nagged at her until finally it melted the fear. Or at least softened it enough to push past it. So here she was, shredded heart and all, observing her grandchild—the bright, funny, forthright grandchild who reminded Lorraine so much of herself she could barely take it in—she'd sworn never to lay eyes on. The child she'd tried so hard to forget.

Except she hadn't. Not even for a moment.

The waitress came; Lorraine ordered coffee, even as she found herself giving grudging props to Melanie for raising the girl on her own. How well she'd obviously done, how she'd clearly refrained from contaminating the child with what had to have been her own asperity about…circumstances.

Remorse battering her psyche like hurricane-churned surf at a seawall, Lorraine slowly pressed a fist to her chest as her soul cried out for the child, images flashing of shopping trips to New York, of debutante and engagement parties, of a lavish, early summer wedding in their backyard…

All fantasy, of course, she thought with a rude thud as she crashed back to earth. Because it was too late, wasn't it—?

She sucked in a little breath.

Honestly, the answer was so obvious, so simple, she couldn't believe it had taken this long for it to come to her. Although she didn't suppose that, relatively speaking, it had taken so long at that. Especially since, once it did, the plan practically exploded in her thought, full-blown.

And with the plan came peace. A sense of having regained her footing, of once more being in control. Because for as long as she could remember, it had always been about The Plan. Naturally The Plan changed according to the needs of the moment, but Lorraine had never been someone given to simply "letting" things happen. That was pure foolishness, as far as she was concerned.

But at least this plan, she mused when the coffee arrived and she removed a couple dollars from her purse to pay for something she had no intention of drinking, should not only make everyone happy, for once, but—and here was the best part—as far as she could tell had already been put into motion years before.

And not by her.

Amazed by her own brilliance, Lorraine dropped the bills on the table, blew a kiss to her husband, and slipped out as unobtrusively as she'd arrived.

Kiss her.

Kissherkissherkissherkissherkissher….

Yeah, it'd been pretty much like that for the past hour or so. Why, Ryder had no idea. Okay, not entirely true. Considering how firmly Mel had been kicking his grief in the butt all afternoon he probably wanted to kiss her out of sheer gratitude, if nothing else.

Which wasn't entirely true, either.

They'd finished up with Moses and were headed back to town. How the old man had recognized her when he rarely recognized Ryder anymore was a mystery in itself. But damned if his bleary, yellowing eyes hadn't lit up when, smiling, Mel had leaned over to give him a hug, then squatted at his knees, tightly holding his gnarled, trembling hand while he rambled on piecemeal about things that had happened years ago…

"Feels like another storm's coming in. The temperature's dropped," she said beside him, hugging herself.

Underneath her breasts.

Fine. He was horny. And lonely. And so bleeping tired of being miserable. And lonely. And horny. And Mel was funny and sexy without even trying, and underneath her grumpiness had a heart as big as her boobs—bigger—and made him laugh, dammit, and how long had it been since he'd laughed without feeling like he was playing the part of a man who was coping just fine, thank you?

"Yeah, looks like," he said, peering up at the glowering sky and away from Mel's…attributes.

But the thing was, wanting to kiss Mel didn't mean he still didn't miss Deanna. Or that being around Mel obliterated the pain, even if it had seemed to recede a bit more than usual. Like the tide.

Which always returned, didn't it?

Then she sighed, making the breasts rise like warm dough—no way to miss it without looking completely to his left—and Ryder thought, *I am a terrible, terrible person.*

A chill rippled through the car; Ryder reached out to punch on the heat. "You warm enough?"

"Me? Yeah, this fleece stuff is warmer than it looks. How about yourself?"

He grimaced at the windbreaker that had seemed more than adequate that morning. "Freezing. In fact, do you mind if we stop by my house so I can grab another jacket? It's on the way."

"'Course not."

"You sure? I know you want get back to Quinn."

Silence reverberated between them for a moment before she said, "It's okay. *I'm* okay." She laughed a little. "And I'm sure Quinn's more than okay. Although your dad's brain cells might be slightly crispy around the edges by now."

"Can't imagine who she gets the chatty gene from," Ryder said, grinning, feeling almost…okay. Normal. Even when Mel squawked.

Especially when Mel squawked.

A few minutes later he pulled up in front of the smallish, gabled concoction he and Deanna had bought two years ago, wondering when—if—the time would ever come that he could look at the house and not feel the pang of unrealized dreams. Mel angled her head to study the place for several seconds before slowly nodding.

"I like it," she said. "It's very 'you.'"

Us. It was supposed to have been very us.

He pushed open his car door. "I'll only be a sec, you can stay here—"

"Like hell," she said, getting out and starting up the flagstone path toward the hundred-year-old, beige-and-white two-story house, the soft denim of her jeans perfectly molding to her shapely bottom, and lust flared. *Whoosh.*

Embrace the horniness, the voice said inside him, and he literally bit his cheek to staunch the thought. Except…

What was, was.

"It's a work in progress," Ryder said, catching up. "I'm doing a lot of the renovation myself and I only have nights and weekends."

"Then I'm even more impressed," Mel said as he reached around her to unlock the front door, catching another whiff of the scent that had been driving him crazy for hours, and his gut cramped again, from longing, from grief, from the guilt slicing him to shreds.

But instead of moving out of his way Mel looked up at him, her eyes soft with understanding, her mouth tilted. A full mouth. Some might even call it luscious, all dewy with the pink lipgloss she'd smeared on in the car after they'd left Moses.

Kill. Him. Now.

"As I recall," she said, "you barely passed woodshop in middle school."

He pushed the door open. "You remember that?"

"It's downright scary, the vast assortment of useless crap stuffed in my brain," she said, stepping inside. "It's worse than my grandmother's house in there…ohhh, nice." She unzipped her fleece hoodie, making herself—and her breasts, and her shiny mouth—right at home. Hips swaying, she crossed to the brick fireplace over freshly varnished oak floors, skimming her fingers over the matching, refinished wood mantel. "Wow. This is *gorgeous.* You stripped it yourself?"

"All twelve coats. And yes, it was hell, thanks for asking."

She chuckled, then slid her hands into her back pockets, lifting her eyes to take in the dove-gray walls, the trio of white-paned windows along the back overlooking a serene, duck-infested tidewater marsh in the distance—the house's main selling point, according to Deanna, Ryder thought on another pang.

"You bought this for her, didn't you?" Mel said, and Ryder's pulse tripped.

"We bought it together, yes."

"And yet, you kept it."

"Yeah," he breathed out. "Although I can't tell you how many times I came this close—" he lifted his hand, thumb and forefinger pinched together "—to listing it. How long it took before I could even set foot in the place without…." He shook his head, his throat closing up.

"I'm sure," Mel said, so much tenderness in her voice, and Ryder thought he would expire from wanting to press close all that warmth and generosity. "And you used the reno as therapy, right?"

"Something like that. Figured I should have something more to show for it than a pile of canceled checks."

She gave him a thumbs-up, then inspected the white wainscoting it'd taken him hours to get right. "After my father died, my mother launched herself into I don't know how many 'projects,' anything and everything to keep her distracted. And when we moved to Baltimore it only got worse, when she finally had a place of her own to decorate however she chose. How much of the house is done?"

"Just downstairs. And…the master bedroom."

She turned, giving him that inscrutable look. "It still hurts, doesn't it?"

"Dammit—how do you do that? Read my mind?"

"Read your face, you mean? Seriously, Ry, it's a fabulous house, but…if it's causing you this much anguish maybe you *should* ditch it. Not that this has anything to do with me—"

"More than you might think," he said, releasing another breath when her eyebrows lifted. "When the sheriff came to my door that night…it was like something broke inside me. Yes, I'm mending, but a lot more slowly than I'd ever imagined. But at least I'd actually gotten to the point where I could walk through the front door and not hear Deanna's voice, or imagine her looking out the window, or sitting on the floor with a bunch of paint samples spread out in front of her. But then, today, being with Quinn…"

He finally grabbed his canvas coat off the rack by the front door. "All those conversations Dee and I had, about having kids…the plans we had… Crap, I hate sounding like this." A short, sharp laugh escaped from his throat. "*Feeling* like this."

Mel took a couple of steps closer. "And who's to say you won't fall in love again? Get married, have those kids—"

"Mel, stop. Please."

"Sorry," she muttered, rezipping her own jacket, jerking when his hand closed around her arm.

"No, you don't understand…" But then, how could she, when he didn't, either?

Ryder sank onto the Shaker bench by the front door, the one they'd found at some flea market or other, his head in his hands. Where it still was when he sensed Mel kneel in front of him, just as she had with Moses. After a moment she reached up and tugged his hands away from his face, her earnest, perplexed expression threatening to rip him in two.

"Hey. Talk to me."

"You've got to get back—"

"Not immediately. What's going on?"

"I can't—"

"Don't even give me that. If you can't be honest with me, then who?"

A raw laugh scraped his dry throat before he met her gaze. "It would appear I have the hots for you so badly I can barely think straight."

And with that, Mel's hormones exploded into flight like a bunch of hyper, hungry, woefully confused moths. Then she burst into laughter.

"You brought me here to have your wicked way with me?"

"*No!* God, no! Why would you even think that? And stop laughing!"

"Ohmigod, Ryder, you're beet-red!"

"It's not funny, Mel!"

"Sorry, Mr. I'm-always-in-control. It's freaking hysterical!"

His gaze bored into hers. "I did not bring you here to have sex with you."

"But you sure as heck thought about it."

After a second or two, he groaned again, then collapsed against the wall behind the bench, his fingertips pressed into his eyelids. "Only about five hundred times."

"Wow."

His hands dropped to his lap. "You really had no clue?"

"None. Then again, I wasn't exactly looking for clues, either. I mean, after our conversation in my grandmother's kitchen, I thought...well. That it was sort of a non-issue?"

"I said I found you appealing."

"*And* that you had no intention of acting on it. So, uh, I take it things have changed?"

His mouth clamped shut, Ryder pushed a long, shaky breath through his nose. "I'm so sorry."

"For being human? Please." He grunted. "Poor baby. How long has it been?"

"Long enough for me to act stupid, apparently."

"*Thinking* is not acting, Ry."

"Not much difference in my book."

Still on her knees, Mel rested her folded arms across his thighs. Thought really, really hard about where to take this. If anywhere. Because either this was an unexpected opportunity she'd kick herself for if she let it go, or a temptation she'd kick herself for if she didn't. No way of telling.

"So what you're saying is, the numbness has worn off. And now everything's..." She fought a smile and lost. "Prickling."

"Not helping, Mel."

"But..." *What the hell, right?* "I...could."

On what sounded like a tortured laugh, Ryder finally

curled forward, capturing her hands in his to tuck against his chest. "Except that would be…" My goodness, *such* a big sigh. "Beyond wrong."

"Depends how you define 'wrong'."

"Mel, I'm—"

"Still mourning Deanna. Got it. No, I swear. I know exactly what this is. Or, more to the point, it isn't. And…oh, for crying out loud—"

Without further ado Mel shifted, gripped his shoulders and laid one on him.

Or tried to.

Clearly startled, Ryder reared back. Frowning. "What are you doing?"

"It's called kissing. Strike a chord, maybe?"

"But—"

"Ryder. One—you know you want to, and two—good news! I'm not sixteen anymore."

"But…" He frowned even harder. She considered telling him his face was going to freeze like that. "But it's *you*."

"Yeah, it's me. Who you just admitted to lusting after, oh, ten seconds ago? And more good news!" She flung out her arms. "I'm okay with that. So pucker up, buster. And if it *does* feel bizarre—because I suppose that's always a possibility, although frankly I'd be surprised—then we'll know and you can stop tormenting yourself." She skootched closer on her knees. "Ready?"

The trembly smile only marginally mitigated the horror in his eyes. "You're insane."

"Goes without saying." She tapped her mouth. "Lips. Here. *Now*—"

The last word was swallowed up—pretty much literally—when he finally booted those pesky qualms and planted one on her for the history books.

Wow. Pent-up volcanoes had nothing on this guy.

And yes, it was everything she could have wished for. And more. All that fantasizing as a kid, about what his mouth would feel like pressed to hers, didn't even begin to compare to the mind-blowing reality. Lordamercy, those poor moths didn't know what to do with themselves.

And yet, Mel mused, shortly after he'd lowered her to the hooked rug in the entry way and their tongues had become intimately acquainted, and despite his pounding heartbeat underneath her palm, we weren't talking wild and wooly, either. Oh, no, homeboy knew exactly what he was doing. And since Mel did, too...well, this was the most fun she'd had in months.

And all they were doing was making out.

For now, she thought with a mental eyebrow waggle as his hand wandered close enough to the outside of one breast to make her hoo-hah quiver in hope. And it was more than evident that she had his *full* attention.

Finally Ryder lifted his head and frowned into her eyes. Mel frowned back. *"What?"*

"It wasn't bizarre."

"Damn me with faint praise, why not?"

Finally the frown eased. A little. "Actually...I liked it. A lot."

"Yeah? Me, too. You kiss good, Caldwell. *Real* good."

That merited a slight grin. Along with—still—no small amount of uncertainty around the eyes, but she'd take whatever she could get. "You, too."

Palming her stomach, Mel propped the back of her head in her other hand. "So you wanna fool around or what?"

He sighed. "I don't know."

"Oh, but I think you do."

"It's not that easy, Mel."

"Only because you're making it complicated. Ryder," she said when he looked away. "I think it's pretty obvious we both need an outlet. Desperately, if that smooching session was anything to go by. So that's all this is. Or will be. Friends helping each other out."

Slowly, his eyes swung back to hers. "This from the woman who a week ago wasn't even sure if she wanted to have dinner with me."

"What can I tell you, things change."

Again with the intense gaze. "You could really put all the other stuff aside?"

"You mean, the family issues? First off, none of that is between us. It never was. Second, it's not often I get to do something just for myself. And I'm guessing you don't, either. So this is for us, okay? Has nothing to do with anyone else. And so help me, if you even *think* of saying you're afraid of hurting me, I will smack you. You don't have to protect me anymore, *capice?*"

Then she reached up to skim a fingertip down that lovely, scratchy, oh-so-male cheek, and his eyes darkened, making her shiver so hard she nearly fell apart right there and then. Pitiful. "S-so. You good to go?"

Blowing a soft laugh through his nose, Ryder grabbed her hand to press a kiss into her palm—uh, yeah, more shivering—then arched one eyebrow. "In fifteen minutes?"

"Right now, sweetcheeks? I'd be good with five."

Laughing softly, Ryder got to his feet and hauled her to his.

And did not lead her upstairs.

"You are so dead," she muttered, only then he took her face in his hands and kissed her again—a nice, long, deep one, too—confusing the hell out of her.

"What—?"

"I need to think about this, for one thing. And for another, I can't do that to you."

"Oh, honey, you can do anything you like—"

"No, I mean…" Somehow he managed to chuckle and sigh at the same time. Talented. "Do you cut corners when you're making one of your fancy dishes?"

"Depends on how much of a hurry I'm in. Because sometimes good enough is, well, good enough."

So what does the turkey do? Wrap her up all nice and close against that warm, solid, soapy-scented chest. Honestly. "You're not making this any easier."

"Neither are you, buster."

He let her go to scoop his coat off the floor where it had landed somewhere along the way, then hunched into it. "And maybe I think you deserve more than 'good enough.' Even though…" He shook his head, then opened the door for her. Frowning.

With an award-worthy eyeroll, Mel plopped her wrists on his shoulders. "Even though this would only be about stress relief. Well, lemme tell you something, bub—if you make love half as well as you kiss, I will count myself one of the luckiest women on the planet. Get it?"

Then—hallelujah!—the doofus smiled. "I think this is what's called a paradigm shift."

"Heck, yeah," Mel said, and kissed him again, and moths went wild.

Normally Quinn was okay with helping Mom make dinner. But after two rainy days where there'd been nothing to do except school stuff and help Mom clean out stinky closets, when the sun finally did appear she was so antsy Mom told her to go outside, for heaven's sake, before she drove her and April—who'd gotten back from Richmond that morning—nuts. Now, sitting with her legs dangling over the edge of the still wet dock behind the house, Quinn squinted against the bright orange rays of the setting sun as the wind gripped her neck, making her shiver.

There he was again.

He was standing on the shore, with the dog, close enough to get a halfway decent look. She'd seen him maybe twice more after that first time, but always from the window or back porch, too far away to talk to. Now she could see he was older than she'd first thought. Taller, too.

He was also looking straight at her, the sun turning his light hair a weird pumpkin color.

"You live here now?" he called out.

"No, just visiting," Quinn yelled back, although she wished that weren't true. The little town with all the really old houses and shops and stuff, and being able to see so much sky, and the way the water changed colors…she felt like she belonged here. And she didn't care what was or wasn't going on between her mom and Ryder's parents; she really liked Ryder's dad, too. Then she remembered the boy. "You can come out here and talk to me, if you want. So we don't have to keep yelling at each other."

So he did, to sit cross-legged on the dock with the dog between them—who was big and black and smelly and kept trying to lick Quinn's face, making her laugh.

"Bear! No! Sit!" The boy grabbed the dog's collar, shoving his butt down to the wood. "Sit!" He sat, sorta, but like he had electricity going through him, his tiny yellow eyes fixed on Quinn as he about wiggled out of his glossy black fur.

Finally the dog calmed down, at least enough for them to introduce themselves. The boy's name was Jack, he said, he was eleven and went to the Friends' school in town, and he lived five houses away—he pointed to a big, blue house with a smaller boat than Ryder's dad's, docked at its own marina—but his father was in congress, so he lived part-time in Washington.

"What about your mom?"

A couple seconds passed before Jack said as he petted the dog, "She died. A year ago. So it's just me and Dad. Well, and my grandparents. What happened to your hand?"

"What? Oh." Quinn glanced at the stitches, which itched something awful but Ryder said they had to stay in for two weeks. "I cut myself on a nail. It doesn't hurt or anything."

"Can I see?"

"Sure."

She stuck out her hand; Jack stared at the wound for a couple of seconds, then nodded. "So are you here with your parents?"

"My mom, yeah. I don't have a dad. In fact, I don't even know who he is."

"Really?" His hand went still in the dog's fur. "You mean, like your mother went to a sperm bank or something?"

Quinn frowned. "What's that?"

"You really don't know?" When she shook her head, he lifted his chin, like he thought he was hot stuff for knowing something she didn't. "It's this place where women go if they wanna have a baby but don't have a husband. There's these two kids in school, their mom did that. So they don't know who their dad is, either."

"Huh." Quinn thought a moment. "I don't know, but maybe. I'll have to ask her." Although if that was true, why didn't Mom simply say that? Honestly.

They were both quiet for a moment before Jack said, "It sucks, not having my mom anymore," and Quinn felt all squirmy inside, although she didn't know why.

"I bet it does. I mean, I never knew my dad, so I can't miss him, but my mom…I can't imagine…" She couldn't even finish the thought, it made her so sad. "I'm sorry. For you, I mean." And she was, even if he did act like a know-it-all. Jack shrugged, and Quinn decided they needed to get off this subject. "Do you know Dr. Caldwell?"

He gave her a funny look. "Which one? The old one or the young one?"

"Young."

Frowning, he picked up a stick that'd blown onto the dock and tossed it into the water and the dog jumped in after it. "Yeah. Why?"

"I think maybe my mother likes him. You know, like a boyfriend."

Jack's eyebrows got all bunched up. "Why are you telling me this?"

Quinn's face got all hot. Because he had a point—why on earth *was* she talking about this? Especially to a complete stranger? Ohmigosh, Mom would *kill* her.

"I don't know. Forget it, it was stupid—"

"Does he like her back?"

She turned to see Jack looking at her with this real strange expression. Huh. "I don't know," Quinn said, sighing. "It's not like anybody tells me anything."

"Tell me about it." The stick clamped in his jaws, Bear swam toward the shore, climbed out, shook, then trotted back to lay the dripping stick on Jack's lap. Jack threw it again, then curled his hands around the edge of the pier, watching the dog. "Dr. Ryder was supposed to marry my cousin."

Quinn's jaw nearly dropped off. Holy cannoli. "You're kidding? What happened?"

"She died. In…in the same car crash that killed my mother."

"Ohmigosh…" Feeling totally dumb and helpless, but mostly dumb, that she'd wanted to change the subject only she'd managed to bring it right back again, Quinn looked out over the water, shivering. Then, not knowing why, she reached for Jack's hand. His head jerked around, looking all shocked and stuff, but he didn't let go. At least not right away. And when he did, to throw the stick *again,* he said, "Um…you wanna come to my house sometime and play Mario Kart?"

"Sure. Okay," she said, and he gave her a shy grin, making her feel like maybe she wasn't so dumb, after all.

And what a fun two days *this* had been, Mel wearily mused as she dropped into a chair at the kitchen table with a mug of tea and her laptop after finally getting her daughter to bed. The hell that was sorting through Amelia's closets, no word from Ryder and—the cherry on the sundae that was her life—Quinn's little bombshell query a half hour before.

Yeah, it was gonna take more than a cup of tea to settle her nerves after that one, she thought, wincing as she scalded her tongue. As for Ryder…she could hardly fault him for wanting time to think things through. This was a big deal, after all. Like he said, paradigm shift. And the dude never had been given to paradigm shifting just because. Of course there was also the distinct possibility he'd realized he wasn't *that* crazy. Which was fine. Really. She would, however, appreciate a head's up sometime before she turned eighty.

April's schlumping into the kitchen in a pair of baggy jammies distracted Mel from her self-torture enough to notice the adorable little frown lines marring that perfect brow. Frown lines that hadn't been in evidence earlier.

"What's up?"

Her cousin gave a short, slightly hysterical laugh. "The inspector was here this afternoon. While you were at the grocery store." Her mouth pulled down at the corners. "There's termites."

"Seriously?" Mel glanced around as though the critters were lined up on the window ledges, smacking their lips, then back at April. "Why didn't you say anything earlier?"

"Because I guess I needed time to process it all."

"All?"

"The heating system has to be replaced, too. Along with the roof."

"And thank you, Nana," Mel mumbled, then reached over to rub her cousin's shoulder. "You *sure* you want to take this on?"

That got a sigh. "At least I can afford to make the repairs. But the house's condition is really going to impact the appraisal—"

"Which it would have, anyway, even if we'd decided to sell it as a fixer-upper. Right? No sense in you paying for the repairs and *then* buying us out."

April smiled. "You're too good to me."

"And don't you forget it."

She laughed, then said, "But I really wanted to get the place up and running by Christmas, to take advantage of the Festival. Now..." She gave a tiny, defeated shrug.

"There's always my idea," Mel said.

April laughed—sort of—then shook her head. "And let the termites win? No way."

Chuckling—and declining to point out that burning the house down would not be to the termites' advantage—Mel got to her feet.

"Tea?"

"Please. And another slice of cheesecake."

Mel put the kettle on, pulled what was left of the pumpkin cheesecake out of the fridge. Yes, it was a week old by now, but any cheesecake is better than no cheesecake. *Like sex,* the termites whispered in their evil little termite voices. "This mean you have to tent the house?"

"Not sure yet. Depends on what the exterminator says. So whatcha doing?" April said with a nod toward the laptop after Mel handed her the cheesecake—which she attacked like a starving locust. Or termite—and her tea.

"Job hunting. And you might want to be careful, eat that too fast and you'll get the bends."

"I'll take my chances," April muttered around a full mouth. "Ohmigosh—I know people who'd *kill* for this."

"Not sure I'd want that on my conscience. And you'd serve cheesecake for breakfast?"

"No," she said slowly, then canted her eyes to Mel. "But I would after dinner. Since once I realized how much money I'm going to have to sink into the place I figured I might as well go for broke and turn the place back into a full-fledged inn." She lifted her fork to Mel. Staring. "With a full dinner menu."

Mel stared back. "You couldn't afford me."

"Oh, but I could. And even you have to admit Quinn's happy as a pig in slop here."

"The kid's on vacation, of course she's happy here. And that's blackmail."

"No, this is blackmail," April said, grabbing Mel's laptop, clicking a few keys, then turning the computer back to her. On which, opened in a new window, gleamed a sixty-inch, six-burner, double-oven gas stove.

In pink.

Mel gaped at her cousin, who shrugged.

"I may be little, but I'm fierce. And your pupils are dilated."

Mel blinked her pupils back to normal, then clicked away from all that gorgeousness before she weakened. "Quinn asked me tonight if her father was a sperm donor."

Now it was April's turn to gape. "Where on earth did she get that?"

"From Jack. Kid who lives a few houses down the road. Congressman's kid." At April's sorry-not-computing look, Mel said, "His mother's dead, which apparently led Quinn to share that she's missing a father. So this Jack helpfully suggested maybe I'd gone to a sperm bank, which is why I've never told her who he is."

"Holy moly. Does Quinn even know what a sperm bank is?"

"She does now," Mel said with a grimace that stretched even further when she added, "And I cannot tell you how tempting it was to just run with that hypothesis."

"But you didn't."

"No," she said, sighing heavily. "And then I changed the subject—"

"A skill at which you excel."

"—which will buy me maybe five minutes, tops. But aside from that, get this—Jack's mother and Deanna were cousins. They were killed in the same accident."

Groaning, April sagged back in her chair, tapping her fork against her now empty plate for several highly annoying seconds before saying, "So…Quinn told me about how she stayed with Ryder's father while you and Ryder went gallivanting around the countryside after the boat ride?"

"We weren't *gallivanting*. Ryder had a house call and David plied my child with ice cream."

"And you let her go?"

"I did," Mel said, trying to concentrate on the Monster.com page in front of her. With scant success, since that frickin' stove was now seared into her retinas and the make-out session with Ryder was seared into…other places.

"Oh, my word! Something happened, didn't it? Between you and Ryder? And don't you dare say 'nothing,' because your red cheeks do not lie."

Mel met her cousin's extremely amused, and equally annoying, gaze. "And this is your business, how?"

"I knew it! Oh, come on, Mel—take my mind off the termites. You wouldn't deny a poor little old widow woman the chance to live vicariously, would you?"

"Nice try. But forget it."

Her cousin's eyes narrowed. "Blythe's coming down tomorrow to show me the final drawings. And I'm not above siccing her on you."

Mel weighed that for a moment, then said, "Fine. We kissed." *Understatement.* "But it didn't mean anything." *To one of us, anyway.*

"And you're blushing again."

"Shut up—"

"So that was it? You just kissed?"

Mel waited a long time before saying. "For now," yelping when itty-bitty April smacked her forearm.

"Get out! Y'all are gonna do the deed?"

"Maybe. And you are way too excited about this."

"And you're not? Mel!" April wagged her hands. "This is Ryder you're talking about—!"

"Who's still hung up on his fiancée. Remember?"

"Ohhh. Right." She sighed. "Guess that puts a different spin on things."

"You might say."

"So you'd be fine with a fling?" This said with the kind of dubious expression one might employ for, say, someone who'd just suggested sledding down Everest. On a flattened cardboard box.

"You kidding? I'd be *thrilled* with a fling."

"With anybody? Or with Ryder?"

"Yeesh, give me *some* credit."

"Just checking."

"Look, I totally get that Ry's head and body aren't in

the same place. I know that, I'm good with that, even, but I'm not sure he is. You loved your husband—you understand, right, how hard this must be for him?"

Something flickered in April's eyes before she wrapped her hand around Mel's. "I understand how hard this is for *you*."

"Me? I told you—"

"Frankly, if I was in your shoes, I don't know that I wouldn't do the same thing. But I also think you're fooling yourself, if you think you can make love with Ryder and then walk away like it was nothing. That's just not you, honey."

Back to Monster. "And maybe I've changed."

After a moment April got up to carry her plate to the sink and wash it. "Lying to me is one thing. But to yourself? That's something else entirely."

The doorbell dinged but forgot to dong. Lordamercy, was there anything in this house that didn't have to be replaced?

Sighing, Mel tromped to the door. Opened it. Fell head first down the rabbit hole that was Ryder's dark, conflicted gaze.

"I thought things through," he said.

Chapter Eight

"You're sure April's okay with sitting?" Ryder asked over his break-dancing pulse as they parked the car by the nearly deserted marina.

"Of course," Mel answered—as she'd done all three times he'd asked—even though Ryder hadn't missed her cousin's concerned gaze as they walked out the door. Yes, even though he'd also caught Mel's mouthed, "I'll be fine," a moment before. "Quinn's been dead asleep for an hour, at least. Kid's down for the count until seven."

Ryder got out of the car and was around to Mel's side before she could open her own door, grabbing her hand and hauling her to her feet, the brisk breeze blowing her bangs off her face. Moonlight speared the pewter clouds, glancing off the motley assortment of small boats languidly bobbing in the night-black water as she smiled up at him.

"You're shaking," she said, her hand soft, warm against his face. "Look, we don't have to—"

"I know. Except…I do."

She took his hand and tugged him toward the boat, their footsteps too loud against the dock. Her suggestion, not his, as though she'd understood how hard it would have been for him to take her to the house.

He helped her on board, shivering from both the chill and the anticipation. But when she tried to hug him, he shook his head.

"Not yet."

She sat beside him as he drove the cuddy out into the bay, to the group of islands they'd passed two days before, to moor at a private dock behind a house he knew had been vacant for months. Silence enveloped them, save for the gentle lapping of water against the boat's hull, the occasional hoot of an owl.

"It's gorgeous," Mel whispered. "Perfect."

Ryder cleared his throat. "I brought wine—"

"Don't need wine. Thanks."

"—and condoms."

She chuckled. "Those, we can use."

His heart jackhammering, Ryder led her into the tiny cabin, the ceiling too low for him to stand upright. He switched on a low light, a small heater, then tossed a cotton blanket across the puzzle of cushions that made up the sleeping area. Then he sat, as if not sure what came next.

Mel kneeled on the bed beside him, taking his face in her hands. "Hey," she whispered. "No pressure. I'm fine with making out. Or sitting outside and admiring the scenery, whatever works for you—"

He silenced her with a kiss, easing her onto the bed, and she opened her mouth, inviting, making sweet little noises in her throat that made him crazy, made his eyes burn—

"It's okay, touching's allowed," she whispered, and he

slipped his hand underneath her hoodie, and she jerked, laughing. "Cold!"

"Sorry—"

"No, keep going, things'll warm up soon enough…*oh*. Yes. Like that."

He responded almost immediately.

Smiling, Mel pressed one hand to his chest. "So we're good?"

When he nodded, she pushed herself up to toe off her Crocs, unzip her jeans, the rocking boat throwing her off balance as she wriggled free. On a startled laugh she grabbed the bulkhead and kicked the jeans behind her, then straddled him, pure devilment in her eyes, her grin, as she slowly unzipped her hoodie. At his undoubtedly stunned expression, she laughed.

"Worth the wait?"

"I'm a doctor, it's not as if I haven't seen…" Ryder swallowed, then laughed. "I'm speechless."

"Good thing, then, this isn't a debate," Mel said, leaning closer—oh, man—to thread her fingers through his hair before joining their mouths, her kiss soft and teasing and making him feel like a rutting teenager. Especially when her nipples got cozy with his chest and every ounce of blood in his body roared south to its happy place, taking any vestige of control right along with it.

Annoyed with himself, Ryder clamped her shoulders in some lame attempt to separate them, except Mel planted her hands on either side of his head and locked their gazes. "Hey. This is my gift to you. Whatever you want, however you want it, I'm just along for the ride. And trust me, *fast* is not a problem—"

He was naked and sheathed and inside her within seconds.

So much for not wanting to rush things.

And yet, amazingly, she cried out before he did, her fingers digging into his bare shoulders as she spasmed underneath, around, *through* him, and he buried his face in her neck, so close, aching to be closer, vaguely aware of her breath coming in short little pants, hot in his ear, and she laced her ankles at the small of his back to pull him in harder and deeper until there was only pleasure, only *this,* bright and hot and blinding.

Tears stung as he drove into her, recklessly, relentlessly, startled when she came a second time, the pulsing finally driving him over an edge he'd shied away from for more than a year.

Afterwards they lay in the dim light, a tangle of sweaty limbs and racing hearts, the boat gently pitching beneath them, until Mel broke the silence with, "Feel better?"

Ryder expelled a short laugh. "I'll let you know in a minute." He looked over to see Mel's eyes trained on his face, her expression unreadable, and shame slammed through the afterglow. His gut cramping, Ryder traced a knuckle down her cheek. "That wasn't exactly finessed."

"After a year? I should hardly think so."

"You deserve better than that."

"Oh, for the love of Mike..." Mel flopped onto her side, palming his chest. "Okay. I've got this cookie recipe that has like, I don't know, twenty steps and twelve ingredients, takes all freaking afternoon to make. Granted, the end result is to die for. But sometimes I'm all about ripping open a bag of Betty Crocker mix, adding an egg and some butter, and boom—ten minutes later, cookies. And you know what? When you want *those* cookies, *those* cookies are every bit as satisfying as the ones that take forever."

Ryder mirrored her position to rest his hand on her hip. Her firm round hip which he'd been too preoccupied before to thoroughly appreciate. Along with the rest of this *gift,* as she called it.

Carefully, deliberately, he slid his hand down her thigh, then back up over her hip again, to her waist, then her breast, warm and soft and irresistible, watching her brows lift, her mouth curve.

"So do you ever get a yen for both kinds of cookies at the same time?" he asked, and she laughed, that wonderful, throaty sound that wrapped around his wounded heart like thick, warm fleece on a stormy night.

"Oh, yeah."

"Glad to hear it," he said, shifting to kiss her.

In a spot, that, judging from her squeal, she clearly hadn't expected.

If Ryder fast was amazing, Ryder slow was…

Was…

Can I get back to you on that? Mel mused drowsily a looooong time later, cradled against that lovely, solid chest, his lovely, strong heart thumping steadily in her ear, even as she knew at any moment the endorphins would wear off and she'd realize she was in a whole heap o' trouble. Not to mention while they'd been satiating the heck out of each other all that other stuff hadn't magically resolved itself.

But until then…

Bliss.

"I suppose I should get you back to the house," he murmured, tracing lovely, lacey circles on her shoulder. "Or April will wonder."

Mel chuckled. "Wonder, nothing. April *knows*."

Although Ryder's flinch might've been nearly imperceptible if she hadn't been smooshed up beside him, all nekkid and what-all, a flinch, it definitely was. "Knows?"

"That we didn't pop out to IHOP for a late-night snack."

He sighed. "Which would no doubt account for the scathing look she gave me."

"Can April even do scathing?"

"Apparently so."

"She's afraid I'll get my heart broken. Even though I assured her that wouldn't happen." At Ryder's silence, she thought, *Oh, hell,* and shifted to look at him. Mustered up the courage to ask, "Were you thinking about her? When we—"

Dude looked thoroughly confused. "Who? April?"

"No."

His sudden grip on her arm was almost painful. "Let's get one thing straight, Mel—I have never in my life had sex with one woman while fantasizing about another. Whatever went on tonight was between us. Period."

Then she saw it. The misgiving, radiating like a damn aura.

"However…?"

He curled forward, plunging a hand through his hair, and Mel would have given almost anything to be stricken deaf at that moment. So she wouldn't have had to hear him say, "This was still probably a mistake."

"A mistake, it should be noted, it took you more than an *hour* to figure out."

He twisted to look at her, his expression ravaged. "I don't do hook-ups, either."

"Is that what you think this was? A *hook-up?*"

"Wasn't it?"

Annoyed as all hell—with him, with herself, with the whole damn situation—Mel lunged forward to search for her clothes scattered across what there was of the floor in the minuscule cabin, knocking the wind out of herself in the process. Panties and jeans found, she clumsily jerked them back on, then grabbed the hoodie.

"Okay, bub, let *me* make something clear—" she shoved her arms into the hoodie, jerked up the zipper "—while I'm more than aware that this was a one-shot deal, believe me, I don't give just anybody access to these—" she pointed to her boobs "—let alone the rest of the package. But if you don't think what we just shared was a rare and wonderful thing…well, I don't suppose I can tell you what to think, can I?"

His own clothes yanked back on, Ryder followed Mel up onto the deck. "And you being upset right now only proves how wrong it was."

Mel wheeled on him, only to lift her hands and suck in a deep breath. Then another. Before she clobbered him like she used to when they were kids. "I'm not upset because of what we did, birdbrain, I'm upset because you're being an *idiot*."

"And maybe that's my point!" Ryder shot back, then shoved out a lungful of air. "I'm sorry—"

"For *what?*"

He gave her an exasperated look. "I thought doing that…with you…would, I don't know. Purge me. Or something. Force me out of this prison I can't seem to leave even though I know I'm the one holding the key. Instead, now I know I can't *make* the doors open. And it kills me that…that I used you."

"Even though I was more than willing to be used?"

"Not sure how that makes it better. Let alone right."

"Oh, Ry, Ry, Ry…" Mel huffed out a breath, then grabbed the railing to keep her balance as the boat lurched. "You are too damn good for your *own* good, you know that? When are you going to stop shouldering the responsibility for everybody else's decisions?"

"I don't—"

"Yes, you do. You always have. I used to find it admirable. Now I just want to slap you silly."

He almost smiled. "It's just…" After a short head shake, he glanced down, then back at her. "I thought, here we are starting over, trying to figure out what we are to each other, to…to forge something solid for Quinn's sake if nothing else, and now…" His shoulders jerked with the force of his sigh. "I was afraid we'd ruined our chance at a do-over. That *I'd* ruined it."

"For crying out loud—are you *listening* to yourself? Like you said, what we are to each other and what you are, or will be, to Quinn…separate issues. So. Did you have a good time tonight?"

Ryder looked out over the water, his jaw clenching, before letting his gaze touch hers again. "Goes without saying."

"Then could you simply own that and not overthink it, for heaven's sake?"

Another several seconds passed before, at long last, his scowl relaxed. Not exactly into a smile, but at least he no longer looked as though he'd accidentally set World War Three in motion.

"I'll try," he said, and Mel released another breath.

"It's a step," she said, even as she sternly told her heart to listen up, to own her own decision, her own actions, for what they were—nothing more than simply helping out a friend in need.

That she'd known going in that *more* was not an option, so no moaning about it now.

Granted, their attempts at normal conversation on the short drive back to Amelia's house were pretty abysmal, but considering all the stuff churning in Mel's head, she could only imagine what was going through Ryder's. She could reassure him until the cows came home, but ultimately he was responsible for finding his own peace.

"You don't have to get out," she said when they pulled up in front of the house, but he did anyway. 'Cause that's the kind of guy he was.

Even took her hand when he walked her to the door, yeesh. Which did not make things *less* strained between them. Once there, however, he let go to ram his hands in his pockets, his distressed gaze steady in hers. "I can't even begin to tell you how much you mean to me," he said quietly, and her heart ka-thudded against her sternum. "How much..." He removed one hand from his pocket to drag it across his downturned mouth before slugging it back into its cave. "How much I...appreciated tonight." Could be a trick of the light, but she could have sworn his eyes glimmered. "How grateful I am it was you."

Her own smile was a little wobbly. "Kinda the point I was trying to make?"

Ryder blew a laugh through his nose. "You're something else, Mel Duncan," he said, then walked back to his car, his footsteps the loneliest sound Mel had ever heard.

And perfectly echoing her own heartbeat.

Except for the occasional fitful, fretful patch of sleep, Ryder had lain awake most of the night, becoming more irritated with each chime of the grandfather clock—another flea market find—downstairs.

Because for all the words he and Mel had tossed at each other after their little tryst, the truth—at least on his part—had deftly sidestepped them all, flitting in and out of the conversation like a ghost. Now, at some unholy hour of the morning as he poured himself a cup of brutally black coffee in the cold, half-finished kitchen, the apparition shimmered more clearly into focus. Still elusive, for sure, but whose unsettling existence he couldn't deny.

Ryder shut his eyes, not against the specter, but so he could will it more clearly into focus, despite the raging headache, and heartache, it brought with it:

That even though he knew he couldn't be what Mel needed and deserved, he wanted her. Especially after last night. Selfishly, irrationally, like a child obsessed with the idea of having something he can't take proper care of.

Because the thing was, he knew Mel too well, knew she was lying about being okay with last night's one-off. As generous as she was, she wasn't *that* generous—as her own admission about how seldom she shared her body attested, he thought with a tight grin. And *he'd* be lying if he didn't admit how much that admission had stoked his ego, even as it made mincemeat out of his already pummeled heart.

Ryder took another swig of the bitter brew, an equally bitter laugh escaping his throat as he thought of what Mel's reaction would be to his musings. At this point, "slapping him silly" seemed fitting, somehow, especially when it hit him that he'd somehow landed right where he'd been ten years ago. Why was it, he wondered, did *he* keep being what he most had to protect her from?

Irony, he thought that was called.

Although this time he couldn't turn tail and run. Nor did he want to. For good or ill he was crazy about this sleepy little town, loved how his practice here was more about people than paperwork and peddling quick "fixes" that rarely were, about being able to offer comfort when there was little else to offer. So Mel's determination not to stick around any longer than necessary was actually a godsend…and at least part of the impetus behind Ryder's resolve, that gray, gloomy morning, to settle this issue about Quinn without further delay.

The other being, of course, his promise to Mel to do what he could to fix this whole sorry mess. Even if that meant alienating his mother—not that he had a whole lot to lose there, he thought peevishly. But if what his father had intimated to Mel was true, if Lorraine was still hanging on to secrets that had in all likelihood played, or were still playing, some part in said mess, then Ryder would do everything in his power to drag them out of her, once and for all and damn the torpedoes. At least he could give Mel that.

He waited until seven, however, to call the woman who'd given him life, both to be sure she was awake and after having consumed enough caffeine to fuel the entire Eastern Shore. She answered on the fourth ring, breathing hard.

"Ry? Why on earth are you calling so early? Is everything okay?"

"I'm fine. Are you?"

"What? Oh, of course. I took the dogs for a walk, the phone was ringing when we got in, I ran to get it—"

"So you haven't had breakfast yet?"

"No. Why?"

"Thought I'd join you."

"Oh. Um, sure. Your father's gone though, he had a delivery last night—"

"That's fine, it's you I want to talk to."

"Really?" A pause. "Actually, since I wanted to talk to you, too, this is good. Don't hurry, though, I look a fright."

A half hour later, Ryder was seated at the round, whitewashed table in the breakfast room in front of a plate of Eggbeaters and toast with some supposedly heart-healthy spread. His parents never replaced Maureen and Tony, opting instead for weekly visits from yard and housekeeping services, his mother declaring it was time she learned how to cook, anyway—after a fashion—although holidays and dinner parties were always catered.

Pulled together in a pair of gray pants and a lavender sweater that clashed violently with her red hair, Lorraine sat across from him, buttering her toast and looking eerily cheerful. "This is nice, don't you think? We so rarely have breakfast together anymore." They'd rarely had breakfast together, ever, but Ryder let it go. "So why are you here?"

"To discuss Quinn," he said, and his mother's eyes shot to his. "It's time to put this whole nonsense to bed, don't you think?"

His mother took a sip of her coffee, the creamy, gold-rimmed Lenox cup rattling slightly when she set it back on the saucer. "Well. Nothing like coming straight to the point."

"I thought so."

His mother's eyes lifted to his, sharp with her customary determination. And something else, something that both caught him slightly off guard and put him on it. But before he could figure out what, she said, "I saw her yesterday."

His glass of fresh-squeezed orange juice halfway to his mouth, Ryder jerked. "Excuse me?"

"At Finnegan's. Your father texted me, told me they were there. Don't be angry," she said when Ryder's brows crashed, "I think he thought I might not get another chance to see her." In the stark morning light, her blush was unmistakable. "And I wrestled with myself for several minutes before curiosity won out over…" She paused. "Over habit. So I went. But I sat at a table a few feet away so she wouldn't see me. Or at least, so she wouldn't have any reason to guess who I was if she did."

Lorraine nibbled her toast, rubbing non-existent crumbs from her fingers when she set the piece back on her plate, then let her gaze drift out the window. "She's quite something, isn't she?"

Bowled over both by this bit of information and the wistfulness in her voice, Ryder sat back in his chair. It couldn't possibly be this easy, could it?

"Yes. She is."

She looked back at him, then lifted one hand to her hair, her diamonds glittering. "You're absolutely right, it is time to put this all behind us. I know how badly I've bungled things—"

"To say the least."

Her nostrils flared with her sigh. "When we found out Jeremy had gotten Melanie pregnant," she said, "it all seemed so wrong. On so many levels. I really did what I thought was best, you have to believe that. But had I realized…"

She glanced down at the oblivious retriever lying beside her, then back up at Ryder. "I want to know my granddaughter. I want to be her grandmother. Especially since Jeremy and Caroline have decided not to have children, and you…" She bit down on whatever she'd been about to say.

"In other words, you think Quinn's your only shot."

"I didn't say that."

"You didn't have to."

"I'm a realist, Ryder. I deal with what's in front of me, not what might be. And who knows how long it's going to take you to get over Deanna—"

"Not here to talk about Deanna, Mom," Ryder said, refusing to let her derail the conversation. Or let his own issues taint it. "Or me. And I suppose you're right—you can only work with what you're given. In fact, one of the reasons *I* want to see this resolved is because I'm already nuts about Quinn, too. But I want a real relationship with her, not one based on lies and secrets. I want her to know

I'm her uncle. However, that's not going to happen until you make things up to Mel. Yes, that's right—you want access to your granddaughter, you're going to have deal with Mel." Images flashed, receded. As did a flash-fire of longing Ryder literally swallowed down. "And me."

His mother gave him a speculative look. "So your friendship…it's back on?"

"It would seem so," he said carefully, even as guilt wrapped icy cold fingers around his heart and squeezed tight. "And whatever my role in all this is, it's as her advocate."

A smile crept across his mother's mouth. "Meaning you're my only hope for fixing this."

"Only to a certain extent. The rest is up to you."

"But she's at least amenable to the idea? That we're all on the same page—?"

"Not so fast. Yes, she's definitely ready to tell Quinn the truth, especially since she keeps asking about her father—"

"Oh, no—we can't bring Jeremy into this."

"Not sure how you think you're going to keep him out. Since not only is it Quinn's right to know whose genes she's carrying, if she finds out you're her grandparents, and I'm not her father, that kind of leaves a pretty big X factor in the equation, don't you think?"

His mother grimaced. "But his marriage…"

"Not our problem, Mom. Not *your* problem. Because guess what? Jeremy's all grown up now." At least, ostensibly. "He will deal, because he has no choice. And so will Caroline."

His mother knuckled the rapidly deepening wrinkle between her brows, then let her hand smack to the table. "God. Secrets are a bitch."

"And there's a revelation that's eleven years too late."

Her eyes shot to his. And there it was again, that look,

like some creature furtively peeking out of a door that had been locked for far too long. "Fine. Just let me…warn him."

"No, actually, I call that one."

"Ryder, no, this has nothing to do with you—"

"Oh, yeah? Jeremy damn well knew how important Mel was to me. So you can't tell me his moving in on her like a cheetah with a wounded gazelle wasn't deliberate. As angry as I am with you, that's got nothing on how I feel about him."

His mother fidgeted with her juice glass. "Then why didn't you call him as soon as you found out?"

"Because Mel would've killed me," he said, and his mother almost smiled. "But before you go planning Quinn's coming-out party, there's a huge gap between telling Quinn who you are and letting her get chummy with you."

His mother looked more chagrined than hurt. "But I… we could give the child so much—"

"To make up for what you stole from her, you mean."

His mother's cheeks colored. "I suppose I deserved that."

"Yes. You do."

"But Mel doesn't seem to have a problem letting Quinn be around your father."

"Actually, she did. But at least I think she trusts Dad. You? Not so much. And why should she?" He leaned forward. "Did you think Mel wouldn't tell me how you treated her? The despicable things you said to her? You did more than hurt Mel, Mother. You made her feel worthless. It's going to take more than a simple apology to undo this damage. In fact, the word *groveling* comes to mind. Especially when you factor in what this little fiasco cost her mother. What you did—"

"For God's sake, Ryder! I get it!" Shaking, Lorraine

pushed herself up from the table and crossed the slate floor to one of the windows overlooking the leaf-flecked backyard and the water beyond, her arms tightly crossed over her ribs. The dogs heaved themselves to their feet and followed, worried. "I panicked, Ryder. And I know that's no excuse, but…"

"But what?" When she pressed her lips together a second time, Ryder rose as well to come up beside her. "You may as well know…Dad already intimated to Mel that there's more going on here than the obvious." His mother's startled eyes shot to his. "And no, I have no clue what that might be. But whatever the truth is, you owe it to her. Because without it, you can probably kiss any shot of having a real relationship with Quinn goodbye."

"Boy's right, Lorraine," his father said from the doorway, making both of them spin around. Rumpled and obviously drained, David crossed to the buffet and poured himself a cup of coffee. "Half-assed isn't going to cut it." He lifted the cup to her. "Time to air the dirty laundry."

Blushing furiously, Lorraine glanced at Ryder, then back at her husband. "But you said—"

"What I said more than thirty years ago," his father said in the most forceful voice Ryder had ever heard, "has no bearing whatsoever on the present." Then his expression softened. "Besides…there's nothing to hold you back anymore, is there?"

Several seconds passed. Then, her eyes trained on David, as though trying to absorb strength from him, Lorraine finally said, "It doesn't have anything to do with Mel directly." Her gaze swung to Ryder. "But it does involve her grandmother. And…" She sucked in a breath. "And what I did to her."

Chapter Nine

"You do realize it's freezing out here?"

Hunkered down in one of the weather-ravaged Adirondack chairs on the equally weather-ravaged back porch, Mel aimed a wan smile from inside her fleece hood at Blythe, standing in the doorway leading from the gathering room. And who, in her ridiculously high-heeled ankle boots—how did anybody walk in those things?—and artfully draped layers looked like a damn goddess. As opposed to Mel, who felt more like a troll. With a hangover. And cramps.

"Suits my mood," Mel said, looking back over the gloomy landscape, the sky and water the same shade of leaden gray, one eagle eye trained on Quinn and her new friend. "You just get in?"

"A few minutes ago, yeah." Blythe rearranged several of the layers to sit in another chair a few feet away, a magnum of designer coffee clutched to her chest. "Can only stay a little while, though. Got an appointment in Falls Church this afternoon." Mel grunted. "Who's the kid with Quinn?"

"Name's Jack something. Father's a newish congressman in Washington."

"Wes Phillips?"

"That would be him. He seems okay." She'd actually met the boy earlier, fed him cookies, tried to get him to talk, decided the sperm bank mention was probably as bad as it was going to get. Then Mel felt a smile push at her unwilling lips. "The kid, I mean, haven't met the dad. He's off legislating. Or whatever our tax dollars pay them to do. I think they're plotting world domination," she said, watching her daughter and the boy, deep in conversation out on the pier. "The kids, I mean. Not congress. Then again…"

Blythe chuckled, then sobered. "So April tells me you went out with Ryder last night?"

Just who she wanted to talk about. The text a half hour ago had been short and to the point, that his mother wanted to "chat." Mel cut her eyes to her cousin, then sank further into her grumpfest. "April sic you on me?"

"Wouldn't be out here freezing my butt off otherwise. And I'm guessing 'went out with' is a euphemism?"

"We went out. On a boat, even."

Blythe snorted. Elegantly, of course. "And you don't think this is going to complicate things? With Quinn?"

"Not that this is any of your business, but it was a one-shot deal. An agreed-upon one-shot-deal, at that. So, no. No complications here."

"For Quinn? Or you?"

"Anybody," Mel said, staring really hard at all that gray.

Because damn her cute little hide, April had been right. If Mel had never been a fan of just-for-fun sex before, what on earth made her think she'd be okay with it now? Even with Ryder? *Especially* with Ryder—? "You tell her yet?"

"Working up to it. I've got a job interview in Baltimore next week, so before then. Depends on…things."

"As in, the Caldwells?"

Mel turned to her cousin. "I assume April's already told you that Quinn met Ryder's father. With whom she instantly bonded, natch. And the thing is…" She looked away again. "He'd make a terrific grandfather. I always did like Dr. David. There's a good guy there."

"Despite his collusion?" Mel felt Blythe's eyes on the side of her face. Or her hoodie, in this case. For a long time. Until Mel finally tugged back the edge of the hood to peer at her cousin. "What?"

"I know you always wondered about Nana's issues with Aunt Maureen."

Mel frowned. "Not really. It was pretty obvious she was irked because Mom went to work for the Caldwells—"

"Apparently it went way beyond that," Blythe said quietly as a besweatered April joined them on the porch, struggling to shut the stubborn patio door behind her before coming to stand beside Mel. Who looked from one to the other, her stomach doing a slow, nauseating turn.

"What's going on?"

"Not what's going on," April said, squatting beside Mel's knees. "What *went* on. Long before any of us were born. You remember those boxes of papers Blythe and I divided up?"

"Yeah…"

Blythe dug inside underneath her many layers of garments to pull out a brittle, yellowing piece of paper which she handed to Mel. "I found this among them."

Lorraine was stacking the few breakfast dishes into the dishwasher when the doorbell rang, making her jump out of her skin and the dogs to their feet, barking.

"Lucy! Ethel! Quiet!"

Already unnerved from the little family meeting that morning, she hurried to the front of the house, the dogs hot on her heels as the chime bong-bonged over and over, as though someone was in dire straits on the other side. David and Ryder had already left for work; the cleaning service wasn't due for another hour yet. Sunlight streamed through the clerestory windows in the two-story foyer as Lorraine opened the door…and felt every drop of blood drain from her face.

"Melanie!"

Cheeks ablaze, eyes sparking, the young woman thrust a folded-up piece of paper practically in Lorraine's face.

"You had an affair with my *grandfather?*"

Oh, hell. Not this way. Not—

"Why don't you come in…?"

"All those names you called me, all that crap you accused me of, when *you'd* slept with *someone else's husband!* So not only were you a snob, but a hypocrite, to boot—!"

"And we are not having this conversation on my doorstep," Lorraine said, attempting to regain control of the situation. She stepped aside, gesturing toward the foyer. "In. Now." The dogs wisely stumbled out of Mel's way as she torpedoed inside. "Go straight ahead—"

"To the den, got it."

Lorraine followed Mel into the same room where they'd had a certain discussion all those years ago, gesturing to the sofa. "Have a seat."

"Not necessary," Mel said as she scanned the room before spearing Lorraine with her gaze, definitely not the same cowering young woman who'd stood here then. "Nothing's changed, I see."

"More than you might guess, actually," Lorraine said, willing her racing heart to still. "I was going to tell you—"

"Yeah, right—"

"I was. You beat me to it." She looked down at the letter, still in Mel's hands. "Where did you find that?"

"I didn't, my cousin did. In my grandmother's things." At the pain and anger—every bit entirely justifiable—in the young woman's eyes, Lorraine felt her own sting.

"May I see it?"

"Go right ahead," Mel said, handing her the letter. "Although I imagine you probably know it by heart. Since you wrote it."

"Very true. On both counts," Lorraine said, carefully unfolding the brittle paper. Her best vellum, a wedding gift from some aunt or other, long dead. Her handwriting had been prettier then. Neater. Her heart cramping, she scanned the apology Amelia Rinehart had demanded she write, three years almost to the day before Ryder's birth, her promise to never see or speak to George Rinehart again. A promise she'd had no trouble keeping, as it happened—Lorraine had been stupid and George a womanizing bastard who apparently continued to assault Lorraine's dignity with pathetic regularity for the rest of his life. But while Amelia had never been able to control her philandering husband, she'd held a hatchet over Lorraine's head for the rest of *her* life.

She refolded the letter, tried to hand it back. Her arms crossed, Mel shook her head. "That's all right, you keep it."

Lorraine set it on a nearby lamp table, tapping her fingers on the polished wood surface for a moment before lifting her eyes to Mel's. "For what it's worth, it didn't last long. And I ended it."

"But who started it?"

"It was…mutual."

"My God, he must've been, what? Thirty years older than you?"

She laughed without humor. "I suppose that was part of the allure." When Mel pulled a face, she said, "I was a newlywed, very young and very lonely—David was away a lot, doing his residency at Johns Hopkins. For two years I rarely saw him, and when I did, he was distracted. And exhausted—"

"Which was no excuse to cheat on him."

"Of course it wasn't. But I was a spoiled daddy's girl who had no clue how to deal with real life," Lorraine said sharply. "Or how to resist temptation. So I made a dreadful error in judgment. One your grandmother never let me forget."

"Does Ryder's father know?"

She nodded. "I told him. Some time before your grandmother found out, in fact."

That seemed to take Mel aback. "And he—"

"Forgave me? Eventually. And a helluva lot more easily than I forgave myself."

For all Mel really, really wanted to hate Lorraine, with every passing minute the fury slipped away a little more. Not that she was ready to fall on Ry's mother's freckled neck and forgive her—woman still had a whole lot of 'splainin' to do—but damned if she wasn't beginning to see her as almost human. Who knew?

"You really never saw my grandfather again?"

"I saw him, of course. It's a small town. But spoke to him? Not one word."

Finally Mel sat on the edge of the sofa, distractedly playing with one dog's ears when the beast wedged herself between the sofa and the coffee table to lay her head on Mel's knees, her big brown eyes nearly as importunate as her mistress's. And slowly but surely things began to make sense. "But that wasn't enough for my grandmother."

"No. As far as she was concerned, what had been done couldn't be undone."

"Yeah," she conceded, "that was Nana, all right. Which was why...crap." Her face lifted to Lorraine's. "Why she could never forgive my mother for marrying my father and coming to work for you."

Lorraine walked over to a small chest by the window, littered with silver-framed family photos, her nervous toying with them reminding Mel so much of Quinn she nearly lost her breath. "Honestly, I had no idea Tony and Maureen were even seeing each other—I guess Maureen somehow knew Amelia wouldn't approve. First I found out about it was after their marriage—you know they eloped?"

"Lord, yes. Mom only told me the story a hundred times."

A slight smile touched Lorraine's lips. "My housekeeper had just retired. Maureen volunteered to replace her. And afterwards, there were...scenes."

"With my grandmother?"

"Yes. She accused me of 'stealing' your mother the same way I'd stolen your grandfather. Even though years had passed since then. And when you were born and Ryder glommed on to you..." Abruptly, Lorraine walked over to the armchair across from Mel and sank onto it, her hands tightly folded in her lap. "Your mother and I both knew Amelia would blow a gasket, but we figured the novelty would pass, that he'd soon lose interest in you. When he didn't..."

Her mouth pressed tight, Lorraine looked at her lap.

"What?"

Her eyes lifted. "Before you were born, Ryder was very quiet. Too quiet. In fact, he barely spoke. David and I took him to every specialist and child psychologist imaginable, and they all said the same thing, that there was nothing physically or neurologically wrong, that he'd outgrow it eventually. Then you came, and he blossomed. No one had any rational explanation for that, either."

Stunned, Mel froze, not moving again until the dog nudged her hand for another pat. "So that's why you turned a blind eye to our friendship."

Lorraine hmmphed. "Blind? Hardly. But within a few months of your birth he was like any other child his age. So his father and I were actually very grateful to you. And no, Ryder doesn't know, since we never said anything."

"So you're saying my grandmother never knew about Ryder and me?"

"No. Your mother and I…we made sure of it. That he never went over to Amelia's to see you girls unless she wasn't there. Or that your mother would pick you all up first when you went on your little…" She smiled. "Excursions."

"Then why the hell did you—"

"Treat you like dirt?" Lorraine's eyes glistened. "Do you have any idea how impressed I am, that you're here?"

"Excuse me?"

"If I'd had half your balls back then none of this would've happened. But I didn't. And I know you have no reason to trust me, or believe me, even, especially considering all those awful things I said to you. But when your grandmother found out what happened, she blamed me. And she threatened to tell everyone in our circle 'the truth' if I didn't send you—and your mother—away."

"Wait…" Mel frowned. "Are you saying she knew I was pregnant before you did?"

Lorraine lifted a hand to her throat, a tear slipping down her cheek. "Yes."

"How—?"

"Because your mother told her."

Her breath leaving her lungs in a rush, Mel collapsed against the back of the sofa. Holy hell. "Why on earth would she do that?"

Lorraine plucked a dog hair off her knee. "Were you aware your mother was trying to reconcile with Amelia?"

"What? No."

The older woman nodded, then sighed. "Your father's death shook your mother to the core. Which you know. And I think it hit her that she didn't have forever to repair the relationship with her mother. And that it was up to her to make it happen, if it was going to happen at all. She had no idea, of course, about…about what had happened between your grandfather and me. And I seriously doubt that Amelia told her."

"So you're saying the reconciliation took?"

"They'd begun to talk, I know that much."

"Enough that my mother felt she could confide in Nana that I was pregnant?" When Lorraine shrugged, Mel belted out a harsh laugh. "Ryder's and my friendship, she kept in the closet, yet she told her I was carrying Jeremy's kid. That's rich."

"I didn't say it made sense. And your mother…she was still grieving. I don't think she was thinking straight in those days. She probably thought there was no one else she could tell."

Mel sat up, pressing her fingertips into her temples. "And Nana used it against you."

"Basically, yes. You see, in her mind her husband's cheating reflected negatively on her almost as much as it did on him. And of course I wasn't exactly keen on anyone discovering my indiscretion. So for a long time we both had a stake in making sure the truth stayed well hidden."

"Hence her making you promise to keep quiet about it."

"Exactly. But at George's death, she discovered…" She blushed again.

"That you hadn't been the only one."

Lorraine nodded. "At which point outing me would have been no skin off her nose. But it still would have been off mine. Not that I didn't want to protect Jeremy—heaven knows I'm not laying the entire blame for this at your grandmother's feet. And I was ashamed, and mortified. But—"

"Nana held it over your head," Mel breathed out.

Hope shone in the older woman's eyes. "So you do believe me?"

"Considering that Nana never spoke to me again? Never responded when I sent her pictures of Quinn after she was born?" She felt her mouth pull to one side. "That if I'm being honest, I remember my grandfather flirting with every female over sixteen who crossed his path? Yeah. I believe you. *But...*"

Mel stood, stepping over the dog to cross to the same window, picking up a picture of darling Jeremy and his cute, perfect, Asian wife, the silver frame cold in her hand. "All this time, I've beaten myself up for *my* mistake, for the misery I caused my mother before she'd even had five minutes to come to terms with my father's death. Not that she ever admitted that to my face, but I knew. Not only that I'd disappointed her, but that my actions had forced her out of what she thought of as her own home. And she did love this place. This house," she said, glancing around before replacing the photo, then once more leveling her gaze on Lorraine. "Leaving it…it devastated her. So it might've been nice to know that it wasn't entirely my fault."

"You don't understand—as long as your grandmother was alive, I didn't dare tell anyone the truth—"

"That's bull, Lorraine. You still had choices—"

"What choices? Your grandmother...you were still a kid, you probably didn't realize how much influence she could still wield in this town. She could have ruined things for us—"

"Not to the point that you couldn't have gotten in touch with me, or my mother, at any time and explained. Apologized. If it's true Nana never told my mother what her real beef with you was, then Mom had no idea, either, why you reacted the way you did. Or, hell, why Nana never spoke to her again. If they had begun to mend fences—ohmigod, that must've devastated my mother. So at least we would have understood. *I* would have understood."

"I was ashamed, Mel," Lorraine said softly. "I still am."

"Sorry. Not good enough."

After a moment Lorraine stood and walked over to Mel, her arms folded over her ribs. "David saw to Amelia's medical needs in her last years. By then she'd alienated everyone she'd ever known. And, according to him, she died a lonely, bitter old woman with, as he put it, only her grudges to keep her company."

"That, and every item anyone's ever hawked on QVC," Mel muttered, and Lorraine sadly smiled.

"I don't want to end up like that, Mel. Having no one give a damn about me." Then she sighed. "I'd also like to think Amelia can't hurt us anymore. But now I'm not so sure."

Mel's face warmed, even as she acknowledged the thing writhing inside her, grown fat and sassy with all the nurturing and coddling and encouragement she'd given it over the years. The only thing she'd been able to count on, she realized with a start. Well, hell.

"What I don't get," she said, almost more to herself than

Lorraine, "is why Nana left me the house. If she disapproved of me so much—"

"Because it was never about you, Melanie. It was about me. And maybe, in your grandmother's head, this was her way of making it up to you? Sounds crazy, I know, but after all she let you stay with your cousins all those summers, despite her rift with your mother. My guess is she did love you, in her own way."

"As in, *bizarre* and *demented?*" Mel muttered, and Lorraine softly laughed.

"You know what I think? That your grandfather hurt her deeply. As I did David," she said, her eyes brimming again. "But at least I've done everything in my power to atone for my reprehensible behavior." Color flooded her cheeks. "To him, at least. Now all I ask is that you let me do the same thing for you. And Quinn?" She unfolded her arms, briefly reaching for Mel before seeming to rethink the gesture. "Come to dinner, both of you. Tomorrow night. Say, seven? What's Quinn's favorite food?"

"Anything but raisins, but—"

"Then it's settled," Lorraine said, finally touching Mel's arm to steer her out of the room, toward the front door.

Settled? Not by a long shot. Even if Mel had gotten some long overdue answers. Still…

"The wounds…they go pretty deep, Lorraine. So you'll understand if I still don't entirely trust you."

"Completely," she said, disappointment wrestling with hope in her eyes. "But…?"

"But…yes, we'll come to dinner. And we'll take it from there, I guess. That's all I can promise."

"That's all I'm asking. Thank you. There's something else, though," Lorraine said, finally opening the door. The dogs slithered past them to galumph around the front yard, tussling with each other in a whirlwind of leaves. "You remember what I said, about how you brought Ryder out of himself when he was a little boy?"

"Yes...?"

Concern softened Lorraine's features. "Deanna's death...it pushed him into a very dark place, Mel. Not so most people could tell, but I can. The moment you returned, though—"

"Oh, no, no—I know where you're going with this—"

"You could bring him back, Melanie. I know it, I can already see the change in him. And then...well. Who knows what the future might bring?" At Mel's eyeroll, she added, "You're a mother, too, you know what I'm talking about."

"Yes, I am. And I appreciate how much you want to see Ryder heal." Mel's eyes burned. "So do I, my heart bleeds for him to see how much he's hurting. But you can't possibly equate what happened when Ryder was five to what's going on now. No, Lorraine, I'm sorry...but it's not up to me or anyone else to bring Ryder 'back,' except Ryder. Which he and I have already discussed," she said when Lorraine's mouth popped open. "And if you're suggesting I manipulate his emotions just to, to patch together a family, even for Quinn's sake..."

Mel paused, took a breath. "I will sacrifice almost anything for my daughter, but no way in hell will I go there," she said, then finally wrenched herself out of Lorraine Caldwell's force field and walked out the door. Except by the time she got around to the driver's side door, she heard Lorraine call to her from a few feet away.

Thinking, *Oh, for pity's sake—what now*? Mel looked up, the older woman's crumpled expression at odds with the stately white portico she stood under.

"I know I'm the last person who should be giving advice," Lorraine said over the bay breeze whipping strands of red hair around her face. "Or at least, the last person you'd want to take it from. But what the hell." She stepped closer. "Don't be a fool, Melanie. Don't let the bad blood between us blind you to what could be a blessing. And for God's sake don't let your hatred of me keep you from loving my son."

For a moment Mel felt as though she'd been knocked off her feet by a fire hose. But she recovered enough to say, "Not to worry. Since it never has."

A slow, knowing smile spread across Lorraine's face. "Good for you," she said, then returned to the house, the dogs trotting loyally behind her.

Ryder gunned out of the clinic's parking lot, cursing the twenty-mile-an-hour speed limit along Main Street until he spotted Mel's Honda headed in his direction on the other side. He honked, catching her attention, then pointed toward a duo of vacant, angled parking spaces in front of the town's only decent—according to his mother—beauty shop, housed in a narrow brick building that matched the brick sidewalk in front of it.

Before she'd cut her engine he was around to her door, holding it open as she climbed out. Then he yanked her into his arms, because he wanted to, had to, even though the clashing emotions as a result nearly made him dizzy. And not in a fun way.

"Let me guess." Mel's voice was muffled against his chest. "You talked to your mother."

Ryder set Mel apart before she suffocated, getting a *What are you* doing*?* look in response. "Just got off the phone, was headed toward your place," he said, amending, at her raised brows, "Fine. April's place."

"Except April took Quinn to the bookstore," she said, nodding toward the quaint little shop down the block, tables of used books half blocking the paned storefront windows, before looking back at him.

A pointed silence ensued, the brisk air swirling around them infused with the scent of the thousands of chrysanthemums crowded into whiskey-barrel planters lining both sides of the five-block stretch.

"They're expecting you, I suppose?"

Another glance toward the shop. More pointed silence. Followed by a sighed-out, "Not really. I just thought, since…never mind." Then her eyes touched his. "But what about you? Don't tell me you left a dozen people sitting in the waiting room, wondering where the heck you are?"

Ryder smiled. Gently chafed her shoulders. "Slow morning," he said, wondering what he *was* doing, to be honest. "Dad can handle things for a little while." Then, finally, he let go to plant one palm on her car's roof. "You okay?"

She sputtered a short laugh. "Sure thing," she said, and Ryder glanced at the town square across the street, then reached for Mel's hand.

"Come on—"

"Ry, no, really, I'm fine, you need to get back to work—"

Ignoring her, he steered her through what passed for traffic this time of day—or any time of day, actually—and into the little park crowded with flame-tinged maples and oaks, toward a black wooden bench badly in need of a fresh paint job. He brushed off a stray crimson leaf and sat, dragging Mel down with him. Still holding her hand, it should be noted.

Which she let him hold, it should also be noted.

Then he sighed. "Well, *that* sure as hell didn't go according to plan." He faced her scowling profile, although whether the hand-holding had anything to do with that, he had no idea. A squirrel scampered toward them across the leaf-littered grass, tail twitching, then seemed to think better of asking for a handout and scampered away again. "I was supposed to be there. For the great confession."

"So you know? That she had a fling with my grandfather?"

"Not until this morning. And only after I dragged it out of her. How *did* you find out, anyway?"

"Dear old Nana left a paper trail," Mel said drily, finally reclaiming her hand to fold her arms over her stomach. "A letter of apology from your mother, to be exact. Blythe discovered it among a stack of papers dating back to colonial days."

Ryder leaned forward to clasp his hands between his knees. "Damn, honey. I can't imagine what you must've thought. Are probably still thinking."

"I'm still…processing. Yeah, it was a million years ago, but at least I now understand the bug up my grandmother's butt. I understand a lot of things I never did before." She paused. "Did your mother tell you the part about how she did what she did—about me and Quinn, I mean—because my grandmother held a metaphorical gun to her head?"

"Yes." Ryder straightened, took her hand again. It was cold. And a little rough. A hand that worked, that fed people. That, along with its mate, had touched and stroked and driven him insane with pleasure, he thought on a rush of heat. That had cupped his face as she'd looked deep into his eyes, tucking him inside her far more deeply than sex ever could. He hauled in a breath. "Do you believe her?"

"I don't know," Mel said on a rush of air. "And I can't exactly go to the source, can I?"

He gently squeezed her hand. Resisted lifting it to his mouth. "I can't believe you bearded the dragon in her own den."

Her soft laugh made his skin prickle. "It's called adrenaline. Act first, think later. But whatever. It's done now, nobody died, and somehow..." She frowned. "Quinn and I are coming to dinner tomorrow night. Still not quite sure how that happened."

"Mom said. She's also ridiculously pleased about it."

"That makes one of us."

"But I thought—"

"I can't help it, Ry, I can't simply slough off the last decade because your parents want me to. Which I told your mother. And yet—" she sighed again "—I keep thinking I need to tell Quinn. Before this dinner. Except whenever I actually picture myself doing it, I get sick to my stomach."

Ryder shifted on the bench to make Mel look straight at him, his hand on her knee. "And to paraphrase something a wise and very beautiful woman once said to *me,* you will tell Quinn when it feels right and not a moment before. Although considering how you stood up to the old gal, something tells me you'll do just fine."

Mel gave a weak laugh. "I don't have to live with your mother. Compared with my daughter? Lorraine is a cupcake."

"I find that hard to believe."

"Quinn carries her genes, remember?" Her mouth flattened. "Not to mention mine. Child is doomed, I tell you. As are the rest of us."

He smiled, as well, then released a breath. "There's one more thing. I'm calling Jeremy tonight. To have a little chat."

"Oh, Lord, Ry..."

"Has to be done, honey."

"I know, I know, you're right, but...yeesh."

"Wanna be in on the call?"

"Not even if you gave me my very own key to the Godiva factory."

Ryder chuckled, then said, "Any messages to pass along?"

"Yeah," she said after a moment. Or six. "That whatever comes next as far as your brother's concerned is up to Quinn. Not him, not your parents. Quinn. If she wants to meet him, I mean. Not that I'm pushing for that, believe me. But no more lies. No more pretending. And no more letting Mama save his sorry ass."

"That's my girl," Ryder said over his cell phone's vibration in his jacket pocket. A text from his father. "Ah. Guess things are getting a little clogged at the clinic."

"I'm sure. And I do need to catch up with the others."

They stood and headed back across the street, both of them with their hands in their pockets. Halfway across, however, Mel glanced up at him, almost shyly.

"Thanks."

"For dealing with my bone-headed brother?"

"Well, yes, that. But also…for being you. Being here."

"I always am, honey. Always will be. Watch out for that car—"

"Oh, for heaven's sake!" she laughed out. "I'm a big girl now. I even beard dragons in their dens, remember?"

They reached his car; Ryder beeped the RAV unlocked, opened the door. Which would be his cue to get in the car. To let her go. Instead, she'd gotten as far as a quivering-leafed ash tree a few feet away when he called out, "So you're sure you're okay?"

She turned, walking backwards. But not quickly. "Yes, Ryder, I'm fine—"

"But you call if you need anything. I mean it. Promise?"

"Promise. But I won't."

"Stubborn little minx, aren't you?"

"Minx?" She stopped, grinning, her bangs fluttering

in the breeze, and his heart kicked him in the ribs. Hard. "Who the heck says minx anymore?"

"A thirty-something dude who stole a certain young *minx's* romance novel when they were kids. And read it."

Mel screeched another laugh, then looked down at the ground for a moment before slowly retracing the few steps she'd just taken, something like apology replacing the laughter in her eyes. "I'm not being stubborn, Ry," she said quietly. "I'm being practical. I know you mean well, really. But Quinn and I…we'll face this together, and we'll face it alone—"

"*Why,* for God's sake? I'm *here,* honey. For both of you. Always will be."

"Of course you are," she said, her eyes steady in his. "On your own terms."

Ryder felt his brows slam together. "What's that supposed to mean?" Except he knew damn well what it meant, long before Mel stepped off the curb to lay a hand on his arm.

"You're the same terrific guy I always knew, okay? And I do know I can count on you. I do. At least as far as knowing you're always on my side, that you'd never knowingly hurt me, or betray my trust. And I have no doubt you'll be the best uncle ever to Quinn. But you know what?" She sucked in a big breath. "I need more than that. I need *real.* I need *now,* and I need forever. If not from you, then from someone whose heart still isn't entailed to someone else."

His mother thought secrets were a bitch? Yeah, well, so was the truth. Especially when it hits you upside the head like a cast-iron skillet. "You said you were okay with… last night," he said stupidly.

"And I was. Am," she said, her expression pleading. *Please understand. Please forgive me.* Except why on earth was *she* asking for understanding? For forgiveness?

"But being around you…" She lowered her hand to clasp his, squeezing tight. "A repeat performance is too damn tempting."

A moment passed before he said, very softly, "Can't argue with you there."

"And that, I wouldn't be okay with." One last squeeze, then she dropped his hand. "Not as things stand now. I *don't* regret last night. And I never will. But it took last night to make me realize…"

She smiled. Not the hero-worship smile of the "little sister" he once knew, but gonna-do-this-if-it-kills-me smile of an adult with the courage to make hard choices.

"Being back here did more than force me to face the past, it's also made me reassess who I am. What I really want. What I really *need*. And that, my sweet friend, is someone who is absolutely nuts about me, who loves me the way my father loved my mother. Hell, who loves me the way *your* father loves *your* mother." Her eyes filled. "Who loves me the way you obviously loved Deanna."

Cue the skillet, Take Two.

Ryder released a long, ragged breath. "Damn, Mel—"

"And you can stop right there. It's not your fault you can't be that person. But that's why I don't dare let myself count on you. Because I'm afraid I'll start seeing things that aren't there. That probably won't ever be there."

His throat working overtime, Ryder looked away to force out a humorless laugh. "The timing—"

"Sucks. I know. Hey. It happens."

He faced Mel again, lifting his hand to thumb away the wetness on her cheek. "How'd you get to be so damn amazing?"

"Copious amounts of bacon," she said, standing on tiptoe to kiss his cheek before walking off.

Chapter Ten

Standing with Mom in front of the blindingly white door with the shiny brass knocker, Quinn lifted one foot to scratch the back of her other leg through her new leggings. Which she loved, don't get her wrong—they were white with polka dots in every color you could imagine—but they were a little itchy. Not so bad that she couldn't deal, though. Besides, they looked totally awesome with her *also* new purple sweater and silvery ballet flats with the big bows across the toes, and anyway, Blythe said sometimes you had to suffer to look good. Mom had rolled her eyes at that. Blythe also said Quinn looked bitchin', but later, when Mom wasn't around.

"You ready for this?" Mom said, taking Quinn's hand, and Quinn thought, *Ready for what?* but she smiled up at her, anyway. Mom looked totally *bitchin'* tonight, too, in this amazing turquoise dress in some real soft fabric that made her look all curvy, with the cutest matching sweater with little beads scattered down the front. And high heels. *Really* high heels. With lots of straps crisscrossing the tops of her feet.

"Sure," she finally said, feeling like it was somehow up to her to make Mom feel better. Even though her mother's hand was cold and kind of damp—ick—Quinn didn't pull away. Because it was pretty obvious how nervous she was. Which Quinn guessed had something to do with Ryder. Again. Or still. She wasn't sure which.

She and April had come out of the bookshop yesterday right when Mom kissed Ryder on the cheek, and after he'd gotten in his car and driven away Mom had noticed them, smiling all fast like everything was good when *anybody* with half a brain in their head could see it wasn't. Then she'd suggested they all go to the outlet mall nearby, because she and Quinn had been invited to dinner at Ryder's parents' house and they could *not* go looking like a couple of bums, she said.

Instead of, for once, maybe actually talking about what had just happened? So, per usual, Quinn got a shopping trip instead of answers. Although, actually, the shopping trip was a new thing. Usually it was cookies. Sometimes a cake or pie, but usually cookies.

One thing was for sure—things hadn't gotten *less* weird over the last few days. Especially since she kept catching Mom staring at nothing with this not-really-there look on her face. Or frowning, like she was trying to figure something out. Or sighing. *Lots* of sighing. And every time Quinn would ask if she was okay, all she'd say was, "Sure, sweetie, why wouldn't I be…?"

"So, you gonna ring the doorbell?" Quinn asked, suddenly realizing how long she'd been standing there thinking about stuff. And that the wind was going right up under her little skirt and freezing her butt.

"Sorry," Mom muttered, and punched the button, the ding-donging making the dogs bark on the other side of the door. Quinn stepped back.

"Don't worry, they're harmless," Mom said, and Quinn wondered how she knew that.

Ryder's dad answered the door, smiling like always and telling both her and Mom how nice they looked. Then he gave Quinn a wink, which made her giggle. The dogs made her giggle, too, so excited to see her she could barely get inside the door.

"Lucy! Ethel! Come! Sit!"

At the sound of the woman's voice, the dogs stopped trying to lick Quinn's face and left to sit by the tall, thin, redheaded woman belonging to the voice. She was really pretty—for somebody that old, anyway—but not dressed up nearly as much as she and Mom were. Black pants and a long, kinda beigey sweater, a chunky gold necklace—that was it. Then she smiled at Quinn, her hand stretched toward her like they already knew each other, and *now* Quinn felt seriously funny inside, like she did know her from somewhere but couldn't remember.

"Quinn, sweetheart," she said, her smile getting brighter, like a light bulb right before it dies. "I'm Lorraine Caldwell. Ryder's mother."

"Nice to meet you," Quinn said, taking her hand, because she hadn't been raised by badgers, as her grandmother used to say, and Mrs. Caldwell said, "Very nice to meet you, too. And don't you look lovely!" and Quinn said, "Thank you, so do you," and she thought *Ohmigosh, this could go on all night.*

"And don't you have the nicest manners, young lady!"

Young lady? Brother. Then again, they were going back to Baltimore in a couple of days—which wasn't sitting all that well, truth be told—so what were the chances she'd ever see Ryder's mother again, anyway?

Then Ryder appeared out of nowhere and Quinn ran to him and he lifted her off her feet in a big hug, and suddenly she felt like crying for no good reason that she could tell.

All through dinner, Ryder could tell Mel was holding her breath as she picked at her food, clearly apprehensive that one or the other of his parents would let something slip. They wouldn't, of course, both well aware how easily this fragile truce could be blown. However, when his mother asked Quinn how she liked St. Mary's, he could practically hear Mel's hammering heart, her eyes wide and even darker than normal as she awaited Quinn's answer.

"It's okay, I guess," the child said with a shrug, her own gaze darting to her mother as though unsure what to say. Then she grinned at him and his heart melted. Again. "I like all the cute little shops and stuff. But mostly I like sitting out on the dock and watching the water and sky. And the birds," she said to his father.

"Are we still on for tomorrow?" David said, and Quinn looked at Mel, who hesitated before nodding, and Quinn did a fist pump, making his mother laugh. His mother. Laughing. At a fist pump. Honestly, Ryder felt as though he'd landed in an alternate universe.

One in which one stunningly beautiful Melanie Duncan was apparently loath to meet his gaze, which was bugging the life out of him. Well, except when he asked her to pass the rolls, and her gray-shadowed eyes had shot to his as though he'd suggested fencing stolen goods, and regret slashed at his gut, that what they'd had lay in ruins between them. That they'd somehow managed to wander into that limbo between friendship and *more,* where they simply didn't fit together anymore.

That here was this incredible woman saying, basically, *I'm yours for the asking,* and he…couldn't.

Can't? Or just too damn afraid?

"Let's have dessert in the living room!" his mother said, rising, sounding more chipper than Ryder ever remembered, and despite the lead weight in his stomach he smiled at how Quinn carefully folded her cloth napkin and laid it atop her empty plate before getting to her own feet, and he caught Mel's eye and winked—because he was perverse like that—making her blush.

Then, remembering, as the others drifted into the formally furnished room that hadn't been used since forever, he snagged her elbow and whispered, "We need to talk."

Her gaze zinged to Quinn, who'd already discovered the baby-grand Steinway by the bay window, her smile enormous when his mother encouraged her to go ahead and try it out, if she liked.

Mel bit her lip. "But—"

"They're not going to do anything stupid, Mel. Way too much at risk." He turned his head, lowering his voice even further. "I talked to Jeremy."

That got her attention. "When?"

"This evening," he said, steering her toward the two-story conservatory at the back of the house, the interior washed in coppery light from the rapidly fading sunset. "I'd called, left a couple of vague messages both on his home phone and cell, but he didn't get back to me until then."

"Oh." She left his side to meander through a virtual jungle of multicolored hibiscus, the trumpet-shaped flowers glowing like jewels, stopping to cup one magnificent coral blossom in her palm. "What did he say? When you told him why you'd called?"

"Not a whole lot. I got the feeling he couldn't talk freely.

Because he wasn't alone, I assume. But he knows. That the jig's up."

"And you told him—?"

"I did."

Mel dropped the flower to press her folded arms to her middle. "So. That's done, then."

"It would appear so." Ryder paused, then said, "I've never seen you in heels before."

Smiling slightly, she glanced down, turning out one foot to pose, then back up at him. "I have to admit, they're strangely…empowering."

"For you, maybe," he said, and she laughed, then shifted to look out over the gardens, a few valiant blooms defying the shorter nights and cooler temperatures.

"We should get back," he said, and she shuddered. Sighed.

"Probably."

Ryder slowly closed the distance between them to drape his arms around her shoulders and pull her close. Unresisting, she melted into him, and he ached. For her, for himself, for what couldn't be.

"So why wouldn't you look at me during dinner?"

She was quiet for a long moment, then said, very softly, "Because despite everything I said yesterday, there's this nasty little voice in my head that will not shut up. A voice that keeps telling me I could fix you." She paused. "Love you enough to heal your heart."

When he found his voice again, all he could say was, "Wow."

"I know, right?"

He chuckled softly into her soft, sweet-smelling hair. "That's incredibly…honest."

"And wrong, on so many levels." After another shrug, she twisted to look up at him. "I hurt so much for you, Ry.

More than I can even begin to put into words. And it slays me, that I *can't* make it better."

Feeling as though he was about to burst into flames, Ryder cradled the back of her neck and lowered his mouth to hers, the kiss soft and deep and bittersweet, before tucking her against his chest, whispering, "Yeah. Me, too."

Because it wasn't that he didn't love her—always had, always would.

It was that he didn't love her enough.

Dude was gonna kill her dead, no lie.

They stood for some time, cocooned in silence and each other's arms, as though they both knew that conversation was over. Not to mention the relationship. Only, see, that's what was driving Mel up a wall, that Ry so obviously wanted…something. To find his way out of his own head, if nothing else. And she could be that something, she knew it. Especially after that kiss. Because that kiss… it hadn't been about lust, and it sure as heck hadn't been about friendship. What it had been about, however, she had no clue.

And neither, she was guessing, did Ryder.

Except that he needed her. But if he couldn't see that, couldn't admit it, couldn't unshackle the pain and fear and grief that rattled and clanked along behind him, there wasn't a blessed thing she could do, was there—?

"So tell me something," he said, making her flinch, "did you put some kind of spell on Quinn before you brought her here tonight?"

Despite everything, Mel laughed. "Talk about a non-sequitur." Then she smiled up into that face she'd always loved, that somehow she'd known, even as a wee little thing, she'd love forever. In one way or the other. "You mean, the Stepford kid routine? That was my mother's doing," she said, forcing herself to let go, to distance herself from all that solidity and warmth and bone-deep goodness. "Since she said it never took with me, she was bound and determined to civilize Quinn. Kid knew how to use a twelve-piece place setting by the time she was five."

"Hmm. Almost as if—"

"She knew she'd need that particular skill someday. I know. Crazy, huh? Then again, I think on some level she understood a lot more than I gave her credit for. Or wanted to believe. Not just that she'd meet her other grandparents someday, but all of it. The *why* behind what happened."

"You mean, about your grandmother?"

"Yeah." Mel walked away to toy with the frond of an immense fern in a majestic, hand-painted urn, her insides pinching at how well Ryder understood *her,* even after all this time. "You know, I never understood my mother's unswerving loyalty to yours. Even after we left, she never, ever said a word against her. I thought she was nuts, frankly. But now...maybe I can see things a little differently. Not that part of me doesn't still wish your mother had stood up to my grandmother. Called her bluff. Because frankly I'm not sure Nana would have ever made good on her threat, never mind how much your mother *believed* she would."

She turned. "However, I've been thinking a lot the past couple of days, about how Mom was able to put everything that happened behind her and move on." Her throat got so tight she could barely get out, "Including forgiving me for screwing up her last chance at patching things up with her mother. While my grandmother hung on to her resentment and grudges every bit as tightly as she held on to all the crap in that house." She gave Ryder a small smile. "And I had to ask myself which example I'd rather emulate, for my own sake as well as Quinn's."

He smiled back. "So you're saying you'll never be a hoarder?"

"Oh, Lord, no," Mel said on a laugh. "But it also means I can't let the past deprive Quinn of something she wants. And needs."

"Sounds like a plan," Ryder said quietly, his features unreadable in quickly fading light. Then, his voice even softer: "Thank you."

Mel nodded, then glanced around the conservatory, the taller specimens ghostly in the near-dark. "We used to play hide-and-seek in here. Remember?"

A beat or two passed before he said, "You were, what? Four? Five?"

"Something like that, yeah." She forced a laugh past her still-clogged throat. "And you were a *such* a jerk, jumping out at me when I'd get close to finding you, making me scream."

"What can I say, I've always loved to make you scream."

Mel pushed out a fake sigh. "Now *how* did I know you'd say that?"

He sighed as well. A genuine one, in his case. "Innocence lost?"

"It *was* innocent, then. I always felt safe with you. Protected. And those memories…they can't be tainted. Can't be taken from us. Ever. I like that."

"Yeah," he said after a long pause. "Me, too."

"And you know something else?" Her eyes burned. "The more I think about the good stuff, the less important the bad stuff seems. And I *really* like that." When he didn't respond, she said, "We're leaving on Monday, by the way."

"Oh. So soon?"

Mel refused to hear disappointment in his voice. Or, far worse, hope in her own head.

"I'm actually holding off an extra day—so Quinn can have her birding adventure with your dad—but April's got things pretty much under control with the house, and, um, I've got three interviews lined up. And this one place, if it pans out—I could start immediately."

Another pause. Then: "So you really won't consider staying? To take April up on her offer."

She thought of that incredible kitchen-to-be, the chance to make up her own menus, to have something that was her own—

"I can't, Ry."

Silence. In the dark, she held her breath. *Your turn,* she thought, closing her eyes and feeling her heart hammering in her chest. *Give me a reason to stay—*

"Are you planning on telling Quinn before or after you leave?"

Tears crowded the corners of her eyes. She blinked them back. "At the moment I'm going with after. I think it'll be better, don't you? Give her a chance to assimilate things away from here. That way if there's fallout, nobody feels it but me. After the dust settles I'll get in touch with your parents, and we can take things from there, I suppose. But whatever happens, it's all about Quinn. Just like always."

If Ryder wondered about her sudden verbal spewage, he didn't let on. Instead he said, "Those stitches can come out in a couple of days," and she said, "Right, I'll see to it," and then he took her hand to lead her out of the dark, and by now treacherous to navigate, space.

They found his parents and her beaming, animated daughter playing Monopoly in the den, her initial shyness with Lorraine apparently dissolved. A quick glance at the board made Mel chuckle. Judging from the nice little stack of play money in front of the kid, clearly Quinn was beating the socks off her grandparents. Who were both, just as clearly, getting an enormous kick out of it. In fact, at Ryder's and Mel's reappearance, Lorraine looked up and smiled at Mel, her hand pressed to her heart as she mouthed, "Thank you."

Then the dogs, who'd been sacked out on the thick rug as close to Lorraine as they could get, both jumped to their feet and bolted from the room, barking. Mel barely caught Lorraine's exchanged glance with David, a frown marring her brow, before, muttering an obscenity, Ryder strode from the room.

Then she heard voices. Ryder's, of course, and a woman's she didn't recognize.

And a man's she did, even if lower than it had been ten years ago.

Her heart rocketing into her throat, Mel whipped around to face a very pale Lorraine as Mel heard Jeremy say behind her, "Well, isn't this convenient, everyone's here for our little reunion…."

This couldn't be happening. Couldn't—

Quinn's puzzled gaze swung to Mel's. "Mom—?"

"Mel, Quinn—" David beckoned them toward the French door leading outside. "Come on—"

But it was too late. There he was, a study in preppy chic trailed by the pretty Asian woman Mel had seen in the photo. Who looked every bit as befuddled as her husband looked determined, his rectangular-framed gaze latched on to Quinn.

"Hello, honey—you must be Quinn—"

"Please, Jeremy, don't," Mel said, her heart shattering, as Ryder grabbed his brother's arm.

"Don't be an idiot, Jer—"

"I'm Quinn, yeah," her daughter said, slowly getting to her feet, confused eyes darting between Mel and Jeremy, and Mel caught his wife's gaze in a frantic, silent plea, saw the horrified understanding dawn in them.

"Jerry, maybe this isn't—"

"Who are you?" Quinn asked.

"Jeremy!" Ryder boomed, at least distracting his brother long enough to allow Mel to grab Quinn's hand and yank her toward the door.

"Mom! What's happening? Ow! You're hurting me!"

"Stop!" Lorraine bellowed, stunning everyone into silence. "Jeremy, shut up and sit down. Mel and Quinn—" Her voice softened, she shut her eyes a moment, then waved them back into the room. "Since I caused the wreck—"

"Mother—"

One hand shot up to ward off whatever Ryder had about to say, but his gaze swung to Mel's as she stood behind Quinn, arms criss-crossed over her chest, feeling her daughter's rapid heartbeat underneath her hands.

Until Quinn wrenched free of Mel's clasp and headed toward Jeremy.

"Quinn!"

"It's okay, Mom. I've got this." Hands plunked on hips, she stared him down, and in that stare Mel saw, with a mixture of pride and sheer terror, all the women whose ballsy genes she carried. "You're my father, huh?"

Chapter Eleven

"Your mom really was going to tell you," Quinn heard Ryder say beside her as they walked along the shore, the moonlight making the marsh grasses look like thousands of wobbly silver spears.

"When she got tired of lying to me, you mean?" She tugged Ryder's way-too-big jacket up around her neck, even though the cold breeze felt good against her hot face. "And *please* don't tell me to calm down."

"Wouldn't dream of it." He paused. "It feels good to be mad, doesn't it?"

"Yeah," she said, except what it felt like, was like she had one of those marsh spears stuck right in the middle of her chest. After all this time of wishing Mom would talk to her, be honest with her, now when she should be talking to Mom…she couldn't. All she wanted was to be left alone. And how messed up was that?

Only, after she'd run outside, Ryder had followed her,

refusing to go away. A thought that tickled her brain in some funny way, but she did not have the energy to figure it out.

"Can I say something?" he said.

"Whatever," Quinn said, knowing she sounded bratty and not really caring.

"You're going to have to let your mother explain the details of what happened, how we all got to this point. Because," he said when Quinn opened her mouth, "she *is* your mother and she loves you more than life itself, that's why. She was also worried sick that this is exactly how you'd feel." Quinn punched the toe of her new shoe into the sandy dirt, probably getting mud all over it. "But you have to understand...she was pretty much forced to keep this all a secret. Until she realized how unrealistic that was. So she'd had a plan. Which was going fine, actually, until my dimwit brother showed up and shot it all to heck and back."

"Yeah, about that..." Quinn turned to Ryder. Who was her uncle, actually, a thought that had a hard time squeezing into what little space was left in her brain. "So this dude knows about me the whole time and just blows me off? And then comes back and expects me to...what? Act like everything's cool? And by the way, you can go ahead and swear, it's not like I've never heard it or anything."

"Noted," he said with a nod, then said, "I have no idea what Jeremy's thinking. But your mom told me a few days ago that it's entirely up to you, whether you want to get to know him or not. He gave up his rights ages ago, so he can't play that card now."

"So you knew all along, too?"

"Not all along, no. Only since you and your mother came back to St. Mary's." They walked for another few seconds before he said, "It's all very complicated, honey.

And trust me, your mother's hurting every bit as much as you are right now."

"So you're taking her side."

"There are no *sides,* Quinn," Ryder said, his voice a little sharp. "Right now you might not want to believe it, but it's true. And God willing from this point forward there won't be any more lies, either. That's the best any of us can do. You either deal with that or you don't."

They'd walked in a big circle and were now coming back to the house, making her insides hurt all over again. "Man, I cannot wait to go home. Back to Baltimore, I mean." Except even as she said it, that didn't feel right, either. Nothing felt right anymore. Quinn half wondered if it ever would.

"Going home with your mom?"

She felt her mouth twist. Along with her insides. "Guess I don't have a whole lot of choice in that."

"None that I can see. But you know, something tells me the two of you will work through this."

"I guess." There was this big porch that stretched across the whole back of the house, so you could go outside from several rooms. In the light from one of them she saw her mother standing. Watching for them, Quinn guessed. "Can I say something?"

"Anything you like."

"Two things, actually. One, thank you for not talking to me like I'm a baby."

"You're welcome—"

"And two..." Her chest all tight, Quinn looked up at Ryder, walking beside her with his hands in his pants pockets. "Why couldn't it've been you? To be my father, I mean?"

He got very quiet, then reached for her hand, holding it tightly as they got closer to the house. And she let him.

"Because I cared too much about your mother to go there," he said softly, which Quinn didn't entirely understand but she got the gist, as her grandmother used to say. "But I'll tell you what—if I were, I'd be the proudest man on the planet. You are one awesome kid. Just like your mom was, when she was your age."

Quinn thought that over a moment, then said, "Do you still think she's awesome?"

"You have no idea," he said, but she had to strain to hear him.

When they reached the bottom of the porch stairs, she threw her arms around Ryder's waist and hugged him, then ran up the stairs before he saw her cry.

Mel's mangled heart lurched into her throat when Quinn flew into her arms, nearly knocking the stuffing out of her.

"I'm sorry I got mad," she said, her voice muffled against Mel's stomach. She looked up, saw Ryder standing at the bottom of the stairs. He gave her a thumbs-up and a forlorn, and yet somehow proud, smile that brought tears to her eyes. Okay, *more* tears.

Then he walked away, back into the night, as if to say *My work here is done,* and Mel buried her face in her daughter's hair, thinking, *Just hell, that's what this is. Just bloody hell.*

"It's okay, you had every right to be upset—"

"Can we go home now? I mean, like tomorrow?"

"But you were looking forward to going birding with David tomorrow—"

"You mean—" Quinn's head arched back, hurt blaring in her eyes. "—my *grandfather?* You lied to me, Mom! You told me you didn't know where my father was—"

"And technically I didn't! And hey—" Clumsily lowering herself to her knees—damn shoes—Mel clamped her hands around Quinn's arms, hooking her daughter's gaze in hers. "You want to be angry with me, fine. But don't take it out on Dav— your grandfather—"

"Or your mother," Lorraine said, she and the dogs emerging from the den onto the porch. "If you want to blame anyone, blame me. Because as I said…this is all my fault. No one else's."

Then, with a heavy sigh, Ryder's mother sank onto a spiffy glider nearby, making it groan. Mel struggled to her feet—damn tight dress—and said, "Where's—?"

"Gone. To a bed and breakfast in town. Poor Caroline was appalled, for whatever it's worth." Mel saw Lorraine's gaze cut to Quinn, standing slightly behind Mel and holding her hand, then back to Mel. "I was just as blindsided as you. I had no idea Jeremy was coming. I swear. And I'm still not entirely sure why he did. What purpose he thought it would serve. Not that I'm not glad it's finally out in the open," she quickly added, once more addressing Quinn. "But this was a terrible way for you to find out. So from the bottom of my heart, I'm sorry. Will you…will you give me a chance to make it up to you?"

At her daughter's silence, Mel looked down and saw Quinn's mulish expression, then returned her gaze to Ryder's mother. "You've got your work cut out for you, Lorraine. Stubbornness running in the family and all."

Lorraine smiled—a small, tired smile—then said, "Then would you at least let me explain? Or try to?"

After several seconds, Quinn finally nodded, and Mel felt a burden she'd carried for way too long finally begin to slide off her shoulders.

Even if the burden didn't seem even remotely interested in taking the heartache with it.

* * *

Despite Lorraine's reasonably thorough explanation—and repeated apology—Quinn still insisted on going home the next day. She did allow David and Lorraine to come say goodbye—with a kitten as a going-away present, Lord help them both—but while the kid had been unable to say no to all that mewing, furry cuteness, she'd been less than committal about rescheduling her outing with her grandfather. Which Mel knew hurt David deeply, even though privately he'd said he understood. That she needed time.

And, after apologizing yet again, Lorraine had hugged Mel hard enough to squeeze whatever lingering resentment was left right out of her. Not that she was ready to call the woman her BFF or anything, but at least they'd laid enough issues to rest between them that Mel could envision future holiday get-togethers without getting twitchy.

Of course, that was all up to Quinn. Who, a week on, was still having a hard time dealing. And who sometimes only seemed to tolerate Mel's presence because otherwise she'd starve to death. Not surprising, Mel supposed as she dragged herself up the front steps to their row-house apartment after getting off work, there being no magic wands handy to wave over the past decade and make it disappear.

Not to mention that damn heartache that had ridden shotgun back from St. Mary's to insinuate itself in Mel's life like an obnoxious, freeloading roommate with no concept whatsoever of personal space. And who kept whispering that her new job—a job there was no reason she shouldn't absolutely love—sucked.

That being back in Baltimore sucked.

That having Ryder as a friend was better than not having any Ryder at all.

That—yet again—she'd screwed up.

The kitten attacked her Crocs, all black-and-white bodaciousness, and Mel scooped up the little purrpot to cradle him underneath her chin. From the living room she heard the *Househunters* theme—Mrs. Davis's fave HGTV show. The elderly woman was sawing logs, of course, although she jerked to attention when Mel plucked the remote off her lap to turn off the TV.

Muttering about how she'd just dozed off for a second, that Quinn had gone to bed an hour ago, she'd been an angel, as usual, she accepted Mel's gentle hug before giving the kitten a pat on the head and then leaving. On a sigh, Mel kicked off her shoes and padded in her socked feet to the kitchen to make herself some chai tea, only to jump when she noticed Quinn standing in the doorway in Target-issue jammies and her Angry Birds slippers. Fitting.

"Mrs. Davis said you were asleep."

"I was. Did you know the whole house shakes when somebody opens the door?"

Mel smiled. "I did. You want something? Hot chocolate? And I brought leftover cheesecake from the restaurant."

"Is it yours?"

"No, they have their own pastry chef."

"Then no. I'm not hungry, anyway. But I do want to talk."

"Oh?"

"Yeah." The birds glared at Mel as Quinn scuffled across the kitchen to drop into a chair, stabbing her hands through her tangled red mop. "And don't worry, I'm over being mad at you. I think. I'm just…confused."

Her tea made, Mel sat across from her daughter. "About?"

"Everything," she said on a dramatic sigh, letting her head flop back against the high-backed chair. "How I can be soooo mad at my…my grandparents and miss them at the same time." Her eyes lowered to Mel's. "How you could

act, like, everything's all fine after what they did to you. To us." Her mouth pulled into a tight little line. "Why you and Uncle Ryder can't see how crazy you are about each other, geez. I mean, *seriously.*"

Oh, dear Lord. Mel stared into her tea, sorely wishing it was something stronger. Like Pine-Sol, maybe, to disinfect her brain.

"Well, in no particular order… Did you ever hear the saying 'Fake it till you make it'?" Quinn nodded. "To be honest, when we first got to St. Mary's I was still extremely angry with the Caldwells. For what certainly seemed to be valid reasons. And I was pretty determined you'd never have a relationship with them."

Quinn's nose wrinkled. "Then how come you changed your mind?"

"A combination of things, I guess. Discovering far more of the truth than I knew before. Realizing how much it takes out of you, being bitter all the time. Angry. And it occurred to me I didn't want to be the kind of person who hangs on to the past like…like—"

"A gazillion old magazines?"

Mel snorted. "Yeah. But realizing something and making it happen are two different things. So I'm still a work in progress on that front. I do believe your grandparents mean well—now, anyway—and I want to believe your grandmother's had a change of heart. But I still get angry sometimes. Like you," she said, and Quinn lowered her eyes, her cheeks coloring. "However, the good news is that each time it has less of a grip on me than the time before."

Suddenly a light went on behind the kid's eyes. "Like the Cherokee wolf story?"

"Huh?"

"Yeah, it's…" One hand went up. "Hold on a sec."

The chair wobbled when Quinn jumped up and ran out

of the room, returning a minute later with a slim three-ring binder which she banged open on the table. "You made me write a report on it," she said, tucking her foot up under her tush as she flipped through the pages. "Here it is."

Cramming her hair behind her ear, she read: "'An old man tells his grandson that there are two wolves fighting inside him. One is evil—hate, anger, resentment, self-pity…' and so on," she said, circling with her hand, then continued, "'The other is good—kindness, love, serenity…'" Her finger skimmed the line until she said, with a pointed look in Mel's direction, "*Forgiveness.* Then the little boy asks which one will win, and the old man says, 'The one I feed.'" Her eyes lifted to Mel's. "So you decided to feed the good wolf, huh?"

Oh, dear God, she loved this kid so much it hurt. Mel grabbed a rumpled napkin from the table and blew her nose. "I guess I did," she said. "In any case I finally had to admit it wasn't right, or fair, to prejudice you against your grandparents. That whatever relationship you end up having with them is between you and them. I won't interfere, one way or the other."

Quinn smacked shut the notebook, then leaned back in the chair, her arms crossed high on her flat little chest. "So it's okay if I like them?"

"Totally okay."

Forehead crunched. "Even if I'm still mad?"

"That's okay, too. But everybody makes mistakes, honey. And I mean everybody. What's important is how you fix them. And what you learn from them."

Judging from Quinn's yelp, the kitten attacked one of the Birds. Her hair quivered as she leaned down to haul the wee thing to her chest, where it started purring like mad, the contented sound at odds with the pain in Quinn's voice when she said, "Like you and Jeremy?"

Damn.

Mel leaned closer to pet the kitten. An invitation, apparently, to teethe on her fingers. "And sometimes," she said, "even the most boneheaded mistakes result in something amazing."

Eventually, a tiny smile peeked out from behind the confusion. "Even when you want to trade me for a dumb model?"

"*Especially* then," Mel said, laughing, and Quinn bounced up to come around and wriggle onto Mel's lap, kitten and all. *Enjoy it while you can,* she thought, twining her arms around her daughter's waist and not even caring that the kid's hair tickled like hell.

"I really liked St. Mary's, too," she said. Cautiously.

"Then I don't suppose you'll mind going back for visits," Mel said. Also cautiously.

"Actually..." She shifted to look down at Mel, her face the picture of earnestness as the kitten gnawed on her hair. "Jack was telling me about his school, it's right there in town and it sounds really cool, and I was thinking maybe it's time I try being in a classroom setting again, anyway—"

Mel sighed. "Not an option, baby."

"But if you married Ryder...?"

"Oh, honey—that's not an option, either."

"Why not? The three of us...we'd be awesome together, don't you think?"

Ice-pick-to-the-heart time. "Probably so. But that's not the point. Quinn, listen to me—remember how you told me about Jack's cousin and his mother, in that accident? Ryder really loved Deanna, and he's still not over it. Not enough to..." She breathed out. "Yes, he cares about me—about you, too—but look what happened with Lance—"

"You mean, about how his girlfriend came back so he

broke up with you? Mom!" Still clutching the oblivious kitten, Quinn slid off Mel's lap. "Hello? Ryder's girlfriend *can't* come back, can she? Okay, that sounded really terrible, but still. Like, totally not the same thing."

"Like, it totally is. *He* may be free, but his heart isn't. And that's what counts. Quinn," she said when her daughter rolled her eyes, "believe me, it breaks *my* heart to see him so unhappy. But I simply can't put myself through that. Not again." She reached over to take Quinn's hand. "Or you."

After several more cog-spinning seconds, Quinn tromped over to the fridge and got out the cheesecake, anyway, lugging the foam carton over to the table and plopping down to pick off pieces with her fingers and shove them into her mouth. "You know, if somebody would explain to me," she said around a full mouth, "why grown-ups make everything so darn complicated, I could die happy."

Sing it, sistah, Mel thought with a gloomy sigh.

The old place was definitely rising out of the ashes, Ryder mused as he pulled up in front of Amelia's house. Already, wheat-colored siding replaced the colorless, decaying clapboard from before, the broken trim restored and repainted a soothing teal-green. The yard, however, was gouged and cratered and muddy, thanks to a slew of pickups and vans from April's having apparently hired every contractor within a fifty-mile radius.

In paint-smeared jeans and a flannel shirt that might've fit Paul Bunyan, she met him at the door.

"Ryder! What brings you here?"

"Mel told me they'd left my jacket here?"

"Oh, right. Come on in. Let me wash my hands real quick and I'll get it for you. Don't bother shutting the door behind you, people are coming and going too much to bother."

He followed her inside, nodding in appreciation at the changes taking place. Light flooded the dust-caked downstairs, thanks to new windows, a wall or two removed, and mountains of clutter banished. "Wow," he said over the shouts and banging and satisfying din of rampant demolition. "This is incredible."

"And we've barely begun," April yelled back. "Blythe assures me it'll be done by early December, but I'm not convinced. Take a gander at the drawings, they're tacked up on the wall over there. I tell you, that woman is a freaking genius."

To say the least, he thought as he scanned the elevations of the proposed kitchen remodel—quartz countertops and pale wood cabinets, bright, white beadboard and restaurant-quality appliances, including a fridge large enough to store a side of beef in, he thought with a smile.

And a six-burner stove and matching double ovens.

In pink.

"Pink?" he said when April returned.

"Of course," she said easily as she handed him his jacket. "Because you know how much Mel loves pink."

Ryder started. "She's coming back?"

"Well, I suppose that's up to you, isn't it?"

"Excuse me?"

April grabbed a half-empty water bottle off a battered radiator cover and took a long swallow, twisting the cap back on as she said, "You've got a choice, you know. And I don't think I need to tell you what that is."

"And you're butting in."

"Damn straight, sugar. But only because you obviously haven't looked in a mirror recently to see how pathetic you look. Long face and everything, mm, mm, mm. People are *talking,* Ryder. In case you didn't know—"

"And maybe I care too much about Mel to offer her only half of myself."

"Lord, men," the blonde said, then jabbed a finger in his direction. "And *there's* a sorry excuse if ever I heard one. Ryder..." She leaned forward. "You're not miserable because of the love you lost, you're miserable because of the one you let get away. The one you're afraid to go after."

And the demolition ruckus now sounded eerily like it was coming from inside his head. "You just want her to come back to work for you."

"Heck, yeah, I want her to work for me. That's a given. Especially after some of the ding-dongs I've interviewed? I wouldn't trust them to feed my dogs. Well, if I had dogs. Anyway. Quinn also needs to be here, with her grandparents. And you. In fact, I'm not sure Quinn might not need you even more than Mel does, but don't quote me on that. I am sure, however, that the person doing the most needing is *you.* Only you're being too much of a scaredy-cat to admit it."

"I'm not afraid, April—"

"Oh, yeah? Then prove it. Not to me. To Mel. And Quinn. But mostly? To yourself."

His heart throbbing under his rib cage, Ryder mumbled, "Thanks for the coat. The place looks great," and got his sorry hide out of there.

Except, if he was angry, it was only because April was right. That this past week had been hell without Mel, that there wasn't a damn thing standing between him and a second chance at happiness except himself. And, yes, fear. Of what, exactly, he wasn't sure. That he'd let Mel down somehow? That he'd lose her like he'd lost Deanna and have to go through the pain again?

Only…he had lost her, hadn't he? And this pain…it was every bit as bad as the grief. Worse, actually.

Because at least with Deanna, it hadn't been his fault.

Although he'd planned on going into the clinic to catch up on some paperwork, he instead found himself driving back to the house—funny, how he'd never, not once, called the place where he lived *home*—through yellowing fields and the occasional clot of trees, gloriously ablaze against a serene, infinitely blue sky…

You have a choice.

His breath left his lungs.

The leaves would return, the crops replanted. The sky was always there. Life, existence, being, whatever you wanted to call it…it never ended, did it? Changed, yes—that whole doors opening and closing thing—but it was never, truly over.

Unless a person believed it was.

You have a choice.

Ryder blew out a long, rough breath as it hit him that what he felt for Mel was only *selfish* if he chose not to share it with her. And how could he not, since…

Since…

Since so much of what he'd loved about Deanna, he realized as his heart tried to pound right out of his chest, he'd loved about Mel, first.

He never made it back to the house. Didn't need to, since the decision pretty much made itself. And at first he considered returning to April's to ask for Mel's address, until he remembered someone else who'd have it.

"Ryder!" his mother said when he walked into his parents' house. "What—?"

"I need—" He paused. "Mel—where does she live?"

Slowly, her lips tilted, before she went to her desk to open her address book and copy something onto a piece of her stationery. When she returned, however, she handed him a set of car keys as well as the address.

"Take the Prius," she said. "It gets better mileage."

It was nearly dark when, as Mel lugged the heavier of the grocery bags the short walk back home—so much for just needing a "few things"—she watched Quinn disappear around the corner ahead of her.

Then heard the shriek.

Her heart in her throat, she rushed to catch up, only to nearly wet herself when she saw Ryder sitting on her porch steps, one arm looped around her hugely grinning daughter.

"You weren't home," he said, as if that made perfect sense.

And Mel burst into tears.

Some hours later, Ryder breathed out a satisfied groan. "That was incredible." He reached for her hand to kiss her knuckles. "*You're* incredible."

Mel grinned. "And there's plenty more where that came from."

"Lord, woman, give a man time to recuperate. I'm not seventeen anymore, you know."

Laughing, Mel got up from the kitchen table to clear their dinner plates. Quinn had bolted down her food as usual and was in her room, reading. Except she'd given Mel a thumbs-up behind Ryder's back as she left the room, which made Mel smile all the harder now. "It was just roast chicken and potatoes, for heaven's sake."

"There was nothing *just* about it." Ryder rose as well to cart the rest of the dishes to the sink, only to slip his arms around her waist from behind as she turned on the water, and Mel thought she'd die from happiness. Heaven knew there were a million details to iron out—fat chance of any real conversation with a hyper-excited ten-year-old commandeering the conversation—but it didn't matter. Because the instant Mel saw him sitting on her steps, she knew. That he'd come for her.

For them.

So the question was, were they both ready for everything that meant?

"Mm. Nice," Ryder murmured into her hair, then gently turned her around to kiss her.

"Even nicer," she said, and he chuckled, his eyes going all crinkly at the corners before he kissed her again, slowly, like they had all the time in the world. Except… "The water's running."

Ryder angled himself around her to turn it off. "Problem solved," he said, then tucked her head under his chin, holding her close. "I'm putting the house on the market."

Mel leaned back to plant her damp hands on his chest. "Really."

"Yep."

"But you loved that house. And all the work you put into it—"

"Deanna loved the house. Frankly I'd rather live in town. And the work…like you said, it was therapy." Then he linked his hands at the small of her back, smiled into her eyes and said, "Where do you keep the coffee?"

"In the fridge," she said, lightly smacking his arm before he released her. "So you're letting it go? Just like that?"

"Just like that," Ryder said, dumping the Trader Joe's blend on the counter. "Filters?"

She reached into the cabinet overhead and handed him one, a little thrill of delight swirling through her at the deliciousness that was watching this man go about something as mundane as making coffee in her kitchen. The coffee started, he opened his arms and she walked into them, where he whispered, "It's okay, it's all over now" into her hair, and she knew what he meant. Except then he said, "Mom said she'd told you that Amelia never knew about our friendship."

Mel's head popped up. "She didn't." Then she frowned. "Did she?"

"I'm pretty sure she did."

"But how—?"

"Who knows? Maybe I left something of mine there when we were kids? In any case, I went out there to check up on the old girl once when Dad was busy, and she asked me if you were okay."

"You're kidding? When was this?"

"Maybe a month before she died?"

A jolt went through Mel. "And what did you say?"

"The truth—that I hadn't seen you in years. And she got this really shrewd look on her face, like she was processing the information." He tugged her close again. "Weird, huh?"

"Yeah," Mel said, her mind going a mile a minute. Speaking of processing information—

"By the way," Ryder said after several seconds had passed, "I'm staying in the old cottage. Until the right place comes along. Is that okay?"

Her heart jumped. "Of course—"

"I mean..." He cleared his throat, then set her apart enough to fish a ring box out of his pants pocket. "Would *you* be okay with living there?"

Wait. What?

"Holy crap, I need to sit," she said, grasping for the nearest chair and letting Ryder lower her into it, before lowering himself to one knee, his grin as unsteady as her legs.

"Ohmigod, Ry...are you sure?"

"Completely." He opened the box. Oooh, sparkly. "This is probably the weirdest proposal ever, but hear me out, okay?"

Struck mute, she could only nod. Ryder set the box on the table and took her hands in his, his eyes shiny. "Baby… I thought you were gone from my life forever. That what we'd had…that it really had been just some childhood thing I needed to let go of. But not until I finally felt free—and believe me, it took a helluva long time—did Deanna appear. And I loved her with all my heart, I truly did. Then, when she…went, I thought, that's it. Not going through that a third time. Except…inexplicably—" Poor guy looked so baffled Mel had to smile through her own tears. "There you were. Back in my life, under the most *extraordinary* circumstances. And all I could think was, what the hell?"

Mel burbled out a laugh, only to bite her lip when Ryder gripped her hands harder. "Fix me, sweetheart. Do whatever it is you do, I'm putting myself in your hands. Because whatever magic you worked on me when you were born, it's still working."

Took a second. "Ohmigosh," she gasped, her eyes wide. "You knew—?"

"I was five, Mel, well aware something was wrong with me. Just as I knew, even if I didn't understand how or why, that being with you released something inside me. Same way it is now. I know what I said, about the timing being all wrong, but…" He smiled. "It actually couldn't be more perfect, could it?"

Her eyes flooded, Mel shook her head, and Ryder finally retrieved the little box, slipping the pretty little pink diamond from its satin bed. "I know what I'm asking of you—"

"Yes," she said, wiping her eyes. Laughing. Sliding off

the chair to throw her arms around his neck. “Yes, and yes, and yes. To all of it.”

“Then give me your hand, woman.”

So she did, admiring the ring as Ryder said, “April will be beside herself—”

“She’s not the only one!” Quinn said from the doorway. With a bark of laughter, Ryder opened his arm to include her in their first official, we’re-a-family-now group hug.

And Mel thought, grinning, *Over? Like hell.*

Because the best part was just beginning.

* * * * *